HOPE BEGINS

VICTORIA NOCK

ISBN: **1500317667**
ISBN-13: **978-1500317669**

DEDICATION

For Kelsie.

ACKNOWLEDGMENTS

To my family, for always being there and for believing in me.
Emma, thank you for reading and loving this story even
through all the rough edits.
Will for your support and encouragement.
To all the long-suffering friends who have put up with me
through this whole adventure.
Kirstie and Ellen, thank you for you much needed input and
support.

I love you all.

When all else is gone...

Hope begins.

PROLOGUE

It was hot this particular evening as Eric Evans peered out of his open window, the breeze cooling him slightly, as he waits patiently in his darkened office.

His workday had started just as every other day, kissing his family goodbye, arriving at the school and yelling at a few rowdy students but as soon as his receptionist gave him that letter, he knew he was in for a long stressful day.

He had finished hours ago, but this impromptu after hours meeting meant he couldn't leave until Henry Caldwell got there and explained the urgency of his unexpected and quite frankly, unwelcome visit. Eric nervously checked his watch before looking out of the open office door into the shadowy hallway.

"I would be much obliged if you turned that watch light off," says a velvety voice from the hallway, making Eric jump out of his seat. He fumbles pulling at the watchstrap with trembling fingers before finally yanking it off his wrist and throwing it unceremoniously into the top drawer.

"I'm sorry Sir," he gasps, his breath escaping his lungs as he moves away from his chair quickly. The owner of the velvety voice glides forward gracefully and the shadowy figure enters the room.

Only the faint glow from the full moon outside illuminates the office and Eric can just make out the curved smile of Henry Caldwell.

"My dear friend it is good to see you again," Henry croons, Eric smiles shakily and nods. "How are your wife and your darling children?" Henry asks as he walks around the desk to Eric's chair. He lowers himself into the chair picking up the framed picture of Eric's family and smiles toothily.

Eric swallows hard as he backs away clearing his throat. His eyes are firmly on Henry's face as he answers.

"*My wife is not doing well Sir. We lost our eldest, our son, to the flu last winter,*" Eric replies, wringing his clammy hands. Henry stares down at the smiling boy in the picture as he strokes the glass with a long slender finger before turning his dark eyes to Eric.

"*That's a pity,*" he says, his tone far from pitying. He then smiles. "*I suppose that means you are already trying for another?*" he asks looking slightly nauseated by the idea. Eric nods quickly and tries to smile.

"*Of course Sir.*"

"*Lovely,*" Henry says with a smile. "*It is good to see a man of your standing and responsibility following the law. You're a role model Eric,*" he states encouragingly and Eric nods.

"*You may sit.*" Henry gestures to the empty seat across the desk as Eric continues to stare down at him. Eric moves slowly towards the chair and lowers himself into the seat at the opposite side of the desk waiting for Henry to go on. Henry looks around the room at all the pictures and certificates on the walls as Eric tries to slow his loud, frantic heartbeat.

"*How was your journey?*" Eric asks unable to stand the silence any longer. Henry turns to him and smiles.

"*Very tiring,*" he says slowly looking over to Eric. "*Are you frightened Eric?*" Henry asks suddenly his eyes darting to Eric's as he nods slowly. "*I can smell it. It's rather distracting hearing your heart race beneath your rib cage. You have no idea what that sound does to us,*" Henry whispers his eyes traveling to Eric's neck. Eric notices the sharp short fangs shining as Henry speaks and this does nothing to calm his pounding heart.

"*I'm sorry; I don't mean to make you uncomfortable.*"

"*It is not your fault Eric, you are only human,*" Henry says in a tone that shows his disgust and pity. Eric cannot help but let that aggravate him, he remains silent as the thought, "*rather human than a monster*", enters his head.

Had he not been a coward and a man who values his life he would have told Henry there and then exactly what he thought of that comment, but he just nods then looks down at the tabletop. Shame washes over him, like the breeze flowing through the open window. The air swirls around him filling the room with Henry's smoky, citrus scent. It seems to cling to Henry almost as if it's permeating through his skin. The smell claws at Eric's throat; he swallows back the bile that rises.

Taking a deep breath he glances up at Henry who is observing him through his black eyes. As the silence lengthens he begins to feel uncomfortable again and even more so as Henry sits forward.

"I'm curious as to why you're here, Sir," Eric says quickly making Henry still. "I hope it's nothing I have done." Henry frowns at Eric before smiling. He sits back relaxing in the comfortable office chair.

"Dear Eric that is not why I am here. You have been very well behaved; I have come as a favour to someone very dear to me," he states and Eric's eyebrows rise in surprise.

"I see."

"Do you?" Henry asks with a chuckle. Eric opens his mouth to reply but closes it shaking his head. Henry sniggers again as he leans back in the chair. "I have a request for you; one I know you will be able to help with."

"Yes sir, anything," Eric quickly replies. Henry smiles, his dark eyes glisten in the little light provided by the moon.

"I would be very careful as to what you say to me Eric, I may take advantage of your kind offer quite literally and drink you dry," Henry croons licking his lips dramatically. He smiles widely and chuckles as Eric pales and he hears his heart skip a beat in horror.

"Is… is that what you want?" Eric stutters. Henry's face turns serious.

"Heavens no! Like I have said you have been very well behaved and where would we find another Principal in such a short time? No, I have a request regarding one of your students."

"A student?" Eric frowns as he sits up in his chair.

"Yes, a Miss Chloe Wood. You know of her?"

"She is one of our best students," Eric says narrowing his eyes. "What could you possibly want from her?" he continues feeling slightly braver as he takes the welfare of his students very seriously. Henry raises his eyebrows in surprise at the man's sudden lack of cowardice. He says nothing as he fishes a letter out of his coat pocket. With a flourish he hands it to Eric who takes it and tears it open.

"Your devotion to your students is touching," Henry muses as he watches Eric read the letter and smiles as his eyes widen in horror. Eric looks up from the letter.

"She will not accept this."

"She has no choice."

"Chloe has worked harder than any other student in the school so she doesn't have to request the change, or become a breeder. We have spoken at length about this; I know this is not what she wants. I have found an excellent position in a hospital for her, it's already arranged," Eric pleads to Henry who shrugs lazily.

"Arrangements can be rearranged." Henry says with a little smile. Eric becomes wary, as despite Henry's smile his voice has picked up a slightly dangerous tone.

Eric looks back down at the handwritten letter shaking his head at the name elegantly scrawled at the bottom.

"Her mother has no right to..."

"Enough!" Henry shouts making Eric jump and crumple the letter in his hand. "She is still the girl's mother, undead or not. You will accept this letter of request. If the girl refuses us you will make arrangements for the girl to become a breeder, do I make myself clear?" Henry threatens, Eric stares at him terror freezing him to the spot.

"I... I don't like this. I was under the impression we had the power..."

Henry is suddenly on his feet, leaning over the desk his face close to Eric's filling his senses with the bittersweet smell that surrounds him.

"We allow your existence! Do your cattle have the right to decide how they live? We allow you to live and give you the honour of changing, should we want you. We are the law, we are the rulers and we decide how your government is run." Henry backs up a little as Eric remains frozen. "You will see this works Eric, or on your family's heads be it. Do I make myself clear?"

Henry asks in a softer, all the more terrifying voice. Eric looks up at him and nods.

"Ye-yes sir," he stutters. Henry smiles, stands up and straightens his coat.

"Good man. I trust you will be able to take care of everything. I have a very busy schedule," Henry says running his tongue over his sharp fangs.

"Yes sir," Eric replies stiffly.

"Very good. Have a pleasant evening Eric. I will be seeing you soon," Henry says as he sweeps out of the room.

As soon as Eric hears the door in the hall closing he rushes to the open window dragging in shaky breaths of the cool night air. Attempting to rid his mouth and nose of that vile smell.

Sitting back down at his desk he sobs loudly, shoulders trembling as he struggles to keep himself quiet. He reaches over his desk, eyes bleary from the tears welling up in them. Loading up his computer it hums to life and the room is flooded with bright blue light.

He struggles to calm his breathing as he waits for the ancient computer to boot, his eyes stinging as he wills the loading bar to move faster. He looks away, hastily wiping away the tears that have rolled down his cheeks.

Unfortunately his eyes land on the picture of his family. He looks at his eldest and only son who is now gone and he's reminded of the pain of losing him. As Henry's threat echoes in his mind, the memory of losing his son makes him turn to the computer, mind made up as he types the girl's name into the search bar. He brings up her files. Chloe's file is filled with extracurricular activities, clubs and excellent grades. He finds the occupation page, hovering over where it says "RESEARCHER" and with a heavy heart hits delete. He quickly types "BREEDER" into the box, with his eyes closed he hits save.

"I'm so sorry Chloe," he whispers and with one last look at his family picture he switches off the computer and in the dark his tears fall onto his desk.

Outside under the moonlight Henry stops beside his long, sleek, black car and looks up towards the school with a smile. He can hear a faint sniffling coming from Eric's open window. Opening the car door he slides in, pulling off his sunglasses, turning in his seat to smile at Lillian, his mate. She looks at him expectantly her dark eyes wide and her face framed by her thick dark hair. He smiles at her before taking her hand kissing it; she lets out a tiny sigh.

"Henry?" she asks as he nods to the driver to drive on and smiles down at her.

"Yes Lillian my dear?" he asks with a knowing smile, received with a frustrated glare, she'd never been the most patient of beings.

"How did it go, did he accept the letter?" she questions as Henry cups her face in his hands.

"My love, has anyone ever denied me anything?" he asks cocking his eyebrow making her smile.

"So she has been registered?"

"It is done?" Henry nods and Lillian pushes forward pressing her lips to his.

"Thank you," she murmurs and Henry smiles.

"Anything for you my love," he says stroking her hair, she smiles sweetly before it flickers and dies.

"What if she refuses? Her father will have poisoned her thoughts towards me," Lillian says in a worried whisper, Henry strokes her cheek.

"Calm dear one. If she does refuse there are other ways to get to her. It just may take a little longer."

"You're right, she will come around; she has to," Lillian realises, as Henry puts his arm around her shoulder and she rests her head against his chest. "Have you seen her?" Lillian asks after a few silent moments.

"I have not, my love," Henry murmurs into her hair and Lillian looks up at him.

"I wonder what she looks like; I wonder what kind of woman she has become?"

"I imagine she is ravishing, just like her mother," Henry says as Lillian smiles happily. "I am sure she will make a beautiful immortal."

Chapter 1

My eyes shoot open as the shrill bell from my alarm startles me out of my light slumber. Damn that thing. I groan internally as I reach over and switch it off. My tired eyes sting slightly as I look up at the ceiling. It's been yet another restless night of tossing and turning, barely any sleep and strange haunting dreams. After waking up from one particularly upsetting dream, only the soft orange light of the sunrise relaxed me enough to catch a few precious hours of much needed rest before today.

Today is a day I have been dreading all year, all my life really, and I can't believe it's actually here. Today is my high school graduation, the day I will be assigned my life career. It's also the last day in my family home. I try not to dwell on this sad fact.

It's safe to say I'm terrified about all of it. I've worked hard for the last six years to assure I'll get a decent placement in a good, respectable field. I want to work in medicine and after six years of hard work that's the placement I'm going to be assigned. I'll get to train in Centrum, the capital city of our small country. I'll have an apartment of my own and will be going to the medical school there. Despite the sadness of the day I can't help but be a little excited.

I roll onto my side hearing a light knock on my bedroom door. I sit up stretching and yawning.

"Come in Dad," I say through my yawn. The door opens and my dad ducks into my room, wearing a tight smile and carrying a cup of coffee, the smell makes my mouth water. I can tell he hasn't slept; his brown eyes are bleary, he's as nervous for me, today, as I am.

"Morning kiddo," he says trying to smile wider as he hovers at the foot of my bed. I smile at him rolling my eyes.

"Dad I'm eighteen. I'm hardly a kid anymore."

"You're my baby, always will be," he huffs. I smile at him as he folds his arms. My smile falls from my face when he begins looking around my room; his face is now showing his sadness.

"What's up?" I ask frowning. Dad isn't very good at all the talking mumbo jumbo, as he calls it. He's what mum used to say "a man's man". He's definitely viewed that way around town; some people are scared of him because he's tall, broad and strong. Also he can be a little intimidating. I find it all very fun as I know better; I know he's really a big softie. He's the gentlest man I know. He just doesn't like to show it very often.

"I'm just making sure you're ok, did you get much sleep?" he says sipping his coffee.

"As much as expected," I say with a shrug. He nods and sits on the end of the bed.

"Me neither," he mumbles raising the coffee to his mouth again.

I knew it, I think as I smile at him. He runs his hand over his face scratching his stubbly chin.

"You'll be fine Chloe. Remember what Mr. Evans said, you were a shoe in. Just go up there, smile and leave. Don't converse with them and you will be just fine, ok?" he says his eyes flashing angrily for a moment.

"Sure Dad. I got it," I nod and I swallow back the sick feeling that rises from my stomach.

"That's my girl," he smiles. I try to return it but I have a feeling my smile isn't quite hitting the mark. "What time are Oliver and his family coming to pick us up?" he asks standing up and turning back towards the door.

"Ten," I say looking at the alarm, "I'd best get up."

"The dress is in the closet in the hallway," he calls over his shoulder as he ducks out of the door.

"Thanks Dad," I say throwing the covers off my legs. He lifts his hand waving me down and I frown remembering the whole debacle a few weeks ago with the dress.

"Dad?" I said, during a rare dinner with my brother Joseph, who had come to visit from the forests where he works. He was luckily assigned a management job there which gave him the luxury of not having to get married or having to father children. He's really smart and if people think my dad and Michael, my other brother, are big then they must think Joseph is a giant.

"Yes, Chloe," Dad said as he looked up from his plate. I looked between him and Joseph who was frowning at me.

It's now or never, I reminded myself as I took a deep, calming, breath. I felt a little embarrassed for bringing it up but I was getting desperate.

"I know that things are tight and you know I wouldn't normally ask but as you know it's my graduation in a few weeks and I don't have a dress," I rushed out in one breath he stared at me with his fork half way up to his mouth. Joseph looked between us with his mouth hanging open, making him look ridiculous. I glared at him and his mouth slammed shut. Joseph may be the eldest of the three of us but he could definitely be the most childish sometimes, despite his ever-growing beard and big muscles. He cleared his throat and Dad looked at him lowering his fork back onto his plate.

"She's right you know Dad. She might not be getting married off or anything, thank god, but she still needs a dress. It's the rules," Joseph said I gave him a grateful smile. I could always count on my brothers to have my back. Dad clenched his jaw and Joseph's eyes dropped to the table and he went back to his dinner.

Maybe not.

"It's ok I will just…" I began but Dad slammed a hand on the table making Joseph and I jump.

9

"No," Dad growled through his teeth.

Oh not good, I thought as Joseph and I both looked at him with wide eyes. We were both startled to see that he was not angry, he was sad and he was crying. I stared at him unsure of what to do.

"Dad?" I whispered, he suddenly stood up, picked up his plate and put it in the sink, including his dinner that was almost untouched. He leaned on the counter and took a deep breath before he cleared his throat and turned around.

"I have something for you," he said in a hoarse voice before he walked down the hallway towards his room. I stared at his retreating back until his door closed with a soft click and Joseph and I stared at each other in shock.

"What was that about?" he asked and I shrugged.

How should I know? I thought.

We ate slowly after that waiting for Dad to come back out and after thirty minutes or so he did, looking stony faced but composed. He was holding a black garment bag and his eyes were on me. I looked between him and the bag and I could feel a smile creep onto my face.

"This was hers," he said in a level tone trying not to sound bitter. The smile fell from my face and I stood up. This was the first time I had received something from my dad that belonged to my mother. I had her ring on a chain that I always wore but I took that. I wasn't given it; Dad was just going to throw it out and after a lengthy argument he gave in and let me keep it.

"Are you sure?" I asked reaching to open the bag and he quickly covered my hand.

"Yes, just..." he sighed and gave me a little smile, "...wait until graduation," he said his eyes pleading. I nodded and smiled up at him.

"Thank you," I said and I hugged him wrapping my arms around his middle.

"Anything for you kiddo," he said gruffly kissing the top of my head.

10

After a rushed breakfast of dry toast and a quick cool shower to wake me up, I rush into the hallway and pull the garment bag out of the small, almost empty closet before heading back into my bedroom, closing the door behind me. I lay the bag carefully on my bed, look around my room and sigh. What was once a room filled with pieces of my life; pictures, trinkets and character is now an empty shell. Everything I cherish is packed away in the heavy standard issue trunk I was sent, as is the rest of the house. As I'm the last child and my dad will be the only one left in a family home he's being moved to a new single occupant apartment. The house is dotted with boxes of his that he's taking with him when he goes. It was a sorry experience clearing the whole house of our belongings and after giving a lot of it away or giving it back to Joseph and Michael there was a depressingly small amount of stuff left that was my dad's or mine. I have a few boxes of precious things that Dad is going to keep for me until I get settled in my new home and I know how much space I will have to work with. My trunk and the clothes I will be wearing today are all I will be taking with me right away. I look back down at the bed and reach for the zip, anxious to see the dress Dad has given me. As I open the bag and realise my fingers are trembling slightly. I gasp a little when I pull back the garment bag and the memory of the dress hits me.

I've seen this before, I think as I unwrap my towel and pull the soft white dress over my head. It's a soft lace dress, which almost falls to the floor. As it slid over my head I caught a faint scent and I feel a strange sensation over my body as my mind tries but fails to place the smell. I look down at the dress as I smooth it down. The lace is intricate and beautiful and covers my arms and chest with a silk rounded neckline making it look very smart. The white lace sits on top of an ivory under dress; the thin delicate material is soft against my skin. I pile my hair

11

onto my head unable to do anything else with the unruly curls. When I finally look at myself in the mirror my eyes widen in surprise.

"I *have* seen this before," I say aloud. I gasp covering my mouth with my hand as my hair tumbles around my shoulders. I walk over to the mirror to inspect myself. Running my hands down my sides and over my tired looking face. Despite the obvious differences, my height, my freckles, I look just like...

"Mum," I whisper in horror straightening up as the realisation startles me. I understand now why my dad didn't want me to wear this dress and why he didn't want me to bring it out. I'm a living reincarnation of my mother. Suddenly the soft material feels itchy and tight and the scent of the fabric makes me feel nauseas. I need to get this off, I think as I'm about to tear the offending garment off my body when there is a loud bang on my bedroom door.

"I'm coming in!"The bedroom door swings open with a bang as Michael bursts in. I spin around, startled. When he sees me he stops short his mouth open in shock. The pain that flashes across his face is clear; he tries but fails to hide it. I feel guilty as I stand there in a state of shock and anger.

"I can't go anywhere in this," I gasp. Frowning, his eyes clear of the pain. He smiles although I can still see his pain flicker beneath the surface.

"You look great," he croaks as he walks over and hugs me. I stand there frozen and disgusted as he gives me a squeeze. "Come on sis. It's only for a few hours then you can burn it," he says and I smile as he pulls back.

"Yeah I suppose so," I agree rubbing my arm.

"How did you get it?"

"Dad," I shrug. I look up at him and he's staring at me with a frown. "What is it?"

"Nothing it's just..." he sighs as he runs his hand through his hair, "you look so much like her." He looks at me apologetically. My shoulders sag a little.

"I know," I say in a small voice and he shoves me with his elbow.

Could this day get any worse? Oh wait, yes it could.

"I'm sorry. It's not your fault, you can't help being ugly," he jokes with smile. I punch his arm and he gives me a hurt look as he rubs his arm.

"Piss off," I growl at him shoving him roughly out of the room. "I need to finish getting ready."

"I don't know why you bother, no amount of makeup can help that face sis," he chuckles. I glare at him and slam the door in his face. I smile and laugh despite the ever-present feeling of dread in my stomach. I shake myself roughly and sit down in front of my mirror with a frustrated huff.

"He may be right," I say running my fingers under my darkened eyes and sighing again.

Once I have finished getting ready and I've packed away all my last-minute things, I take one last look around my bedroom.

I'm going to miss you little room, I think as I back out of the doorway closing the door with a shaky sigh. I hear the rumble of male voices and smile as I walk down the hallway. I hear Dad and Michael but I also hear another familiar voice, the ranting voice of my best friend Oliver.

"So I was thinking about how if they ask me to change, where I'm going to tell them to shove their offer..." I hear a slapping noise and a loud laugh that could only be Michael.

"Oliver Hunter! Mind your manners in other people's homes will you!" yells Rita Hunter, Oliver's sweet but scary mother. I round the corner and see Oliver rubbing the back of his head messing up his already flyaway hair. He stares at his mother with an angry frown on his face, while his dad Jimmy shakes his head in an amused sort of way. Oliver is the first to notice me as I walk towards them. His frown dissolves and his eyes widen before his mouth pops open. I give him an awkward wave and can't help the blush that creeps over my face at his reaction. I see Rita and Jimmy look at each other with little smiles and Rita looks over at me with her hand on her heart.

"You look beautiful sweet heart," she says sweetly. I give her a little smile of thanks. Dad spins around in his seat his eyes widening as he looks me over and I give him a little smile. I'm pleased to see that instead of sadness there is just happiness in his eyes and it makes my smile wider. I see Michael relax in his chair and he gives me a pleased look. I'm hyper aware that everyone is looking at me and I feel awkward standing here in the middle of the room.

"Wow kiddo you look... wow," Dad says as he stands up and hugs me.

"Thanks Dad," I say quietly and I feel myself blush again when I see Rita elbow Oliver who tears his eyes off me and glares back at her.

"What?" he hisses and she looks at him through narrowed eyes.

"Don't you think Chloe looks lovely?" she mutters under her breath but still plenty loud enough for us all to hear. Michael grins widely; I know he'll just love this.

The git!

"Make-up can work miracles, apparently," he says in a, rather carrying whisper. I glare at him but turn away when his smug grin widens. I look at Oliver who is avoiding looking at me and I feel my cheeks heat up. Finally, he looks up and I try not to smile when I see his cheeks flush a little as he looks me over, quickly. Our eyes don't meet.

Oh god.

"Yeah, yeah you look nice," he says avoiding my eyes, still. I nod and try to fight back a smile.

"You too," I say noticing his smart suit. He nods his thanks and chews his lip as he pulls at the sleeve.

"Phew! You can cut the sexual tension in here with a knife," Michael says loudly. My eyes widen and meet

Oliver's wide stare briefly before I look away and to the floor.

"Shut up Michael," Dad hisses as Michael chuckles.

"Can we just go?" I ask, snatching up my coat and stomping to the door. I hear the others moving behind me as I walk down to Oliver's parents' car and wait. I look along the street and see other students leaving their houses. I drag my eyes away from them and look at the car bonnet.

"Your brother's an ass," Oliver says from behind me making me jump. I turn around jumping again at how close he is.

Just calm down Chloe! I scald myself. Oliver raises an eyebrow at me but makes no comment on my scatty behaviour.

"I know he is. I did live with him for fifteen years." I smile at him he nods, his hair flops in front of his green eyes. I reach up and push it back.

"You need a haircut," I say and he smiles.

"You sound like my mother," he sighs as he messes up his unruly red hair more. I roll my eyes. I've always been envious of the dark red colour of his hair and even more so when it shines so brightly in the early morning sun.

"You know we are supposed to look presentable right?" I say with a teasing grin. He scoffs as he looks down at me, his hair sticking out at strange angles making me chuckle.

"They got me in a suit, that's as good as it's going to get," he says tugging on his sleeve again. I shake my head and smile at him. "You ok?" he asks narrowing his eyes, I nod.

"You?" I ask. He shrugs.

"Been better, I just want to get this over with so we can just get on with our lives," he says and I nod. I look back up to the house as Oliver's parents, Michael and Dad head towards us.

"Are you going to miss it?"

15

"Yes," I sigh. "But I'll have you so I will be fine." I nudge his arm and he smiles.

"Yeah. It'll be fine. Even if we are a while apart I can learn to drive and come see you all the time. Plus that also means we can visit the parents."

"Sure," I say trying to sound upbeat and not think about the fact that our homes will be given to some other families as soon as we leave here. The frown on Oliver's face tells me he's not fooled by my fake cheeriness. I smile as Dad walks over to us.

"You kids ready to go?" he asks, his voice sounding upbeat, even though it's totally forced. I look to Oliver he rolls his eyes and I chuckle. I give dad a smile as I open the car. Jimmy pops the boot and he and Michael load my trunks alongside Oliver's.

"Oh Oliver look at your hair! I really wish you would have let me give you a trim," Rita says as Oliver tries to get into the car.

"Oww, mum get off me!" Oliver yells as I scoot down the seat. I chuckle at him as he climbs in after me with a big frown on his face. "Oh shut it," he snaps at me and I snort.

Chapter 2

As we drive down the street Michael groans from the boot of the car making Oliver laugh. Michael is squashed into the boot with our trunks, as there aren't enough seats, he looks thoroughly miserable.

"Are you comfortable enough back there Michael?" Oliver asks with a smirk. Michael shifts with another grunt and glares at him. It does look very uncomfortable back there.

Good, I think. He deserves a little bit of suffering for being such a jackass.

"Bite me Hunter. I have a bloody tire iron trying to climb in my a…"

"That's enough Michael!" Dad says from Oliver's other side, I giggle. Michael grunts pulling said iron out from between his legs. Oliver and I smile at each other.

The car journey is short but after Michael's outburst very quiet, making it seem much longer. I pass the time looking out at the familiar places we drive past. We pass the little playground Oliver and I used to play at, the tree that we used to climb, and lastly the pond that used to freeze over in the bad winters where we would skate. With a big sigh I look back into the car and down at my hands. I jump when Oliver places his hand on mine. I look up at him and he gives me a little smile. I look away but keep hold of his hand. I promised myself I wasn't going to cry today.

Finally, Jimmy parks. As the others get out I watch Rita fixing her short blonde hair, her eyes meet mine in the mirror and she turns to me smiling.

"Are you ok sweet heart?" she asks kindly, I shrug.

17

"I'll be ok."

"Don't worry dear, Oliver will look after you," she says turning away quickly as her lip begins to tremble. She opens her door leaving me staring after her. I've always loved Rita. She's funny and sweet; everything a good mother should be, although she can be a little full-on sometimes.

"Hey are you coming?" Oliver asks popping his head back in the car.

"I'm coming," I sigh. I climb out and we join the throngs of sombre families heading into the school grounds, towards the school's auditorium. Almost every set of eyes looks up to the darkened windows of the observation rooms above the auditorium, mine included. I tear my eyes from the black windows as we begin to get separated almost instantly upon reaching the doors.

"Families to the right students to the left," a man in a black suit commands from the shadowy hallway. I'm barely able to give my dad a quick hug before the other families shunt him and Michael forward. I feel a hand on my back guiding me forward and Oliver smiles down at me.

"Come on, you will see them in a little while," he says and I nod, allowing him to lead me into a faintly lit backstage. His hand on my back makes me feel oddly comforted until it's suddenly gone; I twist looking for him and find him pulling himself off the ground. I rush to help him up, tugging his arm uselessly. He gives me a grateful smile as he dusts off his suit.

"You ok?" I ask. I hear a chuckle and feel Oliver tense under my hands. I sigh and close my eyes in exasperation.

"Clumsy Hunter," the unwelcome voice of Jackson Thompson says from behind me. Jackson is a boy who has been pining after me for years. If it weren't for the fact he was shorter than me, thinner than a twig and at eighteen had a receding hairline and also just happened to be a generally dislikable person, I may like him.

Maybe not even then, I think spitefully.

"Ignore him," I say to Oliver as he sighs deeply.

"How are you so patient?" he hisses through his teeth and I shove him forward as people start to look at us.

"One of us has to be," I say. He looks down at me and shakes his head with a smile. I look upwards and his eyes follow mine towards the dark glass above our heads, his jaw hardening again and he sighs.

"Just remember where we are."

"Thank you," he says in a small voice, I elbow him lightly and give him a little smile.

"I got your back," I wink and he laughs.

"Ladies to the left, gentlemen if you would queue to the right please. You will be graduating men first alphabetically and then the same for the ladies. So if you would like to form a line we are about to begin," I look to Oliver who looks over my head at the queue of boys then down at me.

"See you on the other side then?"

"Yeah," I say frowning slightly. My feet suddenly feel like they are weighed down with rocks.

"You'll be fine. Just smile and get the hell of the stage as quick as possible ok?" he says and I nod.

"Ok. Go. I'm fine." I shove him but he grabs my arms and pulls me into a hug. I crash against his hard chest. He squeezes me and lets me go without a word before he marches over to his line. He stands between two other boys and looks dead ahead. I make my way slowly into my line heading up to the back to wait. The line finally starts to move and there is a polite spattering of applause as we all enter the hall and line up along the wall to await the start of the ceremony.

The hall darkens slightly, accommodating for our hosts and I squint as my eyes adjust to the dark. I feel my hands begin to tremble and I clasp them together. I look down the line of boys and find Oliver looking back at me. He's giving me a worried look, I just nod and he gives me a look that says, "Are you sure?" I nod again and he smiles a little. I take a deep steadying breath and there is another quiet round of clapping as our head teacher steps on stage. He gives us as a little shaky bow and turns to the crowd looking tired and sickly. This time of year is never easy for anyone especially the schools as they are made to put on this farce every year. Then, if they are unlucky enough to have any students who want to go through the change, they have to witness that as well. The last three years there have been no changes so it has been easier for all concerned, but that chain has got to break eventually. There have been a lot of rumors about this year being particularly bad and as Mr. Evans starts the ceremony I try to swallow down my fear.

"Good morning ladies and gentlemen, I am pleased to welcome you on behalf of our leaders. Today is a great day and we are so lucky..." I zone out. I don't even notice that half of the boys in the year have been called to graduate until I hear Oliver's name, his name sounds loud and clear in my fuzzy head. Startled out of my daydream, I blink several times before I realise I was staring up at the blacked out windows. I frown wondering how long I was staring and if anyone noticed. I take one last look towards the windows above the crowd then to the stage where Oliver is making his way. Taking the stairs two at a time. He's obviously keen to get the whole event over and done with as soon as possible.

Mr. Evans casts him a wary look as Oliver stops in front of him. It's fair to say that they had clashed over the last few years when Oliver got a little too out spoken about his hatred for the Fanged. Mr. Evans has attempted to distract Oliver from this by asking him to join one of many clubs but Oliver refused out right.

Mr. Evans glances up at the black windows quickly before turning and retrieving Oliver's diploma. To my shock and the obvious horror on Oliver's face as he's handed, only, his a diploma. There's no silver envelope to be seen. I stare at the stage in complete shock. How did this happen? Oliver never would have put his name forward.

I hear a strangled gasp from the crowd and I recognise Rita's voice. However I can't look away from the stage where Oliver is still stood rigid and unmoving. His words *"Just smile and get the hell of the stage as quick as possible"* echo in my head and I wait for him to move but he hasn't moved an inch. The whole auditorium is deathly silent and I can feel their eyes on Oliver through the glass above us.

"Is this a joke sir?" Oliver asks his voice tight and dangerous, "Because it's not funny." Mr. Evans looks to the high glass windows and back at Oliver. "Do I not even get a gold envelope?" Oliver asks sounding confused

"Mr. Timothy Malcolm," Mr. Evans squeaks and Oliver frowns at the dismissal, he looks up at the black windows. I hear him growl an insult as he storms off the stage.

"God damn parasites," he hisses, the room murmurs in shocked whispers confirming my fear that everyone else heard. Along with half the room I look up to the glass and I see flickering dark movements. My eyes dart back to Oliver's retreating form. It takes all my will not to rush after him but I know I can't. I can only wait. Wait to see if he'll still be there after my name is called and if he is, I'm going to kill him.

I can't help thinking as I wait, that graduation should be one of the happiest days of your life. You're free of school you're technically an adult and that should be celebrated. In the world that we live in you should be thrilled that you even make it to seventeen or eighteen. But as I stand here in the queue awaiting my name to be called, all I can do is shake with fear. Fear for Oliver, fear for the others and fear for myself. If you're strong enough to make it through your life and actually reach the end of your school career you shouldn't have to suffer the horror of the graduation. I would take six more years of study to avoid this moment. It may be morbid for me to think it, but those kids lucky enough to have succumbed to illness before the end of their time in school are free from this nightmare and this world.

I hope they are happy now.

I know it's horrible to think of death as a better option but as I watch my fellow students being handed their life assignments the look on some of their faces makes me think perhaps it is. They are handed a rolled up diploma tied with a crimson bow. For those who will be put to work they will also be handed a silver envelope. For the unlucky majority they're handed a gold envelope that holds their wedding rings.

For those with the gold envelopes they have a chance to go for the change and if you're denied then it's the wedding and that's final.

There is however the last few options either you're 'undetermined' which mean's the government couldn't find something useful for you to do so you're put forward for the change and if the Fanged don't want you then you're married off. Then, last but not least there are the few that opt for the change. You can either be nominated for it, like Oliver, or chose it yourself. The people who choose the change are left out as 'undetermined' as not to upset the general public and alert their unknowing families to their choice but when they are not handed an envelope onstage the rumours start to fly and the bets start.

I watch as a trembling boy is handed his diploma and then much to his horror, a golden envelope. His eyes widen and I hear a cry of anguish from someone in the crowd making my head spin around. There is boy in the crowd who is staring at the stage his eyes wide and hands over his mouth, his silver envelope clutched in one fist. I turn back to the stage and the dark haired boy presses his lips press together to hide his emotions and he walks off the stage and into the crowd. He's smart to hide his emotions unlike his partner, as when he walked off the stage I saw a hint of movement from the darkened windows above us.

"They're watching. They're always watching..." my dad's voice echoes in my head as I look up again. I can barely make out the outlines of the bodies behind them. If they were moving before they aren't now, they are as still as statues. Cold, living statues. I'm shoved forwards and I tear my eyes off of the windows. I stumble over my stupid dress and bump into the girl in front.

"Sorry," I mumble but she doesn't even acknowledge that I have touched her, she stares straight at the stage and I frown. I feel someone watching me and I look around the room. I can't see anyone looking my way but then I feel a prickling on my neck I look up again seeing a slight movement in the dark window before I look back down at the floor. I keep my eyes firmly on the floor, despite the almost overwhelming urge to look up. I fix my eyes on my feet until I hear my name being called out.

"Chloe Wood," Mr. Evans calls. My head snaps up and my eyes widen. I look to the back of the room skimming over the hundreds of faces for Oliver. There's movement to my right and he steps into a shaft of dull light and like a shining beacon my eyes snap to him, his red hair standing out amongst the sea of blonde and brunette.

He is still alive, I think and I can't help the smile that spreads on my face. He returns it, nods at me encouragingly and waves. I swallow as I turn back to the waiting Mr. Evans and hitch the skirt of my dress up a little so my jelly legs will make it up the stairs. Mr. Evans gives me a tight smile as I walk over to him.

"Congratulations Chloe," he says. He holds out his hand and I stare at it. His eyes widen slightly, I take his hand and he shakes mine vigorously. We turn and try to smile as the cameras flash. There is a polite spattering of applause and apart from that the room is eerily quiet. I'm handed my diploma and give Mr. Evans a small smile of thanks holding out my hand for my envelope but he just shakes his head. "I'm so sorry," he mutters, as he turns around, his hands empty when he faces me again. "Try not to lose it," he says with a nervous chuckle looking at the diploma in an attempt at humour but I know it's a warning as his eyes dart upwards. I stare at him in disbelief at not being handed an envelope.

"I should be getting a silver one," I say frowning at him thinking he's making a joke. A horrible joke, but when his head shakes slightly my eyes widen.

No, this can't be happening.

He knows I have worked hard to avoid this very moment, I can't believe it's happening. I pinch myself as I walk slowly down the aisle, when the pain shoots up my arm I know I'm not having a nightmare and I lock my eyes on the exit.

Who could've done this?

Turning my head slightly I spot my dad and brother staring at me in disbelief from their seats. Dad looks like he's going to pass out and he's holding a furious looking Michael in his seat.

"What happened?" Michael mouths angrily; I shake my head wide eyed in fear as I try to think who would have done this. I turn away, unable to look at them anymore. It would never have been them; they look as sick as I feel. I push through the doors ignoring the people who rush to stop me.

"Miss, you have to come back in," another man in a black suit calls from behind me but I ignore him and keep walking away. I walk into the stifling heat, gasping as I try to catch my breath. Who was I kidding? This is no time to celebrate. I lean against the school's rough wall with my hands on my knees as I try and get my head around what has just happened. I can't quite believe the fact that I have worked so hard for six years, joined all the clubs I possibly could, and done all the extracurricular activities to get my grades up. All for a better chance of getting myself out of this situation and it was all for nothing. I push off the wall and walk forwards; I walk around the empty school ground aimlessly with no envelope to show for all my hard work. My promised job has been cruelly snatched away from me.

It's gone. Everything's gone.

Chapter 3

I stop walking and look around realising I'm headed towards the gates, my subconscious telling me to run. I see a small group of people in black suits looking at me curiously. I straighten up, turning away before I lose my composure, I walk slowly back towards the auditorium. I shouldn't have gotten my hopes up, that's what it comes down to. This is what dreaming for something gets you in this world, nothing. I stare up at the top floor of the auditorium and just know that they are watching me. I wonder what they think about my little break down. I can't help but smile.

This is so not funny.

I wonder if they'll still want me when they see how unstable I am, there's a silver lining, I suppose. I start pacing waiting for the graduation to finish.

"No Envelope," I keep saying aloud to myself, to make it real. That means only one thing. Someone put my name up for selection.

But who? I think, as I grip my hair. Who in their right mind would think, I would want to go through the change?

The thought of the change makes me feel sick, especially after what it did to Oliver's and my family. I realise suddenly Oliver didn't receive an envelope either. Why? Out of anyone I know he hates the Fanged the most, especially after what they did to his brother. He's always voicing his hatred towards them loud enough for people to hear. He's not afraid to let anyone know exactly how he feels. *"I would rather die fighting against them; than have them*

26

bleed me dry!" he would always say with fire in his sea green eyes.

I have always feared for Oliver. Feared he would be taken from me in the middle of the night, never to see him again. It's a selfish fear but I would miss him terribly, I'm not sure what I would do without him. On many occasions, I have tried to settle him down, to make him see if he doesn't stop he'll be killed but it has often fallen on deaf ears. The fear of losing him became too much for me one day, a few years back, after one of his more shocking outbursts, where he called the Fanged, 'Leeches' out loud in the cafeteria. I told him then, that every day I was thankful for seeing him at my front door to walk me into school. I even cried a little which shocked him more, I rarely cried. After that day he did tone down his public displays of hatred a little, even though I could see it bothered him to do so.

Despite Oliver being young and strong he's still no match for the Fanged. None of us are, alone. Just as the thought starts to creep into my head about what we could achieve working together, the auditorium doors open and the students start spilling out causing the thought to flit away. I sigh as I look around at all my classmates, I can tell who got the silver envelopes just by the look on their faces. Clearly the relief of being able to live your life more freely is a happy thought, judging but the smiles they wear. They're the lucky ones who have been given a career and therefore the choice of picking a partner; they even have the power to decide if they want to have children or not. I've never been so envious of other people in my whole life.

It should've been me, I think bitterly. I see the sadness on the faces of those poor students who are to become breeders. With the feeling of a brick sliding down my throat I begin to realise that I'm one of them. I clench my fists, as I look around at all their devastated faces. Even the boys look sick to their stomachs.

I had always thought that it would be ideal for a man to get paired off with someone to be able to have a woman look after him tending to his every need. There are very few who think like that but that isn't how the majority thinks, as is evident by their faces. It was of course wrong and foolish of me to think that way. In my defense I have been brought up my whole school life being taught what would be expected of me if I were to be someone's wife.

I, along with every girl in the school, have been taught to believe that's what the wife does; she's the cook, she cleans and she has the children. While the man works and brings home a paycheck. I believed that for a long time, it made me wary towards boys, all except Oliver. I was young and stupid. I hate that I thought like that, but that was before I saw how upset it made my brother.

Three years ago during his graduation Michael bid for a girl who he had liked for a long time. When the hammer fell she became his. He was pleased for a while. She was quiet; she smiled when she met us, then when they got to their new home, she did nothing but cry for a week. Michael came back to the house in tears when he couldn't stand it anymore.

She wasn't eating; he was worried about trying to help her in case she got more upset. I hadn't seen my big brother that upset since mum died. Seeing Millie like that nearly drove him mad. He and dad spoke for hours; just as I was finishing my homework he came into my bedroom, puffy eyed gave me a crushing hug and left looking somewhat better.

I didn't see him for a while, despite him only living an hour away. Then a few weeks later, he and Millie visited, they were holding hands. Millie looked happier, she spoke freely with us, laughed more often and it made me happy to see they were getting on like a house on fire.

Michael told me later that day as we cleared the table that they were just taking it slow. After a year they were together happily and very much in love. They fell pregnant soon after and now they have two great little boys, who I adore. Little Adam and Simon are twins; they were thrilled to have almost filled their quota in one go. They're now expecting their third child and are happier than they have ever been, but it has not been without hard work.

I look around when I hear raised voices, I see the dark haired boy from the stage talking to the other boy from within the crowd. Now I'm out of the hellish room and my mind is a little clearer, I finally notice them. They are the controversial openly gay couple in our school. There was whole assembly about being not being able to choose who you fall in love with and that it was ok. Despite a rocky start for them, especially after one of the boys dumped his girlfriend to be with the other boy they were accepted and even admired. Despite all of that I can't help but think that maybe people weren't as "Ok" with it as they alleged to be.

There is no such thing as choice here, I think as the dark haired boy Damien, with the gold envelope, pleads with his partner. His partner looks angry for some reason and I can't fathom why he would be mad. It was hardly Damien's decision to be a Breeder; he was chosen just like the rest of us. After the publicly of their relationship it's hardly surprising that they were separated.

"Please Tommy, don't do this!" Damien pleads as he holds onto Tommy's arm. Damien stares up at him with wide, scared eyes. Tommy rips his arm free shaking his head as he looks around at the people staring at them.

"I'm sorry Damien; there is nothing I can do. Maybe you can go back to your ex, she might have you back," Tommy says harshly ad Damien stares at him, pain clear in his eyes. Tommy swallows and I see a flicker of regret in his eyes but I see what he's doing. "It's easier this way Damien, you're going to be married tonight. You have to go, I need to go, I'm sorry." He crosses his arms trying desperately to hide the hurt in his eyes as Damien sobs. Tommy turns to look back at him, looking like he's going to crumble, but he shakes his head and just keeps walking.

I, along with the other students, am so engrossed watching poor Damien; that I don't notice the auditorium emptying of families. I'm about to go over to him to try and comfort him, when his family rush towards him, they huddle around him and pull him into their arms. I smile at the touching sight before looking around for my dad and brother. I spot them heading towards me sad faced with pained looks. Michael who pushes past a family, who glare at him, grabs me into his arms and holds me tight.

"Isn't that adorable? Look how your son comforts your daughter," Henry drawls sarcastically from the black window. Lillian slides up to his side watching her son hugging her daughter tightly.

"He has aged well," Lillian says in a bored tone, as she looks down on her middle child, for the first time in eleven years.

"That he has dear one. He is handsome, much like your old mate," Henry says with a smile in Lillian's direction his eyes not leaving her face. She gives a little shrug of indifference before turning away, her head heal high.

"That is none of my concern."

"So heartless my sweet," Henry croons, sensing her discomfort. Lillian turns smiling, shakily.

"I just want my daughter," she says. Henry smiles as he trails his finger down her cheek to her neck.

"And so you shall have her."

"What the hell happened sis? I thought you were a shoe in. Who put your name forward? Do you think maybe mum?" Michael looks at me with surprise on his face and I shrug.

"I don't know," I say and he grips me harder. I feel myself trembling slightly as I start to feel my composure slipping.

"Bitch!" he says loudly, startling me and the other families around us. He looks down at me apologetically. "I'm sorry, I thought you did it," he says sounding embarrassed either about his outburst or his assumption, I'm not sure. I give him a little smile as Dad, politely, pushes through the crowd, his face red from frustration or anger.

"It's ok," I say to them both as dad reaches us. Michael straightens up; he looks down at me his blue eyes dark and angry.

"It's not ok! You've worked your ass off to get, the grades and skills you needed to avoid this," he says loudly, almost yelling. Dad puts his hand on his shoulder to calm him down. I see a flash of pain cross my dad's face, his jaw clenches and he looks away for a moment to compose himself. Michael closes his eyes to reign in his anger as I give dad a grateful smile.

"Just be careful," I say looking over his shoulder to the darkened windows of the Fanged observation rooms that wrap around the top floor of the school. I shudder as another icy chill runs down my spine.

"Sorry," he mutters. He steps to the side breaking my view of the windows. As he crosses his arms across his chest, I give him a small smile. I walk over to Dad and he grips me tightly and in his arms, I nearly break down.

I'm not going to cry, I need to stay strong. I bury my head in his broad chest and steady my breathing.

"I'm so sorry Chloe, I had no idea she would do this. I can try and have a word with them to explain the situation," he murmurs into my hair. I shake my head.

"No Dad, you know they never change their mind. None of us knew this would happen, I will just have to…"

"You'll be fine," Dad grips my arms and holds me at arm's length to look at me; I swallow the lump in my throat and nod.

"Ladies and gentlemen, could I please have your attention?" Mr. Evans calls from the entryway to the auditorium. We all turn to face him and he gives us a strained smile. "Thank you. Now could I have all the remaining students who have not been allocated a career and those who hold the golden envelopes over here in a nice orderly line? You will be taken inside for presentation," his voice breaks on the last word. I look at Dad and Michael who are staring at me with wide fearful eyes. I hand Dad my diploma and Michael narrows his eyes.

"Don't do anything hasty," he warns and I smile.

"I'll be back," I say and they nod. I give them each a kiss on the cheek, smiling at them as I back up. "I love you both," I call over my shoulder. Dad opens his mouth to say something. I turn away before I change my mind and actually consider running away.

Chapter 4

As I approach the auditorium I see Oliver hanging at the back of the line, he's chewing his lip nervously, something he rarely does. He smiles when he sees me rushing towards him.

"I can't believe it Chloe!" he says angrily when I'm in earshot and I sigh.

You and me both.

"You deserved freedom more than all of those goons put together," he says with a scowl. I see a few other students glaring at him but he either doesn't see it or he just ignores them.

"I don't know who I was kidding really. I should've known I wouldn't get a career, I was being stupid." I shrug. He huffs angrily.

"You weren't being stupid," he says putting his arm around my shoulders; I give him a little smile.

"Thanks. I can't believe you were picked though. Do you know who would have done it?" I ask.

"Not a clue. Do you know who put your name in?" he asks. I chuckle darkly.

"One guess," I hiss under my breath he stares at me. Then like a light switch being turned on his eyes widen.

"She wouldn't?" he lets out in a shocked breath. "I can't believe she would do that, it's just..." I put my hand on his arm and flick my eyes to the windows nervously as his voice gets louder and angrier. He clamps his mouth shut, I know that he was going to go into a rant like he always does when he's upset or angry. He huffs and rubs his neck. "I'm sorry," he says and I smile gratefully.

"Yeah you too."

"I'm ok. I kind of knew this was coming. I was expecting a gold envelope though," he says with a humorless chuckle. I stare at him in shock.

Why did he not tell me about this?

"I've been in too much trouble for them to give me a position of responsibility," he says running his hand through his hair, I nod in agreement. I did tell him that he was probably not going to get picked to work in the offices at the town hall like he applied for and at the time he went in a mood with me. Now however he doesn't seem that bothered.

"Yeah, could you imagine you helping the Mayor?" I look at him in mock horror, making him laugh. "There would be riots in the streets." He elbows me lightly and I shove him back.

"Easy there princess," he chuckles. I scowl at him and look down at my dress.

"How awful do I look? You can be honest," I say tugging at the skirt. He's silent, I look up at him and his green eyes are staring.

"You look beautiful," he blurts out, I blink, a little shocked, he goes a little red. "I mean for you," he adds trying to mask his embarrassment by shoving me.

"Thanks I guess." I frown as I rub my arm. He nods before he looks down at the ground. We start to move forward. I look back outside, I can just make out Dad and Michael looking back at me and I wave. They both raise their hands at the same time, I smile at the almost mirror image of them.

The doors are sealed shut as we make our way towards a seat in the middle of the dimly lit room. Groups of friends and some family sit together, dotted haphazardly around the hall. When we are all seated we fall silent and wait for something to happen.

"When we tell them where to shove the change I wonder what we'll be given for work?" Oliver says, after a few minutes of tense silence, I frown at him.

"Oliver I won't..." I begin but Mr. Evans walks up onto the stage and the whispers all around us die as butterflies' assault my stomach.

"Attention students," Mr. Evans calls from the podium and I turn to face the front. "Welcome to this year's presentation," I can see Oliver is still staring at me in my peripheral vision.

"You won't what Chloe?" he hisses in my ear, I nudge him to get him to shut up. A few people turn around and I stare at the front feeling my face redden. Mr. Evans doesn't notice and continues on.

"Today you lucky remaining students will be presented before the Council. You may or may not be asked to join their ranks. Some of you have already been selected as breeders so if that's not your wish this will be your last chance to impress the Council official. If they change their mind, you will be allowed the honour of being turned." He doesn't look quite convinced by his own words, but smiles and plows on.

"Those of you who have had or put your own name forward will be presented and the Council will decide if they want you in their ranks. As I said it's a real honour," he says with as much fake enthusiasm as he can muster. "If you are chosen to join the Fanged you will be turned here." Mr. Evans looks up as a huge glass dome is lowered until it's suspended above our heads. "This dome will contain you while the rest of us watch as you are transformed," Mr. Evans explains. There is a murmur of excitement from a small group of six further down the auditorium. I glance over at them and catch Oliver looking away from them shaking his head in disgust. I turn away back to the stage.

"The students who choose 'the life' will be shown the ways of our gracious Fanged leaders and bathed in riches," Mr. Evans says, attempting a dazzling smile, but falling short. His face drops as he goes on. "Those who decline the generous offer of eternal life and beauty will be

35

married off and will return to their lives to live it out raising children and working until they reach their farming date," Mr. Evans says in a flat tone. Oliver stiffens in his seat and I know the reality has just hit him that he's talking about us.

"One more exciting piece of news, we are being joined today by a very special guest official. We are very honoured to have him with us today and let me tell you it's extremely rare that he takes time out of his busy schedule to attend these ceremonies." Mr. Evan's smile twitches before he turns, exits the stage and the room fills with quiet nervous murmurs.

"Who could it be?" someone whispers loudly but I couldn't care less. I can't help but think how awful Mr. Evans looks. Normally this time of year is never good for him but this year he looks especially thin and worn down. His greying hair looks unclean and his suit hangs off him a lot more than usual.

"Shit," Oliver says in a hushed voice. He turns towards me in his seat as I focus on the stage. "Look Chloe I know he's not really selling the human life but you can't start to think the change is a good idea," Oliver says, worry clear in his voice. I roll my eyes drawing them off of Mr. Evans' retreating form. I stare around the room at the thirty or so students left over and I wonder which of them will do it, who will chose 'the life'? I know that this is the opportune moment for humans to be turned into a Fanged, as they are generally healthy enough to survive the transformation. It's also the ideal stage in a human's life for the change as it's when they're deemed the most beautiful. This means that the Fanged will be forever young and beautiful. I know, however, that someone can be changed at any stage of their life as long as they have the right mentality and have retained their beauty, like my mother. I don't see how wanting to be a living corpse is the right mentality but it's what they look for. I glance up at the dark glass and I swear I can feel their dark eyes on

36

us. *"They're watching, they're always watching"*. Oliver puts his hand on my arm and I turn to face him, his shining eyes are full of worry as they meet mine.

"What?" he whispers frowning slightly. I shake my head and I see worry flicker on his face as I glance at Jackson who is staring at me again. His face is pinched, like he's sucking a lemon. I look away feeling angry and fearful.

He's going to try and buy me, I think grimly. Oliver stares between Jackson and me, looking disgruntled. His attention is diverted to the group of six when they laugh quietly.

"They're all up to something," he whispers, as he looks down at the small group consisting of two girls and four boys. I see a raven-haired girl called Rachel chatting amongst them and I'm momentarily shocked to see her there. She was in a few of my classes and she always seemed nice, normal even, despite her excessive use of make-up. She always made an effort to try and talk to me in classes and I feel a pang of sadness seeing her sitting there. Her attention is drawn to us, her eyes flickering between Oliver and me before settling on him. She gives him a big smile and he looks away quickly.

"I think they're all for the Turners," he says his tone dripping disgust.

"I know," I reply and he sighs. I see them all looking this way and I turn away not wanting to draw more attention to myself. We are quiet for a moment until Oliver starts to fidget and huff.

"What is it?" I ask, knowing he wants to say something. He looks up into the darkened windows and then at me.

"I saw Jackson looking over at you," he says quietly, I look away frowning.

"And?" I say as he turns in his chair.

"When you decline their offer... It means you... that we're going to have to..." he frowns unable to finish his

sentence but I nod confirming his thought. I'm glad the fact, that when we decline the Fang's invitation to be turned we'll become Breeders and forced to marry, has finally dawned on him. Oliver frowns looking back at Jackson and his jaw clenches. "He's going to try and…"

"Yes probably," I snap, the frustration of the whole thing getting to me. Especially now I know that in a matter of a few minutes the years of harassment Jackson has inflicted on me, my constant refusal to date him, might all be for nothing. In a few minutes he could buy me and own me and I'll be unable to do anything about it. I glance at Oliver out of the corner of my eye, he looks angry. I wonder if he's thinking the same thing. "I really don't want to think about it though," I add quickly and he nods. His eyes are fiercely staring towards where Jackson is sitting.

"If he…" He clenches his teeth and sighs, "… I'll kill him." he says and I frown.

"If we are paired he can do whatever he wants."

"Stop," he says closing his eyes. I put my hand on his arm.

"If it's him, I would rather let them have me," I say in a low voice. His eyes snap open meeting mine instantly.

"You wouldn't? Chloe that's not funny. You can't be serious?" he says angrily.

"Serious? Of course I am Oliver, think of it from my point of view," I say staring him down. "Could you imagine having *that* all over you every day and being powerless to refuse him? I would take death over that any day," I say, his eyes widen.

"Why didn't you… you're serious aren't you?" he asks and I shrug. "Chloe I…" his voice fails him as the room is plummeted into darkness. I look back at the stage squinting to see it. I've never liked the darkness and for good reason, there are monsters in the dark. Oliver reaches over and puts his hand on mine holding it tightly as I tense. I give him a grateful smile I hope he sees but when I see his teeth flash I know he did. The doors and windows are shuttered closed and after a short but deafening silence a set of doors creak open at the back of the stage and three shadowy figures emerge from the pitch dark. My eyes have adjusted and I see the leader, a tall, sleek man in a black robe who gracefully walks to the podium followed closely by two red-cloaked followers.

"The Turners," Oliver croaks and I feel my palms begin to sweat. I have of course heard about and been warned about this ceremony. It's legend in schools. It's one of the only times you have your own choice when it comes to how you live your life. There are always three Fanged present at a graduation, a high-ranking official, normally a Fang who works for the leader of our country and his two most trusted and controlled Turners. The official gets to decide who, from the volunteer and nominated humans, he thinks is worthy to join his ranks and the Turners well they get the messy job. They're made to do all the biting without killing the volunteer. It's gone horribly wrong a few times but that's very rare. When it comes to Turners they're the best at what they do.

The leader shakes Mr. Evans' hand and leans into whisper something into his ear before straightening up. Mr. Evans nods back and backs up, visibly shaking from head to toe. The leader turns to us and lowers his hood. There is an intake of startled breath from the crowd. I lean forwards to get a better look at the angel in front of me. He's quite a specimen, with dazzling dark eyes and high strong cheekbones giving him a regal look.

"Bloody hell," Oliver says behind me, I blink and sit up. I turn to him; he looks at me and blushes furiously. If it weren't such a serious moment I might have laughed at him. I have heard of the power that the Fanged have over us, how they can draw us in with just their looks, dazzling us long enough to tear our throats out.

The thought makes me shiver; I didn't believe the rumours until right now in this moment. Oliver shifts in his seat, folding his arms looking embarrassed at his outburst. I turn back to look at the front making sure not to look too long at the Fang in front of me.

"Good afternoon Ladies and Gentlemen. My name is Henry Caldwell."

Wow that voice, it's soft and deep but his tone is gentle. There's a spattering of polite applause started by Mr. Evans and Henry waves us down looking extremely embarrassed.

"Oh please, you are too kind. I am, as you may know, the leader of this charming country." My eyebrows shoot up in surprise. I'm shocked by this information; it's not very often that the leader of the country comes out of Centrum, especially not to come to something as mundane as a graduation. I stare at him as the feeling of dread washes over me again.

Something's not right...

Chapter 5

"I forgive you of course if you didn't recognise me." Henry smiles brightly at us all as we stare at him. "I don't get out much and there are not very many paintings of me after all," he chuckles at his own joke and looks around the darkened room at us all with a beautiful smile. The Fanged, of course, have great night vision but light a room even with a torch they will be dazzled. If the light is too intense they will even be momentarily blinded. Not that that would stop them finding you, only slow them down.

Not dismayed by our silence following his joke Henry clasps his hands and walks up and down the stage slowly looking at us all in turn.

"You are all looking lovely today," he says. His black eyes land on me, his lips curling upwards slightly. I sit up in my chair leaning forward slightly. I feel Oliver stiffen next to me and he grips my hand. Henry's eyes leave mine and flit to Oliver then to our joined hands before he slowly turns around to face us all again. "I am thrilled to see so many potential humans here in front of me. More potential here than was requested, you have a charming group here Mr. Evans. Some good stock," he says turning to him smile at him. Mr. Evans sits up in his chair and nods.

"Oh yes, lovely. It's a very bright year," Mr. Evans says with a rushed breath. Henry doesn't seem to notice or care about the fear clear in his voice. Henry closes his eyes before taking in a large breath through his nose. A small but slightly sinister smile crosses his face.

"Truly lovely," he says opening his eyes and I feel the hair rise up on my arms as they land instantly on me again. Oliver shifts in his seat clearing his throat noisily. "I am hoping that some of you lovely dears if not all of you choose this life. We have a lot to offer you and for those whom I deem worthy of a life full of pleasure," he says. This time when his eyes land squarely on me I shiver. I feel my face redden, he looks away smirking. "So without further ado let's get under way." He bows to us before taking the seat Mr. Evans offers him with a wide smile. Mr. Evans wipes his damp brow with the back of his sleeve and pulls out a roll of paper, opening it with trembling hands.

"Anthony Adams," he calls out. Anthony makes his way down the aisle and on to the stage.

"Stand on the X my dear boy," Henry says. Anthony nods and faces him. He wipes his trembling hands on his trousers, standing up straight while Henry looks him over. Henry's eyes narrowing before he nods. "So what say you?" Henry asks after a few moments.

This is what we'll all get asked if Henry wishes to have you. Anthony shakes his head quickly and confidently holding his golden envelope tightly in his clenched fist.

"No," he says. A one word answer that's all that's required.

"Don't converse with them." my dad's voice says in my head.

"So be it," Henry says, unflinchingly, with a nod. "Head to donation and good luck with your pairing." Anthony nods quickly and walks off the stage into the small side room where the donations must be being taken. Donation is something we have to do every month once we turn the age of fourteen. It's how we supply the Fanged with blood without them hunting us to extinction, which would not benefit them at all.

The ceremony continues with everyone following Anthony, either refusing or being refused the change, until Rachel Hunt is called forward. She strides onto the stage and waits patiently for Henry to appraise her.

42

"You put your name forward am I correct?" Henry asks surprising us all, Rachel nods. He almost smiles. After a moment Henry nods at her. "What say you?" Rachel is still for a moment before she nods.

"Yes," she says in a shaky voice. The Turners heads snap up as the room falls silent. I hear a little groan from Oliver as Henry holds out his hand from his chair smiling.

"Come child," he says. She takes his hand and he sits her next to him. She looks out into the dark room looking frightened but determined. "Continue," Henry says to Mr. Evans who is staring at Rachel in disbelief. She's the first student in three years to say yes and the first under his watch. If I thought he looked pale earlier that's nothing in comparison to how he looks now.

"Oh, of course," he bumbles and he looks down at the piece of paper that's shaking like a leaf in his hands. I don't need to hear it to know who is next. I look over to Oliver and his jaw is tense. "Oliver Hun-hunter," Mr. Evans stutters still clearly shocked by the turn of events. Oliver stands up quickly and gives me a tight smile. I watch him as he makes his way down the aisle his shoulders tense and his jaw set. He takes the steps two at a time and stands in front of Henry with his hands behind his back. His fists are clenched tightly. Henry considers him for a few seconds and just as I think he's about to tell him to move on he actually smiles.

"Your name was put forward by your older brother Ethan. He sang your praise in the application," Henry says smiling at Oliver. I see Oliver stiffen and his muscles tighten in his back.

"My brother was sick," Oliver says tightly. "He was not in his right mind."

Don't converse with them. Don't converse with them! I chant in my head as I stare at Oliver's back hoping my silent message will reach him.

"I am well aware of his state of mind that is why we denied him entry," Henry says with a little smile. Oliver

43

says nothing I know how hard the subject of Ethan is for him. I'm surprised and impressed that he's remaining so calm. I'm also shocked to realise that I have stood up as if to rush to him if it gets out of hand. Henry's eyes drift towards me, he smiles at me. "You may sit down Miss Wood," he chuckles. Oliver turns around and squints through the darkened auditorium towards me. I sit down embarrassed by my actions. Henry turns back to Oliver and smiles up at him again. "Your mind is not sick. You are a determined young man. I have heard a lot about you Mr. Hunter. I believe you would make an inspiring vampire. However I can practically taste your hostility as I talk to you now." Henry pauses. Oliver stays mercifully quiet. "I almost feel foolish asking this Oliver. What say you?" Henry asks with a little knowing smile. Oliver straightens up and takes a deep breath. My whole body tenses as I wait for his answer.

Careful Oliver.

"No. I do not want to be like you," he says sharply and I smile. Rachel Hunts head droops and her gaze that was lingering on Oliver drops to the ground. Henry's eyes dart to me again and my smile vanishes. Oliver turns around, frowning, looking out into the crowd for me but I know he can't see me. His frown deepens when Henry doesn't look away from me and he clears his throat. "I said no," he says a little louder and Henry turns back to him and smiles.

"I thought as much, such a shame your brother would be so disappointed. It seems his death was for nothing after all," Henry says casually leaning back in his chair and Oliver freezes where he stands. I can feel the tension of their stare; Oliver begins to advance on Henry and is instantly blocked by the red-hooded Turners.

"Don't you dare, you know nothing! You know nothing you filthy…" Oliver growls as the Turners push him back.

"Oliver!" I yelp from my seat and he freezes. He stumbles back as he's shoved hard.

"Such spirit wasted." Henry's lips quirk but his eyes don't leave Oliver.

"Can I leave?" Oliver hisses through his teeth and Henry smiles brightly. I watch as Henry stands up and slowly looks him over again. My heart is racing in my chest as my hands grip the armrests of the chair. Henry gets threateningly close to Oliver before answering.

"So be it," he says with a little laugh, "Head to donation and good luck with your pairing." He shoves a golden envelope roughly into Oliver's hand. Oliver looks down at it, nods and walks down towards the tent. Before he disappears from my view he shoots me a nervous glance. I stare back at him hoping he can see the anger and exasperation on my face.

What are you playing at Oliver?

After he has disappeared from my view I look back to the stage and wait patiently and nervously for my name to be called. I pay no attention to what is happening my mind is too busy reeling from Oliver's foolishness. I try my best not to worry about him too much right now, as my name is getting closer. I hardly notice when four others decide to join the Fanged. It's only when myself; Damien and Colin Young who are cousins are left, that I notice the small group sitting around Henry.

Mr. Evans looks like he's going to pass out. I stare at them in disbelief when my name is finally called. I nearly miss it but then I see Henry smile and sit up in his seat. I look to Mr. Evans who looks at me wide-eyed and desperate. Henry, who was beginning to look bored despite the group of five he has around him, now looks positively captivated.

This is it.

I get up slowly and I see Oliver and Jackson looking over at me from the group of the sorted. Funny, I don't recall Jackson's name being called, I wonder if he was offered the change? I think, as I slowly make my way down the aisle. I make my way down between the rows of chairs lifting my skirt a little so I don't fall over my gown. As I start to climb the stairs my teeth begin to chatter in my skull, the sound is deafening in my head. I see the Turners turning their heads towards me at the noise and I try and calm myself. There's a chilled air being blown onto the stage, as the Fanged like it a bit cooler. I cannot help but tremble due to my flimsy gown.

"Ah, Miss Wood. I have been looking forward to meeting you in person," Henry says sweetly. I frown a little when He stands up gracefully and makes his way over to me. I freeze. He never got up for anyone else. Except Oliver, but he was being an idiot. I watch him wearily as he circles me. He's pale and dazzling in this light. If the Fanged only want the most beautiful of the humans in their ranks, I can definitely see why he was chosen with his high cheekbones and big shining eyes. I can't help but wonder what colour they were before they turned jet black. I realise then that his eyes are on mine and I have been staring. I feel myself leaning towards him drawn by his tangy, limey smell.

Strange.

There is a loud cough from the crowd and I jump. I straighten up and look away from Henry, shaking my woozy head. I know without looking it was Oliver and I know, with a pang of embarrassment that he knew I was getting drawn in. I have never been so grateful for him having my back. I hear a low growl from Henry. I close my eyes to steady my red face and embarrassingly accelerated breath. I focus on breathing through my mouth to lessen the intoxicating smell of his cologne.

"You look just like her," Henry says, his smooth voice close making my eyes pop open. He's stood right in front of me his eyes burning into mine; I tear my eyes from his and look at his throat.

"What?"I ask I hear a gasp from the others on the stage.

"Do not converse with them," my dad repeats in my head. I swallow hard my mouth dry. Henry smiles widely,

I look at his mouth his short sharp fangs shine in the dark, as does his smile. Another cough and I feel my face flame. Henry just keeps smiling and I focus on his chest like my life depends on it.

Well I suppose it does.

His smile however, is hard to ignore. I have to fight with my eyes for them to stay in place.

"Your mother dear child. You are her double." This makes me look him in the face his lips quirk like he's pleased to have my full attention.

"My mother is dead," I say stiffly.

Shut up! I think as Henry chuckles.

"Far from it, her heart may not beat but she is very much thriving," he says I scowl at him and meet his eyes again.

"She is dead. She died when her heart stopped beating," I say defiantly a flicker of annoyance flashes on Henry's face.

"Her request for you stands despite her still heart," Henry says and I grind my teeth. How dare she, she left us she has no right to make these decisions for me. I look Henry in the eyes and glare at him until he asks, obviously bored with our conversation, "So what say you?"

"My mother has no say in my life. You can tell her from me she does not get to make decisions for me. I say no," I say as his eyes narrow. He walks angrily to Mr. Evans, who looks like he's about to feint, and snatches up an envelope. He jams it into my hand not looking at me, like he's ashamed of me. He walks to his chair and sits down before staring at the spot above my head.

"So be it. Head to donation and good luck with your, pairing," he says spitting the last word sounding thoroughly disgusted. I stare at the people in the five chairs beside him and they all look away. I nod quickly and grip the envelope tightly. I feel the small metal band through the thin paper. I storm off the stage and head into the room where the nurse is waiting. Her eyes widen when she sees me. She rushes to sit me down. She gives me an impressed little smile as she presses the needle into the crook of my elbow. I look away from her, failing to hide my own smile.

Chapter 6

I watch as the small bag of blood fills slowly, while the nurse hooks Damien up to his machine. Our machines whir and gurgle as we sit silently. Despite what the machines are used for they really are interesting. They draw the blood out of your arm through the little needle. Your blood is then run through the diagnostic and any sort of illness or disease is detected. Testing for any illnesses is important, not because the Fanged can get sick but because the purer your blood, the more money they get for it. If your blood is tainted then it will go for a low price and if untainted for example, young and virgin, it will sell for the highest price. It's quite the delicacy, apparently.

My machine beeps and the nurse smiles down at me as she disconnects me. I'm given a horrible salt and sugar drink to replace any that I lost during the donation and a small sweet biscuit. The nurse points me to where I'm supposed to go before she rushes back to Damien whose machine starts to beep. Damien was the last of the students to come into the little room; he wandered in looking a little startled. Not only was he separated from his boyfriend to be married off to, but also his cousin who was called before him decided he wanted to be turned. I get up and pass him giving him what I hope is a reassuring smile which he weakly returns.

I make my way through the auditorium to the group of students opting out of becoming a Fanged. I spot Oliver who looks anxious as he talks to a boy whose face I can't see. Oliver spots me; he excuses himself before he pushes his way through the crowd. As he rushes towards me the boy he was speaking to turns and I recognise him as one of Oliver's friends, David. He smiles at me and I wave awkwardly just as Oliver reaches me.

"Thank god," he sighs as he catches me in a tight hug nearly lifting me off the floor. "You had me scared for a minute there," he says into my hair. I chuckle as I wrap my arms around his waist.

"Look who's talking!" I snap and I remember that I'm mad at him. He lets me go and I hit him hard on the chest making him frown. "Why the hell would you do that? They could've killed you."

"I'm sorry I just lost it. When he mentioned Ethan I just saw red," he mutters having the good grace to look embarrassed.

"Oliver," I groan.

"I know I was stupid. I'm sorry. Well you weren't much smarter. He was really gunning for you." I arch my eyebrow at him and he chuckles. I frown remembering the embarrassing staring and my strange connection to the Fang.

"I know. Thanks for having my back," I say with a little smile. He pulls me back into his arms and sighs.

"That's alright."

"I'm sorry."

"What for?" he asks frowning.

"I nearly broke our promise. If you weren't there to snap me out of it I don't know what would've happened. What I might've said," I say and he hugs me tighter.

Ever since the cold November morning, a few years ago, when I woke up and found out my mother had left us to be changed, Oliver and I, who were only seven at the time, agreed never to let anything no matter how bad drive us to that.

I remember waking from my dream, of chasing butterflies around our beautiful spring garden, to a howl that sounded like a wounded animal. I'd never heard something so sad in my life; the sound chilled my already cold body. I crept out of bed and tiptoed to my bedroom door, fear coursing through my veins. I opened my door and peeked through the crack. What I opened the door to find caused my heart to stutter in my chest and tears to fill my eyes instantly. My dad was on the floor being held down by Joseph and Michael as he thrashed around.

"Dad, please stop!" Michael, who was only ten at the time, begged as my dad's struggling arms almost threw him off and into the kitchen table. I saw Michael's teeth clench as he held on tightly while Joseph held Dad's shoulders down.

"Dad you're going to wake Chloe, don't let her see you like this," Joseph pleaded quietly as my dad wriggled beneath them but as soon as the words left his mouth, dad looked up and his eyes locked with mine. He leapt up from the ground sending the boys flying across the room, the kitchen table crashed in to the wall his wake. He rushed towards me and for a moment I thought he was going to attack me, but he veered off into his room. The whole house shook as he slammed his door. After a few seconds of silence the house was filled with more yells of rage, loud bangs and smashing. Michael rushed over to me, picked me up and carried me out of the house while a startled and bleeding Joseph rushed to dad's bedroom door and began trying to get inside. I heard the angry yells and the sound of Joseph throwing his, large body against the door. Even though he was only sixteen Joseph managed to crash through the door with ease. Michael closed the front door and put his trembling hands on my shoulders before looking me in the eye.

"Just wait here until we've calmed him down," he said to me. I nodded and grabbed his hand tightly.

"What happened Michael?" I asked. He handed me a letter. I stared at it for a moment as Michael shut the door again muffling the sound of the screams and smashing. I opened the letter and read it the best I could.

Dear Christopher,

I am sorry; I cannot do this anymore. I cannot stand the waiting. I will not wait around here any longer to be picked off. You and the children can join me, when they are older.

I want you to join me and we can be together forever. We do not deserve to be torn apart at a moment's notice. We should decide how we live our lives. I choose to be changed; I hope you can respect that.

I love you,
Your Lillian.

Even at seven years old I could see the contradiction in her letter, even if I didn't quite understand what it meant at the time. As I read it I could feel the anger in me rising up at her words.

"She's left us," I said over and over again. As the realisation sunk in I slid down the house wall that's where Oliver found me. He had heard the commotion from down the street and came running out with his family. A crowd had gathered when people started hearing my dad's yelling. Oliver found me huddled at the side of our house and ran straight for me. He hugged me until I stopped crying. All the while his dad, brother and mum, who had run into the house, attempted to calm my dad. After I had settled a little Oliver asked what happened. I told him everything. He listened with a shocked, pained face and when I showed him the note his gentle smiley face turned hard.

Oliver and I made a promise to each other that day never to accept the change; it's something we never talk about but something that we both hold onto with every fibre of our being. That day shook us to our core and it changed us both for good.

That was the first, but not the last, time I saw the traces of the real anger and hatred show on Oliver's young face. It was that day that ignited the flicker of real hatred towards the Fanged for both of us, that day was only the beginning. A few years later after Ethan, Oliver's older brother was turned down by the Fanged, he went mad. When he saw no way out he ended his own life. Ethan ended up setting fire to the family shed before locking himself in, so that his blood would be gone and the Fanged couldn't use it. He apparently wrote that if they didn't want him to join their ranks then they could never have him. That day was the start of Oliver's real rage and resentment towards the Fanged and with age it has only gotten worse. It tore his family apart. His sister, the eldest of the three hasn't spoken to the family ever since Ethan's funeral and Jimmy and Rita had to go through the government to put in a plea so they didn't have to have another child. The whole ordeal was horrible. Oliver suffered greatly, he still does. The only relief they got is that their plea was allowed, as the government did not want another unstable human to deal with.

Unlike Oliver whose anger boils on the surface, my anger towards them is deeply buried, hidden almost. I've used it to fuel my passion of wanting to help others but now, as I stand here in Oliver's arms I realise maybe Oliver had it right all along.

Oliver shuffles his feet and I blink back tears that are threatening to spill over at my upsetting thoughts.

"I knew you wouldn't do it Chloe," he says as I blink up at him.

"How could you possibly have known that?" I ask looking down at the floor not wanting to openly admit that turning really did sound more appealing than having Jackson pawing at me for the rest of my life. Another scary thought is that if Henry hadn't mentioned my mother and the resentment and anger hadn't come flooding back, we may not have been having this conversation. Oliver puts his hand on my shoulder I look up at him feeling embarrassed about even contemplating it.

"I just knew you wouldn't have, you're good Chloe. You wouldn't have done that to your brothers or your dad, you're not your mother. No matter how much you look like her. Also you wouldn't have done it to me either." He shoves me playfully with his shoulder and I smile. "You know I would've had to change my mind. I would've changed just to look after you and then I would be pissed at you forever!" he says. I stare at him feeling the smile slip from my face. I'm about to ask him if he's being serious but the look in his eyes tells me everything I need to know.

"You really would wouldn't you?" I ask. He nods. "You're the best but I can look after myself you know," I say. He smiles widely.

"I know. I feel sorry for the poor soul you get paired with... I'm sorry," he says quickly as I frown, his smile faltering. I look back down at the ground not able to look him in the eye.

"After today..." I begin but find myself unable to continue.

Neither of us has brought up the subject of what would happen if we were to be married off because we really didn't think it was going to come to this. We both had hoped for a career and with that, the option to meet someone when or if we wanted to. We were hoping to both work for the government, Oliver in the Mayor's office and I with the hospital but now because of the selection, we are both to be breeders and that's something we have not spoken about. We both know that married women aren't supposed to be associated with men other than their husbands or direct family, regardless of how long they have known each other. Once they are married they are especially not allowed to be alone with other men. Now when I'm sold off, to another man, I'm not going to be able to see Oliver, unless my husband is there. Then there's the horrible fact that we may not even live in the same place; we could live hundreds of miles apart. He could be sent off to a totally different region to me and that means I will hardly see him, if at all.

What am I going to do?

It's just not going to be the same. All of this dawns on me in a matter of seconds and my eyes fill with tears quicker than I can stop them.

"Chloe, what is it? You're killing me here," Oliver says his voice sounding strained. I look up at him, he frowns when he sees my tears.

"We are never going to get to see each other," I say finally, my voice shaking. He lets out a sad little sigh. "You're going to be working, you may not even live near me anymore and you're..." I can't seem to say the word 'wife' out loud but by the look on his face he knows what I'm trying to say. "You could be miles away and I'm going to be..." His eyes fall to my stomach where I have unconsciously placed my hands; he grabs me in yet another hug and squeezes me.

"Hey look, we'll work it out, try not to worry," he says into my hair. I let him hold me standing there limply just trying to hold back the tears that blur my vision threatening to spill over. We're silent for a moment when he takes a deep steadying breath. He unwraps his arms from around me, holding me at arm's length. "Look Chloe, I have an idea but..." he begins. There's a rumbling groan from above making us jump apart. I look around and notice a few people staring at us. Embarrassment floods through me, I look away when I spot Jackson looking between us. I had forgotten that we were in a room with other people. I look up at the glass dome as it descends from the ceiling, the ropes and runners squeaking loudly.

"Ladies and Gentlemen," Mr. Evans calls from the dark stage. We all turn towards him. "We're going to have a five minute break. Some of you may want to have a breath of fresh air..."

"Those who are turning I advise you to get one last look at the sun," Henry interrupts and they all look at each other wide eyed. "It will be the last time you ever see it, after all."

55

"Quite," Mr. Evans nods. He points a trembling hand to a set of doors towards the other end of the auditorium. "Five minutes everyone," he says and he makes a hasty retreat after Henry, who left quickly through the back of the stage.

"You think he's going to throw up?" Oliver asks, his eyes following Mr. Evans' retreat. I shrug as I follow him towards the doors that lead to the school courtyard, feeling deflated. We step out into the sun and I take a deep breath. The courtyard is quiet and empty. It's quite disconcerting when you're so used to it being filled with students. "I need the bathroom. Are you going to be ok for a minute?" Oliver asks. I nod as I take a seat on a bench. "I'll be right back."

"I'll be fine," I say and he nods, before rushing off towards the bathrooms. I stare down at my envelope and pinch myself to make sure that I'm not having some horribly realistic nightmare. The throbbing in my arm tells me that I'm very much awake. It's strange; I certainly feel as if I'm in a nightmare. The sort where you know you're asleep and there's nothing you can do to escape your terror. But this is not a nightmare. The threat is here, it's very real, high in its dark nest watching us as we mill around in the sunshine. The chilling realisation that no matter what I do I can't escape washes over me like an icy wave. I'm trapped, trapped to live my life under their rules. I must comply or it's game over.

I'll have to have children; the very thought chills me to the bone. I'll have to watch them grow, I'll fall in love with each of them and then I'll have to sit and watch them go through the same horror I'm going through today. It'll be made so much worse because I'll know deep down what they're feeling.

The sickening feeling of absolute terror and exploitation, the feeling of being used, like a vessel to bring more lives into the world, to feed our dark owners. I'll have to put on a brave face and tell them that everything will be ok despite, knowing it's an outright lie. We have absolutely no hope.

This is not my dream. I wanted to go through my life free from the pressure of breeding. I wanted to help people, make cures for illnesses and heal the sick. Now I'm just going to be another vessel. Sold off to the highest bidder and impregnated, whether I agree or not, to fill my quota of three children. Three is the minimum, I must fill it or it will be to the donation with me. I feel physically sick as I think about having to bring one child into this sinister world let alone three. Having a child should be a happy experience, not something you dread with every fibre of your being.

Another horrible realisation is: who will I have to do it all with? Who's going to be the father of my children? I have to swallow hard to fight back the urge to be sick. I take a deep steadying breath as I get up and walk alone towards a low wall surrounding a small garden. I sit on the wall and glance around the students again. I start looking for Oliver but I still can't see him. I look over at the courtyard exits, I stand up to make my way back to the doors before I do anything stupid like try to run away. I bump into someone as I look back towards the exits. I stumble and look up, groaning when I realise its Jackson.

"Excuse me," I say, trying to step past him; he steps in front of me grinning from ear to ear.

"I see you got a marriage certificate then," he says looking down at my golden envelope with his watery eyes. I sigh.

"Looks like it," I say in the most bored voice I can muster.

"I thought you were going to be shipped out of here to work? Can't say I'm disappointed to see you here," he says. I clench my teeth as he smiles.

"That makes one of us. Excuse me," I try to get by but he blocks my way again. "Get out of my way Jackson," I say, my voice sharp.

57

"Hmm, feisty as usual. Where's Hunter?" he asks looking over his shoulder, nervously. "I saw you two earlier, looked kind of cozy."

"He's inside," I say snappily. He looks back at me knowing he's safe to continue talking to me, because if Oliver were here he would have chased him off by now.

"I see. Your dress is very..." he looks down at my chest. "Pretty."

Don't punch him, I chant in my head.

I cross my arms protectively across my chest to block myself from his view and so I can't hit him; he looks up at my face again. I hope he sees the rage there and he sees that if it weren't for the events of the day and the amount of people milling around I would have slapped his stupid face by now. He smiles and lifts his hand to touch my face; I hit it away.

"Do. Not. Touch. Me!" I say through gritted teeth. He rubs his arm where I knocked him back, I clearly hurt him. I look at his arm and smile. He notices my smug look, he scowls and flaps his envelope in front of my face looking me over again, making my skin crawl.

"When, I buy you," he begins threateningly. "Touching you is all I'll be doing." I stare at him trying not to show any emotion even if my muscles shudder at the thought. I clench my teeth fighting back the nauseous feeling, breathing slowly through my nose. He smiles triumphantly when he sees he has gotten to me. "See you tonight honey. During the honeymoon I'll want to get right down to the baby making," he says with a wink. He saunters off brushing past me. I stand stock still until I know he's gone. I rush back towards the little garden to empty the contents of my stomach over the flowers. As I straighten up I wipe my mouth and see people staring at me.

"What?" I snap. They look away as I walk over to the doors to wait for Oliver.

Chapter 7

"Chloe!" someone calls over the quiet murmuring of the students. I spin around seeing a group of people walking towards us. Dad and Michael are amongst them. They're both smiling. As I rush over to them both of their eyes fall to the golden envelope clutched in my hand.

"Oh Kiddo," Dad says sounding sad but relieved. He gives me an apologetic look as I wrap my arms around him.

"What're you doing here?" I ask into his chest.

"They let the families in to let them say good luck before, you know..." Michael says. I nod. I spot Jackson staring and my blood runs cold. "Has that little runt been bothering you?" I grip his arm as he moves towards him.

"Just leave it Michael. Please," I say. Michael looks down at me his face stony.

"Fine."

"It won't be him," Dad says. I stare up at him.

"How do you know?" I ask my voice sounding defeated he just looks down at me shrugging.

"It just, it can't be," he says sadly. I know it's wishful thinking. We both know that Jackson has had a thing for me. If it's even possible my dad and brothers hate him more than I do.

"That little slime ball better stop looking at you like that. If Joseph was here he would have smacked the nose off of his face, Leeches be damned," Michael says in a hushed tone. I turn to him and see him staring daggers at Jackson who has now turned away. Joseph was always over protective of Michael and me. I have always appreciated my dad and brothers' protectiveness over me.

Although they have never done anything to anyone other than deliver some impressive death glares; their size and their dark dangerous stares are enough to put anyone off talking to me. I also have Oliver for that when they are not available. Oliver is one of the few people I know not to be frightened off by them and for that they respect him; also they know how well he looks out for me.

"Hey maybe you and Ollie…" Michael says but I stare at him, he shuts up but smiles a little.

"Oliver's a good choice," my dad says brightly. I roll my eyes.

"Sure he is, but remember I don't get to choose," I say. They both look at each other glumly. I spot Oliver standing amongst his family as he glances up looking around the courtyard. I watch him as his eyes scan the crowd. I smile, waving when he finally spots me. He waves back before his mum puts her hand on his cheek. She's crying and talking seriously to him. He nods before looking over at me again. He looks away quickly. I turn around frowning as he hugs Rita. Dad and Michael exchange a look, I frown at them.

"You had better hope for him," Michael whispers in my ear. I sigh deeply feeling too tired to argue anymore. I'm definitely not going to bother hoping for anything else. I know he means well saying that but it does nothing to help me. If it were a case of us just getting married, living happily ever after that would be great. But the fact we must have children, throws a spanner in the works. I would happily be with Oliver all the time, we basically are anyway, but to be forced into a physical relationship with him would be too strange and it might ruin what we have. We've kissed once; it was for a dare when we were fourteen. We just closed our eyes and bumped lips before Oliver pulled back and wiped his lips.

"That was gross," he said sticking his tongue out. I didn't even get offended; it was weird for me too. He did

60

avoid me for a few days after it but I thought nothing of it. It's not that he's unappealing either, far from it. I'm sure he'll have many girls hoping to be bought by him but I would find the whole thing difficult. We have known each other since we were children it would be unbelievably awkward, as I'm sure it would be for him.

"Families your time is up, if you would come this way," a tall man in a suit calls from the gates. I feel my heart flutter painfully as Dad lets me go so I can quickly hug Michael.

"See you soon," I say over Michael's shoulder, he nods. I turn quickly heading over towards Oliver; I smile at his parents as they pass me. Rita tries to reach for me but Jimmy pulls her along giving me a sorry smile as she slows me a tear-filled kiss I smile at her. I smile gratefully at him as I reach Oliver who is waiting for me. I understand that she'll hang on to me for just that little bit too long and that Jimmy is doing me a favour.

"She's a nightmare," Oliver says watching Jimmy pulling Rita away. I look up at him expecting him to look annoyed, instead he's just staring after his parents his face expressionless. "I forgot to ask, did you get a vocation?" he asks his voice full of hope. After everything, I've forgotten to look at my envelope to check if I had been given a job as well. It's uncommon for the female to be assigned a vocation once they have been chosen as a breeder as they should be looking after the children and the home. Occasionally, though, the female is given little jobs such as a cleaner, washer or something to do with household chores. Unable to face looking, I hand Oliver my envelope. I watch his face falling. I groan internally and look down at the envelope and see, 'BREEDER', in bold black ink. He turns it over looking for anything else, when he finds nothing he shakes his head angrily.

"I'm sorry," he says. I just shrug as he hands me the envelope back.

"What about you?" I ask my voice quiet, sounding more defeated. He glances down at me showing me the back of his envelope. I see "BREEDER" and directly under that "FARMING". "Really?" I ask shocked that they are making him do a job he has never done in his life. I'm not even sure he likes animals that much. It also means he'll be heading to the north where the farmlands are located.

"Could be worse," he shrugs.

"Have you ever held a shovel in your life?" I ask in an attempt at a joke. He chuckles and gives me a little smile before the room falls into darkness and we are stood trying to adjust for a moment. I notice the floor has been cleared of the chairs.

Someone clears his throat in the darkness. We look around, frowning, jumping when a voice commands, "Everybody take your seats. Ladies if you would sit to the left, gentlemen to the right of the dome please. That's lovely." Henry claps as he steps out of the shadows followed by a horrified looking Mr. Evans. Oliver takes my hand giving it a squeeze; I stare up at him with wide eyes. I try to smile, failing I return the pressure.

"I'll see you soon," he says. I nod unable to speak. I spy Jackson behind him glaring at the back of Oliver's head. I let him go, knowing that this may be the last time I ever speak to him. I wish I could think of something profound to say, maybe how much I'm going to miss him, how he's my best friend and that I love him, but my tongue is not working. He walks under the now lower dome towards the other end of the hall as I sit on a chair. I watch him as he takes the seat across from me. I can't seem to take my eyes off of him. His face is cold and stony but I see the real pain in his eyes as he stares into mine, it breaks my heart. We stare at each other until 'the six', who come out of a door beside the stage breaks our line of sight. There's no point remembering their names now, they're dead. The six of them stand in a straight, uniform line under the dome as the remainder of it lowers, covering them like spiders under a glass. Their eyes dart around nervously; there's a heavy click as a hatch at the top of the dome is opened. A small wooden platform descends; I can see the Turners standing atop it, still shrouded in their blood-red cloaks. They're lowered into the dome slowly. As the Turners get closer and closer the six all watch nervously. When the platform reaches halfway the Turners spring off landing gracefully at the bottom, they straighten up tossing off their cloaks with a flourish. The platform is brought back out and the hatch is closed. I watch the group inside the dome with fascination; it's an almost unbelievable scenario to witness. I can see their bodies trembling as the Turners mouths move in sync. The six seem to be repeating after them, I presume it's an oath they are taking. I lean to my left slightly and see Oliver looking at the group with an angry scowl. His jaw clenches and unclenches before he looks away shaking his head. His eyes meet mine; the look on his face speaks volumes. He's disgusted, horrified, angry and scared all at once.

I know by the way he's tensed and coiled like a spring that he could explode at any second. I give him a pleading look shaking my head slightly, I see him exhale before sagging in his chair. With him calmed down, I allow myself to relax a little. He knows he has no option but to watch this. Watch people we have grown up around being slaughtered in front of our own eyes. I straighten up and I meet the gaze of the girl sitting next to me, she gives me a nervous smile. Rose, I think that's her name. I try to return the smile but she gasps making me jump. I spin around as the Turners slice across their hands with identical blades before clenching their hands in a fist. I watch in horror as they offer each of the six their hands. Starting with the girls, making them suck some of the blood that oozes out. They all drink before pulling back with disgusted, bloody faces that are paler than they were before. There is a collective gasp from all of us outside the bowl as the Turners drop their knives and in a flash are leaping into the group. They tackle the two girls to the floor first biting into their neck. The girls' eyes widen with shock as their mouths widen with silent screams. The boys in the dome start trembling violently clutching their stomachs; they back away quickly as the Turners drink their fill of the girls. I watch transfixed as the life in the girls eyes slowly begin to dim, their bodies wilting in the Turners arms. The boy's collapse to the ground one by one their trembling arms wrapped around their stomachs as they double over in pain.

That's the simplicity of the turning, once you have drunk the blood from the Turners you're as good as dead anyway. No changing your mind. Fang blood is toxic even if you ingest the smallest amount it will kill you, eventually. So if the Turners decide not to drink from you, you will die anyway. It's said that if you're not fully turned you could take up to five days to die, the poison keeping you alive longer. Through the whole experience you will be in agony. Eventually, if your heart doesn't give in first you will die of dehydration and malnourishment; nothing anyone does for you will save your life. So, after you have drunk the Turners blood you had better hope for a speedy turning.

There has never been a case where the Turners have been able to resist drinking the blood for too long so most people don't have to suffer for long. However there have been plenty of cases of people being bitten and just left to die. A little reminder to us all of who's really in charge.

The Turners spring up making quick work of the boys after they have had their fill of the girls. The human female is favored when it comes to a turning, as it's rare to get fresh, young, and straight from the source, female blood. During the farming, the females despite their age are sold off at a higher price than the males. Some are kept alive for years longer than they should be once they have been purchased it's against the laws, apparently. In the rare and unfortunate instance of a woman not being able to bear children they too are sold off to the Fanged, alive. If she can't produce children then she's of no use to them for anything other than for her blood. I have heard horror stories about a few people we once knew that suffered that very fate. It makes me shiver in my seat. Having children has never been something I worried about; I planned to never have children. Why the hell would I? But now that it's to be my future I can't seem to get it out of my head.

The room has fallen deathly quiet and I find myself staring into the dome as the Turners stand up from their last kill. I watch as they wipe the blood off their chins. They pick up their cloaks and throw them on as the six on the ground start writhing around like they are being electrocuted. I jump when the hatch above them pops open causing the room to be filled with screams of agony and the metallic blood stench. I cover my ears, I'm glad to see that I'm not the only one with the same idea. Damien is staring at his cousin with a horrified, desperately sad look. I look away from Damien to Oliver who is looking at me again; his face is pale and sickly. Suddenly the screaming stops, I tear my eyes from Oliver noticing that the six are still writhing on the floor. I look up as the hatch is securely shut again. The Turners are nowhere to be seen. I feel Rose shaking next to me; I jump in my seat as someone clears their throat again in the silent room.

"La-ladies and-and Gentle-men," Mr. Evans stutters his voice pitchy and breaking. We all look over at him; he's standing on the stage at the podium his eyes wide and horrified. They keep glancing to the six in the dome. Henry is standing behind him smiling as he observes the six changing with great interest. There is now another man on the stage; he looks to be only a few years older than myself. However in this light and with the shock of what he just witnessed he looks twenty years older. I notice he's holding a stack of papers in his arms, I realise with revulsion, that he must be the government official here to witness the signing of the wedding documents. He keeps glancing nervously at Henry, his Adams apple bobbing in his throat making it look like he's struggling to breathe. Henry turns his eyes from the dome smiling out at us all.

"Shall we begin?" he says, his smile widening as he rubs his hands together. He looks toward me and the other girls. "Ladies if you would like to join us on stage please," he says sweetly. There is a pause before we make our way to the stage none of us wanting to go up first. We line up along the stage facing out at the small group of boys who have all sat down. I see other girls straightening out their dresses and fixing their hair while I scowl out into the room trying to ignore the now still bodies of the six in the dome. The official leaves the stage quickly heading to a little podium to the left of the stage. He sets down a small stack of paperwork before looking back up at us. Henry walks along the stage in front of us smiling at each of us in turn. I avoid his distracting gaze, knowing it has some sort of power over me.

And he knows it.

Then just to prove my point he stops in front of me and I stare at his chest determined not to look him in the eye. His long, pale finger comes under my chin lifting my head up; his icy finger on my skin makes it hard to avoid his eyes.

"Smile dear one. This is the happiest day of your life," he says mockingly. I can't help but glare at him making him smile. I narrow my eyes and grit my teeth holding back what I want to scream at him. I say nothing but settle for clenching my jaw in frustration. I just look away. I hear him chuckle as he walks to the first girl. "What is your name dear?" he asks pulling the first girl to the front of us all.

"Grace Sir," she says. He nods as he circles her once then turns to the boys.

"Who would like to start the bidding for the voluptuous Grace?" he says. I see Grace's face redden.

"Six months," one boy calls out, Henry smiles.

"Lovely, do we have any further advances on six months?" he asks and then several hands fly up into the air.

The bidding is simple enough. A girl is offered up and the boys bid with time. The cost for a wife of your choice is paid with months or years of your life. So for example if a man offers up five years of his life for his chosen bride he'll be farmed at sixty-five instead of seventy. Seventy is the cut off even for the unpaired. Everyone is farmed. It's the easiest way to pick your bride. As you're offering years of your life for them you had best be sure about whom you choose.

As the group of girl's whittles down I notice that Jackson has not made a move yet and his eyes are fixed on me. I swallow nervously waiting as girls exit the stage some crying, some with emotionless faces. Then one girl, Mary, squeals with delight as her boyfriend, Oliver's friend, David buys he. Not one other boy bothered try, David and Mary have been dating for years and the death glares David gave them all, were enough to deter anyone. Mary lunges off the stage into his open arms, her intricately styled brunette hair falling free of its restraints. I can't help but smile as she cries into his shoulder while he kisses her hair.

"Oh, how sweet, young love is so charming," Henry whispers in my ear. I shiver the smile falling from my face as he steps around in front of me holding out his hand. "Miss Wood, please step forward." I ignore his offered hand, stepping forwards. I look out into the smaller crowd of boys; I look everywhere but at Oliver who is looking up at me. He's behind Jackson so it's hard for me not to stare at him as I feel both of their eyes burning into me. I focus my eyes on the dome and the six who are beginning to stir. They're looking up at their hands, looking at their reflections in the dome, two are even looking right back at me with a hungry look in their eyes. Henry slides over to me again stepping in front of me.

"There is still time you know." He moves a bit of loose hair out of my face before leaning forward. "You could still join us. I would love to turn you myself," he says his eyes roaming over me as his long white finger traces my neck. I look him in the eyes as soon as he has dragged them from my body.

"No thank you," I say, he huffs.

"Your mother will be so disappointed," he says in a hushed voice. I look away to the back of the room feeling the shock on my face. I ignore his smile as he turns to the crowd. "Who would like to start the bidding?"

"Two years," Damien calls. My eyebrows shoot up in surprise as I turn to him. He avoids my eyes as I stare at him in disbelief. I didn't think anyone else would bother with me but now he has started I can't help but feel hopeful that he gets me. I know he wouldn't be a horrible husband; also he'll probably want to sleep with me less than I would him. Best of all I know he wouldn't stop me from seeing Oliver.

"Three years," Jackson's unwelcome voice shouts. I cringe.

"Four," Damien says. He looks over at Jackson whose face is an angry red colour. Jackson scowls at Damien; I look between the two of them. They are staring at each other, Jackson looks furious but Damien just stares coolly back at him.

"Four years," Henry says sounding impressed. "Going once, going twice." I look over at Damien; he gives me a little smile that I return trying to portray how grateful I am. He nods a little. "Sol…"

"Five years!" Jackson nearly screams. I stare wide-eyed at Damien who bites his lip; he looks over to Jackson who is smiling smugly.

"Well this is exciting. Young man do you wish to bid further?" Henry asks Damien sounding positively gleeful. Damien meets my eyes; I feel my stomach drop knowing he's not going to.

You fool Chloe, I think sadly as I feel my body lose strength. I nod at him and give him a grateful smile for trying.

"No, I'm sorry Chloe," he says. He sits back in his chair. I look down at my feet feeling foolish for getting my hopes up again. I can't bear to look at Jackson's smug face. I chew my lip hard as it starts to quiver trying to hold back the tears that have threatened to spill over all day. *There is still time you know...I would love to turn you myself* Henry's voice replays in my head. I look over at him desperate and destroyed.

"To the young man in the front row, going once, going twice..." I open my mouth to beg him to stop but I'm cut off.

"Ten years!" My eyes close in pain and I nearly bite through my lip. It's like the words are a blade to my heart.

Oh no...

Chapter 8

"Ten years!" Oliver says again, louder.

Please no.

"We have a new bidder," Henry says, clapping his hands together, excitement oozing off him. "This really is dramatic." I look over to the row where Oliver is sat, his hand in the air; he has a terrified look on his face. The room is filled with shocked murmurs; our eyes meet and the look he gives me makes me feel ashamed.

He knows what I was going to do.

He lowers his hand mouthing, "I'm sorry." I look away.

He can't do this.

I see Jackson out the corner of my eye, his face contorted in rage. Damien is smiling, I know why; no one is going to outbid ten years. It's stupid, foolish, a waste of his life. I'm so mad at him for this, I think as I glare down at my feet while Henry paces in front of me.

"Any further bids?" Henry asks looking out at them hopefully. Jackson looks at Oliver whose face twitches with a little smile. "Come now young man surely she is worth a few more years. She will give you some very attractive children." Henry is obviously enjoying this dramatic turn of events. I can't help but look at Oliver who is glaring at the back of Jackson's head as he stews in his seat.

"I..." Jackson stutters. I feel him looking at me but I don't care. I know that he knows he has no chance. Even if he was to keep going Oliver is going to be stupid and outbid him each time. He's not brave enough to risk Oliver bowing out at any moment.

"No," Jackson says spitting the word. "No I'm done, he can have her."

"Very well. Sold!" Henry calls happily. I frown, sagging a little as Oliver stands up his face unreadable as he walks towards the stage. He walks past Jackson who glares up at him from his seat. He looks like he wants to tear Oliver limb from limb.

Get in line pal! I think as I walk off the stage. Oliver waits for me at the edge of the stage, when I reach him he offers me his hand. I glare at him as I walk down the stairs without his help.

"Oh dear, trouble in paradise already," Henry says with a chuckle from directly behind me. Oliver's eyes flash angrily over my shoulder, I glare at him.

"Stop it," I say anger clear in my voice. He looks at me nervously. Ignoring Henry's laughter, I storm towards the official awaiting us in the corner of the room. I hear Henry start the bidding on the girl next to me, Alex. I reach the official before Oliver does thrusting my crumpled envelope in his face. He takes it from me with a little smile that I don't return. He looks over my shoulder to Oliver as he hands him his smooth, crease free envelope. This irritates me for some reason and I fold my arms across my chest. The official looks between us keeping a forced smile on his face.

"Congratulations," he says trying to sound jolly. I huff while Oliver remains silent, his smile falters. He looks down at Oliver's envelope and for the first time smiles genuinely at us. "Oh farming. My brother works in a wheat farm out there, it's a good trade."

"So they say," Oliver says shrugging. I sigh loudly getting impatient. They both look down at me.

"Can we get on with this?" I snap. The official clears his throat while Oliver frowns at me.

"I'm sorry," the official says. When neither of us answers he just goes on. He tears open our envelopes pulling out our documents. He shoots me a little smile while smoothing mine down. "You will both have to sign each other's certificates then exchange rings," he says tipping them into his palm. We both stay silent but we are both looking down at the rings. The official hands us both an expensive looking pen. I lean forward scratching angrily at the paper almost tearing it while Oliver calmly signs his half. He glances up at me looking upset. I look away. He straightens up as we are handed the rings. I stare down at the silver band in my hand then up at Oliver who is chewing his lip.

I can't believe this is actually happening.

"You have both signed each other's certificates so now with these rings do you vow to honour and respect one another until your last days on earth?" the official asks.

"I do," Oliver says. I'm startled by the readiness of his answer.

"Miss Wood?" the official asks nervously. I ignore him as I continue to stare up at Oliver, who is looking nervously at me. I suddenly become very aware of the silent room. I know I shouldn't be mad at him, he stopped me making a terrible decision but I can't help it. I can tell by the look on his face that he feels bad, that he thinks he's doing me a favour. I suppose he is, but ten years! Ten years of his life he has wasted on me that I will never be able to forgive. I can also see the anger in his eyes. He's mad at me and he has every right to be. I feel horrible. It's my fault he had to do this. He said he would change for me, I should've known he would've done something this crazy.

I look to the side, I see Jackson standing beside a horrified looking Alex. Looking back at Oliver, the relief that floods through me comes as a surprise.

"Yes. I do," I say quickly, Oliver's tense shoulders relax as the official lets out a relieved breath.

"Oh great," he squeaks. I shake my head sighing a little as Oliver rolls his eyes but he's smiling, with what I guess is relief. He clears his throat and blushes. "I mean, please exchange rings." I push the band onto Oliver's finger and he slides a matching one onto mine. "Congratulations. I now pronounce you husband and wife." I notice Oliver looking over my shoulder with a smile playing on his lips. I can practically feel Jacksons stare burning holes in the back of my head. I clear my throat; Oliver looks down at me chuckling.

"Really mature," I murmur as he smiles innocently.

"You may kiss your bride," Henry says from behind the official, who squeaks and jumps to the side, nearly falling on the floor. We turn to look at him, Oliver's face turning stony as he steps out of the dark.

"Sir that's not a mandatory part of the ceremony," the official says bravely as he straightens up. Henry raises his hand silencing the man.

"Oh, but I insist," Henry says with a dark smile. I look at him; he's not looking at me but at Oliver who is staring back at him with a cold hard stare. He and Henry stare at each other for the longest time before Oliver opens his mouth to say something. In a desperate move I step in between them, reach up and pull Oliver's head nearer mine pressing my lips to his. It's quick but it's just enough to startle him and divert his attention from Henry. He looks down at me with a little frown as I stare up at him.

"Please Ollie, don't," I say in a whisper as I pull away from him, I hear Henry chuckle. Oliver's frown deepens as he turns back to Henry who is staring between us with an amused smile.

"You had better listen to your wife Mr. Hunter." Henry smirks at him before looking down at me. "You really think she is worth ten years of your life?" Henry asks, his gaze lingering on me, making an icy tingle run down my spine. Oliver steps in front of me slightly. Henry peels his eyes from me and looks at him.

"She's worth every second," Oliver says causing me to gawk up at him in surprise.

What?

Oliver smiles at Henry, looking pleased with himself.

"But you knew that already. Didn't you?" Oliver asks. Henry's eyebrows shoot up in humour and he scoffs.

"Is that so?" Henry asks, Oliver chuckles, smiling brightly. I gaze at him as he stares down the head vampire brazenly. Oliver leans forward getting right in his face. Henry doesn't move except for a tiny twitch in his lip, I stiffen and attempt to pull Oliver back but he doesn't budge.

"Yes she is. Otherwise why would you have tried so hard to keep her for yourself?" Henry's face falls. Oliver leans back smiling, wrapping an arm around my waist as Henry tries to regain his composure.

"It almost worked," he says turning to me once he has resumed his cool demeanour. I feel the icy tingle again before the pull of his stare. This time it's stronger, so strong that I nearly step towards him. It's only the feel of Oliver's arm tightening around me that stops me. Henry growls low and the tug stops. I gasp for air like I had just been submerged in water. He turns to face Oliver again, his dark eyes narrow and dangerous. "You will not always be there to protect her," Henry says threateningly. Oliver's eyes harden.

"Yes I will," he says. I stare up at him, seeing his bright eyes stare Henry down makes me smile, despite the seriousness of what he's doing. He turns his back on Henry to look down at me. "Come on lets go home," he says. I nod allowing him to pull me along the hall.

"Oh, Mrs. Hunter," Henry calls making us both stop midstride. "Your mother says you look beautiful. I'm sure she is just thrilled to know that she is to become a grandmother again." I stare at the floor frowning.

"Come on Chloe," Oliver says quickly taking my hand, I follow him stiffly. He holds the door for me as I slide past him. The door slams closed behind us; I reach blindly for the other door handle. "Don't listen to him Chloe," he says in the dark.

"He said she *is* thrilled, that I *look* beautiful. He must have talked to her..." I gasp as I push the door open. "Oliver she's here!"

Despite the heat, I feel myself shiver at the thought of my mother being here, being so close. The bright sun hits us in the face making us shield our eyes. It takes a moment for my eyes to adjust after the dark of the auditorium. I see small clusters of people waiting outside looking nervous while they await their children. I see Jackson's family looking disappointed as I step into the sun with Oliver. They turn away when I meet their gaze. I see the families of the six who turned; I feel pity for them as they look expectantly at the doors for their children.

"Should we tell them?" Oliver asks.

"No, it's none of our business," I shake my head not wanting to waste any of my time on other families when I want so desperately to see mine. I spot David and Mary looking our way. David is looking between us with a shocked expression while Mary smiles knowingly. I look up at Oliver whose face has turned a bright shade of pink. I frown as his eyes meet mine and quickly dart away as we hear an excited squeal from Rita who is waving as she rushes forwards. I spot Dad and Michael following Rita and Jimmy. They look at me before looking around expecting to see Jackson. Then when Oliver follows after me their eyes widen and Michael smiles.

"Don't tell them Oliver. Don't tell them she's here," I whisper hurriedly before Rita and Jimmy reach to us. He gives me a dark look as we are engulfed in a hug from them. Rita crushes me in a surprisingly strong hug; I pat her back and try to smile only really managing a small grin.

"I was hoping he would pick you dear," Rita says putting her hand on my cheeks. I see Oliver who is being congratulated by Jimmy turn to face us his face now a bright red.

"Shut up mum," he says sounding cross.

When our eyes meet, the hidden anger flashes on his face and I know that we're going to start this whole arrangement on an argument. I give Rita a little smile as I look away from him, not wanting to see that look in his eyes anymore.

Dad hovers by us and as soon as Rita lets me go I rush to him crashing against his chest.

"My baby," he says happily. "I honestly thought... when you came out with an envelope. I know you didn't want this." He pauses as he looks at Oliver, who throws me a knowing glance before continuing his conversation with Jimmy and Michael. "I'm so happy to see you. I honestly thought..." dad goes on, his voice tightening. I squeeze his middle knowing what he was going to say, feeling sick that I almost did.

"I would never do that Dad," I lie and he squeezes me. I feel Oliver's eyes burning into me and my face burns with shame.

"I know kiddo," he chuckles. I look up at him; he smiles as he inclines his head towards Oliver and Michael. Michael is ruffling Oliver's hair as Oliver shoves him. He attempts to smooth it down with little success.

"Congrats man," Michael says seriously, I hear Oliver grumble a thank you. "How much of a fight did that little rat put up for her?" he asks, I stare between them. Oliver chews on his lip glancing at his mum and dad who are smiling at him with pleased looks on their faces.

"Tell them," I say. Oliver glares at me; I know he was hoping to keep the number of years a secret but I want him to be in trouble.

He was a damn fool.

"Why don't I tell them everything that happened?" he threatens angrily. I stare at him wide eyed. As our families look between us nervously.

I should've seen that coming.

"I'm sure they would love to hear the whole story," he says his eyes stormy; his jaw is tense as he fights back his obvious anger. I stare at him but can see the confused faces of our families in my peripheral vision.

No they can't know!

"Oliver..." I beg.

"He offered up five," Oliver says, cutting me off angrily. Rita gasps, I see Oliver cringe. He knows that offering more than five is stupid and the fact he offered ten is just insane. I feel intense guilt and I hate myself for making Oliver out to be the bad guy here. I'm the one who was about to give up, the one who was going to break my promise for the second time that day. I look at him and I can see the hurt in his eyes. I open my mouth to apologise, to beg for his forgiveness, when Rita sobs.

"Oh Oliver," she says sadly, I stare at him. He looks up at me his eyes wide and pleading.

"Chloe I'm sorry."

What, no I'm the one that should be apologising what is he doing?

"I couldn't let them take you like that," he says defensively. I look away from the intensity of his gaze. "I'm sorry Chloe. Please don't hate me, I couldn't just sit there and watch that happen," he says. I look up at him my heart throbbing painfully when I meet his sad eyes.

"Ollie, I don't hate you," I say quietly.

"You should've heard the things Jackson was saying. Then your face on the stage, Chloe I haven't seen you that sad for years." He looks over at my dad who is staring at him startled.

"Ollie please..." I beg, his apology making me feel an inch tall. I'm so ashamed of myself for making him do this.

"How many years?" Jimmy asks Oliver who looks at the floor. "How many Oliver?"

"Ten," he says quietly. The others all gasp while I keep my eyes on him, watching him cringe at their reactions.

"Oh, Oliver!" Rita gasps loudly. Jimmy wraps his arms around her while she sobs into his chest.

"Shit!" Michael says.

"I'm as mad as you all are," I say, they all look at me and I swallow nervously, Oliver looks up lifting his eyebrow.

"He wasn't going to outbid me," he says making me roll my eyes.

"That's because it was beyond stupid!" I snap, I instantly regret it when his face reddens. He's about to argue back when my dad steps forward. Oliver stares at him and he visibly relaxes as Dad puts a hand on his shoulder.

"Thank you son," Dad says. Michael nods from beside me. "I'll be forever in your debt for what you've done to protect my girl." Oliver looks at me quickly then back at Dad.

"You don't owe me anything. Chloe's my friend. I'm just trying to look out for her." Oliver is, of course, being honest. I know he knows what he did was impulsive and that he didn't think it through fully but it was also very brave and noble. He has saved me from a fate I want less than the one we are left with; but damn it I'm still mad! There's still something that's nagging at me but I can't quite put my finger on it. I stare between them all; an overwhelming feeling of guilt and awkwardness makes me feel like I shouldn't be witnessing this conversation. I can see that Oliver is embarrassed, I know he would rather not be talking about this with everyone watching, especially me. If Dad had time he probably would've taken him to the side to speak to him privately, but today we are limited for time. Rita steps forward her eyes red and cheeks flushed, she puts her little hand on Oliver's arm.

"Come on you two, we need to get you to the bus," she says shakily, reminding us all how little time we have together. She pulls us along towards the school gates as the other follow silently behind. There's a long queue of white busses along the roadside. Each of them is allocated to a different group. We look among the crowds and find our bus with FARMING printed on the sign. We all stand beside it. Rita gives Oliver a little shove; he breaks off from us and heads over to the driver.

"Name?" The driver asks sounding thoroughly bored.

"Oliver Hunter." The driver checks down the list for his name.

"Where's your wife?" Oliver turns to face me; the driver looks over and nods curtly. "What's her name?"

"It's Chloe Wood, I mean Chloe Hunter." Oliver runs his hand through his hair as the driver writes my name down.

"The bus leaves in ten minutes," the driver says and Oliver nods before rejoining the group. I look up from the ground to his face.

"Wife," I mutter under my breath. Oliver looks down at me apologetically. I turn away to face Dad and Michael.

"Call us as soon as you get settled. I'll call Joseph; he'll be going mad not knowing what is going on. Don't forget to give us your new address, we'll come and visit as soon as we can," Dad says and I nod.

"Yes Dad," I say. He smiles as Michael wraps his arms around me. He looks over at Oliver then back at me.

"Take care sis and just try and enjoy the next few days. Go exploring and just... go easy on him. He'll be feeling crappy as well." I glare at him knowing he's right and for making me feel worse. "You could do a lot worse sis." I reluctantly nod as dad hugs me. Michael heads over to Oliver.

"He's a good man," Dad whispers. I look at Oliver as Michael shakes his hand. I try to smile.

"I know," I mutter.

"Look after my sister Oliver, or so help me. I will have to hunt you down," Michael says threateningly Oliver smiles. "Or worse I'll let Joseph at you."

"I'll look after her, you know that," Oliver says. Michael nods clapping him on the shoulder. Dad holds me at arm's length and smiles down at me.

"Your brothers and I are only a phone call away. Anything, anytime."

"I know dad," my voice cracks. My eyes burn with unshed tears, I blink them back as I take a deep, shuddering, breath.

No, not now.

"I love you kiddo," Dad says. I smile widely as I wrap my arms around him again.

"Love you too old man," I say into his coat. He chuckles before pulling me to the side. I look up at Oliver who is looking at us nervously.

"Oliver, she's my everything. Please..." Dad's voice breaks.

"I promise Christopher," Oliver says his face tight with emotion.

"You're a good man son," Dad says pulling Oliver into a one armed hug squashing me between them. Oliver awkwardly pats dad's back his eyes looking everywhere but at me.

"Thank you," he says as dad lets us go. I look down at the ground as Oliver steps back from us.

"We have to go," Rita says. Oliver looks down at me. I bite my lip hard to stop it trembling. I give Michael and dad another quick hug as Rita latches onto Oliver for a last hug.

"See you soon," I say waving to everyone as they're ushered away from the busses. I watch as they disappear around the side of the building and I chew my lip to hold back the tears stinging my eyes.

Chapter 9

Lillian paces up and down the observation room her hands folded in front of her chest, fury radiating from her. The others in the room cast her curious looks.

"What?" she snaps. They turn away getting back to their menial observing work. The doors open with a bang. She hisses quietly when she sees Henry walking in. "What the hell happened down there?" Lillian asks looking at Henry who is pulling his robe off slowly.

"I could not get through to her my love," Henry says in a level tone. Lillian looks at him in disbelief as a crash sounds behind him followed by a series of yells. Henry rolls his eyes taking a deep, steadying breath as he turns around. One of his Turners is pinning down one of the female recruits. "Samuel, I suggest you control her or I will have to undo your hard work and rip her throat out!" he says his voice getting louder and more strained.

The exhaustion of the day was really wearing on him. He didn't think it would be quite so hard to manipulate the girl, if it weren't for that young man. Henry thought angrily. That young man, he interested Henry more than the girl. He was feisty. Henry smirked to himself moving further into the room, he wanted nothing more than to rest but the impatient huff of his mate told him that wouldn't be happening anytime soon.

"You promised me that I would have my girl back Henry. I thought you said you would be able to change her mind," Lillian says her arms crossed stubbornly across her chest. She watches as Henry pinches the bridge of his nose and closes his eyes. Then within the blink of an eye she is thrown across the room hitting into the opposite wall with such force she is knocked to the floor. Henry advances on her his eyes dark and dangerous.

"You will not speak. I have done everything you have asked of me. Your daughter does not want you; her heart does not belong to you anymore. She is taken."

"But she…"

"SILENCE! Your daughter is gone, she is no longer yours. Move on my dear, I am growing tired of your whimpering," *Henry says before sweeping out of the room; leaving Lillian on the floor while the Turners herd the new recruits out after him. Lillian gets up dusting herself off with a growl. Moving towards the window she looks out at the busses. She spots her daughter in the crowd standing next to her new husband while she waves away their family. Lillian smiles when she realises that if she wants her girl back she will have to do it herself.*

"Shall we?" Oliver asks a few moments after our families have disappeared around the corner. I can tell he's trying to hide the hurt in his voice. I look up at him and he indicates to the bus, I nod. I feel a shiver down my spine and I look back at the black windows frowning. "What is it?" Oliver asks. I turn away from the black windows shaking my head.

"Nothing," I say, he sighs obviously not believing my answer. He offers me his hand; I stare at it for a moment. Just when it looks like he's going to take it back I take hold and the tingles stop. I frown as I look down at our joined hands. That was weird.

He gives my hand a little squeeze as we make our way to the bus. I see David and Mary getting on, David and Oliver exchange a quick smile as we approach their bus. I know Oliver will be pleased that he'll be living near David. David and Mary are closely followed by Damien and Rose. Rose notices us moving towards them, she smiles and waves when she sees us join the queue. I look to my right when I hear a commotion. I notice Jackson pushing his way through his bus line. He's marching towards us, his face furious.

"Oh for god sake!" Oliver says, with a sigh, stepping in front of me slightly. Jackson glares at him.

"You think you're so smart don't you?" he practically screams, pointing his finger at me angrily. I raise my eyebrows at him in surprise.

"Excuse me?" I ask as he glares at me.

"I should've known you two would pull something like this." He steps closer to me, getting in my face. Oliver puts his arm between us. I shake my head in frustration.

"Just give it up Jackson, its over," Oliver says putting a hand on Jackson's chest making him back up. Jackson shrugs Oliver's hand off, ignoring him.

"You think you can embarrass me in front of everyone like that and get away with it? You're just like your whore mother." I stare at him in disbelief before he spits in my face. I recoil with a gasp and wipe my face quickly. I straighten up and I'm about to lunge at him but I notice he's gone. I blink once confused and then with a smile, I see he has been knocked to the floor. Oliver is shaking his hand looking down at him. Jackson groans loudly clutching his cheek while Oliver turns to me.

"Are you ok?" he asks looking at my face and wiping it gently with his sleeve. Jackson scrabbles up, his lip bleeding, he rolls his jaw. Oliver turns around lifting his hand up to hit him again; I grab him holding him back.

"Don't, he's not worth it," I say, he relaxes a little but I keep hold of his arm.

"You two are well suited, the whore and her thug husband," Jackson says. I groan as Oliver's arm slips from my grip and lunges for him again. Damien, who has rushed off the bus, grabs hold of him keeping him back.

"Just leave it Oliver!" he says through his teeth as he struggles to restrain Oliver. "He's just bitter you have Chloe." Jackson laughs loudly, despite his wide alarmed eyes, and wipes his bleeding lip.

"Shut up you faggot. I feel sorry for your poor girl. At least mine has a real man," Jackson spits at Damien. He just scoffs rolling his eyes as he pulls Oliver back towards the bus.

"I'm sure Alex is just thrilled, come on Chloe," Damien says. I turn away but Jackson grabs my arm spinning me around. He steps up to me his face inches from mine.

"This is not over!" he hisses at me.

"I think it is Jackson. Now let me go." I yank my arm free from his grip. He turns away spitting blood onto the road before pushing through the gathered crowd. I turn to follow Damien and a furious looking Oliver.

"What did he say?" Oliver asks wrestling out of Damien's grip. I give Damien a grateful smile as he lets Oliver go.

"You ok?" Damien asks as Oliver stares at me waiting for an answer. I give Damien a little smile; he nods before heading back onto the bus. I watch as he sits down next to a worried looking Rose. They whisper to each other and Damien shrugs.

"What did he just say?" Oliver says sounding desperate and I look over at him.

"He just said this wasn't over. Just leave it Oliver we're probably never going to see him again." Oliver's teeth grind audibly as I turn, climbing on the bus, he follows closely behind me. I walk up the aisle of the bus avoiding the stares of the other passengers who witnessed the embarrassing spectacle. We take the back seat behind David and Mary, who smile at us. I return their gesture before I squeeze in by the window. Oliver sits down, after a quick exchange with David, rubbing his hand. I look down at it, it looks a little red, I frown as I look up at him. He gives me a tentative smile.

"You ok?" I ask and he shrugs.

"I'm fine, his skull it thicker than I originally thought, explains a lot…" he replies. I smile shaking my head.

"I'm pretty mad at you by the way. I kind of wanted to hit him," I say with a little smile, he chuckles looking relieved.

"Sorry," he says. I look up at him.

"It's ok. Oh, and thank you," I say.

I hope he knows that I'm not thanking him just for hitting Jackson, but for everything.

"Anytime," he smiles, I look down at my hands just knowing that I'm going to have to apologise so much, for the way I have acted. I'll wait until we get to our new home. He won't appreciate talking about it in a crowded bus. Especially considering, I'm sure, he's going to want to scream at me. The bus roars to life making me jump. I look out of the window as it slowly moves off. I watch with a heavy heart, as the town I grew up in gets further away. As we start to leave the less populated areas I see the familiar, clustered together Fanged watch towers start to become further and further apart. There are fewer towers out in the countryside as there are fewer people for the Fanged to monitor. It's a small comfort knowing that where we are going there will be very few towers. Their presence will be less obvious than it is in Centrum. I continue looking out of the window until I don't recognise our surroundings anymore.

"This is the furthest I have ever been from home," I say quietly. Oliver takes my hand giving it a reassuring squeeze. I look at him from the corner of my eyes; I can see the worry on his face. How can he stand being near me after what I nearly did?

He should hate me. The horrible thought makes me close my eyes at the pain in my chest. I look back out of the window unable to deal with the guilty feeling Oliver's concerned face is giving me. As soon as we are out on the open road a lady in a dark tailored suit stands up holding a microphone. She faces us all smiling and is met with our blank stares. When it's clear we are not in the smiling mood she lets hers fall off her face.

"Good evening Ladies and Gentlemen. My name is Miriam and I'm here from Greenbelt city to allocate housing and tell you a little about where we are heading," she says in a bored tone. I turn away from her looking back out of the window. "We are heading to a lovely county up in the lowlands of the north of our beautiful country. Just above the industrial midlands. It's quite beautiful. As you have probably guessed it's called The Greenbelt. I know you will all have heard of it. It is, of course, our biggest farming region with its fertile ground and habitat for our livestock. It's the main source of food in this county, apart from the items we have shipped into the docks and the little farms elsewhere. Those of you who are uncoupled will be living in the city and will be responsible for the running and distribution of food throughout the whole of our country. It's a very important job and will take up most of your time. Which is why you are uncoupled," she pauses and looks at her clipboard.

"Those of you who have been paired off, firstly congratulations." She smiles at us again and again it falls from her face when she's met with more silence. I look up at Oliver realising he's playing with his ring. Not one person thanks her and she stares awkwardly at us and clears her throat. "Well anyway, you will, of course, be responsible for the continuation of our people. Without you ladies and gentlemen, we will not survive. Ladies, your male counterparts will be responsible for bringing home the money. He will be in charge of his own little farm or land. The contents of which will be given to you along with your house allocation. Additionally with that he will work with the other farms during the busy seasons. It's a very tight knit community, everyone does their part," she says flipping a sheet of paper over on her clipboard. She starts to reel off names letting everyone know where he or she will be working and living. The uncoupled are all being housed in large apartment buildings in the city to save space but the coupled are given a small house situated on the edges of the farmlands so they have space to raise children.

"Mr. and Mrs. Green?" Miriam calls. David and Mary look up together. "You will be in farm house fourteen, you will be farming potatoes," Miriam says. David frowns but nods. Other couples are given a house and a farm ranging from cattle to fruit. Then it gets to us.

"Mr. and Mrs. Hunter?" she calls. Oliver raises his hand. "You will be in house thirteen; you will be in charge of the work horses." Oliver frowns. She ignores his frown moving quickly on.

"What the hell am I supposed to do with a bunch of horses?" he whispers. I shrug. Finally, after Damien is assigned poultry and house twelve Miriam sits back down. The bus goes quiet, I lean my head on the window thankful for the silence. It's raining outside now. I close my eyes listening to the drops pounding on my window. It's cold; I try to stop myself shivering by focusing on keeping myself together.

I must've fallen asleep because I'm being shaken awake. I open my eyes feeling a little disorientated by the dark inside the bus. I'm also very warm, despite the open windows. I frown when I notice I'm covered in Oliver's suit jacket.

"Hey, we are nearly there," Oliver says making me jump. I realise I'm resting my head on his shoulder; I sit up rubbing my eyes.

"Already?" I ask. He chuckles as he stretches.

"It's been five hours," he says. My eyes widen.

"Really?"

"Just about," he says with a nod.

"Why didn't you wake me sooner?" I ask, feeling bad for dozing off.

"You looked peaceful," he says shrugging. I open my mouth to speak but he just smiles. "Shut up Chloe, its fine. We'll be there in five minutes."

"Well thank you for covering me," I say pulling the coat off of myself, folding it on my lap.

"You were shivering," he says with a little shrug. I have a lot of apologising to do, I think grimly.

I look back out of the windows as the guilt and dread starts creeping over me again. I see a line of tiny houses coming towards us. Some brightly lit with the lights inside showing signs of life; others are darkened and are clearly vacant. From what I can see from the village through the dark, it looks nice.

Nice enough to raise children, my sudden thought makes me gasp quietly. Don't go there.

The bus eventually pulls to a stop after bumping down the dirt road. Oliver gets up stepping aside so I can walk ahead of him. I notice only a few of us getting up. All of the uncoupled, as well as some of the other pairs look at us as we exit the bus. We must be the first of the drop offs. As soon as we are off the bus each of the guys are given an envelope from Miriam.

"Good night and good luck," she says stepping back onto the bus with a guilty look on her face. I frown at her as the door closes. We all stand watching as it drives off, spraying us with dust and pebbles, with the same lost look on our faces.

"Children," someone calls from behind us we turn around as a man approaches us from one of the houses down the street. He looks between us frowning as he hobbles towards us. "My name is Norman. Welcome to the Greenbelt," he says with a low bow. The six of us look around the little village where we have been dropped off; I can hear a few loud voices. I guess it must be from the centre where I imagine there is a little pub. I look back around at the houses; they line either side of the road the even numbers on the right, odd numbers on the left.

"There has been a sight change of plan this evening," Norman says rising from his bow. I look at the others who all look as confused as I feel. Norman gives us a toothless smile.

"What change of plan?" Oliver snaps. I can tell instantly he doesn't like this man. I don't blame him; he looks like an older sleazier version of Jackson. Norman looks behind us making us all turn around. There is set of bright headlights heading towards us on the road. I look up at Oliver who is scowling.

"What the hell is going on?" Damien say with a deep frown.

"You boys are to be taken to the Hillcroft farm for an introduction this evening. It's lambing season and all hands are needed," Norman explains. Oliver's eyes widen. He looks down at me as I stare at him in horror.

"You can't be serious? This week is supposed to be our free time; it's our wedding night man," David says angrily as Mary clings to him. Norman straightens up staring at David.

"I'm deadly serious boy. It'll have to wait. This is part of your livelihood and now your job so you will do as you are damn well told. I will make sure your ladies are settled in," Norman says as the car comes to a stop beside us.

"How long will they be away?" I ask.

"Your husbands will be back when they are no longer needed," Norman says shrugging.

"Yes, but how long will that be?" Damien asks. Norman groans loudly before scowling at him.

"I don't know nor do I care." Mary starts to cry. David holds her as he tries to soothe her. I look over at Oliver, he looks furious. The car horn beeps as the driver sticks his head out of the car.

"We don't have all night Norman!" he snaps. Oliver clenches his jaw.

"I will see you later then. Hey, its fine, you need to do this," I say, tugging on his hand. He looks down at me his eyes stormy as he looks over my shoulder at the car. Norman steps up beside us.

"Don't worry son your girl will be waiting for you, won't you sweet heart?" He pats my shoulder and I scowl at him. Oliver throws his hand roughly off me.

"Take your hand off her." He looks like he's going to jump the guy but I tug on his arm again, he looks away as Norman backs up.

"Just go and I'll see you soon," I say. He hands me the envelope with the keys in it.

"You going to be ok?" he asks looking worried. I nod. "Lock the doors and don't let anyone in unless you know them," he says pleadingly.

"I won't," I promise. He takes his coat from my tight grip and swings it over my chilled shoulder before he pulls me in for a hug. He kisses the top of my head shocking me slightly.

"See you soon," he says letting me go. I pull the coat around me as I watch him climb into the car beside Damien. Rose stands next to me her arms crossed looking angry. We have to take hold of Mary when she refuses to let David go.

"I love you," he says to her as she sobs. I look in the car to Oliver; he gives me a little smile. David finally climbs into the car and we watch them drive off. Mary sobs on Rose's shoulder, Norman clears his throat.

"Very touching," Norman says mockingly. "Ladies, if you would follow me I'm to take you to your class while the men are away," he says I frown at him.

What the hell?

"What class? I didn't sign up for any class, did you guys?" I look at the other two and they shake their heads at me. "You said we were to go home."

"Plans change," Norman says smiling.

"In the ten seconds we have been here?" I snap.

"You need a lot of work done on you," Norman says.

He walks down into the village leaving me staring at him my mouth hanging open. The other two stare at me.

"We should just go," Rose says as Norman gets further away. We have no choice but to follow him, we don't know where we are. He leads us down the village. We turn towards a large red brick building. I see the words 'Training Centre' and my blood runs cold. I feel bile rise up in my stomach as Rose gasps.

Chapter 10

"Oh god."

"Is this a..."

"Yes it's a training facility. We have them everywhere for women to learn how to care for their husbands. You three were not supposed to be coming here until your honeymoon was over but due to the changes Miss Love thought why not take you now?" Norman says as he opens the door ushering us in. I walk stiffly stopping at the foot of a small, steep, set of stairs. I know I should have more fight; feel more shocked, horrified even but the events of today have completely drained me. I have absolutely no energy left. I try to imagine Oliver's reaction to this place. The thought alone makes me shiver. I could only imagine the colourful things he would have to say about a place like this.

"Good evening ladies," comes a high-pitched voice from our right. I spin around as a tall thin woman with dark brown eyes and a bun, so tight it has pulled her face back, smiles at us. She wears a long grey skirt and a white shirt covered by a thick grey cardigan. "I am Miss Love and I will be your tutor until your gentlemen return." I frown, her sharp eyes land on me. "First rule of being a lady we do not scowl and second rule." Her eyes dart to Mary who sniffles. "We do not blubber. Our job is to look after the family; there is no time for emotions," she says coldly, Mary looks down at the floor, a tear rolling down her nose.

"Now follow me, we will have an early night, you all need some sleep. Thank you Norman that will be all." She sweeps out of the room calling over her shoulder. Norman backs out of the room with one last leering look as he closes the big wooden doors behind him. Rose follows Miss Love leaving Mary and I to tag along after her. we're shown into a draughty, concrete walled room that has eight little beds lined along the wall. The image of a prison comes to mind. I suddenly miss home terribly. Miss Love turns to us opening her arms.

"This will be your room for the time being. You will each have a bed which you will make each morning before you leave this room. You will have a regulatory set of clothes." She indicates to her grey outfit. "The trunks contain a variety of sizes. You must wear them at all times while in this institution. We will take care of your dresses in the morning. You will have them cleaned for the arrival of your gentlemen," she says. I stare at her in disbelief.

"We're to wear them again?" I ask. She turns to me, her eyes narrow slits. She doesn't like me.

Well the feeling is mutual, hag, I think. I struggle to keep my face neutral.

"Well of course. You want to look your best for your husband after he returns from the hard labour. Do you not?" she says in a disbelieving tone. I sigh and she shakes her head looking completely flummoxed by the fact I'm unenthusiastic about the whole thing. "Now off to bed, all lights will go out in five minutes." She leaves the room looking a little bemused. I hear the door lock; I turn to look at the other two who are staring wide-eyed at the door.

"Did either of you know anything about this?" I ask and they both shake their heads.

"Nothing. I just thought we were to be left to it," Rose says and I nod. "I mean after everything we have taught to us in school I didn't think these places would be needed." It was true but what shocks me the most is that we were never told not once, about this sort of place even existing. In school, girls were taught from a very young age of the importance of keeping their husband happy. We were taught how to bake, cook, sew and do the laundry, as well as minor repairs and maintenance around the home. The woman is supposed to be in sole control of running the house, as the man will be working long hard hours to feed the family. The fact that this place exists may be proof that the women here may not be up to the Fang's standards; the thought makes me smile for some reason.

"Do you think they do this all over the country?" Mary asks as she looks into the trunks. She groans loudly as she pulls out a long grey skirt holding it up against herself. I look away not needing to see what else is in there.

"There probably are other places. I suppose they think the schools didn't do a good enough job drilling the 'Wives Duties' into us," I say pulling back the covers of one of the beds angrily. There is a thin, itchy looking nightdress under the sheets. I unzip my dress kicking it to the corner of the room before I quickly get changed.

"Should you not hang that up?" Rose asks. I glare at the offending item.

"I was planning on burning it after today," I mutter as I pull my nightdress over my head. I don't miss the concerned look on Mary and Rose's faces as I climb into the bed. I pull Oliver's jacket around me breathing in the familiar smell of his home. The cold room has made my teeth chatter loudly so I bury myself into the bed trying to get warm under the thin sheets. The room falls silent when the lights flicker off. I can only hear our breaths until I hear Mary and Rose start to cry. I frown angrily at the noise but it's not long before I join them. I cry for the longest time. My breath comes out in pants as I struggle to breathe. I curl into a ball smothering the worst sobs into my thin pillow. I cry for myself, being stuck here in this cell only to be set free to have babies and die. I cry because I should be doing something better with my life. I cry for Oliver who is, no doubt, furious with me. I cry because he has saved me from a life of misery and wasted ten precious years of his life on me. I cry out of guilt for making him feel bad, despite the kind thing he has done for me. I cry because I miss him and I wish he were here with me, he wouldn't allow this. I cry because I'm already missing home. I cry for the poor families of the six who were turned. Finally my tears run dry when I run out of new things to cry about. I turn and stare up at the ceiling with burning eyes until light starts to come through the thin curtains. I close my eyes, sighing.

I jump awake when I hear a shrill, painfully loud, bell. I sit up shivering. Miss Love is standing in the doorway holding a bell looking like she's enjoying every minute of the rude awakening.

"Up, get up," she says. I throw the covers off myself groaning when my feet touch the cold stone floor. I pull out some clothes from the trunk. I quickly get dressed and make my bed remembering Miss Love's instructions from the previous night; I'm just too exhausted to start any arguments today.

Tomorrow, I will make a stand tomorrow.

I stand, waiting for the others when Miss Love barges in again. She picks up our dresses from their spots on the floor or over the ends of the beds.

"Your first job, before you eat I want you to make those dresses spotless. Come with me," she says throwing our dresses at us, hitting me in the face with mine. She turns on the spot before briskly walking out of the room. We follow her as she leads us through the surprisingly large building, into a large hot laundry room filled with many other women of all ages. "This is Agnes. She'll show you what to do." She introduces us to a small plump woman, who smiles at us sweetly, before turning on her heel and leaving in a blur of grey. I look back at the small lady who smiles a little wider.

"Don't worry dear I won't bite your head off," she says in a kind, motherly voice. I can't help the smile that crosses my face. I look around the room when I notice the other women looking at us all with interest. "On with your work ladies, stop making the girls uncomfortable. We've all been here. Come with me girls I will get you set up," Agnes says. The other women look away, getting on with what they were doing before we came in. She leads us into a quiet corner at the back of the room. She shows us how to mix up a suitable cleaning solution. She shows us how best to clean our delicate dresses; she leaves us to it while our dresses soak before we start scrubbing. "Oh, don't forget to do the inside, Miss will check," she says, with a wink, while patting Rose on the cheek.

"She's nice," Rose says as she watches Agnes pick up a full laundry bag and swing it over her shoulder.

"Yeah, *she* is," I mutter. Mary and Rose stare at each other again.

We're left to ourselves and after a few hours my hands are stinging and my stomach aches from hunger. Rose is giggling to herself as her stomach rumbles loudly; I can't help but chuckle at her, I think she may be going mad. Mary works quietly and diligently. I think it's because she really does want to impress David. Rose tosses her brush down with a smile; Mary and I look at her curiously.

"I don't know why I bother. Damien isn't even going to come near me," I look at her; she doesn't look upset or even that bothered about it.

"I'm sure he'll think you look nice," I say. She snorts loudly.

"Oh please, he's as gay as they come. I think it might just be me and a turkey baster to make the babies," she says. I stare at her in shock while Mary snorts.

"You never know," Mary says uttering the first words she has spoken all day; she looks up at Rose smiling. "He might surprise you. I mean he's got to be with you for, well forever. He might want to have some fun. He went out with that girl before he got with Tommy. He may be into guys just now but he wasn't always. He's still a man."

"I'm not going to hold my breath," Rose says with a shrug. I look down at my soapy dress focusing on scrubbing, while I think about Oliver. *"He's still a man"* rings in my head like an alarm. Oliver's a guy, I know he'll want that, eventually. I wonder if I could give him that. I mean the thought of doing it isn't repellent. I know he's good looking. He will make some pretty babies with their red hair and beautiful eyes but its Oliver; he's my best friend. It could be… no, will be weird! Rose shoves me a little with her elbow. I blink at her.

Was she talking to me?

"Sorry?" I mutter, her and Mary chuckle.

"Mary asked if you and Oliver are more than friends," Rose asks. I stare between them.

"No we aren't," I say. Rose smiles but Mary looks unconvinced.

"I knew it. You looked so shocked when he bought you," Rose says. Mary smiles the same knowing smile she gave me the day before making my cheeks turn red.

"The whole day was pretty shocking," I mutter looking down at my dress as I try to hide my face.

What is with that smile?

"Yeah it was. But you two have always been so close," Rose goes on. Mary puts down her dress looking very interested in the conversation now.

"He's my best friend." I shrug trying to emphasis the point.

"And now your husband. Soon to be the father of your children, oh come on now. It could be worse. Your husband could prefer men or even worse, he could be Jackson," she groans, shivering dramatically. I smile despite the awkward subject. Mary sticks her tongue out in disgust.

"Jackson tried damn hard to get you. David said that he was practically jumping for joy when you didn't get an envelope," Mary says.

Don't remind me.

"I suppose it could be worse. At least I like Oliver," I say, dunking my dress into a basin of warm water.

"Just don't think about it when it comes, sex is natural. Oliver is a hottie, it shouldn't be too horrible," Rose says matter of factly. I feel myself blush, I'm thankful now I have my back to them and I focus back on my dress. I try to zone out while Rose and Mary chat amongst themselves. I try my very best not to blush, but sadly they notice and laugh at me. The direction of the girls' conversation is taking an extremely promiscuous route. No matter how hard I try I keep blushing at the things they are saying, making them giggle more. They manage to weed it out of me that I'm a virgin, then for some unknown reason, they then think that I need them to give me pointers. I'm actually thrilled when Miss Love enters the washroom to inspect our dresses. I sigh in relief when she walks over to us as they begin talking about the do's and don'ts. I have a feeling the conversation was about to get way out of hand.

"Mediocre at best," Miss Love says as she inspects Rose's dress. Rose just shrugs as she inspects mine. She nods but says nothing. Mary gets a glowing review she smiles, looking pleased with herself while Rose and I roll our eyes at her. Finally we're shown out of the hot room. I give Agnes a small wave as I pass; she smiles back and waves at me. We're shown into the kitchen where we're served a bowl of barely warm, lumpy porridge. Despite that we're all so hungry that we don't even complain as we wolf it down.

Through the rest of the day we're given jobs like cleaning, dusting and sweeping the outside yard. Arriving at night really didn't show off the size of the building but as we sweep and pull up weeds we get a fair idea of how big it is.

"It looks about the same size as the school," Mary comments. I nod in agreement. It even has the blacked out observation windows on the top. As I look around at the high fence surrounding it and the flat concrete grounds I see it.

"I think you're right Mary. It must be an old school," I say looking around shielding my eyes from the sun. It would make sense, although most of the schools are now in the main towns and cities these small villages used to have their own big schools. Most of them got closed down around thirty or so years ago when the human population was ravaged by a strain of flu that wiped out a large number of children and adults. It was after the flu died out and it was contained that the new rules came into effect. More people were chosen to become breeders. That's when the three-child rule came into effect. The Fanged needed to rebuild their population. They needed to do it as quick as they could. It was also made a law that every child was to be inoculated against a range of illnesses that could spread and cause problems like before.

"I see it now," Mary says as she looks around. "There must have been a hell of a lot of kids that lived around here to have a school this big."

"Enough chit chat!" Miss Love says as she storms towards us. "Come now inside it is time for lessons." She shows us where to hang our brooms; we follow her into the building through the maze of hallways. We pass doors all along the walls. As she shows us into our lesson room it's filled with desks and chairs. We all look at each other with little smiles. "Take a seat in the middle, one behind the other and no talking or you shall spend the night in the kitchen peeling potatoes," Miss Love snaps. I take a seat in between Mary and Rose not really wanting to be peeling potatoes all night.

For the next two hours we sit and listen to a lecture about how our husband is the main provider for the family so for that reason should be looked after. He should have a hot dinner ready for him returning from work and should be catered to in any area.

"You ladies are there to keep house and keep your husband happy. He will father your children. An unhealthy man will result in sick babies," Miss Love says after a horribly descriptive lecture about how to get pregnant. We all stare at her in shock, even Mary and Rose looking as disgusted as I feel. I know that the woman in the marriage had to do all of this but I still feel sick to my stomach that I'm here, having to listen to this.

"Has it always been like this?" I ask without thinking. I hear Mary and Rose gasp while Miss Love looks at me like I have slapped her. "I just mean… have we always been like this?" Miss Love stares around the room in shock.

"Yes. Now don't ask such stupid questions," she declares finally. She looks away quickly as I frown. After our horrible lectures are finished we're sent into the kitchen to make our own dinners with limited supplies. After a disappointing dinner of potatoes and a small bit of cheese, we're ushered back into the bedroom and the door is locked behind us. We get dressed for bed in silence. I collapse on to my bed with a groan. I'm nearly asleep when Rose clears her throat.

"Hey Chloe? What was going on with you and that Henry from graduation? You know the Fang?" she says. I groan into my pillow before I lift my head up, to see her and Mary looking over at me.

"Nothing, I've never seen him before," I say honestly.

"Yeah, I guessed as much, your jaw nearly hit the floor as well when you saw him," she says looking pleased with my answer; I thump my head back on the pillow. "I just mean he was really keen on you. I have never heard of a Fanged trying so hard to change someone's mind."

"It's not even allowed," Mary says. I turn to face them.

"I don't know what was going on but he um…" I sigh looking back at the ceiling, "I think he knows my mum," I say. I can feel them staring at me.

"You don't think she was there do you?" Mary asks.

"I think so. She apparently put my name up for registration. I'm pretty sure she was there. She hasn't tried to contact me before and even if she did I wouldn't respond," I say

"God that sucks, I'm sorry," Rose says. I turn away hiding my face.

"She's dead as far as I'm concerned, don't worry about it," I say honestly, closing my eyes as they start to sting. I hear her sigh.

"Hey Chloe, about what you said in the class room?" Mary says in a low voice. I sit up wiping my eyes hastily.

"Yeah?"

"Well, I bet it wasn't always like this." I look over at her, she's looking up at the ceiling, smiling. "I bet people didn't have to go through all of this. I mean isn't it a little strange that we have no history books apart from really, really old ones. There are hundreds of years of our history missing. I think that they show that we weren't always like this. I think the Fanged just want us like this to suppress us, to control us." She frowns her eyes still on the ceiling. I stare at her, then Rose, who raises her eyebrows looking impressed. "I bet women were doing the same things as men and weren't used just to have babies," she adds with a dramatic loud sigh, making me smile.

"It's a nice thought," Rose says and I hear a smile on her voice. I nod in agreement.

"It is…"

Chapter 11

I can't wait for this to be over.

The past few days have been horrible. We were forced to clean our way around the whole of the building. We scrubbed the floors by hand as, according to Miss Love, "It is the best way". Today is our fourth day in this horrible place; we're achy and even more miserable than before. Especially after the last lecture that consisted of horror stories of disobedient wives. We were told stories of wives being killed by their partners when they didn't do their duties. Then, even worse horrors, when the woman turned out to be sterile and unable to reproduce. The women and sometimes men would be shipped off before being sold at auction. We'd never been taught about men being sold off as well, which was a bit of a shock to the system. The fate of those poor men and women, who were unlucky enough to be sterile, has apparently been leaked out. Miss Love told us about them in great, upsetting detail. They've found out that the men and women, who were bought for obscene amounts of money, were ravished by the Fanged. They say it's their only chance to really let the 'monster out'. These events are called Feasts. I couldn't help but think that these stories might have 'leaked' on purpose just to keep us all in line. If I'm truly honest it's worked on me.

After Miss Love has scared us half to death we're escorted out of the lecture room pale and horrified. We're shown back to our room and left to clean up. Mary cries as she showers while Rose and I sit on our beds listening to her sobs. I can't help the feeling of helplessness and the overwhelming feeling of defeat. This place has completely crushed my spirit. I have found myself unable to protest or fight any longer. The only thing getting me through the day is the fact that the boys will be picking us up in a few hours.

Oliver will be back.

The thought of him coming to get me out of this place sets of a little fire in my heart, warming me from the inside. The lambing is finally over and they have been released. We have been granted the coming weekend off to settle in to our homes and for them to recover, before they started their real work.

"Call it a honeymoon," Miss Love says as she helps Mary into her dress. My dress feels a little looser than it did a few days ago. It's probably due to the fact I have barely eaten or stopped for much longer than the six hours a day we were allocated for sleep.

"Are you really going to leave your hair down?" Rose asks me, for the fourth time, as we get ready. She looks at me in the mirror, her blonde hair all prettily pulled up. She looks great in her cream dress, as does Mary who has really made an effort for David. Her ivory dress clings to her albeit slightly less, as her black hair falls in ringlets over her shoulder.

"Yes," I hiss feeling stressed. She smiles at me raising her hands up in surrender.

"Ok," she chuckles. She turns as the crunch of gravel comes through the open window. Miss Love moves swiftly, a grey blur, out of the room. I stare after her.

"Ohhh, that will be them," Mary says excitedly. She rushes towards the window. I peer out over her shoulder. I see Damien stepping out looking tired and filthy. He stretches before stepping aside for David to get out. They both look up at the building frowning. I smile widely when Oliver gets out the front, looking equally as filthy. They all look like they haven't slept the whole time they've been away, they are unshaved and bleary eyed. Oliver shuts the car door loudly while looking up at the front of the building with Damien and David. His tired, dirty face hardens. Rage spills off him, I can feel it from where I'm stood. His lips move angrily, his teeth snarling, before he marches toward the building. Damien rushes after him with a worried, exhausted, look. David follows them running his hands over his tired face as I hear a door crash open.

"Shit!" I hiss as I rush away from the window, snatching his crumpled jacket off my bed.

"Chloe! Where is she?" I hear him yell from down the hall. I rush across the room nearly tripping on my dress.

"Oh he's mad," Rose says as I pull open the door rushing through it, I jog down the hall. I hear him talking angrily as Damien tries to calm him down. I round the corner to see him facing off with Miss Love as Damien pulls him back. David is looking on angrily but he looks too tired to do much else but stand. Oliver is staring furiously at Miss Love; he turns when he sees me enter.

"Chloe, what the hell is going on? Why are you not at the house?" he asks. I stare between him and Miss Love. She's eyeing me suspiciously and I know she's wondering how I'm going to handle this situation. *"A good wife will always know how to handle an upset husband."*

"Chloe?" he says again. I turn to him smiling. His face falls, his eyes narrow as I make my way towards him. I place a calming hand on his arm. He stares down at me looking utterly lost and confused.

"Your wife is here to learn her trade," Miss Love says. Oliver spins around staring at her. He turns back to me frowning deeply.

"Trade? They've given you a job?" he asks hopefully. I shake my head, making him frown. Then something like realisation crosses his face, he straightens up looking around.

"This place, is it a... what the hell is this place?" he almost yells. I pat his now trembling arm as Damien eyes him warily.

"Its fine Oliver," I say calmly his eyes search my face for something. We both jump when Mary screeches behind me as she runs into David's arms. He smiles widely before she kisses him. Rose makes her way over to Damien who kisses her cheek, she looks at the two of us, Damien shakes his head in a, don't ask sort of way. Olivier's eyes never leave my face; I try to keep my smile in place. Finally he huffs putting his hand on my face to make me look at him. I stare up at him; the anger in his eyes scares me a little.

"This isn't fine Chloe, for god sake!" he says angrily. I try not to sigh at him as Miss Love glares at me.

"Everything is fine. Can we just go home?" I plead. He frowns dropping his hand from my face. The others take this as their cue and make for the exit. I follow after Rose and Damien while Oliver follows after me wordlessly. We walk behind the others through the busy village; I grip his coat hard trying to hold on to my nerve. People stare at us as we pass giving Oliver and me curious looks, probably because I'm walking with my arms crossed over my chest while Oliver shoots me glances from the corner of his eye.

Finally we reach the outskirts of the village. The others are talking in hushed voices about what we were doing in that place while I stay silent. Knowing if I talk Oliver might... will lose it.

David and Damien don't look too happy either, as Mary and Rose fill them in on what they had to do. I silently wish they would shut the hell up as I watch Oliver's face redden. We slow down as we reach a narrow road with houses either side all numbered in the teens. We come to a sudden stop when we find our house numbers amongst the rows of houses; we're all quiet as we look at the tiny vacant homes.

"Well I guess we'll see you around," David says he shaking Damien and Oliver's hands. They exchange a strange scheming look. I frown at them; David glances at me quickly before looking back to Oliver. "Just don't freak out," he says warningly to Oliver, whose jaw tightens as he looks at me.

Freak out? What is he talking about? Did Oliver tell him what I was going to do?

I stare between them wide eyed as David takes Mary's hand. He pulls her towards one of the vacant homes. We watch as he picks her up to walk her over the threshold of their new home smiling as he does.

"Suppose it's nice they're together," Damien says and Rose sniffs, I see her hastily wipe away a tear. I stare ahead wishing I hadn't seen her crying. I spot house thirteen, without saying goodbye I walk towards it. I hear Oliver saying goodnight to the others before following after me. I push the little gate open. I look around the blank little garden then at the front door. Oliver joins me on the threshold I turn to him handing him the envelope. He tears it open tipping a set of keys into his hand. We seem to stare at them for the longest time before he reaches round me to open the door. It opens without a creak; I stare into the dark unfamiliar hallway. Oliver steps up onto my step and we both stare into the strange house for a little while until he sighs and picks me up. I stiffen in his arms as he walks us into the house, our house.

"Welcome home," he says flatly, before putting me back down. He flicks on the lights as he closes the front door locking its many locks. I look around the small hallway. I spot a little kitchen adjoining the living room. The living room has a small TV, a few blank cabinets and a small couch and arm chair. There is a little dining table straddling the living room and kitchen. I walk in further, thorough an open door on the right; I see a little bathroom with a little shower and a small tub. I look at Oliver who is in the living room looking around; he looks huge in this little house. I wonder how he's going to fit into this stuff; I just know he's far too big to fit in the tub comfortably. I push away the thought as I open the door to the right of the bathroom. I gasp when I open it. It's a small

105

rectangular room that's plainly decorated, but sitting in the middle of the room is a pure white baby's crib. I slam the door closed feeling the sudden urge to get the hell out of there. As I spin around I bump into Oliver who is staring wide-eyed at the door. Judging by his look on his face he saw exactly what the room contained. He looks down at me and swallows hard.

This, this is what has been niggling at me since Oliver bought me. We're going to have to have children. In the back of our heads of course we knew it, but with everything else going on it hadn't really registered. Now, seeing that crib, it really hammered it home. I know I have been saved from the utter humiliation of having Jackson pawing at me constantly or even fathering my children but as I turn to face him the look on Oliver's face tells me that he had not thought this the whole way through. I turn away making my way to the last door, pushing it open. It's the master bedroom, I hear Oliver following me. I look down at the small double bed and back at him.

"So how do you want to do this?" I ask. He frowns at me.

"Do-do what?"

"This. It's not technically our wedding night but aren't we supposed to... you know?" I say indicating to the bed his face reddens.I glance back in the direction of the crib room, his eyes widen. "Chloe. I don't expect..." he says gently and I frown.

"Why delay the inevitable?" I reach round unzipping my dress.

"Jesus Christ Chloe. Stop!" he yells as I lower the straps. I pause as he sighs turning away a little. "Please just stop," he says eyes wide and his voice tight.

"Why?" I ask and he looks at the floor.

"I don't want..."

"You don't want me? Well you shouldn't have bought me then!" I snap frowning. His head shoots up; he stares at me in disbelief.

"What and let you allow yourself to be turned?" he doesn't shout but the anger in his voice is evident, making it all the more terrifying. "I saw what you were going to do Chloe. I saw you look at that Leech. Tell me you weren't going to do it and I will apologise," I stare at him unable to speak; an angry smile crosses his face. "I knew it. Why? Why would you do that?"

"I didn't see any other option. Oliver, you should've heard what Jackson said to me when you weren't there. He would have made my life a misery. I would never have been able to see you again," I say honestly, he frowns at me.

"What about Damien?" he asks. I frown up at him.

"What about him?"

"You were smiling when he was going against Jackson," he says, sounding frustrated. I'm surprised to see he looks a little jealous.

"Well I, I guess I was hopeful because he would have been less interested in me than I was him and he's nice."

"You still would have had to have children with him."

Good point.

"I know but it was a better option than Jackson. It wouldn't have been as repellent if it was with Damien," I say desperately.

"And what about me?" he asks. I stare at him my mouth hanging open.

"I-I don't…"

"Are you mad at me for picking you?" he asks sounding confused; I frown at him shaking my head to clear it.

"I'm furious. You didn't have to waste ten years," I say slowly.

"I know I didn't Chloe, but I knew he wouldn't do something so…"

"Stupid?" I say. His lips twitch in a smile.

"Well I suppose so. I was going to choose you anyway," he says with a shrug. I look at him surprised.

107

Really?

"You said at the school you weren't mad at me," he says crossing his arms. I stare at him totally confused by this mile a second conversation.

"Well I lied, this is a mess." I grip my dress staring at him desperately. I know I shouldn't be mad at him but there is no one else here. "Look we have to have children Oliver. So if you don't want to have..." I blush.

"Sex?" Oliver says, making my face redden more.

"Yes, sex," I say stiffly, he just stares at me. "If you didn't want that, then why did you choose me?"

"I couldn't be without you," he says matter of factly as he steps towards me. I jump a little; he stills his eyes full of anger and hurt.

Why am I flinching from him? It's Oliver.

"I'm sorry, I never thought about what might happen in this situation I never in a million years thought it would come to this. I panicked ok?" he says as he grips his messy hair, he drops his hands and they flop to his sides. He looks completely defeated. I realise then that he must be totally exhausted and he's filthy.

"Let me run you a bath," I say as the good wife code clicks on. I step around him and I hear him sighing.

"I don't want you to do that," he says from behind me.

"You are tired and dirty let me do this," I say turning back around to face him.

"What is going on with you? Why are you acting like this?" he asks frowning deeply. I stare at him, the horror stories of the misbehaving wives still fresh in my mind.

"It's my job to look after you," I say. He closes his eyes sighing.

"It's not your job. I don't expect anything from you ok? Look, please don't be mad at me, I was stupid. I get it but I've said sorry," he says trying to keep his voice calm. "I couldn't lose you Chloe. You're my best friend, I didn't want to never see you again," he stays startling me. "I saw Jackson's envelope. He was going to the forests. You would have been miles away. I know Joseph's there but if Jackson bought you, not even he could have helped you. I knew if Jackson got you I would never see you again. I even hoped Damien might have won the bidding. He would have been here and you're right, I knew he would let you see me. He's a good guy." The truth in his words startles me. "But when Jackson was winning I had to do something. Even if he was coming here with you I don't think I could've stood seeing you having to live with him. Then I would have seen you pregnant, with his kid, knowing what he would have done to you, that would have killed me," he says looking horrified at the thought. I just stare at him a little bit shocked at the whole confession.

"He doesn't deserve you. You're too good for him, for anyone. I'm sorry, I know it was selfish but I panicked," he says and I swallow hard. He walks over to me and I freeze. Hurt flashes across his face again and he sighs. "You're the only person left in this damn world that I trust Chloe. I didn't want you taken away from me like everything else," he says. He leans forward, I think he's going to kiss me but he just grabs the comforter off of the bed. He turns to walk out of the room. I let out a breath I didn't realise I was holding.

"Where are you going?" I ask he stills in the doorway.

"I'm sleeping on the sofa. Good night Chloe," he says without looking back at me. He closes the door lightly. I slump down on the bed; I start to cry instantly

.

Chapter 12

I lie in my new, too soft bed, staring up at the ceiling. It's long been silent in the house; it was filled with the sounds of Oliver walking around then the rumble of the pipes as he showered. The silence is unnerving; despite my exhaustion I give up trying to rest. I shakily get out of bed, all my limbs weak and heavy as I walk around the room. I go through a set of drawers finding it contains some standard issue clothes. I pull out a pair of soft cotton pyjamas that are about my size. I wriggle out of my dress letting it fall to the floor, I kick it into a dark corner of the room.

I really must get around to burning that.

I pull on the pyjamas, having to roll them up a little at the leg. I continue exploring the room looking through the little closet. There's nothing in there but a slight smell of other people. I try and imagine another family living here. Then I wonder what happened to them. As my thoughts begin to take a dark route I close the door. I head over to the other set of drawers. In it there are identical sets of clothes to the ones that are in mine, all except for their size. I realise they must be for Oliver. I turn, looking at the door, when I realise he's sleeping on that tiny sofa after all the hard work he has just gone through. I close the drawers quietly as guilt floods through me I walk over to the door and out into the hallway. I tiptoe into the living room where I find him hanging off of the sofa. One of his long bare legs is hanging over the arm while the other foot is planted on the floor. His arm is slung over his eyes. He's freshly showered, shaved and I see his hair is still darkened by the dampness. I can smell the soap. His pile of dirty clothes is folded neatly on the chair. He has the comforter wrapped around his torso like a sleeping bag. The sight of him there breaks my heart. I pad over to the couch and kneel down by his head.

"Oliver," I say. I shake him a little making him groan.

"What?" he grumbles.

"Oliver, wake up," I say a little louder. He jumps his eyes wide and startled.

"Chloe what... what's wrong?" he asks sitting up rubbing his neck.

"Nothing I'm ok," I say as he rubs his eyes, that I notice are red. He must have been crying. I'm silent for a moment feeling awkward, not really sure why I came in here.

"What is it?" he asks. I quickly look at him then the floor.

"You shouldn't be sleeping in here. You're too big. Will you... I mean it's your bed too," I say quickly. I see him frown.

"Chloe I'm fine here."

"No you're not. Let me take the couch at least you're hanging off of it. You need some proper sleep you look like you haven't slept in days," I say. He just stares at me.

"I'm fine. I don't want to make you uncomfortable."

"I'm uncomfortable anyway. This place is strange, it's too quiet. I can't sleep." I look up, I see him chewing his lip. "Please Oliver," I beg and he considers me for a moment and then he nods slowly.

"Ok. But you aren't sleeping in here alone," he says quietly. He stands up, wrapping the comforter around himself tighter, and offers me his hand to pull me up. I lead him into the bedroom he closes the door behind him. I climb into the bed pulling the covers up to my chin.

"There are pyjamas in the drawers over there," I say pointing to his chest of drawers very aware he's naked under the comforter. He nods pulling the drawers open. I lie down turning away so he can get dressed in privacy. I hear him get dressed then the bed dips as he climbs in. He switches off his light, the room falls into darkness and I stare at the dark wall. As he gets comfortable I can feel the big gap between us. I try not to cry again, scrunching my eyes shut. I hear Oliver sniff and my eyes shoot open.

"Oliver?" I whisper. He clears his throat.

"Yeah?" he croaks. I roll over facing his back.

"I missed you," I say. He chuckles making the bed wobble.

"I missed you too. Good night Chloe," he says. I hear the smile on his voice.

"Good night," I say smiling and we fall silent. I close my eyes counting Oliver's steady breaths. I thank my lucky stars for him knowing how this night could have been going of it weren't for him. I sigh contently. I feel Oliver move before I fall into a restless sleep.

Warm, it's really warm.

I start to wake up; from behind my eyelids I can see that it's finally daylight. The sun is shining through the window it feels hot on my skin. I hear a deep sigh or rather feel it, my eyes snap open. I look around I realise that my pillow is not a pillow but Oliver's chest. My eyes widen. I slowly lift my head trying not to disturb him but then my eyes meet his blue-green ones. He's not moving; I feel his arm tense around my waist.

"Morning," he croaks. I smile nervously.

"Hi. I'm sorry I didn't mean..." I say as I sit up, he moves his arm.

"It's fine," he says quickly. I look down at him my eyes widening in horror.

"Oh my god!" I gasp covering my face in embarrassment.

"What, what is it?" he asks nervously he shuffles about as I laugh into my hands.

"I drooled on you," I say through my fingers.

"Oh! Thank god," he breathes sounding relieved. I frown at him as his face reddens slightly. "So you're a drooler eh?" he asks with a nervous chuckle.

"Shut up! Well you fart," I say. He laughs as he sits up wrapping his arms around his knees. I scowl at him shoving him so he nearly falls of the bed.

"Hey! Well I'm a guy, it's what we do," he says proudly as he rights himself. I shake my head smiling.

"You're gross," I say.

"Oh please! Don't pretend you don't do it," he says. I narrow my eyes at him.

"Not intentionally I don't," I say. He rolls his eyes.

"Well I suppose we're going to get used to each other's normally hidden disgusting habits," he says. I stare down at my feet; I catch a glimpse of the ring on my finger. I look down at it. I see him looking at me nervously.

"I suppose. I don't think I'll ever get used to your smelly backside though," I say with a smile. He shoves me with his shoulder, making me fall to the side still grinning.

"I'm sure you'll be fine. You grew up in a house full of men," he says. I nod smiling.

"True." I stare at him and despite the last week and our argument the night before, I feel almost happy. I just know that it's because he's here. "How was the farm?" I ask crossing my legs. He lies back heavily blowing out a deep breath.

"Exhausting, there were so many ewes that were pregnant. A ewe is a female sheep by the way," he says.

"Interesting," I say mockingly. He narrows his eyes.

"Shut up, I didn't know. Anyway there were hundreds of them and there were lambs…" he goes on. I smirk.

"Baby sheep," I interrupt. He smiles shoving me with his foot.

"Yes smart ass. Well they were popping out all over the place. I had to help pull a few free, it was gross at first but I kind of got used to it. It's what I'll be doing with the horses apparently, if the female has trouble."

"Sounds exciting," I say pulling a face.

"It was actually. It was cool seeing something being born, like it wasn't there one minute and then pop, it's a little thing," he says and I stare down at him as he smiles up at the ceiling. His smile slowly fades though. "There were quite a few who died though it was sad, a couple of mums and a few babies. We had to hand feed a few. That was cool though. The lambs are really cute," he says. I smile, he sighs loudly as he stretches. "What do you want to do today?" he asks. I shrug.

"I don't know but I have to get something to eat I'm starving. Do you think there is food in here?" I ask looking towards the kitchen. He throws the covers off himself getting up.

"Let's find out shall we?" he says stretching. I giggle at the sight of him, his pyjama legs are a good few inches too short and he's showing off quite a bit of ankle. He opens the door looking back at me frowning. He looks down at his legs rolling his eyes. "Come on then," he says walking out of the room. I follow him still smiling. He's crashing around the kitchen when I walk in. I watch as he pulls out a carton of eggs from our pre-stocked fridge. I walk around to have a look inside and spot large green bottle.

"I suppose it's our wedding gift?" I ask pointing to it. He picks it out looking at the label.

"To Mr. and Mrs. Hunter." His eyes dart to me then back down at the bottle. "Congratulations on your betrothal. Do you want me to throw it out?" he asks as his nose wrinkles, I shake my head.

"We should drink it, it's for us after all and it looks expensive," I say. He smiles looking back down at the bottle.

"Really? *You* want to drink this?" he chuckles. I frown at him before shoving him.

"Sure why not? It's not like we're ever going to be able to afford it again so why not enjoy it?" I ask. He smiles shaking his head.

"I'm not a kid anymore I can do what I want."

"What has gotten into you?" he asks his eyebrow arched. I smile.

114

"I only didn't do anything reckless before because I wanted to be placed in work but now..."

"You're stuck here," he says sadly. I shake my head knowing he feels guilty.

"That's not what I mean. I just mean I can cut loose a bit," I say. He looks down at me smiling widely.

"Good. Well shall we crack it open for breakfast?" he asks, with a huge grin. I take it from him putting it back in the fridge. He laughs.

"Ok, not that loose. Let me ease into it," I say as he continues to chuckle.

"Whatever you say," he says closing the door.

"So what do you want for breakfast?" I ask. He shakes his head steering me to a chair.

"Just sit, I've got this," he says. I narrow my eyes suspiciously.

"What are you making?" I ask eyeing the eggs as he pops them open.

"My famous omelette," he says with a flourish. I shake my head; he puts his hands on his hips sighing. "What's wrong with my omelette?"

"You mean the same 'famous omelette' that made me sick for days?" I ask.

"The very same," he says smiling. I feel my stomach clench in nervous anticipation.

"Ok, but just make sure it's cooked properly this time. Burnt is better than raw," I plead. He rolls his eyes.

"It was hardly my fault you have a weak stomach. You need to toughen up your gut," he says.

"Or you could just not poison me," I suggest and he chuckles. I watch as he rolls up his sleeves beginning to mix the egg mixture. His hair is a mess, his eyes are still slightly red and he still looks exhausted. I swear that he, too, has lost weight since the last time I saw him. His pajama bottoms hang low on his hips. As he starts to whistle tunelessly, I notice the drying drool mark on his chest. I blush again at the fact I dribbled on him. I look up at him realising that I've been staring at him. When his eyes meet mine I give him an embarrassed little smile that he returns.

"Did you get a chance to call your Dad?" he asks. I shake my head and bite my lip.

Damn it.

"I totally forgot. They didn't have a phone in the um..." his eyes flash angrily.

"I bet they didn't," he says acidly. "You better call him he'll be worried." I spring up grabbing the phone off the wall. I quickly dial Dad's new number, the phone rings twice before it's answered.

"Hello?" Dad says. I smile at his voice.

"Hey Dad," I say smiling. I hear him sigh.

"Hey kiddo, I was beginning to wonder if you had forgotten about your old man," he says a smile in his voice. I chuckle.

"Sorry Dad. It had been a crazy couple of days," I say. I explain about Oliver being taken off to the farms on the night we arrived.

"So you were left all alone?" he asks sounding angry. I give a noncommittal hum of agreement.

"It was ok. I got to get to know the girls I came here with," I say. I notice Oliver staring at me frowning, with his arms crossed. I turn away from him knowing he's mad that I'm not telling Dad about the training I went through.

"How has it been, settling in?" Dad asks.

"It's been ok, the house is strange though. It's really bare you know. It doesn't feel like home yet," I say and I see Oliver nod in agreement as he watches the breakfast cook. "How is your new apartment?"

"It's ok but I know what you mean about a place not feeling like home. Your mum and I felt that way about our old place too. You will grow to like it when you make it your own. Don't worry about that," he says.

"How's work going? How are the kids?" I ask not wanting to think about mum.

116

"They're ok. I got a few more come to me after the graduation; apparently there were a lot of changes all over. The families are struggling but that's what I'm here for," he says and I nod.

Dad had done a great thing after mum left. He put in a request to open up a little office to help people with the grief and loss that comes with the change or the Farmings. He used his experience of losing mum to help others. Since he started he has been constantly busy, but he's made a great difference in the community and everyone loves him for it.

"How's Oliver?" Dad asks. I look over to Oliver, who is busy flipping an omelet.

"Oliver is ok, I think," I say. Oliver gives me a thumb up, making me chuckle. "Yeah he's ok, he's tired from the farms I think but he's busy making breakfast just now."

"Got him well trained already. That's impressive," Dad chuckles. I laugh, making Oliver stare at me like I'm losing the plot.

"Oh yeah, he's well trained," I say smiling. Oliver raises his eyebrows at me; I stick my tongue out at him making him smile.

"I got a call from Joseph. He told me that Jackson is going to be part of his team," Dad says. I laugh loudly again.

"No way," I say happily making Dad chuckle.

"What is it?" Oliver asks. I turn to face him a big smile on my face.

"Jackson's going to be working with Joseph," I say. Oliver's eyes widen before he bursts out laughing, Dad chuckles at our reaction.

"I thought you two would like that," Dad says. I giggle as Oliver wipes away a tear with the back of his hand.

"That's the funniest thing I've heard in a long time," Oliver sniggers. I shake my head at Oliver.

"That's the best news. Hey Dad, I have to go breakfast, is ready but I'm glad I caught you. Say hello to Joseph and

Michael for me when you hear from them and let me know how Millie is doing."

"Sure will, take care Chloe. I'll see you as soon as I can."

"Ok Dad, I love you. Miss you already," I say. I hear him smiling.

"Love you too Chloe. Say bye to Oliver for me and tell him good luck for Monday," he says, I nod and smile.

"I will. Bye Dad."

"Bye Christopher," Oliver calls. Dad chuckles.

"Bye guys," he says. He hangs up the phone. I put the receiver back on the wall turning around as Oliver is placing our breakfast on the table.

"Dad says bye and good luck for Monday," I say, taking a seat.

"That's nice," he says as I look down at the plate. "Well eat up before it goes cold," he says. I pick up my fork stabbing at a corner of the omelet. He smiles as I look at it warily. "Come on what is the likelihood of me poisoning you twice?" he jokes with a smile. I arch an eyebrow at him as I put the eggs in my mouth and chew. He looks at me expectantly. I swallow meeting his eyes.

"These are good," I say making him smile.

"You sound surprised."

"I was sick for five days. I'm allowed to be a little cautious," I say as he chuckles.

"That was five years ago, I didn't know how to cook back then. I can cook eggs now, among other things," he says proudly. I nod and continue to stuff my face. After hardly eating all week I'm starving. I eat quickly and very ungracefully.

Once I'm finished I push the plate away sighing contently.

"Thank you that was great," I say and he nods as he chews. "Well at least now you don't need to bother with the cooking anymore," I say. He looks up from his half eaten omelet frowning.

"What do you mean?"

"Well you will be working. I'll have nothing better to do so I can cook your meals," I say.

"I like cooking. You don't have to do that," he says.

"Yes I do, like I said I will have nothing better to do. I won't have much to do in here," I explain. His frown deepens.

"You can go out. Explore this place, its huge there will be plenty for you to do, do whatever you want. You didn't really expect me to make you stay here all day did you?" he asks looking taken aback.

"I don't know, I guess I kind of did. They told me at the training place that that's what our husbands would expect," I justify. As the words leave my mouth I instantly want to take them back but he slams his fork down folding his arms angrily.

"Look Chloe, I don't expect anything from you. You can go out and enjoy yourself. Meet new people, another guy, if you really want to. You're free to do what you want," he says sounding furious and hurt at the same time. I stare at him as he stands up, he picks up my empty plate and his half full one.

"Are you not going to eat that?" I ask. He looks at me with angry stormy eyes.

Oh dear.

"I've lost my appetite," he says. I flinch slightly at his words knowing that they were supposed to wound me.

It worked.

I can see that he's disappointed in me for thinking that way. He tips his breakfast into the bin and tosses the plates in the sink where they clatter loudly, making me cringe. He doesn't even look at me as he storms into the bathroom, slamming the door behind him.

Chapter 13

I stare at the door in shock; I can't quite believe how the mood went from comfortable to horrible, in the blink of an eye. I'm mostly shocked that he got upset over my offer to cook for him. I thought he would have appreciated it. I cringe a little when I realise that it's how I put it across. He thinks I feel obligated to do it, not that I want to do it. I frown, standing up. I'm cross at him for being mad at me over something so silly. It's hardly my fault that I have had it drilled into me all my life that a wife should cater to her husband's every need. That they should make sure he's well fed when he comes home from a hard day at work. Ok I admit I probably shouldn't have mentioned what the training place said as it clearly upsets him. I know that he thinks it's his fault that I'm here. What he doesn't realise is that I'm glad to be here with him.

Maybe I should tell him that? Instead of assuming he knows. Ignoring my thoughts I slam the bedroom door before quickly getting changed. I need to get out for some fresh air to clear my head.

I walk past the bathroom on my way to the front door. I hear the shower running. I don't wait until he's finished. I just walk straight out of the house, slamming the door for good measure. I walk down the quiet dirt road past Mary and David's house. I notice the house is still dark, the curtains still drawn. I look away; angrily realising they are probably still having the traditional honeymoon. I glance back looking for Damien and Rose's house. I'm shocked to see theirs is just the same. I frown as I wonder if they are doing the same thing.

Is it really that easy to just give yourself to someone?

I chew on my lip as I walk down the road away from the houses and I think about what Oliver said. Did he really think I would go out to find another man? Where would I even start with that? I have never really let boys cross my mind at all; I always had my life planned. Work hard and hope to get a good job. Then maybe meet someone. Not this. Not having to think about having children with my best friend. I groan loudly rubbing my face with both hands. Does everyone have this problem when they're forced into marriage? I remember poor Michael and Millie. I suddenly feel bad for my whining. At least I know Oliver. I know it can't be easy for everyone but I wonder if giving myself to someone would have been easier if it were someone else and not Oliver.

My mind flashes to Jackson and I shudder. No, no that would have been far worse. He would have forced himself on me. Made me sleep with him where Oliver would never do that. He isn't forcing himself on me. He's my friend and he's kind. I trust him. If I have to give myself completely to someone I guess I'm glad that someone is Oliver. I mean would it really be that horrible? Like Rose said it's natural.

The kiss I gave him on graduation wasn't bad.

I stop in my tracks startled by my train of thought. I look around, trying to see how far I have gone. I'm at the end of a track unsure how far I have walked. I spot a tower to my left with their blacked out windows. I scowl at it before I look back. I can just make out the village, there are a few more towers dotted around. There are not as many of them here as there was back home, there was one every mile or so back home but I suppose there are less people up here. I look around again, taking in the view of the village and sigh. *"They're always watching"* my dad's voice rings in my head. I stare back at the nearest tower moving off again cursing the damn Fanged under my breath as I come to a field. I look over to the tower and right into the window. I know I probably shouldn't do it but I hop over the fence. I continue walking, sticking to the hedge line. I walk in the opposite direction to the tower and my mind drifts back to Oliver.

Maybe I should just do it, just walk up to him and kiss him, see how he handles that. I know we'll have to eventually, I know he'll wait for me to be ready; there'll be no pressure. He's probably not expecting it; I mean, he told me I could meet someone else.

He probably doesn't want me, I think, startling myself. I don't know what to make of this; did he not say he was going to choose me? I frown as I power through the field. This should be something I want to do when I'm good and ready. I shouldn't be thinking about forcing myself on Oliver. I shouldn't be thinking about how I'm going to do it. It should happen naturally. We should both have a choice in the matter. It's our lives after all, I scoff loudly, glaring back at the tower.

The only thing is that, if the decision is left until it's too late, we'll be forced into it. Into having babies, it'll feel wrong. It will be horrible for both of us. I pause in the middle of the field looking back at the village surrounded by morning mist. It really is beautiful up here.

"Just do it," I say aloud before taking a deep breath and squaring my shoulders in determination, I turn and head back. I walk quickly, for a short time, stumbling when I see a movement in the corner of my eyes, I can tell it's big; I freeze. I slowly turn round, squeaking when I see a huge bull eyeing me with its big head low.

"Hello Mr. Bull," I say raising my hands. I immediately regret it, as it lowers its head further, the whites of its eyes showing. I step back lowering my hands and it rushes forward a few paces. I panic and before I know it, I'm turning and running away. I immediately regret the decision when I hear its huge body moving quickly behind me. I probably should've stood my ground. I spot the gate, my heart falls when I realise how far it is, I push myself on faster beginning to panic when I hear the beast closing in on me. I spot a big circular hay feeder to my right, I veer off towards it, running as fast as I can. When reach it I throw myself through the bars hitting my shoulder, painfully, on one of them. I cry out, hauling my legs through after me, before the bull reaches me. He skids to a halt as I tug my legs into my chest as its big head bangs against the side. I curl myself into a ball as it paces angrily around me.

That was too close.

The bull eyeballs me, occasionally bumping into the feeder, as I sit silently in the dry itchy hay and wait. I realise how lucky I am, to have gotten out of the way of this brute, he's huge. Those horns, short as they may be, would have done some serious damage. I glare over at the tower knowing they are probably having the time of their lives in there watching me sitting here, hiding from a damn bull.

That's right. It's hilarious when food fights back.

I look up at the tower wondering if they're actually watching me, I'm close enough to see the windows so they must be watching. I glare at the bull, embarrassed and angry, as the thought of being any form of entertainment to the Fanged washes over me. The bull finally seems to lose interest. I try to move but I moan as my shoulder starts throbbing. I breathe heavily trying to catch my breath. I shift again, my leg slipping, making the bull snort angrily. I pull my leg back up and freeze.

It feels like hours before the bull finally gets bored and walks off. I wait until he's far enough away before I pull myself up slowly. My shoulder aches but I ignore it as I swing my legs over the side falling to the ground as quietly as I can. I land on soft squishy ground, my nose wrinkles at the realisation of what I have landed in. I don't look down but keep my eye on the bull; he has looked up at the noise. I'm ready to throw myself back into the feeder but after he observes me for a moment he looks back down and continues grazing. I walk slowly towards the gate looking over my shoulder every now and then to the still grazing bull. Feeling brave and just desperately wanting to get out of there, I start running. When I reach the gate I throw myself over gracelessly nearly falling on my face on the other side. I right myself just in time, my arms flailing wildly as I keep running. I run down the long road, my breath burning my lungs. I pass curious villagers and all of the other houses without a second glance, I actually run past our house, skidding to a halt when I realise I've run too far down the street. I find number thirteen; I crash through the gate and the front door slamming it behind me. I lean against it breathing heavily clutching my trembling knees. My heart pounds in my ears making me feel woozy. Oliver runs out of the living room his eyes wide.

"Hey where were... what the hell happened to you?" he asks rushing forward looking me over.

"Bull in field... Chased me," I gasp, clutching my side as I straighten up, his eyes widen.

"What were you doing in a field?"

"Walking, had to think," I splutter. He nods before he walks into the bathroom, while I try to steady my breathing.

I need to get fit.

I hear the shower turning on. Soon after, he comes back out, drying his hands on his jeans.

"Go have a shower. You stink of cow shit," he says. I burst into laughter making the stitch in my side burn more.

"I hid in a hay feeder," I admit. He smiles pulling a strand from my hair.

"I can see that. Go on go get washed up, on you go," he says rolling his eyes when I don't move. He pulls my arm slightly; he instantly drops my arm when I wince, sucking in a pained breath cupping my shoulder. "I hardly touched you," he says backing away. He looks down at me, concern clear on his face. I shake my head.

124

"I hurt my shoulder jumping into the feeder. Hit it off the bars," I say rubbing it lightly.

"Let me have a look," he says as I shake my head. "Chloe stop being a big baby."

"Fine," I huff trying to pull my arm out of my jumper. I groan when it throbs. "Could you give me a hand?" I mumble trying and failing to shimmy out of the jumper. He grips the hem pulling it up slowly. He wriggles it upwards as I manoeuver my arm. I can tell he's trying to not hurt me. When I get my good arm free he pulls it over my head then slides it down my bad arm. As the adrenaline wears off it really starts to throb. He hisses through his teeth when he looks down at my shoulder.

"Damn that looks sore. You bruise like a peach," he says gently touching my shoulder. I stare up at him as he examines the bruise. He begins rolling my arm. "Is that sore?" he asks softly and I shake my head. He looks down at me through narrowed eyes he clearly doesn't believe me and I realise that my breathing has accelerated. "Hey are you..."

Now! My brain screams at me.

I lunge forward pressing my lips to his. I close my eyes when he freezes. His hand tightens on my arm a little; I know he's standing there with his eyes wide open. I pull away peeking up at him as I do. He blinks before he stares down at me. His eyes meet mine and I panic. I rush past him into the hot bathroom. I close the door leaning against it heavily. I cover my face in disbelief.

What did I just do?

I breathe slowly as I stare into the steamy room. When I catch my reflection in the mirror a smile breaks on my face. I can't believe I just did that. It wasn't so bad, I think as I lean off of the door. I quickly undress, stepping into the shower. I discard my filthy clothes in the wash basket where they join Oliver's suit, dirty from the farm, and close the curtain.

Chapter 14

After my shower, I stand in the bathroom with my hand on the door handle, listening for any sign of movement. I can't hear anything, so opening the door slightly I peek out. I'm half expecting to see Oliver still standing there, frozen to the same spot. I'm glad to see the hallway is clear. I tiptoe past the living room where I see him sitting on the sofa staring at the opposite wall. I'm not looking where I'm going so it's not a surprise when I stub my toe against a side table. I cry out muttering curse words under my breath. Oliver spins round his eyes locking eyes with mine. He turns back around when his eyes flicker down to the towel I'm wearing.

"We have to talk," he says, staring intently at the wall.

"Ok." I say nervously. His face is giving away nothing. I have no idea if he's embarrassed about what I did or just plain old mad.

"Get changed. I'll wait here," he says. I walk into the bedroom shutting the door before pulling on my pyjamas. Wanting to avoid this conversation for as long as I can I detour back into the bathroom, quickly brush my hair and grab our dirty clothes. I pass him on the way to the kitchen. He doesn't look at me. I bite my lip as I throw the clothes in the washer before turning it on.

You're procrastinating. Ok, so what if I am? I really don't want to have this conversation.

Oliver hasn't moved from his spot on the couch but when I sit down next to him he glances at me from the corner of his eye.

"They brought our clothes from home," he says and I pull nervously ay my sleep shirt.

"Oh, ok." I notice he's wearing jeans and a t-shirt and I feel silly sitting in my pyjamas in the middle of the day. I wait for him to speak. He looks over at me.

"Chloe what were you doing earlier? Why did you kiss me?" he questions.

"I don't know," I say my eyes falling to my lap as his stare burns into me.

"You don't know?"

"I just thought..."

"I told you, I don't expect anything," he interrupts. I sigh and look back up at him feeling determined.

"I know, let me finish," I say, he looks at me and nods. "I just thought that this should be something I decided on." He arches his eyebrow at me. "That we decided on. Look, I get why you chose me, I do. You were trying to protect me and I owe you for that."

"You don't owe me for anything."

"Yes I do Ollie. You've saved me from horrible life I did not want," I say emphasising my words. It's true I didn't want to be turned; I just had a moment of madness and desperation. "You also saved me from an unbearable life with Jackson, even if you think you were being selfish. Which you weren't, by the way." He looks down at his knees. "I'm the one who's being selfish. I have been horrible to you even after everything you did for me. I owe you everything. Despite what you think I'm glad you did it, I'm glad you chose me," I say. He looks up from his knees frowning.

"Really? Even with everything that comes with it?" he asks still sounding doubtful.

"Yes really. It might have been a bit of a shock, it still is. It's going to take time to get used to, for both of us. I know I won't have to change for you," I admit looking into his eyes. "I know you and you know me. I know what we're going through isn't ideal but it could be worse. We could be apart and neither of us wanted that." I shove him making him smile a little. "Most of all I trust you and you can trust me, right?" I ask. I smile when he nods. I chew on my lip before taking a deep breath. What I'm about to propose is something that terrifies me beyond anything I can think of. Asking Oliver to think of me as something other than his friend, is a big ask, but I know that it's the only option we have. It has to work.

"Well I have decided, if you will have me of course, that I would like to give us a try. The whole more than best friend's thing, you know? Try and give us a chance," I blurt out. He just looks at me like he's scared and confused all at the same time. "I mean if Damien can manage it..." I trail off, he chuckles shaking his head.

I try to keep looking at him, despite the overwhelming embarrassment of offering myself to him. I'm seconds away from getting up, running back to the bull and letting it finish me of because of the embarrassment. He stays silent but keeps his eyes on me. I can tell he's thinking hard. His jaw is flexing like he does sometimes when he thinks. Unable to take the silence I try another route.

"If we're going to be here together, we may at least try. If it doesn't work, you know if you don't like me or whatever, then at least we tried." His frown deepens. I look down realising he's playing with his ring. When I look back up he's still looking at me.

"Liking you isn't going to be a problem," he says his voice quite. My mouth pops open, he looks away as my face turns red. "But Chloe this isn't just about me. Do you think that you can do it? You know, with me?" he asks, his voice showing he's clearly embarrassed. I take the time to look at him while he's looking elsewhere. Of course he's good looking with his wild red hair and sea coloured eyes. He's tall, strong, kind and fiercely loyal. But the only thing that really matters is that he is my best friend and I trust him with my life. He looks up as the silence stretches out. I meet his eyes, biting my lip I nod at him.

"I think I could yes. It might be a little weird but I think that maybe we should make the decision so we won't have it forced on us when the time comes. We can take it slow. Just take our time to get comfortable with each other like this," I say. He nods in agreement.

"Ok."

"Will you be able to see me that way?" I ask nervously he nods quickly. I bite my lip to stop giggling as his face flushes.

"I had thought about it before," he says. I feel the smile slide off my face as my eyes widen.

"Really?" I stare at him completely and utterly shocked.

"I always just thought it would be weird or you know gross, but I don't know you just grew up and well…"

"Ugh!" I shove him. He chuckles.

"I'm a guy. I couldn't help it."

"I can't believe you didn't say anything. You never usually have a problem telling me you're thinking."

"I didn't want to make it awkward. Everything with you is just so… easy. I knew you didn't want to meet a guy, so I just hung back," he says. I stare at him shaking my head when I suddenly realise something.

"Duncan. Are you the reason why he stopped talking to me at the start of the year?" I probe. He chews his lip before smiling at me guiltily.

"Maybe?"

"Oliver!" I say crossly, making him stare at me and frown.

"Well the poor guy was hanging around like a bad smell. You were totally oblivious so I just saved him the heartbreak," he says. I cross my arms making him smile.

"I was not oblivious," I say defensively, also lying completely. He arches his eyebrow at me and I try not to smile.

"You were oblivious; I've never seen anything like it in my life. He tried giving you his number about five times. I felt bad for him," he says. I try not to laugh, remembering the times Duncan had tried giving me his number.

"Poor Duncan. What did you say to him?" I ask. He smiles.

"I just said we were secretly dating," he reveals. I roll my eyes.

"You could have warned me, I thought he had fallen out with me. I even yelled at him for being standoffish," I say trying hard not to laugh.

"Poor Duncan," he pouts. I slap his arm making him laugh. He rubs his arm as we sit in silence for a moment.

"I'm sorry about earlier," I say. He frowns at me looking confused.

"What for?"

"Kissing you like that, I shouldn't have," I say. He smiles before looking away.

"I didn't mind, but maybe a little warning next time? You nearly knocked my tooth out."

"Next time eh?" I ask. He turns, smiling at me. I feel my face flush; he opens his mouth to say something when someone raps on the front door. We both jump, Oliver springs up rushing to answer it. I watch as he opens the door then look away sighing.

Well that was awkward!

Secretly, I'm also glad to have gotten everything out in the open. It feels like a huge weight has been lifted off my chest.

"Hey look who's here," Oliver says walking back into the house followed by Damien and Rose.

"Hi Chloe," Rose says smiling widely. I smile at her and wave from my seat.

"Hi," I say giving Damien a smile.

"How are you enjoying the new house?" he asks sitting down. I look at Oliver as he and Rose sit on the chair, her on his lap.

Interesting.

"We hate it," we answer together. Rose and Damien smile.

"What about you guys?" Oliver asks.

"It's ok," Damien says taking Rose's hand. My eyes flicker to their now joined hands; I can't help but frown a little.

"It's too quiet," Rose adds. Damien nods looking up at her. I nod in agreement. These houses all must be the same, we're all used to a little more traffic and people around us. There's a long pause when Rose nudges Damien's leg.

"Oh, Rose and I wondered if you two would like to come to the pub with us. We're going to have dinner and a few drinks. You know to celebrate; it's our honeymoon after all," he says. Oliver and I look at each other, I can tell he really doesn't want to.

"Well we…" I begin. Rose looks between us her eyes widening.

"Shit, we're so sorry guys," she says. She gets up pulling Damien up with her. He stares at her looking confused. "We should've known you guys would still be…"she makes a crude hand gesture and my mouth falls open in embarrassment.

"No we weren't," Oliver says quickly, he blushes looking at me desperately. I get up, blushing furiously, only now realising how it must look with me in my pyjamas.

"We would love to come out with you," I say. Oliver shoots me a smile of thanks.

"Ok great. We'll meet you down there in an hour or so then," Rose says we nod as they make their way to the door.

"Sure," I say as Oliver rushes to open it for them, I follow.

"What about David and Mary?" Oliver asks. Damien smiles as Rose shakes her head.

"We checked on them but they are otherwise engaged," he says.

"They yelled at us and told us to piss off," Rose says chuckling. Damien smiles while Oliver chuckles. I roll my eyes; I notice Rose staring at Damien who gives her a little smile that makes her blush. I catch Oliver's eyes; his eyebrows rise up in surprise. Rose giggles as we turn to look at them; Damien has his hand around her waist.

"I was as shocked as you two. Get half a bottle of champagne in this one and he'll do anything," she says noticing our reaction and bumping her hip off of Damien, who smiles.

"Not anything," he says looking a little shocked at Roses bluntness.

"Sorry it's none of our business," Oliver says. Damien takes Rose's hand.

"It's alright. You've just got to accept the hand you're dealt right? No point bitching about it," he explains. Rose chuckles.

"That's very romantic," she says. He squeezes her hand.

"That's not what I mean and you know it," he says kissing her cheek. She smiles before shoving him again. "I may not favor girls but she's pretty any guy can see that. She's mine. I'm hers. We've talked about it and we're fine with that," he says. Rose squeezes his hand, as he smiles at her. I look enviously at them, I'm acutely aware of the distance between Oliver and me. It may be only a foot or two but compared to how Damien and Rose are pressed together it may as well be a mile.

Why is it not that easy for us?

"So, we'll see you both there?" Rose asks snapping me out of my thoughts I nod and smile. "Cool, well we'll see you soon." They wave as they walk down our path chatting and laughing. Oliver closes the door turning towards me.

"I guess a double date is as good a place to start as any," he says.

"I guess so," I agree failing to hide my smile.

"Let's go get ready," he says with a grin as he walks into the bedroom. I follow slowly after him still reeling slightly over the revelation of Damien and Rose actually consummating their marriage. I walk into the room as Oliver is pulling out a trunk from the closet. He smiles at me as he plops it down on the bed.

"Is that my stuff from home?" I ask, with a smile, running my hand over the chest.

"Yeah," he says with a nod. I pop the lid open smiling when the smell of home flows out from the clothing and few belongings I packed. I start pulling out pictures and little ornaments that used to be in my old room. As I look over them I suddenly don't feel like going out. I slump down on the bed sighing.

"I miss home," I say, my voice sounding sad even to my own ears. Oliver looks up from his trunk and gives me a sad little smile.

"I know," he says. He closes his trunk and walks over to me smiling. "Hey is that the snow globe I got you for your Christmas when we were like ten?" he asks looking into my trunk. I reach in pulling it out with a smile.

"Yeah and we were seven. You got me it the same year my mum left," I say looking up at him.

"I remember," he says sitting down next to me. "You opened it and looked at me like I had given you a dead rabbit. You said, and I quote, *what the hell do I do with this?*" you were a real bitch," he chuckles. I bite my lip trying not to laugh as I remember his startled seven-year-old face.

"Oh god yeah, sorry about that. I love it really," I promise, as I smile at him. I don't miss his wide grin as he turns to his trunk.

"Good. It cost me a fortune," he says. I roll my eyes.

"I know it cost you less than ten pounds," I say, he looks at me shrugging.

"I was seven, I had a tight budget. It cost more than the gift you got me," he says. I stare at him frowning.

"I didn't get you anything."

"Exactly!" he says rolling his eyes.

I laugh as I shake the globe. The little cottage inside now sits amidst a glittery blizzard. We watch as the snow slowly swirls to the ground.

"Looks nice in there," I say, I look over at him giving him a little smile.

"It does," he says. He nudges me with his arm before standing up. "Come on, let's get ready or we'll be late," he says. I nod and put the snow globe down on my bedside table next to the picture of my dad, Joseph, Michael and his family. He looks at the little collection of items, smiling, as I look in the trunk for something to wear.

I pull on a pair of my favourite worn but very comfortable jeans and my favourite red shirt as Oliver changes in the bathroom. I open the bedroom door bumping into him as he comes out of the bathroom. I bounce off of him, nearly falling to the floor until he grabs me around the waist steadying me.

"Sorry," I mumble as he rights me. He lets me go stepping aside to let me past. I grab my hairbrush from the bathroom before heading back into the bedroom. I freeze in the door way as Oliver pulls off his t-shirt throwing it onto the bed. I can't help but stare at his broad, muscled back as it stretches. I feel my face flush as he leans forward picking up his shirt and pulling it back on. I don't know what my body is doing to me; it has never reacted this way to a topless man before, especially Oliver! Or, maybe it did but I just ignored it before. Back when I was too busy focusing on getting a job. It's fair to say that I didn't let much distract me during that time. I do remember when we were younger and the time we went swimming with the school. I saw him and the other boys without tops on that day. I remember looking over them curiously but as I began comparing their bodies I stopped myself from looking. Obviously it was just my teenage hormones out of control. I do remember Oliver always being bigger and broader than the other boys. However, I don't remember the smooth rolling muscles that move under his pale skin as he swings the shirt over his head. I shake my head trying to clear it from such thoughts as I walk, slightly unsteadily into the room. He turns around and my mouth dries at the sight of his chest. If I thought his back was beautiful then his chest should be outlawed.

"I was hot," he says as he buttons up, I shamelessly roam my eyes up his torso then eventually to his face.

"What?" I ask after too long a pause. He smiles a little knowing smile. I look away blushing.

"I said I got hot, I had to change," he says his tone slower so I can take in the words. I nod as I sit down in front of the mirror busying myself with brushing my hair. It's none of my business.

"Ok," I say with an indifferent shrug but my voice is breathy and completely embarrassing. I don't miss his big smug smile in the reflection in the mirror. I feel myself redden as I groan internally.

What's wrong with me?

I silently curse Rose and Mary for their stupid conversation in the laundry room also for putting all those thoughts in my head. That's right blame them. I've seen Oliver topless many times before. It never bothered me then. I endured days of him roaming round in just his shorts when the weather was good and I never thought anything of it. But now, now here he is and we're sharing a room, a bed, and for the first time, the sight of him half naked makes me nervous.

Has he been working out?

I glare at myself in the mirror. I can't ignore the undeniable racing of my heart, the flush of my cheeks or the slight acceleration of my breath. I pause in brushing my hair as he moves towards the door.

"I will just be in the living room," he says I nod, meeting his eyes in the mirror. I see a strange look in his eyes and I can't quite place it but he just smiles before walking out of the room. I stare back at myself shake, my head and sigh.

"Get a grip!" I whisper tossing my brush into a drawer. I get up, slipping my shoes on. I take a deep breath before flicking off the light and closing the door. Oliver is waiting for me in the next room he smiles when I enter.

"Are you ready?" he asks. I nod he gets up from the sofa joining me in the hall. "Let's get going then, they will probably be waiting." He opens the door letting me walk out first. I turn waiting for him to lock the door. He joins me on the path and we walk down the garden path together. We walk along the road towards the village centre. As we pass homes the people all look at us. We cast them nervous smiles some return them, nod or wave but others just stare at us. There are children playing in their gardens or in the street. They look at us curiously but they all smile or wave after a few moments. I smile as I return their waves; Oliver looks down at me with a little smile.

"What? I like kids," I say, he rolls his eyes but keeps on smiling. As we reach the middle of the village a group of rowdy men walk our way. They slow slightly leering at me, pointing and laughing. I move closer to Oliver instinctively, he reaches for my hand without any provocation. I give him a little smile as he keeps his eyes on the men. They wolf whistle but we ignore them as we continue down to the pub, The Wheat Sheaf. It's an old white building with a grey slate roof. It's larger than I thought it would be and there is bright yellow light spilling from its many windows. The entrance is surrounded with a trellis covered in ivy, which is making its way across the front of the building like green veins. As Oliver opens the door for me I'm hit by a wall of sound. It's crowded, as we enter some people spot us then it's like the volume got turned down and everyone stares at us, it's quite unnerving. Oliver and I just stare at them unsure what to do. I'm about to back out of the building when I see Damien and Rose.

"Hey guys!" Damien says standing up from his and Rose's little table, he waves us over. I feel eyes following us as we walk over to them thankful that we weren't coming here alone; otherwise I think we might have just gone home. I see Damien's eyes falling to our linked hands, I don't miss the smile on his face. I realise I'm squeezing Oliver's hand in a death grip. I let him go before shooting him a sorry look. He smiles as he rubs some life back into his hand.

"Weird isn't it?" Rose says looking around the room as the people start talking again. I pull out the seat across from her.

"It is a bit," Oliver says sitting down next to me.

"It's like they haven't seen strangers before," I add looking around at some of the people who are still looking at us. Rose nods leaning forward.

"It's creepy, did the people outside stare at you too?" she asks. I nod, she straightens up her eyes widening. "Weird!" she whispers Damien chuckles as he stands up.

"What do you guys want to drink?" he asks, I shrug. I look down at Rose's glass, her drink looks nice.

"I'll have what Rose has, if that's ok?" I ask. He nods before turning to Oliver.

"Pint?" Damien asks. Oliver nods.

"I'll come up with you," he says getting up giving me a quick smile. They head over to the bar, many sets of eyes following them. Oliver nods at a short, surly looking man who turns away.

"So weird," Rose mutters, as I turn back to her. "So…" she says with a mischievous smile, as she leans forward, I lean back in my seat cringing.

"Don't," I warn. She looks at me innocently.

"What? I was only going to ask how your first night in your new house was… And if you've done it yet," she says with a little smile. I feel myself blush. I narrow my eyes at her. "I take it from that reaction that's a no." I groan crossing my arms, she laughs.

"I'm not saying anything," I say looking down at the table. I see her smile and my cheeks heat up.

"You don't need to. Your body says it all. You look miserable," she says with a chuckle. I frown at her before looking around the pub to make sure no one is looking at us.

"Of course I do. This is a shitty situation, I can't believe you and Damien. How can you guys just ignore everything and just do it?" I ask my voice low.

"I don't know. I guess because I wasn't expecting anything it was a nice shock. A very nice shock," she says as she grins at me; I roll my eyes sitting back in my chair.

"You're telling me," I mutter, making her smile.

"Look I know it's weird, but like Damien said, I'm his and he's mine, no matter how much we wish it wasn't true. He doesn't want me to be miserable and he doesn't want to be miserable either. It's not ideal for him but he seemed to enjoy it anyway." I look down at the table. "Come on Chloe we just want to be happy, to get on and this is the best way."

"You could just be friends," I say and she laughs loudly.

"Being friends won't make babies," she says. I look up at her. I see the pain flash in her eyes; I give her a little smile.

"I'm sorry," I say and she smiles.

"It's ok. I'm very lucky to have Damien. He's sweet; I just want to make him happy, as well as myself. We have been dealt a shit hand but we can, and will, make it work. You never know later on it may get easier. You're lucky you have Oliver." I frown knowing I really do have it a lot easier than she does.

"I know I am."

"Well, stop looking so sorry for yourself and just enjoy it," she says with a smile. I stare at her in disbelief.

"It's going to be weird though," I say, she shrugs and leans over patting my hand.

"Maybe, but you two have something that most of us don't," she says. I raise my eyebrows scoffing.

"Oh yeah, what's that?"

"You love each other," she says, like it's the most obvious thing in the world. I stare at her my mouth wide; she shakes her head at me. "Maybe you're not 'in love' yet, but you have that. You guys are so lucky." I look back over to the bar, I see Oliver joking with Damien. When I look back at her, she smiles. "You'll be fine. You have plenty of time to get used to each other. You'll get it," she says and I let out a long breath.

"Yeah maybe, we're going to try," I say. She looks up smiling, looking pleased.

"Really?"

"Yeah, this is kind of like a date or whatever."

"Oh, that's adorable. Mary will be so sad she missed this momentous occasion!"

"Shut up." I groan, she laughs as she looks behind me.

"Did you notice the picture when you came in?"

"What picture? I didn't see a picture, all I noticed was the whole village staring at us," I say turning around in my seat. I stiffen when I notice the picture she's talking about, it's Henry. A dark, lifelike oil painting sits pride of place on the wall behind me. I stare into Henry's black, lifeless eyes. I can't help the shiver that runs down my spine at the little knowing smirk on his painted lips. "Why do they have that?" I croak as I turn away from it.

"I don't know but I hate it. It's like he's here, watching. I can't stop looking at it," she says visibly shivering. Her eyes dart to where the picture hangs again; she shakes herself before looking me in the eyes. "So how's your 'training' going?" she asks before taking a sip of her wine. I smile at her blatant attempt at trying to change the subject.

"He won't let me do anything," I say. Rose smiles and rolls her eyes.

"That's because you're not my slave," Oliver's says loudly from behind me. I hadn't heard him approach; I shake my head as he puts Rose's and my drink down.

139

"He doesn't see the logic; if he's out working all day while I'm not doing anything, then I should at least make the dinner," I say trying to sound reasonable. He huffs as he sits down.

"Men!" Rose says dramatically, I smile as Oliver crosses his arms.

"What about men?" Damien says, as he joins us, putting down the pints in front of himself and Oliver before sitting back down next to Rose.

"We were just saying how annoying they are," I tease glancing at Oliver, who narrows his eyes at me.

"Tell me about it," Damien says. Oliver looks at him like he just slapped him.

"Come on man, you should be backing me up here," Oliver moans. Damien shrugs while looking at him apologetically.

"Sorry Oliver, but I know first-hand how irritating guys can be," he says. I smile triumphantly at Oliver while Damien and Rose laugh.

"Oh shut it you," he says snatching up his pint moodily and taking a big drink.

Chapter 15

A few hours later after a lovely dinner and a good few glasses of wine that I have to say, I'm rather enjoying, we're the only people left in the pub. We're all laughing so hard about a story Damien is telling us, about a time when he and Tommy were caught in a school cupboard by the janitor, that we don't realise when the pub door opens and Rose goes quiet. I notice her face fall, I stare at her, still chuckling.

"What is it?" I ask. When she doesn't answer and when Oliver and Damien still in their seats, I turn around. My mouth pops open audibly when I clock the couple that has just entered. They're very clearly a pair of Fanged. They look around the room and the male frowns a little when he spots us. He looks at the clock on the wall while his mate sniffs the air hungrily. I hear a crash but can't seem to tear my eyes off of the female, who has her eyes locked on me. I see the barman bumbling into the room gasping for air.

"You, you're early," he stutters looking at the male, his eyes wide and scared, as they dart between the Fanged and us. The female turns to look at him, her nose wrinkling in disgust.

"Is *that* why you dragged me out here at this ungodly hour?" the female asks with a hiss, looking from the barman to her mate.

"The bar is closed," the barman says rushing around the bar, giving the Fanged pair a wide berth as he hurries towards us.

"What's going on?" Oliver says standing up quickly, his chair to clatters to the ground.

"Oliver," Damien says in a warning voice as he stands beside him.

"Out," the barman says shakily as he shoves at Oliver and Damien, who grabs Rose's hand. The Fanged stand still as statues by the door watching us intently, only their eyes giving away any sign of life.

"They're not supposed to be here," Oliver says looking over at the Fang couple. The barman looks nervously between the Fanged and us, wringing his hands. The male is standing with his hands held behind his back with an amused look on his face, while his mate is poised in a slight crouch, with her eyes on me. I walk slowly and cautiously towards them. I can hear my heart racing in my ears; I curse it for giving away my fear. I have never come across a loose Fanged before, why would I have? They aren't supposed to be out so early. The female twitches as we near her. Her mate slides over to her putting a hand on her shoulder making her still again. The thought that this pair must be a couple of rule breakers is making me increasingly nervous. The male's eyes wander over us all, but the female; her eyes remain locked on me. Oliver steps around me blocking me from her view. I hear her hiss as he blocks her line of sight. He takes my hand tightly before pulling me along faster. The barman looks nervous as he holds open the door; sweat beading on his forehead and upper lip. Damien leads the way, pushing Rose out before him. They walk quickly towards the road. Suddenly, as Oliver pulls me along, I'm snatched back painfully. I call out in agony as I'm torn from Oliver's grip. As soon as my hand leaves his it feels like slow motion, as the female Fanged spins me towards her. The pain in my arm and chest, as I thump against her, tells me it wasn't as slow as I thought. I hear a series of muffled, angry yells as the black eyed female stares at me hungrily.

"Now see here!" the bar man calls.

"Hey! Let her go!" Oliver roars, he wraps his arms around my waist and pulls hard as my eyes stare into the dark lifeless pits that are locked on mine. The female lifts my arm up towards her mouth. I try to wriggle it free but she has a tight grip on me. I stare at her wide-eyed and unable to move as she lowers her head to my arm. I see Oliver's free hand trying to pull my arm back but nothing else is happening.

"Please," the bar man pleads as the female sniffs my wrist her eyes closing with pleasure. Oliver's hand grips my arm harder and I feel like I'm watching this all unfold from outside my body. Jack steps forward slowly smiling politely.

"My mate means no harm," the male assures us but I can't help but doubt his words as I see his hand tighten on her shoulder. The female's grip tightens on my wrist, painfully. I try not to wince or call out, in fear it will startle her and make her bite me.

"If she means no harm then tell her to let her go," Oliver says fiercely, standing between the female and me. He takes hold of my arm with both of his hands. Through a gap in Oliver's arms I see the male stepping forward, his fangs lengthening threateningly, as Oliver nears his mate.

"Be very careful human," the male says in a low but dangerous voice. Oliver straightens up but doesn't back off.

"Can you not smell her Jack?" the female asks oblivious to the tense standoff. Jack nods, before talking directly to Oliver.

"It's quite mouthwatering. You see young male, your mate's virgin blood is intoxicating," he says. Despite my deadly situation I blush.

"Tell *your* mate to let her go, or I will break her fingers," Oliver says ignoring the Fang, Jack quirks an eyebrow looking amused but he turns to his hungry mate.

"Sara my love, let the young female go, her mate is very serious. I can smell his rage," Jack says. Sara who I have had my eyes on the whole time groans. She opens her mouth her white fangs shining. I panic and start tugging my arm painfully. Oliver lunges at the female but is knocked back, hard, by Jack. He flies to the floor groaning, but he gets up quickly before rushing forward to attack again. His face looks angry and terrified, his eyes are on me, as he rushes back towards us. Jack grabs him, pulling him tightly against him, restraining his arms as he thrashes to get free. I stare at Oliver while he wriggles frantically in Jacks arms.

This is it, I think sadly.

Oliver's eyes meet mine; they're filled with anger and a desperate kind of fear.

"Watch young human," Jack hisses in Oliver's ear, his black eyes on me. Oliver recoils from the voice, his teeth clenched.

"No please!" Oliver says desperately, struggling against the male as the female opens her mouth. I see her fangs lengthen in my peripherals but my eyes are on Oliver. He watches wide-eyed and terrified as Sara's mouth hovers over my arm. I gasp when something cold and wet travels up my arm; I turn as she licks my wrist. I stare at the female in shock and our eyes meet.

"Delicious," she says in a breathy exhale. I see her fangs lengthen more but she drops my hand. I back up as Jack lets Oliver go. He rushes over to me as I grip my arm tightly, he quickly grabs me practically carrying me out of the pub. I see Damien and Rose staring at us in shock. Damien rushes over to help Oliver with me.

"Good evening young humans," Jack calls as the door to the pub closes taking with it the sliver of bright light, that was shining into the dark street.

I wriggle in Oliver and Damien's arms until they let go of me. I walk quickly ahead of them, my legs trying but failing to run. I hear Oliver and Damien talking hurriedly about laws being broken and I hear a lot of muted cursing. I'm not sure how I'm still walking as my legs feel like jelly. Rose is muttering to herself about how scary the whole thing was. It's taking all my willpower not to vomit. I rub my wrist, hard, where she grabbed me; I can see the bruises already forming all the way up my arm where I was held tightly. I feel Oliver wrap an arm around me as my knees give out and I begin to fall to the ground.

"Chloe..." he says his voice sounding miles away. I frown and shake my head trying to clear my senses. I stumble again as my world starts to spin. My breathing has become quick and I'm finding it harder to catch my breath. I lurch forwards; Oliver catches me again his grip tightening.

Oh no, I'm going to pass out.

"I think she's having an anxiety attack," Damien says his voice clear and overly loud. I hear someone say my name, I look up and Oliver's face swims in front of me then my world goes black.

I wake with a start when I hear a crash and a lot of whispered swearing. My eyes open but it's still dark. I sit up momentarily thinking I have gone blind. Then a lamp switches on bathing the room in a bright yellow glow making my eyes scrunch shut.

"I'm sorry I never meant to wake you," Oliver says looking up at me from the floor as he mops up a puddle of water with one of his t-shirts.

"What happened?" I ask groggily as he stands up tossing the t-shirt into the wash basket.

"I tripped over your dress and dropped my water," he says picking up the offending dress, I frown rubbing my eyes.

"Earlier, what happened earlier?"

"You blacked out, I think. You kept muttering things, you were sick," he says, folding the dress and putting it in the cupboard.

"I don't remember any of that," I say watching him as he makes his way back over to the bed. I look down realising I'm in my pyjamas. I feel my face redden. "Did you...?"

"No," he says quickly. "Rose, she cleaned you up too."

"Thank you," I say, as he sits down.

"I didn't do anything. I couldn't," he says sounding frustrated. I put my hand on his. He looks up at me looking upset.

"Oliver don't, you did everything you could. You stood between a Fang and me. You attacked her! Are you insane?" I say hysterically, making him smile.

"I must be. How do you feel?" he asks, as his thumb brushes over my knuckles.

"Embarrassed, and like I need to brush my teeth," I say, as I smell my breath he smiles and nods. I throw the covers off myself as I climb out of bed.

"Um, Chloe you may want to put these on," he says with a chuckle. I turn and look down I'm only wearing the top half of my pyjamas and a pair of knickers. I snatch the trousers from Oliver who looks away smiling.

"Bloody Rose, I'm going to kill her!" I hiss as I tug them on he chuckles as he climbs into bed. I rush to the bathroom closing the door quietly. I quickly make sure I don't smell of vomit. When I'm happy I don't, I vigorously scrub my teeth. I rinse and look at myself in the mirror. I move a strand of hair out of my face and spot a bruise on my wrist. I pull my sleeve up and wince. I'm shocked to see, most of my forearm, a horrible black and blue, under the colour I notice an, almost perfect, hand shape and I sigh. I pull at my sleeve, revealing the bruise from the bull attack; rolling my eyes, I cover it again before heading back into the bedroom. Oliver looks up as I enter.

"Feel better?"

"Much," I say as he pulls back the covers for me. I smile before hopping into the bed. I lie back heavily sighing as my head sinks into my pillows.

"How's your arm?" he asks. I lift up my sleeve to show him. His jaw tenses as he sits forward taking my arm lightly. "That looks sore, are you in pain?" I shake my head, he sighs. "It looks swollen. I should've put some ice on it."

"Its fine, I bruise like a peach remember?" I say trying to rid his face of the guilty look plastered there, he chuckles darkly before letting my arm go.

"Yeah well, he got me pretty good too," he says, rubbing his chest. I raise my eyebrows.

"Let me see," I say sitting up. He starts unbuttoning his sleep shirt. As he pulls it to the side I see a prefect handprint on his ribs. I look up at his face to see him watching me nervously. "Is it sore?" I ask. He shakes his head. I don't realise what I'm doing until it's too late but I place my hand lightly over the bruise and his breathing stops. I pull my hand away quickly and give him an apologetic look. "I'm sorry did I hurt you?" I ask. He shakes his head again. His eyes are dark; the intensity of his stare is making it hard to look at him. My mouth dries and I feel my heart rate pick up.

"Chloe," he says. I frown before looking down at my hands.

"I don't know what to do," I say. I blush at my words, I feel him move. I look up at him through my lashes; he's buttoning up his shirt.

"Just come here," he says holding open his arms. I stare at him for a moment before shimmying over and lying myself against him. He wraps his arms around me, letting out a big breath.

"I'm sorry Oliver," I say closing my eyes and his chest rises and falls with a deep sigh.

"It's ok Chloe we'll work it out. Just get some sleep," he says. I snuggle into him and when I settle he kisses my forehead.

"Oliver?" I say sleepily. He hums, his chest rumbling below my ear. "Thank you for tonight. I had a nice time," I say. He chuckles as his arms tighten around me.

"Apart from us all nearly being eaten alive?" he says. I smile.

"Well yeah. Good night Oliver," I say and he squeezes me a little.

"Night Chloe," he says. He yawns as I drift off into a safe sleep.

The next morning when I wake up I'm still wrapped in Oliver's arms. During the night I have slung a leg over his and wrapped an arm around him effectively pinning him to the bed. As I lift my head he continues snoring lightly, I'm thankful to see I haven't dribbled on him. I pull my leg off his, stilling when he groans and frowns in his sleep. I smile at his angry, sleepy scowl then I watch as he relaxes and the years fall off his face. I see the memory of what his face used to look like, carefree and happy. He looks so much younger when he sleeps.

I never knew that.

I wouldn't really have much cause to, I suppose. I've never shared a bed with him before. I like his sleeping face it's so different to when he's awake, he always looks much older than his eighteen years. He's normally scowling or angry at something. He very rarely lets his guard down to have a real laugh or joke, I can't help but miss his carefree face terribly. I lay looking at him wishing there was something I could do to make him happy. I would love to hear him laugh freely, without the fear of anyone watching or judging him. I smile to myself as a thought comes into my head.

Oh this will be perfect.

I'm unsure if I'll be able to pull it off, but it's worth a try. I owe him so much. I pull myself free of his grip sliding out of bed quietly. I worry he's going to wake up but he just grunts before rolling over and snoring on. I smile as I tip-toe out of the room into the kitchen, a nervous excitement rushing through me. I rummage through the drawers smiling when I find the little village telephone directory. I rush over to the phone and dial.

I sneak back into the house a few hours later. I smile when I see Oliver is still sleeping. I tip-toe into the kitchen putting the borrowed cool bag on the table. I rummage in the fridge for a quick breakfast, stuffing it in the bag, before closing it and putting it in the living room. I head to the bedroom, smiling to myself as I put my hand on the door handle; opening the door as quietly as I peer in. He's still snoring loudly. I chuckle before I crash into the room causing the door to slam off the wall. I laugh when Oliver jumps and nearly falls out of bed.

"Rise and shine!" I shout.

"What the hell Chloe?" he groans. I ignore him, marching into the room opening the curtains. He moans loudly, covering his eyes.

"I have a surprise for you," I tease. He lifts his arm to frown at me. I smile as he runs his hand through his hair looking very confused. "You really need a haircut."

"Don't tell me you woke me up to tell me I need a haircut. What are you up to?" he asks looking at me suspiciously. I smile wickedly and he narrows his eyes.

"Just get up. I want you dressed and out in the living room in ten minutes," I say as I walk back to the door.

"What should I wear?" he asks. I lean back into the room to see him smiling at me.

"Bring trunks," I say. His face brightens; he throws off the covers and springs to his feet. I close the door as he rushes towards his trunk, a big smile on his face. I wait patiently in the kitchen for him and to give him his credit he's ready in seven minutes. He rounds the corner wearing a pair of black swim shorts, a white t-shirt and a big goofy grin. I smile at him as I stand up from the sofa.

"You ready?" I ask. He nods but his hand falls to his stomach.

"Can I grab something to eat?" he asks rubbing his stomach. I shake my head, toeing the cool bag at my feet.

"I have breakfast covered," I say picking up the bag. I sling it over my shoulder as I walk. I lean down grabbing my rucksack, he frowns at me as I pass it to him.

"What're you up to?" he asks, his smile getting bigger I just shrug and he chuckles.

"You'll see," I say and he smiles.

"Minx," he says pulling on the rucksack. I laugh as I open the door for him.

Chapter 16

We walk quietly into town, but comfortably so. I smile as I round the corner and see our ride for the morning waiting for us; a horse drawn cart. I smile widely as the man waves at me from his seat in the carriage. Oliver slows and looks down at me. I smile at him and his eyes widen for a moment before he looks back at the cart.

"No way, did you really arrange this?" he asks with a disbelieving chuckle, I simply shrug and walk on, leaving him behind me looking flabbergasted. I smile when I hear him laugh quietly. I wave to Billy, the driver, as I approach. I smile at him when he looks at me with an approving look, before jumping down from his seat.

"You're early kid. I'm impressed," he says with a chuckle. I smile at him again turning to Oliver who is looking between us clearly confused.

"Oliver this is Billy," I say introducing my new friend, as he smiles at Oliver. Billy is an older man, just a little older than my dad and just as sweet. I met him earlier in the morning, in the rental shop, as I pleaded with the shop owner for a trade for the day. When the man started being difficult he stepped in, vouching for me despite having never met me before. After I had thanked him a good twenty times, we got talking and I found out he worked on the horse farms that Oliver would be working in. After I told him that's what Oliver was going to be doing, he was more than willing to help me with my plan. He was very interested in meeting Oliver so he offered to help me get set up and the use of his cart.

"Oliver, Billy works at the horse farms so you'll be working with him, he's the breeder there. He's going to be driving us to where we need to go," I say smiling between the two of them. Oliver shakes Billy's hand.

"Good to meet you sir," Oliver says. Billy smiles and chuckles.

"You too son, good to see we've a strong young man comin' onto the farm. Your predecessor is gettin' a bit tired," he says, trying to hide a grim expression. The air is tense for a moment until Oliver chuckles and looks over to the horse.

"I'm sure I will be no match for these beasts," Oliver says clapping the horse on its shoulder.

"Oh, it ain't the horses gotta worry 'bout, it's the riders, highly strung divas if you ask me. You'll be, luckily, avoidin' that lot though. You will be workin' with the workhorses, takin' over from old Rick. He's excited for you to start," Billy says rubbing the horse's nose. "We weren't expectin' anyone to take over from Rick for a few years yet. We just got the call on Saturday there."

"We weren't supposed to be here. Last minute changes," Oliver says with a hint of bitterness in his tone. I glance at Billy who looks away, his mouth set in a grim line.

"Sorry 'bout that," he says gruffly. "Should we head off? Your girl's hella excited 'bout what she has planned for today, ain't you kid?" Billy says looking back at me and winking, making me blush. I plaster a smile on my face to hide my embarrassment. Luckily Oliver just smiles before turning to me offering me a hand into the cart. I sit down smiling for real.

"Thank you," I say as he passes up the cool bag. He smiles climbing in after me.

"No problem," he says squeezing on the narrow bench next to me, jamming the bag between his legs. Billy pulls himself into the driver's seat picking up the reins. He clicks his tongue and the horse moves off. We're shunted back a little; I can't help but smile as we bump along the cobbled streets. We look around the village, I point out some of the shops to Oliver as we pass. Billy points out a few of the less used stores, I take a mental note. Oliver waves at some children who are pointing up at us. They wave back at him. I can't help but smile. The further out of the village we get the rougher the road gets. The motion of the cart bumps us off each other, I laugh when one particularly big bump sends us up in the air. Oliver chuckles as he sits himself up. I look up at him smiling, I can already see his face beginning to relax as he smiles down at me.

"Are you going to tell me where we're going?" he asks his voice low. I shake my head making him pout. "Not fair."

"You have a clue," I say looking down at his legs.

"We are going swimming?" he asks with a smile.

"Maybe," I shrug. He groans but I can still see the smile on his face from the corner of my eye. After another bumpy ten minutes, the cart slows and finally stops. We stop by a thick line of trees and Oliver hops out of the cart. I slide to the edge of the seat handing him the bags, which he puts down. As I stand at the edge he lifts me out effortlessly. He puts me down carefully and I smile up at him. Billy clears his throat loudly. We step apart both blushing. I busy myself with picking up the bags as Oliver thanks Billy who is smiling widely.

"No problem son. You two have a nice day. Where you want is just through those trees there. It should all be set up," he says giving me a wink. I feel myself blush deeper but he just keeps grinning.

"Thank you so much Billy," I say ignoring my red face. I like this man even if he's trying to embarrass me.

"Have fun," he says his tone taking on a suggestive tone. I bite my lip, as my face turns crimson. He winks at Oliver who has the good grace to turn red as well. "See you tomorrow."

"I look forward to it," Oliver says shaking Billy's hand again. Billy climbs back into the cart clicking his tongue.

He turns the cart and with another click the horse trots off. We watch until it disappears behind a wall of trees. We stay still and quiet until I take Oliver's hand; he looks down at me curiously.

"Come on," I say unable to hide the excitement in my voice. He smiles and nods before taking the bags off of me, then allows me to pull him along. I push through the thick trees and bushes holding back the branches for Oliver as he follows me closely. I smile when I finally spot what I'm looking for, the shimmering, smoothness of the lake. I push through the last few branches stepping out into the sunlight, in front of the beautiful secluded lake. It truly is a beautiful place; a small but wide lake surrounded on all sides by thick trees. Oliver grunts with effort as he ducks under a thick branch, tugging the bags from the twisted branches. He lets out a long deep breath then, as he straightens up, he stills next to me. I look up at him trying to gauge his reaction. He's staring, wide-eyed, at the sight in front of us. His lips curl upwards as he takes in the view, my breath releases in a long, relieved breathe when a smile breaks across his face.

"It's part of a farmer's land that Billy knows. He asked for us to be allowed here for the day as well as a few... special privileges," I say with a smile

"Wow," Oliver says breathlessly.

"You like it?" I ask, feeling nervous. He blinks, dragging his eyes from the lake, to look down at me.

"Are you kidding?" he asks with a chuckle. "It is amazing, you're amazing. How did you come up with all this?" he asks smiling.

"I'm a woman, we have mad skills," I say with a smug, teasing, look. He smiles, looking back out to the lake.

"You sure do," he says as he takes in the view once again.

"Come on there is one last thing I want to show you," I say pulling him along the shoreline. He follows me willingly.

"More?" he asks sounding shocked. I nod dropping his hand and turning to him.

"Ok close your eyes. Just do it, it's a surprise," I say quickly when he looks like he's about to argue. He looks down at me confused for a moment then he puts the bags down and covers his eyes. I wave my hands frantically in front of his face to make sure he isn't peaking. When I'm convinced he isn't I back up towards the old mossy log, near the waters edge, keeping my eyes on him the whole time, in case he peeks. He shuffles his feet with nervous anticipation and I can see is smile beneath his hands. I wave my arms again to see if he's peeking. When he doesn't move I know he isn't cheating. I turn, leaning over the log, smiling when I see what I'm looking for.

"Come on Chloe, this is killing me," he says desperately. I smile as I make my way back to him.

"Ok, I know you haven't done this in a while but it should be like riding a bike. You never forget. Hold out your hands," I say, trying hard to keep my smile at bay. His smile widens under his hands before he lowers them and holds them out. He keeps his eyes scrunched tightly closed. I place the rod in his open hands. His face falls as his fingers wrap around the pole. His eyes spring open and he stares down at it in shock.

"Chloe, I can't believe you..." he breathes, his voice tight with emotion. He looks up at me and I just smile.

"You like it?" I ask. He shakes his head looking completely shocked but he smiles widely.

There's the old Oliver, I think happily as he looks at me.

"I love it," he says. I smile feeling relief flooding through me. I was in two minds about doing this, as I know how precious fishing is to Oliver. He used to talk my ear off about it when we were younger. He used to go fishing with his granddad on the occasional weekend but sadly, after his grandfather was taken, he never did it again. I never admitted it but I missed his stories after that.

I needn't have been so worried about upsetting him as the smile on his face shows how truly happy he is.

"Glad you like it. It's kind of my way of saying sorry for everything," I say giving him a little smile, he stares down at me looking a little speechless then he surprises me by stepping forward, cupping my face in his hands, leaning down and kissing me. My eyes are wide as his lips press to mine. They're firm but soft on mine; my whole body feels like it has turned red. He straightens up smiling at me.

"This, is the nicest thing anyone has ever done for me. Thank you," he says his hands still cradling my face. I smile slightly awkwardly at the feelings shooting through me. I definitely didn't expect it to be that nice.

"You're welcome. I um, made breakfast are you still hungry?" I ask my face feeling rather warm under his hands, his smile widens.

"I'm starving," he says, letting me go. "I really don't think you could get any more perfect right now if you tried. What've you made?" he asks. I look down at the ground grabbing the cool bag trying to hide my pleasure at the compliment. I unzip the bag with trembling hands. I bite my lip as I dig through the bag.

"Well, with sorting this entire thing, I didn't really have time to make anything. So it's not much," I say as I pull out some bagels, soft cheese and grapes. I pull out a blanket and lay it on the ground.

"It looks great."

"It's only part of my plan," I add as we sit down on the blanket.

"Oh?" he says with a frown as he kneels down next to me. I nod.

"Yeah well we're allowed to catch as many fish as we want but we have to throw them back. But..." I say teasingly. "We're allowed to keep one, to cook, so I was thinking we could make it for lunch," I say with a chuckle as his eyes widen in excitement.

"We can really cook one?" he asks sounding like a kid. As I nod he springs up, his breakfast forgotten. I watch him with a frown as he starts looking over the trees. After a moment he pulls off a slim but sturdy looking tree branch. He bites into it; I'm about to ask what the hell he's doing when he starts stripping off the bark. He looks down at me smiling as I frown at him.

"What's with the stick?"

"You'll see, trust me," he says with a grin as I look at him doubtfully. He walks over to the rotting log and, with the air of someone who knows exactly what they're doing, he starts digging. I watch for a while, as he digs through the soft mud under the log. He uses his hands to tear off some of the tree's soggy bark. "Would you go and collect some dry wood for a fire?" he asks stabbing into the ground again with his stick.

"Sure," I say getting up. I wander into the tree line gathering up an arm full of wood and dry leaves. I make sure they're extra dry, so they will catch fire easily. I move back through the trees and see he's still digging; he has made quite a large hole already. He's smiling as he starts tugging on a worm. His smile vanishes when the worm clearly refuses to leave the ground. So with the sharp end of his stick he chops it in half. I chuckle as I place the firewood down.

"What?" he asks turning to me. He looks up at me with a big grin. He has a smudge of dirt under his left eye, his eyes are shining brightly up at me; it makes my heart squeeze uncomfortably in my chest. I try to ignore the fact that seeing him this happy makes me very happy too.

"That worm giving you a bit of hassle there?" I joke, my voice shaking slightly.

"Yeah he was being difficult so I chopped his head off. Or his ass, I'm not sure what end it was. Whatever it was, he's having a really bad day," he says holding up the halved worm, sounding younger than I ever remember him sounding before.

157

"Sorry little worm your day is about to get worse," I say as I look down at the worm as I sit down next to the pile of firewood. Oliver picks up the hook sticking it through the worm. I sort through the wood.

"Poor bugger," Oliver says as he throws the line out into the lake. He lays the rod against a rock propping it up with other rocks. He shuffles over and starts to dig in another area of the log. He keeps glancing at me as I make a start on the fire. "You know how to do that?" he asks smiling slightly as I throw the wood haphazardly into a pile.

"It can't be that hard, can it?" I ask holding out the leaves. He rolls his eyes and shakes his head. "You want a shot?"

"No, no you're doing a fine job," he says smiling. I narrow my eyes at him knowing full well he's mocking my lack of skills.

"Just show me how to do it, I want to do it right," I say, he looks at me, considering me for a moment, like he's unsure if it's some sort of trap.

"You sure?" he asks cautiously as he digs around the mouldy log.

"Yes. I'm sure, I don't want to make a rubbish fire," I say trying not to smile at his worry. He nods putting the stick down. He smiles a little when he sees me trying not to laugh. He gathers up the sticks clearing a patch of the stony sand. He puts the leaves in the middle and stacks the sticks neatly, smiling when it's complete.

"You have a lighter or matches I assume?" I nod grabbing my bag. I dig around for a moment before pulling out a box of matches. I throw them over to him. "You can do the honours," he says throwing them back to me. He moves back over to his log scooping up his stick.

"Thanks," I say sarcastically. He chuckles as I strike the match, holding it to the leaves. I watch as they blacken and curl, they catch very quickly. He then piles on some little twigs.

"Keep it going with these little ones until it properly catches then we'll need more," he says. I nod as I load the flames with some more leaves and dry, thin twigs. I tend to the fire while he digs around the log some more.

"Is this ok?" I ask after a few minutes, he looks over to me nodding.

"Yeah great," he says with a smile. The fishing line starts to whiz loudly; Oliver scurries over to it, quickly. He grabs the rod giving it a tug, and then groans. "Damn it, it got away," he says reeling the line back in. I watch as he brings in the hook I notice our little worm friend is gone.

"It took the worm," I say, he nods and checks the hook.

"They do that a lot. I used to get really mad about it, then Granddad would just tell me to shut up and simmer down. Fishing is about patience the reward is the catch at the end," he says smiling fondly. I smile as he sits back down next to the log. I start sorting out breakfast, finally, as he digs into the bark of the soft log again.

"Come and eat," I say as I dish out the food.

"Two seconds I think I... Oh, hey look, I found a grub or something," he says holding it up smiling. I grimace making him laugh. "Ah, it bit me!" he says angrily throwing it to the floor. I lean in closer for a better look at the wriggling insect as he picks up the fishing rod. He leans to pick up the wriggling grub carefully avoiding the head end. I look at it struggling between his fingers.

"That's gross," I say as I see its insides writhe about under its translucent skin. I feel the warmth of his breath on my face as he laughs. I realise that we're inches apart and it snaps me back to my senses making me lean back a little. He spikes the grub angrily with the hook before tossing the line out.

"I hope he gets eaten," he says as he props the line up again. He looks down at his finger and I see a little blood. He sucks on his finger and I snatch it out of his mouth.

"Ugh gross, don't do that, let me see. Your hands are filthy. Stop being a baby," I say when he tries to pull his hand back. It's still bleeding a little so I reach into my bag pulling out a little first aid kit.

"What do you have in that bag?" he asks, as I rummage in the little pouch, I look up at him smiling.

"In a world full of Fanged you don't want to be bleeding all over the place," I say. He frowns as we both look over to the tower that's just visible in the distance. I pull out a wipe to clean the cut before wrapping it in tape.

"Thanks," he says I smile as I put the little first aid kit away.

"It's ok."

"You think I'll live?" he asks making me chuckle.

"It will be touch and go for the next twenty-four hours," I joke and he laughs. He holds his finger up in front of my face and I frown at him.

"Kiss it better?" he asks, I laugh and shake my head at him. He smiles sheepishly as I lean forward to kiss his plaster.

"Better?" I ask as he smiles widely at me.

"Much," he says still grinning from ear to ear. I look away, but smile, as I finish dishing out breakfast.

"Big baby," I mutter.

"Thank you," he says as I hand him his little plate of food. "Not for the food, well that too, but for this," he says looking around then back at me.

"It's ok. I'm glad you like it. It's nice to see you happy," I say. He frowns deeply, his first frown of the day.

It was going so well.

"I'm not unhappy," he says.

"I know, I just mean it's just hard to be relaxed and to be able to enjoy stuff you know? It's been hard over the last few months, years really, you just seem to be angry a lot," I say rambling. He looks at me sadly.

"There's a lot to be angry about," he says popping a grape in his mouth. I sigh placing my plate down.

"I know, I just…" I sigh deeply, feeling frustrated with myself. "You're misunderstanding me. I just wanted you to have a nice day and to say sorry. That's all. Nothing else," I say feeling annoyed at myself for making him look upset. I feel him staring at me as I start on my breakfast.

"What about you?" he asks. I look up at him wiping my mouth with the back of my hand in case any cheese is on my face.

"What about me?" I ask after I swallow.

"You're always unhappy too but you never let it show. Even after everything you wanted got taken from you, how do you do it?" he asks.

"Do what?" I ask frowning while he smiles a little.

"Just keep going. Your whole world got flipped upside-down and you're so... calm. Well, apart from the normal mood swings," he says. I arch my eyebrow at him making him chuckle.

"I've been a bitch."

"You have a reason to be."

"No I don't. I'm lucky, I'm here with you when I could be stuck somewhere with Jackson. You always have my back, you stopped me doing something I would've regretted and I can't thank you enough for that."

"Today makes us even," he says. I shake my head.

"I don't deserve you. You should hate me," I say looking at my feet.

"Well I don't, so get over it," he says tossing another grape in his mouth.

"How could you not hate me?" I ask, genuinely curious. He takes a moment before he answers.

"Because you're Chloe, you're my best friend. I suppose if we're together life won't be too horrible." I stare at him a little taken aback by his honesty. "I wish we could just, I don't know... leave here. I wish we could get away from this place away from the Fanged and their power over us," he says. I keep staring at my feet but nod.

"We should," I say.

"I wish," he says in a low voice his face remains calm but I can see his breathing has accelerated.

"Why not?" I ask. His reaction is instant, he looks up at me chewing on a grape and my eyes flicker to him. He narrows his eyes as he places his plate down.

"It's not possible. We would be found."

"Maybe not," I say.

"I couldn't do it. We have our families to worry about what would happen to them?" he asks.

"Then, we fight back," I say quickly. He sucks in a startled breath. He stares at me looking a bit like I have just slapped him.

"What has gotten into you?" he asks a devious smile creeping on his face despite the touchy subject matter.

"I hate this," I say. He nods sitting up a little, his eyes not leaving mine. "I hate that we're made to live like animals and breed like dogs to sustain their lives," I say angrily pointing to the tower; Oliver's eyes follow my hand. "We should be in charge of our own lives. Who are they to tell us that we can't do something? They are dead! I didn't think dead people had rights. They had their chance at life and they threw it away for what? To always be young, beautiful? That's not a life," I say unable to stop myself. I'm internally shocked about what is spilling out of my mouth but the floodgates are open now. There's no stopping me, and it feels great.

"I want to be free to choose when, or if, I have children. I don't want to have to live in fear that they will eventually be farmed and either eaten alive or kept alive for their blood. That's not right. I can't live in a world knowing the date people I love are going to be taken away from me. Dad, my brothers, you," I say staring at him through bleary eyes. I wipe at my eyes, embarrassed that I had nearly cried. He stares at me wide-eyed and I look down at my hands. I realise I have crushed my bagel in my hand. I wipe it off my fingers as my blood rushes through my veins. I'm so irritated all of a sudden. I frown down at the ground and I start when Oliver puts his hand under my chin.

"I've *never* heard you talk like that before," he says his voice a little hushed; I look up at him, his eyes are wide and full of something I have never seen before; adoration. I shrug slightly squirming under his gaze.

"I've never had the time; I've always thought it though. After mum left, Michael and I would talk about how we would run the country if it were up to us," I say with a little shrug.

"You always surprise me," he says with a huge smile. I feel myself blush under his stare. I realise that his breathing is matching mine, it's quick, excited. He licks his lips before he moves towards me. I stare at him a little startled; we freeze when the fishing rod twitches violently he looks at me with wide eyes. We spring apart as the pole starts to come loose from the rocks. He quickly scrambles to the pole grabbing it, as it breaks loose.

"Oh my god you've got a bite, bring it in!" I say breathlessly, shakily rushing to his side and sitting next to him. "Is it on?" I ask. He nods as he pulls the rod back, the line goes tight and the rod bends almost in half. Its a few minutes before anything else happens. He keeps reeling in the line and after a hefty tug the fish finally splashes out of the water.

"Did you see that?" he says standing up he looks down at me excitedly. I nod as I get up looking into the water. I see the fish's shadow as he pulls it nearer to the shore. I look up at him and can't help but smile at his grinning face. The fish jumps out of the water again splashing loudly as it flops on the water's surface.

"Wow, it's huge! I can't believe it, don't let it go." He nods before giving one last tug of the pole. He swings the pole around with the fish flapping madly on the end of the line. He swings the pole over my head before the fish lands on the ground.

"It's a trout," he says as he moves over to the fish that's flapping furiously in the sand, trying to get back to the water. He picks up his stick as he kneels down next to the

163

fish holding it still. He shields the fish from my view, killing it quickly and without hesitation. I clap as he picks it up and beams at me giving me a little bow.

"Good for a second attempt eh?" he says proudly I nod my head, smiling widely.

"I can't believe it. I thought I would be out here for hours without you catching anything."

"Believe it baby. Sorry…" he says quickly as he blushes. I bite my lip and try not to smile.

"It's fine, well done though. We should cook it now, make it for lunch," I say pretending that what he said didn't take my breath away. He cleans the fish the best he can with his stick and the lake water. He brings the gutted fish and his stick back with him, smiling widely. He pokes the fire with the stick in an exaggerated way and I groan.

"Ok, I get it the stick is useful," I say. He chuckles as he pokes the stick through the fish placing it on the wobbly stone pillars I built so we could cook it. He sits down carefully smiling to himself as he picks up the rest of his breakfast. We eat our breakfast in silence. When we're done he sets up the pole again before stretching out on the ground using my bag as a pillow.

"It's nice out here. I think I will spend a lot of time out here, it's so… peaceful," he yawns loudly; I nod as he lifts his arms up resting his head on them. His stomach is revealed, I stare at it for a moment watching it move as he breathes. His plentiful muscles move under his pale skin hypnotically. I eventually tear my eyes away blushing at my stupidity; I get back to poking the fire and turning the fish, focusing really hard on it. I keep glancing over to him catching myself staring. I notice he has fallen asleep, his mouth slightly open; his breathing is slow and even. I glance back at him, my eyes sliding down his body. I look at his arms, he has nice arms, and they look strong.

Strong enough to lift me up; no stop it! I blush.

His chest is broad; I can see through his t-shirt that it's as muscular as his stomach. He may be muscled but not

164

horribly so, his muscles are subtle and beautiful, I noticed that last night when I watched him change. His legs are strong and lean I noticed that the other day when they were hanging over the sofa.

What am I doing?!

I look away, feeling bad for staring but as my eyes flick back to him I find that I can't help myself. Now that I'm allowing myself to think this way, I admit to myself that he's nice to look at. I shouldn't be embarrassed about it; he's my husband after all and he did admit that he was looking at me differently for a while.

I'm allowed to look at my husband, I think defensively before shaking my head knowing this can mean nothing but trouble. I shouldn't have gawked at him like that when he was...

His sea green eyes meet mine and my mouth falls open.

Oh no!

Chapter 17

"You're awake!" I squeak.

"Yep," he says sitting up slowly, with a smile on his face. I turn away feeling completely and utterly mortified. I want to throw myself in the lake and drown myself.

"Oh my god! I...I'm...UGH!" I say stumbling as I get up, he just stares at me.

"What?" he asks chuckling.

"How long have you been awake?" I ask angrily.

"A while," he says. I groan loudly as my face flames.

"I didn't mean to..."

"Stare?" he offers me with a little smile.

"Don't you dare smile, this is so embarrassing," I say pacing up and down, really wanting to just run away leaving him there.

"It's ok," he says crossing his legs as he looks up at me. I can tell he's really trying not to laugh.

Git.

"It's not; I'm not like that. I'm not some sort of... well I don't normally," I splutter.

"I know you don't normally, I'm flattered. It's nice to be looked at," he says. I stare at him starting to feel sick with embarrassment.

"Ugh, god. Can we just pretend this didn't happen?" I beg.

"I can't do that I'm afraid, but I promise to keep it to myself," he says.

"It's you I want to keep it from!" I moan.

"Chloe, please don't feel embarrassed, I'm not."

"You're not?"

"No! Having a girl like you check me out is good for the ego," he says smiling as I frown at him. I scoff before looking away.

A girl like me?

"Yeah whatever."

"Come on Chloe, I've know you forever, that's better you're pretty when you smile," he says startling me. I didn't realise I was, I blush as he stands up. He clears his throat and stretches. "So if you're quite finished gawking at me, can we go for a swim?" he asks with a cheeky grin.

"I wasn't…" He arches his eyebrow at me and I look away. "Fine, let's go for a swim," I say rolling my eyes. He smiles widely pulling off his t-shirt. I pull off my shorts and top.

"Those bruises looks bad," he says, his eyes flickering between my arm and my shoulder. I look down at my bruised left side and sigh. I had actively avoided looking at it as I changed in the morning but now he came to mention it, it was a little stiff, and it looked awful.

"It's ok," I say moving the arm around. My shoulder twinges a little but it's not unbearable. "Yours ok?" I ask looking at his chest and the hand shaped bruise there.

"Yeah, just a bit tender. I'll live," he says.

"Good," I say smiling. He smiles back at me.

"Nice suit by the way," he says letting his eyes linger shamelessly on my bikini.

"Shut up," I say pushing past him hiding my smile. I crouch at the lake testing the temperature as I try to get over the embarrassment. I'm mortified that he caught me staring at him and more than that I can't believe he doesn't mind. What did he mean when he said a "girl like you"?

"Come on Chloe just jump in," he says from behind me, startling me. I straighten up and he wraps his arms around my waist making me scream.

"Don't you dare!" I squeal as I try to wriggle free, making him chuckle.

"Too late," he says before he throws me into the air.

I hear him laughing before I'm plunged into the murky water. The taste of the lake fills my mouth as I struggle to right myself on the slippery floor. I break through the surface of the water coughing and spluttering. I hear Oliver still laughing. I scowl at him through my messy hair. I stick my middle finger up at him while I scrape my hair out of my face. I turn facing away from him coughing harder, pretending I'm struggling. I hear him wade into the water quickly and I smile to myself.

"You ok?" he asks as he reaches me. I turn still smiling. It takes him a few seconds to register my deception but it's enough time for me to leap at him and wrestle him into the water. He calls out before he goes under, pulling me down with him. I manage to keep my head above the water. I stand up as he comes out of the water. His hair flops over his eyes, his mouth set in a pout. I smile triumphantly at him while he rubs his eyes.

"Pay back is sweet," I say. He scowls but it's quickly replaced by a smile as he pushes his hair out of his eyes.

"You're a good actress, I thought you were choking," he says.

"I was, I may have exaggerated it slightly but you threw me into the lake!" I say slapping his arm, he laughs.

"It's warmer than I thought it was going to be," he says sounding a little disappointed. I sink down into the warm water swinging my arms along the surface.

"It's nice but I'm freaking out a little bit," I admit. He chuckles.

"Why?"

"I don't like that I can't see what I'm standing on, it feels squishy," I say feeling the bottom of the lake gingerly with my toes. I cringe not wanting to know what is down there. "And if anything touches me I'm going to go run out of here," I add looking into the murky water. He smiles.

"Let's go for a swim," he says. I nod, feeling brave I dive into the water and come up smiling. I don't really

Victoria Nock

enjoy swimming but as I propel myself along the surface of the water I feel my troubles melt away. I swim around until my shoulder starts aching. I motion to Oliver that I'm heading in; he nods before he follows after me. I get to the shallow edge rolling my shoulder as I start walking out.

"You ok?" he asks from behind me. I turn and nod as I grip my shoulder.

"I'm just a bit sore. I'm done anyway," I say. He nods moving his hair out of his eyes as he approaches me. I scream loudly when something slides across my thigh causing me to leap out of the water and crash into him. He wraps his arms around me. "Something just touched me!" I groan. He laughs loudly gripping me tighter as I wriggle to get free and run out of the lake.

"Calm down. It was me Chloe, calm down." I stare up at him as he smiles down at me.

"Really?" I ask unconvinced. He nods and I scowl at him before slapping his shoulder, hurting my hand.

"Ouch! Is this how it's going to be for the rest of our lives? You always hitting me?" he asks. I glare at him again as I place my hands on his arms.

"Only if you continue to act like an ass," I say making him smile widely.

"Well, I best get used to it then hadn't I?" he says making me laugh. "I'm going to go for another few laps ok?" he asks. I nod unwrapping myself from him.

"Sure. I'll go and check on the fish. I don't want to be in here anymore," I say eyeing the water suspiciously. He smiles before letting me go. I turn around slowly feeling my way through the water back to the shore. I jump when he takes hold of my arm turning me around. He gives me a little smile his eyes sparkling and I feel all the air leaving my body.

"I have wanted to do this all day," he says before he lowers his head to mine. He stills waiting for me to slap him or push him away but I take a steadying breath before nodding slightly in encouragement. He lets out a little

169

relieved breath before smiling and kissing me. I stand frozen for a second but then my lips begin to move with his. My eyes flutter closed as his breath mingles with mine and I feel my body heat up. He moves closer to me and presses his cool chest to mine as I wrap my arms around his neck. After a moment I feel him smiling, I open my eyes before pulling back, my eyes meeting his. He bites his lip as he smiles, before letting me go, turning around and diving into the water without a word. I brush my fingers over my lips and smile. I watch him as he swims out into the lake.

Maybe this won't be so hard after all, I think as I turn and wade out of the water. I dig my towel out of my bag wrapping it around myself before I turn the fish over again, the smell makes my mouth water. I'm tempted to sneak a taste but instead I just pop a few grapes in my mouth. As I lay down on the blanket in the warm sun, I stretch, sighing contently as the sun soaks into my skin. I open the towel and close my eyes.

Sometime later I hear a splash and look up to see Oliver walking out of the lake. I feel my face redden as I watch him coming out, glistening in the sun, his hair messy and dripping wet. I lie my head back down before he catches me staring, again. I feel him sit down next to me as droplets of water splash on me. I frown before opening my eyes to glare at him. He's shaking his head, spraying the water everywhere. Once he stops he looks down at me smiling.

"That was nice," he says as I wipe the water off my stomach.

"I'm not much of a swimmer. I only swim when absolutely necessary," I say. He chuckles drying off his hair with the other towel. I close my eyes and settle back down.

"Like when?" he asks his voice startling me as it's closer than before. I hadn't noticed he had lain down too. I look round at him; his face is inches from mine.

"Life or death," I say my voice quiet.

"Or flooding?" he asks with a smile, his voice teasing and playful.

"Or flooding," I agree with a smile. He chuckles before stretching. I hear a few bones creak and pop but he sighs contently.

"Were you serious earlier?" he asks a few moments later and I look round at him again frowning.

"About what?" I ask. He rolls onto his side moving closer to me, almost touching, almost hovering over me. I look up at him as he rests his head on his hand. He looks down at me his eyes darting all over my face.

"About leaving, about wanting to do something," he clarifies. I look away from him for a moment absentmindedly playing with my wedding ring.

"I don't know," I say honestly and he looks a little disappointed and I frown. "I mean obviously I want to do something but what can I do? What can any of us do Ollie? They're strong," I say looking down at his bruised chest.

He takes up my bruised wrist looking at it while his fingers lightly trace my bruised shoulder. His touch is distracting; I have to mentally shake myself before I can speak again. "I mean you're strong but you know how easily that Fang knocked you down," I say. He looks down at my towel with a frown.

"There has to be something we can do," he says in a low voice I turn onto my side to face him.

"There's nothing. If there was something don't you think we would have tried it by now?" I ask. He looks up at me, I can see that the carefree Oliver is gone and has been replaced by the shielded angry Oliver. No, this is wrong. "I shouldn't have said anything earlier. It was stupid. If I was heard... we have to be careful," I say glancing towards the tower and back at Oliver who is still staring at me. His hand, which is still wrapped around my wrist, tightens slightly.

"I hate this!" he says angrily as a frown wrinkles his forehead.

"What's brought this on?" I ask. He looks at me a little shocked.

"I've always felt like this, you know that," he says. I nod before looking down at his hand as his fingers trace circles on my wrist. "It's mainly because of you," he adds startling me. I stare at him with my mouth open.

"Me? Why me?"

"You make me want to fight. Ever since your mum left, when I saw you that day, I have wanted to do something. Then, with what happened to Ethan..." He looks down at the towel again. I take his hand and he looks up at me. "That's why I wanted to do work in the Mayor's office, to make a difference. Then with what happened at graduation, that was the last straw. I hate seeing you suffer, I hate seeing anyone suffer," he says. I nod.

"None of those things were your fault though Ollie. She chose to leave and Ethan, he was unwell," I say a delicately as possible. "The whole graduation thing no one could have guessed that was going to happen. I should've known but I would never have guessed." He huffs angrily.

"What your mum did was really shitty. She chose to change. She cut her connections to you and your family; she had no right to ruin your life for a second time by putting your name in for selection, making you think you had no way out." He sighs.

"Ollie I..." I try to apologise again but he plows on.

"When someone is dead they should remain dead. It's like when Ethan killed himself, everyone was saying he would go to hell for what he did. Why is it ok for someone to die and live on without judgment then when someone kills themselves they're shamed?"

"It's not," I say so quietly I'm surprised he heard me, despite our closeness.

"The Fanged have no right to die and expect to live on. Living the life of luxury and feeding off of us. It's wrong and it has to be stopped. I want it to stop," he says his eyes flaring dangerously.

"I want that as well," I say. His eyes meet mine.

"Really?" he asks. I nod once making him smile.

"Of course I do."

"Then let's do it. Let's find a way to bring this hell to an end."

"How?" I ask, trying not to smile at the excitement on his face. He lies back down with a huff.

"I haven't got that far yet," he says giving me a sheepish smile. I snort loudly and laugh, making him chuckle. I lay down, still laughing. He takes my hand winding his fingers with mine. I look over at him smiling.

"We'll figure something out," I say. He smiles and squeezes my hand.

"Yeah, we will."

We lie under the hot sun quietly letting the excitement die down. I can feel my heart beating fast after his speech. I lay there contemplating how we could possibly win against the Fanged. We have one distinct advantage over them and that's the sun. It's the only weakness we were taught about in school, as it's too obvious to hide from us. I'm sure there are plenty more they are hiding. Oliver sits up suddenly startling me out of my thoughts, he turns the fish again before laying back down, all the while, keeping hold of my hand. We'll work this out, together.

"Hey Ollie," I say. He hums to let me know he's listening. "Do you think that if we could, we could count a tent as our home?" I ask my voice low, he looks over at me.

"You mean to keep them out?" he asks catching my drift, I nod. "I don't know. I suppose if we were living in it then yes but I don't really want to have to test that. I'm not even sure that them not being able to come into our homes is true. Why, what were you thinking?" he asks. I shrug, chewing on my lip.

"Nothing really, just thinking."

"About?"

"I'm just trying to come up with a plan. If we were to run we would need shelter..." I say.

"Hey don't worry about it now, let's try and enjoy the rest of the day. Lunch will be ready soon," he says looking back at the fish.

"Ok," I say but then I remember something and I sit up.

"What is it?" he asks sitting up as well.

"What were those two Fanged up to last night, at the pub? I mean they shouldn't have been there at all but they were there so early. What could they possibly want with a pub?" I ask frowning. Oliver runs his hands through his hair.

"Damien and I were talking about that last night while Rose was helping you out," he says as I blush a little at the embarrassment of passing out. "He reckons that they were there to feed,"

"Really?" I ask breathily, my embarrassment instantly forgotten as he nods.

"Yeah I mean you saw how hyped-up the female was. When she saw the barman she looked a bit ill, but when she smelled you she was practically drooling." I nod, rubbing my wrist frowning when I remember how she commented on my virgin blood. "Damien reckons she thought we were there to let them drink from us," he says snapping me out of my thoughts.

"What?" I gasp. He nods, his face set in a grim line.

"Damien thinks that the barman is feeding them or getting others in to donate blood for money," Oliver says. I feel my eyes widen even more.

"So you think it's like a brothel for blood?" I ask, horror clear in my voice.

"Damien says they are common in little villages, his sister told him, apparently. He thinks that people go to donate or give blood when they are struggling financially."

"Can you really sell it?" I ask. He nods.

"Why not? People sell their bodies. Fangs have no use for our bodies, in that way, but they do want our blood. It would be risky, though, because if you give too much, when it comes to the donation, you can make yourself sick," Oliver says and I nod.

"How do you know so much?" I ask. He shrugs.

"It's just basic stuff I found out. We only have so much blood to give before we're drained, right?" he asks. I sigh knowing him to be right; I did want to be a doctor after all. I just never realised that Oliver paid much attention in class.

"How did I miss you doing all of this?" I ask sounding as guilty as I feel. He shrugs with a little smile.

"You have had your head buried in a book for the last three years; I had a lot of quiet time to do my own studying," he says. I lift my hand, brushing a strand of hair out of his eyes.

"I'm sorry," I say. He takes hold of my hand holding it against his face. His eyes are darting over my face again. I see him swallow nervously.

"Can I kiss you again?" he asks. I smile at him thinking how sweet it was to be asked and nod.

He smiles as he leans into me. He brushes his lips against mine lightly before pulling away a little to look at me. "Weird?" he asks with a worried look. I bite my lip, which still tingles and shake my head.

"Not weird, more unexpected," I say, trying not to smile.

"Why unexpected. Did you think it would be bad?" he asks his lips twitching in a little smile.

"No I just…" I chew my lip again feeling embarrassed.

"What Chloe?" he asks, his voice low and I look into his eyes.

"I just never thought I would ever be kissing you and I didn't expect to like it as much as I do," I say feeling my face heat up. His eyes widen a little then he smiles smugly.

"Oh really?" he says sounding pleased. I shove him making him laugh and fall backwards.

"You are such an ass," I say as he sits up trying to wipe the smile off his face.

"I'm sorry, it's just nice you giving me a compliment," he says smiling. I narrow my eyes at him.

"I bet it is," I say rolling my eyes.

"You're a good kisser too, if that makes you feel any better?" he says. I scowl at him desperately trying not to blush and show how secretly relieved I am, as he smiles at me.

"Really?" I ask before I realise I have said it. Embarrassed, I look down at my feet my blush in full effect now. He chuckles and I glare at my sandy toes.

"Yes, you are," he says after a little moment. I glance over at him; he looks sincere so I smile.

"Thanks," I say, the smile pulling at my lips. He crawls over to the fish pulling it off the stones. He chews on his lip while he balances it carefully on two stones to cool. "What is it?" I ask knowing he wants to ask something.

"Nothing," he says. I arch my eyebrow at him.

"What Ollie?" I push. He looks up at me from the fish.

"Well, it makes me wonder."

"About what? What're you talking about?" I ask frowning. He chews his lips before continuing, he looks like he's trying to find the right words.

"It makes me wonder how many guys you sneaked off with without my knowing," he says carefully. I know he didn't mean to offend me but the question beings me up short and I straighten up where I sit. I can tell when his face falls that he knows he said the wrong thing. "No wait! I just mean..."

"You mean how many guys did I fool around with?" I ask, trying not to sound hurt by what he thinks of me.

"No I just... it was good so I assumed..."

"None," I say quickly. He stares at me with his mouth open. I'm so mortified I don't bother fighting my blush. I never fooled around with boys at all through school. I was always with Oliver and apparently, even when some boys showed interest, I was so oblivious that Oliver had to spare their feelings and pretend he was dating me.

Was I really that oblivious?

"None? What about Duncan and the other guys?" he asks sounding surprised. I shake my head.

"Well you got rid of Duncan and what 'other guys'?" I groan.

"Come on Chloe. I know you were blind but you had to have noticed?" he says, I shake my head. "Jeez, Chloe."

"Look I'm sorry I'm not some sort of…"

"Hey, wow. Stop there. I'm not saying anything like that. Ok? I'm just in shock," he says, making me frown.

"Why though? I was constantly with you!" I say. He nods and looks away with a guilty look on his face.

"Yeah you were," he says in a quiet voice. His face looks like it has fallen slightly and my eyes widen.

"Oliver," I gasp. "Who?" He cringes as he fidgets with his trusty stick and prods the fish. He clears his throat and avoids my eyes. I see his cheeks redden as he looks my way. "Who Oliver?" I ask suddenly feeling a little angry. He looks up at me through his eyelashes.

"Rachel Hunt," he says. I stare at him for a moment trying to place the name. My mind catches up and my mouth falls open in shock. I remember her; she was one of the six. The tall, black haired, preened within an inch of her life girl, I shared a few classes with. Her staring at him during graduation makes sense now.

"She was one of the…"

"The ones who turned, yes," he finishes for me. She must have still liked him. That's why she was staring at him and why she was being so friendly with me towards the end of the year, this explains everything.

"When?" I ask. He looks at me pleadingly, like he would rather talk about anything but this.

"Do we have to discuss this?" he asks.

"Why did you not tell me you were seeing her?" I ask as he worries his lip.

"We weren't 'dating' exactly," he says and my eyes widen. I picture the tall athletic Rachel wrapped around Oliver and I feel my blood begin to boil. "It was nothing," he says desperately. I look away out to the water.

"Sleeping with someone isn't nothing," I mutter trying not to get upset.

What is wrong with me?

I know it's stupid to be so mad, it was none of my business. I had on claim Oliver, well I didn't, but I'm supposed to be his friend I'm allowed to be mad that he never told me.

…and jealous. Oh shut up!

"I just wish you had told me. Why didn't you?" I ask, sadness clear in my voice. He crawls back over beside me, his eyes still looking guiltily at me.

"I only didn't because there really was nothing to talk about. It was only a few times then we never spoke again. You were so busy I didn't want to bother you with something so trivial," he says. I turn and face him.

"You are my best friend. Trivial is what we do best. When did you first get together?" I ask, trying to sound casual. He runs his hands through his hair.

"David's party at Christmas, the one I begged you to come to. Remember? You were too busy studying," he says. I remember perfectly. He was desperate for me to come, he all but got on his knees to beg me, but I insisted I had to study. I didn't see him for a few days after that. Now I know why.

"I'm sorry," he says. I look up at him frowning.

"What for?"

"For not telling you."

"Then I am too," I say, he shouldn't have to apologize for going out and enjoying himself. Even if I think it is a little bit gross.

"Why are you sorry?" he asks with a chuckle.

"For making you feel like I wasn't there for you," I say.

"You're impossible," he says rolling his eyes.

"How long did it go on?" I ask without meaning to. He stares at me for a little moment before answering.

"A few weeks, on and off. She just called me when she wanted... well when she was bored," he says his face turning red. "It really meant nothing," he adds sounding embarrassed and a little bit desperate. I nod slightly and shove him a little.

"I can't believe you slept with Rachel Hunt, gross Ollie!" I say with a chuckle. He covers his face with his hands groaning loudly.

"That's why I didn't say anything. I knew you would think that," he says through his hands. I smile.

"She's *so* fake. That's why she was being all friendly with me a few months ago, because you and she were..." I shudder as Oliver groans in embarrassment.

"I think she thought if she became your friend then something might happen between us," he says with a sigh.

"Who broke up with who?"

"We weren't dating Chloe," he says, I roll my eyes at him and he chuckles. "I stopped seeing her, she didn't want to 'date' she just wanted... fun. I didn't want that so I stopped it." I stare at him with a little frown.

"Why didn't you want it?" I ask, his eyes meet mine and his stare makes my heart flutter. "Tell me, is she that bright orange all over or is it just where the general public can see?" I blurt out, not wanting to hear his answer after all. He laughs before shuddering a little.

"Let's move on shall we?" he says in a pleading voice.

"Fine, we'll move on." I say as I shake my head at him, in mock disappointment; he narrows his eyes and I giggle before he tackles me to the ground.

"So you forgive me?" he asks. I nod up at him, smiling.

"There is nothing to forgive. You weren't mine then," I say, his eyes widen and I quickly blush over my word slip. "I actually feel a little sorry for you," I say, he laughs.

"Good," he says before leaning down and kissing me softly. "You ready for lunch?" he asks resting his forehead on mine. I nod again; he gets up moving back towards the fish. I lay there feeling a little overwhelmed. With a groan, I sit up, watching as he rummages through the food bag and pulls out the remainder of the food.

I'm relieved that he didn't comment on me saying he was mine as I think I might have actually died of embarrassment. I watch as he sorts lunch realising that, he is in fact mine now, as I'm his. A smile pulls at my lips as I watch him dish out the food, he separates it onto the two plates before he pulls some of the flesh from one side of the fish, piling it onto the plates. The cuts the last bagel in two and spreads the last dollop of cheese onto them before handing me a plate. I notice that the plate he's holding out to me has the bigger helping on it, I arch my eyebrow at him.

"What?" he asks looking confused. I pick up the plate with the smaller helping and he rolls his eyes.

"You need more energy than I do. You have work tomorrow," I say. He just shakes his head but doesn't say anything else. I pick up a little bit of the fish popping it into my mouth. My eyes close and I make a low moan. "That's amazing!" I say pointing to the fish on my plate. I open my eyes, Oliver smiles at me and I see a little flush on his cheeks.

"I learned from the best. Granddad taught me everything I know," he says.

"Thank you," I say with a smile. He looks up at me frowning.

"What for?" he asks. I shrug unsure why I actually said it.

"For everything I suppose. This week would have been a lot worse if it weren't for you. I don't think I have properly thanked you yet," I say. He scoffs.

"Thank me for what? Bringing you here to get chased by a bull, attacked by a Fanged and sent to some wife training centre?" he asks. I chuckle and shake my head at how ridiculous it all sounds.

"Well, there is all that but I could be sharing a bed with Jackson every night so I will take the near misses any day," I say. Oliver shudders and frowns. "It wasn't all bad. The training place was just like school only a more concentrated version. The bull I can handle and the Fanged, I knew you had my back," I say looking up at him. He snorts as I rub my still bruised wrist.

"Hardly, you got hurt and I was thrown to the ground like it was nothing to him," he says looking down at his bruised ribs. I take his hand and he looks back at me.

"You would've found a way. You would have burned that place to the ground if you needed to," I say.

"I would have. I would've done anything to keep you safe. I promised," he says his voice lower than normal, I smile. I know that he would have done anything to stop me being hurt and I have an overwhelming surge of gratitude towards him.

"I know," I say placing my plate down. I shuffle over towards him on my knees. He puts his plate down his eyes locked to mine. He tenderly puts his hands on my waist as I cup his face. "We will keep each other safe. Agreed?" I ask. He nods up at me and swallows.

"Agreed," he croaks. I smile as I lower my head to kiss him. A bright flash and a deafening crash sounds above us making us jump. His hands grip me tighter as we both look up.

"It looks like it's going to..." I begin, before I can say it a fat, icy drop of rain lands on my chest. I look down as Oliver's eyes follow its descent into my bikini top.

"Rain?" he asks, as the drop darkens the material. He looks up at me and a drop hits him on the face. I smile before moving to grab up my things. I pull on my clothes as he throws the towels into my backpack.

"How do we put out the fire?" I ask as I wrap the fish up best I can and put it in the cool bag.

"I'll get it," Oliver says, he starts to pile damp sand onto it, it hisses and smokes for a few seconds then dies. "Have you got everything?" he asks, straightening up, as he looks up at the dark grey clouds rolling towards us. I hear a distant rumble as I take one last look around. I nod, gripping the fishing rod, as I throw my backpack over my shoulder.

"I'm ready," I say. He slings the food bag over his shoulder taking one last look out to the lake. "We'll come back," I promise, he turns to me smiling.

"Yeah, I hope so," he says. He takes my face in his warm smoky-smelling hands and kisses me. My whole body shivers, I feel him sigh contently. He pulls back, only slightly, resting his forehead against mine as he looks into my eyes. In the few seconds it takes for him to say something the extent of how much our relationship has changed over a short week nearly floors me. From best friends who spent all their time together just being friends, to a couple of people forced to marry. To separated and angry at each other and now, as his hot breath heats my skin I can't seem to want to stop looking at him, thinking about him and kissing him. My best friend, I never thought I would, or could, feel this way about him not in a million years. It's amazing how just accepting something can change you so quickly.

He is mine.

"This is the best time I have had in a long time Chloe. Only you could have done this for me. Thank you," he kisses me again, I lean forward and I feel him smile. I take a little steadying breath to control my breathing; it has become a little erratic.

"You're welcome. I had fun too," I say. He smiles widely as he takes my hand.

"Let's go home," he says. I nod and we walk hand and hand through the dense woods out onto the road. The thunder rumbles above us as we walk the short distance back into town.

I drop off the fishing rod off at the little rental shop. The man hands me my mother's ring back after he has checked the rod over thoroughly.

"Why'd he have that?" Oliver asks as we walk back out of the shop. I secure the chain around my neck.

"He needed something valuable so that I would bring back the rod. I offered him my wedding ring but he wanted this so I gave him it," I say, tucking it back under my t-shirt.

"Why do you still wear that?" Oliver asks curiously, I smile at him before shrugging.

"Same reason you carry Ethan's picture in your wallet; I miss her," I say. Oliver stares at me as I walk off.

Chapter 18

The heavens finally open as we hit the outskirts of the village and we set off at a run. We splash through the muddy roads, laughing as we run towards our little cottage. As we reach it Oliver leaps the fence sprinting to the door, while I wrestle with the gate. I crash it open sprinting down the sodden path and through the open front door, Oliver is holding open for me. I come to a sliding stop dropping my bag as Oliver closes the door, sliding the locks shut. He turns to me and we stare at each other smiling. There is a steady dripping coming from both of us and I chuckle.

"What's funny?" he asks his smile widening.

"I have never been caught in rain like that before. I feel like I have jumped in the lake," I say. He laughs.

"You look like it too," he says and I scowl. "Well they did say it was colder and wetter up in the north than the south, guess this proves it," he says holding out his drenched arms and sniffing. I see goose bumps on his arms. I turn, heading into the bathroom. "Hey, where are you going?" he calls as I push the door open, and start running him a bath.

"I'm running you a bath."

"Come on Chloe don't start all this again," he moans from behind me. I turn around looking at him from the doorway. He looks moody.

"I'm not starting anything Ollie." I touch his arm and he looks down. "You're cold; you start your new job tomorrow. You can't get sick."

"I'm fine," he says and I glare at him.

"Just shut up and take a bath," I say crossing my arms.

"What about you?" he asks.

"What about me?"

"You're cold too," he says. I notice my risen skin as well.

"I'll go and dry off and head in after you," I say walking past him into the bedroom. I pull off my cold wet clothes and towel myself off; I wrap the towel around myself waiting for my turn in the bathroom. I sit on the edge of the bed and wait patiently. I hear an occasional splash or hum coming from the bathroom and I realise I'm smiling. Today was a good day. It didn't go quite according to plan. The plan being to get a lot more fishing done and have less talk of running away and overthrowing our dead leaders.

Oh yes and less kissing.

Ok that was not an altogether awful change to the day but it was unexpected. The most thrilling part of the day, no matter how amazing the kisses were was finding out how on the same page Oliver and I are. For the fifteen years I have known him not once have we discussed actually doing something to regain our freedom. Only he had openly expressed his opinions. I had nodded in agreement or if I didn't agree kept my mouth shut. But today, today I let him know how much we thought alike and how that, if he truly wanted to do something to get out of here, I would back him one hundred percent. It just made me more determined to do something knowing he would back me too... I just need to figure out what.

"Hey."

"Jeez!" I jump to my feet spinning to the door where Oliver stands trying not to smile. "You nearly scared me to death," I say clutching my towel.

"Sorry. I said your name like four times, you looked deep in thought," he says. I nod looking away from him noticing his state of undress, how the towel wrapped around his hips is hung low...

"Bathroom free?" I ask looking everywhere but at him.

"It is."

"Thanks," I say as I rush past him. I don't miss his sigh before I shut the bathroom door. I take my time in the shower letting the water soothe my chilled skin and muscles. I jump when the water suddenly spurts and goes cold.

"Damn it!" I squeal reaching for the taps and switching them off. I grab my towel wrapping it around myself tightly. I stomp out of the bathroom my teeth chattering and my hair still soapy.

"What happened?" Oliver asks coming out of the kitchen wearing a white apron and holding a knife.

"W-w-wat-t-ter w-w-ent c-cold!" I chatter as I shiver on the spot. His lips lift in a little smile.

"Do you just need to rinse your hair?" he asks looking at my soapy head; I nod as my teeth chatter loudly. "Ok, go into the kitchen, it's warm and I will grab you something warm to wear." I nod again. He hands me the knife and I take it with a shaking hand, he makes me grip it tight. "Don't drop it on your toes," he says. I grip the handle tighter as I walk into the kitchen. I feel the heat straight away from the oven. I put the knife down on the table as I walk over to the oven. I hold my chilly fingers over the stove where there are some potatoes simmering and a pan of boiling water sitting atop it. I see a little pile of broccoli on the side and I peek in the oven and see a little foil parcel in there.

"I thought we could finish the fish," Oliver says as he comes back into the room, I nod as I turn to him. He has a big royal blue bundle slung over his arm and he opens it open for me. It's his dressing gown. "Come here, you're going to freeze," he says. I walk over turning around and securing my towel before slipping my arms into the dressing gowns huge arms. Oliver places it onto my shoulders chuckling as it nearly hits the ground.

"Sh-shut up," I mutter, wrapping it around myself and tying the ties securely. The robe is very long, but it's

Victoria Nock

Oliver's and he's ridiculously tall, so I'm not that shocked. It is very warm despite it being a little thread bare, it's soft and smells like his home, which is a comfort. I snuggle into it and he smiles at me.

"Better?"

"Yes, thank you."

"No problem. Now let's get those bubbles out of your hair."

"How?"

"Have you never washed your hair in the sink?" he asks as he steers me towards it. I frown up at him when I spot the peelings from the potatoes. "Oh... let me clean that up," he says quickly scooping them out and putting them in a bowl with some trimmings from the broccoli.

"Why are you not just throwing them out?" I ask. He smiles at me as he washes his hands.

"I'm going to start a compost pile, you know to help with growing our own food, it's less expensive and it's an easier way to get fresh stuff," he says, I smile when I spot a little pile of leaflets behind him on the table. He notices me looking and shrugs. "Well you were taking ages in the shower, I got bored. Plus it's a good idea."

"I'm not saying anything, I think it's a great idea," I say. He smiles and rolls his eyes.

"I know it is. Now come here before that stuff dries and you scratch all your hair out." He takes my hand before pulling me over to the sink. He positions me in front of the sink and picks up a plastic jug. I stare at him.

"I can do it," I insist but he just ignores me, while he waits for me to concede he crosses his arms. "Fine," I say after a few moments. He smiles triumphantly.

He begins to run the water as I lean forward over the deep sink. The hot steam warms my face immediately. I open my mouth to ask why this water is hot when Oliver speaks.

"This water is from a smaller tank," he says reading my mind. I smile at just how well he knows me.

187

"Oh," Is all I say as he pours a little water onto my head. I jump a little at the unexpectedness of it.

"Sorry was that too hot," he says apologetically. I shake my head.

"No it's perfect I just got a fright I wasn't expecting it," I mumble.

"I thought I'd scalded you," he says. I shake my head again and he puts his hand on my head. "Ok, just about to pour, close your eyes," he says. I nod, closing my eyes. The water feels nice on my cold head, I sigh a little as it warms me. "Is that warm enough?"

"Yes," I say quietly as he moves my hair forward and the collar of the robe back down my shoulders a little before pouring again. It feels great to have someone else wash my hair, it's relaxing. I feel my body turn to jelly as Oliver's fingers rub my scalp. I can't suppress the yawn that passes my lips.

"Is that nice?" Oliver asks after a few minutes. I hum lazily. "Just about done," he says. I feel him rinse my hair ringing it with his hands and I straighten up. I smile up at him feeling sleepy. He lifts the towel up to my face patting it dry.

"Thank you," I say as he hands me the towel. I wipe my eyes, clearing any soap from them.

"Its fine," he says with a little shrug and I lean up and press a little kiss to his jaw.

"I'll be right back."

"Kay," he says his cheeks turning a little pink. I smile as I walk back into the bedroom careful not to trip on the long robe. "Dinner will be five minutes."

"Ok," I call over my shoulder smiling as I close the door behind myself. I quickly throw on some comfortable clothes. I brush the knots out of my hair before heading back out into the living room to the delicious smell of dinner.

I round the corner; Oliver is mashing the potatoes in a bowl. He smiles at me as I enter.

"Hey it's nearly done. Sit down," he says. I walk over to our loaded plates and he tries to shoo me out.

"Do you need a hand with anything?" I ask as I try stepping around him, unsuccessfully.

"I got this Chloe just sit down," he says with a wide bright smile as he threatens me with the potato masher. I stare at it smiling before I lick it.

What the hell am I doing? I think as his eyes widen for a moment. I smile sheepishly.

"It's good," I say. He stares at me as I sit down. He blinks a few times before he composes himself enough to return to what he was doing while I smile at him. I play with my knife as I watch him finish serving up the meal. I smile at him as he shoots me little looks every now and then. I even admire his butt when he bends down to pull the foil parcel out of the oven.

What is wrong with me?

He hisses loudly, as the steam bursts out of the foil burning his fingers.

"You ok?" I ask getting up as he moves to the sink to run his fingers under the water.

"I'm fine. Just wasn't paying attention," he says staring down at his hand.

"Let me see," I say. He shakes his head, I take his wrist and he pulls away. He looks at me and I gasp. His eyes are dark; the intensity of his gaze takes me by surprise. My heart does a little skip and I freeze to the spot. I notice he's breathing harder than normal and I swallow nervously.

"Oliver?" I say quietly. He puts both of his hands on his my face. I blink up at him. He stares at me like he's asking my permission to kiss me. My head moves up and down of its own accord, he lets out a little growl before his lips crash to mine. My eyes widen at the force of the kiss but they quickly close as his breath mingles with mine. My hands find their way into his hair tugging lightly making him sigh. He pulls me against him holding me there tightly, like he doesn't want to let go. Truth be told, I don't want him to either. I don't know how long we stand there for but when we come up for air it's too soon. We stare at each other wide-eyed and smiling.

"I'm sorry," Oliver says.

"What for," I croak, tightening my grip around his neck, he smiles sensing my worry.

"Not about the kiss," he says and just to prove his point he kisses me again. He pulls away again, too soon. I groan, making him chuckle. "I meant for being rough. I just... I don't know what happened. I'm sorry." He runs a hand through his hair and chews his lip before putting his forehead against mine and I smile.

"It's ok. I kind of liked it," I say feeling my blush spread. He smiles widely.

"You did?" he asks looking a little smug. I smile and tug his hair. "Ouch! Ok sorry."

"Your hand ok?" I ask. He straightens up looking down at it. It looks a little red but otherwise ok, the plaster from the grub bite still tightly wrapped around his finger.

"I'll live," he says.

"You've been in the wars today," I say. He chuckles and he kisses my forehead.

"I know. You still hungry?" he asks as he lets me go. I nod as my stomach grumbles in agreement. His eyes fall to my stomach in surprise at the loud noise. I wrap my arms around it and he laughs.

"Starving," I say as he chuckles.

"Sit and I will bring it over," he says. I pull out my chair; he quickly serves up the meal and places it down in front of me. "It's a little bit colder than I hoped," he says giving me a little smirk. I feel my face flush. His smile tells me he knows I'm thinking about the kiss. He sits down grinning from ear to ear. I look down at my plate, my mouth watering, it looks and smells delicious. I take a bite of the broccoli; it's still crunchy, slightly cool but still tasty.

"So good," I say through my mouthful. He smiles as he chews. We eat in silence for the rest of the meal stealing glances at each other every now and then. When we're both finished I get up, collecting the plates and filling the sink.

"Do you want a hand?" Oliver asks placing our glasses down next to me.

"No it's ok, you made dinner," I say, but he ignores me and picks up the dishcloth and begins drying and putting away the plates. I just smile and keep going. It only takes a few minutes for us to finish tidying the kitchen. Once we're done we both head into the living room feeling full and sleepy. I glance at the clock I'm surprised that it's only eight in the evening, it feels much later.

"I'm ready for bed," I moan as I slump onto the sofa next to Oliver.

"It was a tiring day. It was a good day," he says taking my hand.

"Yeah, it was nice. I'm glad you enjoyed it," I say squeezing his hand. His head rolls to the side so he can look at me.

"Did you... did you enjoy it?" he asks looking a little worried.

"Yeah I did," I say smiling. His face relaxes and he smiles. "What I said earlier Ollie about us getting out..." His eyes widen and he surges towards me. His lips are suddenly on mine and I stare at him with wide eyes as he pulls back shaking his head ever so slightly.

"Not here," he whispers in me ear. To an outsider the way he was acting may have looked like a man trying to seduce his wife but the force of his kiss and the harshness of his whisper were anything but romantic. "Remember what your dad always said?"

"What?" I ask completely startled and confused.

"Remember Chloe, what does he always say?" He leans forward. I shiver when I feel his lips against my ear. "They are always watching," he breathes against my ear, I shudder with fear. He moves back a little, I stare at him wide eyed.

"Here?" I wheeze out. He nods, my eyes dart around the room nervously. He cups my cheek bringing my attention back to him.

"I haven't checked yet but I will, don't worry, I heard you loud and clear," he says giving me a wide smile that I find hard not to return even if mine is a little weak. "I will get on it in the morning. I was talking to some guys when lambing they were quite interesting. I will see how the land lays there. All I ask from you is for you to keep your feelers out as well and be careful," he says almost pleading.

"I will," I promise. He smiles widely before standing up in a smooth motion holding out his hand.

"You ready for bed?" he asks I take his offered hand.

"Definitely," I say. I look around the room expecting to see a camera or something but I can't see anything. We walk into the bedroom flicking lights off as we go. I climb into bed throwing the covers over myself as Oliver pulls off his jumper and socks. He crawls in next to me.

"I'm so tired," he says as he tugs the covers out from under himself. He flops down heavily on the bed bouncing me on the mattress making me chuckle. I roll onto my side. He smiles at me from his position on his stomach. "Hey," he says and I smile. "Quite a day we had today."

"It was," I say moving a bit of his unruly hair out of his eyes. They flutter closed as my finger touches his forehead. "Are you nervous about tomorrow?" I ask. He shakes his head and opens his eyes. I notice they are darker again; my stomach does a little flip again. I look away as he rolls onto his side.

"Not now I've met Billy. It'll be interesting I think," he says. I look up at him, he's looking at me his eyes heavy with sleep.

"I don't know what I'm going to do," I say with a sigh.

"Do whatever you want. I think you should explore, just try and avoid cow fields. Oh, and I take back what I said about meeting someone else," he says. I prod his ribs making him snort with laughter.

"Well there goes my plan," I say. He narrows his eyes at me.

"Ha-ha very funny."

"I will have you know I'm hilarious," I smile at him mischievously before prodding him in the ribs again making him laugh loudly. "See," I say grinning. He shakes his head, his tired eyes widen as my hand creeps towards him again.

"Don't you dare!" he warns and I smile at him innocently.

"I didn't do anything," I protest.

"No but you were thinking about it," he says. I fold my arms away. He relaxes a little knowing I'm not going to attack him and lets out a relieved little sigh. He may be nearly a foot taller than me and much stronger but he can be brought down by anybody, big or small, with one simple tickle to the ribs. It's his one and little known weakness but it works every time.

"I might look around this place and see if it has a library," I say. My eyes widen and dart around the room before pull the covers up over my head.

"What? What are you doing?" Oliver asks tugging on the covers. I hold them tightly and he gives up, joining me under them.

"Will they be... you know... listening in here?" I whisper. He stares at me in the dark, finally I see him shake his head.

"I've checked in here, there's nothing. They have no interest in what goes on in a human's bedroom. I don't see why they would be interested in watching or hearing us have sex and sleep is boring," Oliver says. I see him chewing on his lip as he obviously realized what he just said. It's suddenly very hot under the covers.

"Do you think they do it? Have sex?" I ask. I see his eyes meet mine then dart away again.

"Apparently but I don't think it quite works the same way after you have died," he says. I can't help but laugh loudly, I hear him chuckle.

"Maybe we should tell them there are pills for that?" I suggest. He laughs joining in with me. We pull the covers off our heads laughing into the room for a while. We're unable to look at each other without bursting into fresh waves of laughter. When I start to get a sore side I have to turn away from him to calm myself down. Oliver stops first. I hear him sigh as he tries to regain some control. After a little while we have calmed down and it's quiet.

"The thought makes me sick," he says suddenly, shuddering slightly. I turn around to look at him. He's staring angrily at the ceiling. I don't ask what he's talking about but I know it must have something to do with the Fanged mating or just with the Fanged in general. I just nod in agreement and he closes his eyes. We're silent for some time before I hear a light snore come from Oliver. I look over at him, smiling. He's wearing a little frown even in sleep, he has his hands clasped on his chest and his mouth is slightly open. I lean over and kiss his cheek before I lie back on my pillow.

"Good night Oliver," I breathe as I close my eyes, one of Oliver's hands takes hold of mine and squeezes.

"Good night Chloe," he murmurs.

Chapter 19

It has been just over two months since Oliver and I moved up north to our new life in the countryside. Our new life as a married couple, except from the day we had together fishing, has been downright miserable. The storm seemed to have brought an onslaught of rain with it. Ever since that last sunny day it has rained every day. The day after our little fishing trip, Oliver started his new job. He got out of bed at four in the morning after waking up and being unable to get back to sleep. He let me make him breakfast, as he got dressed. I could see he was nervous; I tried to reassure him, as he stared into his coffee cup, but I'm sure it fell on deaf ears despite the smiles he gave me. He rushed down his porridge and coffee in silence. He kissed my cheek before leaving, at half past five, so he could find his way there in time.

I was left alone from then on. I knew I had twelve hours to kill before he would be home and I had some form of company so I tidied, cleaned and did everything else that came to mind. I pottered around the house all day unpacking all of our things. I familiarized myself with the things that came with the house and rummaged through the drawers while cleaning the house top to bottom. I even had time to organise the food for the week, arranging it into meals for each day. By the time Oliver came home, looking tired, muddy and wet his dinner was on the stove, ready to be served. He smiled widely when he saw me and as soon as his boots and sodden jacket were off he pulled me into a hug and kissed the top of my head.

"How was work?" I asked as I breathed in a sweet smell from his jumper.

"Interesting," he said as he squeezed me. He leaned down to kiss me, I felt him smile before he let me go. "I'm glad to be home. Dinner smells amazing. Do I have time for a shower?" he asked, I nodded. He smiled and rushed into the bathroom.

He came out five minutes later in his pyjamas and sat down with a big sigh.

"I feel human again," he said. I smiled as I put his dinner in front of him. He gave me a grateful smile. As I sat down he started telling me about his day. He told me how he was shown the ropes and how he would be in training for a few weeks before he would be left in charge. "They're giving me the work horses. They're huge. The guy there, Rick is close to sixty now he's close to retirement," he said casting me a glance that I knew said that the man was nearing his Farming age. The man was apparently thrilled that Oliver was there, as he wanted the last few years of his life to be relaxing, rather than working himself into the grave. I nodded a little understanding. I looked back down at my plate as sadness washed over me for the older man. "They are teaching me to drive the tractor," he said changing the subject after the silence began to drag out. I stared up at him. He nodded smiling at the obvious shock on my face.

"Really, you?" I said. "They must be mad," I said shaking my head, he laughed loudly. He shoved me playfully, making me giggle

"I know, that's what I said," he said. "Just you wait, I will be the best tractor driver ever," he said. I looked at him with my eyebrows raised.

"I'll bet. Just don't kill anyone ok?" I said smiling. He smiled and got up as he finished his dinner.

"I'm not promising anything, but I will try my damn hardest not too," he said.

"I guess that's the best I can hope for I suppose," I chuckled joining him at the sink. He took my plate while he smiled at me.

196

"The house looks great; you were busy I see," he said. I nodded.

"I thought I would do something. It won't always be this tidy," I said as I picked up a dishtowel to help with the dishes. He smiled at me.

"Good." Is all he said and I smiled as I put the glasses away. That was the last evening that was semi normal, where we spent more time talking than just going through the motions of cooking, eating, showering and bed.

After that morning and after realising his work was closer to home than he thought Oliver began leaving later in the mornings. Until the morning after we received a call from my very excited brother.

"Hello?" Oliver answered hesitantly; I heard a yell and Oliver held the receiver away from his face. He looked at me as he held it out to me. "It's your brother," he said groggily. He had been getting grumpier in the mornings. He slumped back down in his seat as I picked up the phone.

"Hello?" I said. I heard a squeal and then a laugh.

"Simon, don't pull Adam's hair!" Michael said from the other end. I rolled my eyes.

"Michael?" I said. I heard him gasp.

"Oh, you're there, I never heard you. The kids are mad, they're all excited," he said.

"What is it Michael? It's like six in the morning," I groaned. Oliver sighed loudly as he ate his toast, like hearing the time was painful. Michael just laughed loudly down the phone. I held the receiver away from my ear. Oliver's eyes met mine as he swirled his finger by his temple.

"He's finally lost it," he mumbled. I nodded in agreement.

"Michael why're you calling, is everything ok?" I asked as he chuckled to himself.

"Better than ok sis, Millie had the baby," he said his smile clear in his voice. I felt my eyes widen.

"What is it?" I asked. Oliver sat up in his chair and looked directly at me.

"Baby?" he mouthed. I couldn't help the smile on my face as I nodded. "Boy or girl?" I shrugged, waiting to hear when I realised Michael was crying.

"Oh no... please tell me it's not..." I said my hand over my mouth. Oliver's eyes turned sad.

"No. God no Chloe, she's perfect. It's a little girl." I groaned in relief while Oliver stared at me with expectant eyes.

"A girl, she's perfect," I said to Oliver as I wiped my tear filled eyes, his shoulders slumped as he smiled.

"Thank god. Tell them congratulations."

"Oliver says congratulations. So do I Michael, that's just great. How is Millie?" I asked as Michael laughed.

"She's perfect, tired but she's great. She's over the moon. She got her girl."

"What is her name?" I asked.

"Alice. Her name's Alice. She's so beautiful Chloe; I will send you a picture as soon as possible."

"Ok, wow I can't wait to see her," I said swirling the phone wire around my finger. Michael sighed happily.

"Miss you sis, wish you were here."

"I miss you too. Get back to your family and keep me up to date. I love you all," I said as Michael sniffed.

"Love you too sis. Tell Oliver we send our love. We'll see you soon ok?" he said a smile clear in his voice and I nodded.

"Sure, I will do. Speak soon. Bye," I said and as soon as the phone was down my eyes filled with tears and Oliver had his arms around me.

"You ok?" he asked into my hair. I nodded and sniffed.

"I just miss them," I said.

"I know," he nodded.

After that morning Oliver began leaving earlier for work again just saying he was needed, as he was in training. I just went with it but then he started coming back later and later at night in a worse mood every evening. It was getting hard to put up with. When I asked him what was wrong he would either say he was tired or he had a hard day. Even on his days off he would be distant. It would be like talking to a mannequin sometimes.

Today was one of those days. I had been patient with him; I even let him yell at me when he was really stressed out. I never retaliated, knowing he would just get more upset but not today.

Today I was pissed, two months of silent treatment and snapping and I was done. For the last ten minutes I have been explaining to him about what I've been doing in my spare time. How I have been visiting the library, looking through the dusty stacks for any sort of book that would give us some sort of background on the Fanged. Anything on how they came to rule over us.

"… I mean I have hunted high and low and I have come away with nothing, yet. I have looked in Local books and as many history books as I can find, but they only have a limited number of them. I don't want to ask anyone I don't know because I don't know if they can be trusted," I say, putting the mugs away from the tea we'd just had.

"Mary made a good point at the Training Centre; we're missing so much of our history. They can't have erased everything, there has to be something. It has been two whole months; I have to find something eventually right?" I ask. When I don't get any response, I look around to see Oliver staring out of the window with a completely vacant look on his face. I know right off he hasn't been listening to a word I have been saying.

Something in me snaps. I grip the mug tightly in my hand and before I know it it's flying across the room. It smashes into the brick wall behind his head shattering loudly. He jumps up spinning around, his eyes wide and startled.

"Chloe, what the hell?"

199

"How long have I been talking to myself?" I ask in a low measured tone. It makes him straighten his back and look around the room quickly.

"What?"

"I have been talking to you about the plan for the last ten minutes. Have you been listening at all?" I ask through my teeth.

"Why are you so mad?" he asks. I feel my eyes widen to a dangerous level.

"Screw you Ollie!" I say with as much venom as I can. He recoils like I have slapped him. I storm past him into the bedroom where I slam the door making the whole house shudder.

Good! Maybe it will fall on his stupid head and knock some sense into him?

I shove my feet into my boots before pulling on my rain jacket, all the while muttering angrily under my breath. I throw open the window swinging my legs out, they dangle for a little moment, before I jump down into the muddy flowerbed below. I know it's childish to escape out of a window but I can't stand looking at his moping face for another moment. So the window is my only escape route. I stomp through the mud, through the garden and I make my way straight over to Rose's. I see her in her kitchen window. She looks up waving when she sees me approaching. I don't wave back, her eyes widen at my murderous glare. She looks over her shoulder and a few moments later the door swings open and Damien stands there smiling.

"What's he done?" he asks. My face falls and I smile sheepishly.

"Am I that easy to read?" I ask. He just gives me a little shrug.

"Let her in Damien it's freezing," Rose says from inside the house. He moves aside gesturing me in; I smile.

"Thanks," I say as Rose comes out of the kitchen smiling.

"So he told you then?" she asks drying her hands on a dishtowel. I see Damien's eyes widen as I frown at her. "I told him he should've told you sooner but he's just so…ugh! I said to him, just because she can't go doesn't mean she shouldn't know." She stops talking and looks at me frowning. I look at Damien who smiles nervously.

"He hasn't done anything, that's the problem," I say slowly. I frown deeper noticing her cheeks redden.

Something is up.

"What're you talking about; he should've told me what? Where can't I go?" I ask. She and Damien exchange a worried look.

"Look Chloe, Rose shouldn't have said anything," Damien says his tone soft but he throws Rose an angry look, I feel my jaw tighten.

"What is going on?" I demand. I look at them both through narrowed eyes. It takes a little moment for it to click in my brain then I realise Oliver is up to something, he has a plan, they know. Rose and Damien know. What do they know? Why do they know? I stare between them, they both look desperately guilty, Rose more so. Damien puts a soft comforting hand on my shoulder, my eyes dart to him. He drops his hand, backing away looking a little scared.

"He told us not to say anything," Damien says lamely. I hear my teeth grind as I turn around. I storm through their still open front door. "You need to learn to keep your damn mouth shut!" I hear Damien snap.

"Well he should've told her!" Rose barks back; I hear their door slam shut as I power walk down their path towards our house.

I can't believe he didn't tell me. Why didn't he tell me?

I cross the road without looking. I kick open our gate breaking the latch, sending it flying across the path; I kick it out of my way as I stomp up the path. I hammer on the locked front door. I hear Oliver curse on the other side of the door my lips quirk in an angry, manic smile.

"What?" he snaps as he swings the door open. He only has a second to register confusion as to why I'm outside before I slap him hard. I shove past him; he's thrown slightly to the side as I slam the front door closed. "Chloe?" he gasps his hand on his red cheek.

"How dare you! How dare you keep me in the dark? You don't have the right to do that!" I scream in his shocked face.

"Shh! Keep your voice down!" he hisses.

"Don't you shush me Oliver Hunter," I say, prodding him in the chest. "Who the hell do you think you are? How could you not tell me about..." He covers my mouth with his hand, my eyes widen in anger before he wraps an arm around me, pulling me off of my feet carrying me screaming into the bedroom. He throws me onto the bed, muddy boots and all, making me call out in surprise. "Oliver!" I yell. He covers my mouth as he pins me to the bed pulling the covers over our heads, as he does.

"Stop yelling!" he says his tone quiet, but angry. I stare up at him with angry eyes before I nod. He removes his hand sighing. "Believe it or not Chloe I was trying to protect you."

"Protect me? Protect me from what? I'm not a child!" I hiss at him.

"I know Chloe, but I made your dad a promise," he says. I remember him promising my dad at graduation to keep me safe.

"He isn't here! He wouldn't want me to be kept in the dark about this," I snap. He nods knowing I'm right.

"I know, but I didn't want to put you in danger having you know anything. Ignorance is bliss," he says. I scoff.

"Not if you're ignoring me it isn't," I say. He looks down at me frowning.

"I... I didn't..." I see the hurt in his eyes. I shake my head I don't want to feel bad for him now, I'm still angry.

"Anyway it's not up to you what I know. You don't get to make those sorts of decisions for me. You know how I feel and what I want. You can't keep that from me. It's not fair," I say. He frowns but nods a little accepting my words.

"I'm sorry I never meant to make you feel like..."

"Your breeder wife?" I say harshly. He winces as he looks down at me. I can see the moment the realisation of what he did hits him.

"I never wanted that," he says his face pained. "I'm so sorry. I just didn't know what to do. They made me promise not to tell a soul. I panicked. I wanted to tell you."

"Damien and Rose know," I say unable to hide the hurt in my voice. I hear and feel him sigh as he hovers over me. He puts his free hand on my cheek wiping a tear away I hadn't realised had escaped. I look up at him under the darkened tent of our bed covers, I move my head out of his warm hand. Hurt flashes across his eyes, I bite my lip to stop myself feeling bad about it.

"I'm so sorry. I should've told you everything. I will. Damien is obviously a better person than I am," he says. I just stare at him; I'm not going to disagree with him there.

"It hurts more because you're supposed to be my best friend," I say as he chews his lip.

"I am Chloe. I'm so sorry," he says his voice low. I huff feeling my resolve crumbling.

"I shouldn't forgive you for this. Just don't keep anything like this from me again. I want to know everything that's going on ok?" I say sternly. He nods and crosses his heart but I can see him trying not to smile.

"I promise," he says. I nod as he smiles a little.

"What?"

"Did we just have our first argument as a married couple?" he asks. I frown at him trying not to laugh.

Stupid idiot. He's always able to make me smile, even when I'm crazy mad.

"Well you were an arse," I say. He nods.

"I was, I am. I can't believe you slapped me!" he says his eyes wide. I bite my lip really trying not to smile now.

"I'm sorry. I was, am, so mad," I say. He shifts and I realise he's still holding my hands above my head and is pressed against me and I can't find it in myself to care.

"I noticed. It bloody hurt by the way. How did you end up outside?" he says with a chuckle

"The window, I climbed out," I say. He looks down as if noticing my boots and raincoat for the first time. He releases my hands as he sits up taking all the heat and covers with him.

"Shall I take those off?" he asks looking down at my boots. I nod as he reaches down pulling at the laces. I watch as he loosens the laces. I can feel my heart begin to race.

Behave!

He looks up at me as he tugs the first boot off a little smile on his lips like he heard my thought.

"I've missed you, you know," I say catching us both of guard. His shoulders slump a little as he tugs off the second boot. He places them both at the foot of the bed. I lean up on my elbows as he looks round at me. He moves forwards leaning over me and I hold my breath.

"I've missed you too," he says. I let go of the breath as he kisses my forehead. "Get into something warm and I'll make you something hot to drink," he says getting up from the bed; I frown at him as he smiles. "I'll be back. We have some catching up to do," he says. I feel a little blush spread on my cheeks. He just smiles before rushing out of the room.

Chapter 20

I flop down on the mattress as he exits the bedroom. My stomach begins to flutter at the prospect of finding out about what has been happening right under my nose. More so at just being able to spend some time with Oliver. I quickly undress getting into my pyjamas. As I'm pulling my top down the bedroom door opens.

"Shit sorry," Oliver yelps. I tug my t-shirt down looking over my shoulder.

"Its ok, come in," I say. He sticks his head back in the room looking quite flushed.

"I should've knocked."

"It's ok, my back was turned," I say. His face gets redder as his eyes flit to the mirror. He looks back at me offering me a steaming mug of tea, giving me an awkward smile.

"Hope its ok, we're running low on tea so I used the same bag," he says as I take it from him.

"I'm sure it's fine it's hot that's the main thing," I say.

Since our starter provisions have started to dwindle we have become thriftier with everything. We're doing anything we can to save any money we can. Like when making tea we tend to share the bag unless it's in the morning cup. Things like left-over's get put into a pot where we make a nice homemade soup that changes every day or so as we add the different ingredients. It's something Oliver's mum used to do. I have to agree it's a great idea.

We've been using paper until there is no space left to write then it goes into the compost heap that's coming along nicely now, thanks to Oliver bringing home some horse droppings to start it off. Oliver has promised Damien and David first pick from his little vegetable patch for keeping us in supply of fresh eggs and potatoes, which they were struggling to get through in their own houses. They were more than willing to trade for some fresh produce. We've been saving our firewood for when the nights get truly cold. Knowing that, for now, putting on an extra layer will keep us warm enough. Anything we can do to make our lives that little bit easier the better.

Oliver shifts awkwardly from foot to foot before he sits back down on the bed and crosses his legs. He pats the space next to him. I walk around the bed setting my drink down before I settle down next to him.

"So what do you want to know?" he asks as I turn to face him crossing my legs and cupping my tea in both my chilly hands.

"Everything, start from the start," I say. He smiles at my eagerness but he sits up sipping his tea.

"Ok well do you remember me telling you that I met some guys at the lambing?" he asks. I frown and then I recall our conversation after the fishing, he smiles when I nod. "Well I was watching these guys; they seemed pretty chummy and were kind of keeping to themselves, so I got curious. They were younger than most of the other guys there, older than us but only like thirty or something. Anyway, I overheard them talking about bringing down a tower. So naturally that caught my interest." I stare at him with a disapproving look. "I know I'm too nosey for my own good but these guys were up to something and I wanted to know what. So I followed them. I heard them saying they were just going to drive a tractor into it and be done with it," he says shaking his head. I frown.

"Hang on, a tower? You mean a watch tower?" I ask in a whisper. He nods.

"Yes," he says. I stare at him in disbelief.

"How? I mean they are big. It wouldn't be possible," I say in a low voice. He smiles and shakes his head.

"You'd be surprised. Have you seen one up close?" he asks.

"Of course not, why would I have?" I say frowning.

"Exactly, they're old, Chloe, they're weaker than they look. With the right amount of power they can be brought down," he says. I shake my head a little.

"How do you know all of this?" I ask and he shrugs.

"I have one in my field and I checked it out, that's what we have been doing the last seven weeks. Planning," he says with a hint of bitterness. Before I can comment on it he smiles.

"So where was I? Oh yeah, the guys were planning the tractor move. Well I heard them say that and I kind of laughed so they caught me. Well they would have caught me if they were fit and not so clumsy. I managed to dodge them before they caught me and beat the crap out of me. Which, they have no problem reminding me all the time that, they would have done if they had caught me."

"Why didn't they stop to listen to you?"

"Would you have Chloe? Do you remember how everyone in the pub looked at us when we first moved here?" he asks. I nod remembering the whole place falling silent. "Could you imagine how it looked to them seeing me standing there? Listening to their plans on how to bring down a Fanged tower? They had every right to be nervous." I nod in agreement.

"They are always watching," I say so quietly I'm surprised he even hears me but he nods, taking one of my hands.

"Exactly," he says. I give him a sad smile. "We know that there are some Fang fans in this town. We just have to be really careful."

During an evening walk a few weeks ago Damien and Rose saw a small group of people rushing in the back door of the pub only thirty minutes before curfew. It had been quite a shocking revelation to us all. It only spurred Oliver's anger and distrust of this place, making him hunt through the house for something out of the ordinary. After nearly tearing the house apart he found a hidden recording device. It was taped underneath our television. It was hidden so well he nearly missed it. As soon as he stomped it into dust he went over to David and Damien's showing them what he found. They also found one under their televisions and after they had been destroyed they too searched the rest of their houses.

We had no idea who would have done it. It made us nervous to talk to anyone in the village so we all just kept to ourselves. The thought of someone in the village helping the Fanged didn't sit right with me. It made me feel sick that we were being spied on like that.

"What happened after they stopped chasing you?" I ask shaking myself out of my thoughts. He looks up at me running his thumb over my knuckles before he continues.

"Once they had calmed down a little and got their breath back," he says with a little smile making me roll my eyes, "they listened long enough to hear what I had to say. Now what you have to remember is that all of this happened before I spoke to you at the lake, about any of this. I had an idea about how you felt but I didn't know it was that strong," he says. I nod. "Ok, so I told them that I had a better idea to bring down the tower. When I told them their faces lit up and they promised they wouldn't kill me."

"I'm glad they didn't," I say making him smile. "So what was the plan?" I ask. He chews on his lip; I can see his reluctance to tell me. I yank my hand out of his crossing my arms and staring at him.

"You promised," I huff. He looks at me pleadingly

"I know. I just think that if you don't know this specific detail then you will be ok. You can't be hurt," he says.

"Oliver," I say my tone dripping with anger.

"Ok, just let me tell you everything else then I will tell you the plan ok?" he says, as I continue glare at him.

"I won't forget if that's what you're hoping," I say. He smiles as he swirls his tea in his cup.

"I am but I know you won't. You're far too stubborn for that," he says with a hint of pride. I roll my eyes as he drains his cup. I stare down at my half full mug.

"So this is what you have been doing the whole time you haven't been here?" I ask as I swirl my warm tea around.

"Yes. I've had to go to meetings at dawn, as that's the safest and the only time we can all meet as the towers are unoccupied from half five until half six every morning." I feel my eyebrows shoot up.

"Really? How do you know that for sure?" I ask.

"We have some inside information." I scoff.

"From where?"

"An ex-government worker, he used to live in Centrum. He got fired and sent here to do some filing job because he was so bad at his old one. He hates it here but he hates the Fanged more."

"Wow," I say with a hushed sigh. I sit up feeling a little overwhelmed with all this information.

"I know," Oliver says but I frown.

"How do you know he can be trusted if he worked alongside them, how do you know he isn't the one working with them to ferret out people like us?" I say. Oliver shakes his head.

"I doubt very much he's a spy. He isn't exactly the sharpest tool in the box. He's barely able to keep him and his wife alive never mind trick all of us. He's a miserable swine but he has had a lot of contact with them. He's privy to some quite useful information on them. Plus Billy trusts him." I ignore the twinge of annoyance that threatens to spill over, at finding out Billy knows and force a smile. I trust Billy's judgement, so this guy's probably ok.

"What information does this guy have?" I ask leaning forward very interested in what this ex-government worker has to share.

"Well apparently they do sleep," Oliver says as I look at him shocked. "I know right, who knew? Well he says it's not quite sleep; it's like a trance they go into. Once they're in it they can't come out for a few hours so they have to make sure they are totally safe when they do it. They can go for days without rest and sleep but they become groggy and because of that they become more dangerous and unpredictable. Apparently they avoid doing that because they don't like the feeling of not having total control of themselves. Also light is not only blinding to them but if applied directly and the wattage is strong enough it can cause them pain. That's why they're so strict about lights when they're in rooms with us. It's all about them being in control. If they can't see us properly they can't control us. Marcus said that he had seen some Fangs with burns on their faces. He thinks that someone did it trying to protect themselves."

"We can hurt them?" I gasp.

"I don't know for sure but I want to find out. Having any sort of defence is an advantage."

"Do you remember what Henry said at graduation? He said that there were not very many paintings of him. Do you think that he only has paintings because of the flash?" I ask, frowning, as I put the little pieces together.

"I suppose so. That's a good point. I will bring it up at the next meeting," he says smiling. "The best thing that we found out for sure is that a Fanged can't enter a human's homeland without permission. They must be invited."

"Really all of their land?" I ask running my hand through my hair. He nods.

"That is why the towers are in the sky. They're not technically stepping foot on a humans land so they are able to keep watch on us. So if they're brought down…"

"Then they can't watch us all the time," I breathe.

"Exactly. Also, as long as you're at home you will always be safe," he says. I can't help the smile that spreads on my face at this news.

"Does that count for the farm land as well? They are owned by people," I ask. He shakes his head.

"Not all of it no, more home lands, where we live," he says. I nod, looking back down at my now cold tea.

"I want you to take me," I say after a little while. I look up at him, he's staring at me, shock plastered across his face.

"Wh-what?"

"To the next meeting," I add hurriedly.

"Oh right," he says letting out a little breath, "I don't know if..."

"Oliver Hunter you will take me to the next meeting or I will just have to follow you," I say crossly, prodding his chest.

"Ouch, okay," he says rubbing where I prodded him. "I will just need to say to everyone that I want to bring you. I don't want to upset anyone." I stare at him. He returns the stare with a pleading look. "Please Chloe, just one more day. Let me speak to everyone."

"Fine, just know that no matter what they say I will come anyway," I say crossing my arms; he chuckles.

"I bet you will," he says with a laugh. I shove him.

"You are a jerk you know? You should never have kept all of this from me. I'm your..."

"Wife?" he asks with a little smile that falls off his face as I narrow my eyes at him, still not in the mood for joking.

"Friend," I glare at him.

"I know, I was kidding. I really didn't want to keep it from you Chloe I just thought it was for the best but I was wrong. I'm really sorry."

"I know I'm just mad that I'm the last to know, well except from David and Mary I suppose." Oliver looks away guiltily. My mouth hangs open as my still simmering anger flares up striking again. "Them too?" I shout. Oliver hunches his shoulders like a dog that's being yelled at.

"David has been in on it from the lambing. He told Mary. She's been to a few meetings."

"What?" I rage.

"Chloe…"

Chapter 21

I can't believe him!

"For god sake Oliver, how could you not have told me especially after Mary, of all people, turned up at one of your little meetings?" I say, harshly, feeling beyond angry. He frowns.

"She's actually very smart, she's doing a lot of research," he says defensively. I grind my teeth.

"So have I for the last two months. Wasting my time apparently!"

"Come on Chloe," he says as I turn away from him, hanging my legs over the side of the bed. He tries to reach for me but I shrug him off.

"No Ollie, you knew I was in that damn library everyday and you never said a word," I say. My voice is filled with the hurt I'm feeling. I stand up as my lip starts to tremble.

Damn, I'm going to cry.

"Wait. Please," he says taking hold of my arm, I still and sigh.

"What?" I say my voice quite; he turns me around to face him. He crawls towards me on his knees despite my standing up and him kneeling on the bed he's still a head taller than me.

"Please don't be mad. I know I have been a dick. I'm sorry. You have no idea how sorry I am. I thought if you went to the library every day then you wouldn't be suspected if something went bad," he says pleadingly. He's just looking out for me, I think, but it makes me angrier.

"I'm not a child Oliver. I can keep secrets. I can be discreet. What do you think would happen to me if you got taken away? They would never believe I was not involved," I say. He stares at me before dropping his eyes sadly.

"I know. I just didn't know how to tell you. I knew you were going to be mad no matter when I told you," he says. I scoff loudly.

"I'm not mad Ollie, I'm sad." As if to prove a point my voice quivers. "I hate that you never told me." He frowns like my words are uncomfortable to hear.

"I'm telling you now," he says pathetically.

"Would you have though, if I hadn't found out?" I ask looking into his green eyes; they change from sorry to truthful in a flash.

"Yes. I would have. I was going to tell you today. That's why I was so quiet. I didn't know how to tell you," he says. I plunk back down on the bed feeling exhausted. He watches me.

"Tell me the plan," I say shortly. He nods letting go of me knowing I'm not going to leave now.

"Horses," he says. I stare at him unsure that I actually heard what he said. It's enough to shock the anger out of me when he doesn't say anything else.

"What?"

"Horses," he says with a smirk.

"How are horses going to help fight the Fanged? They are big but they are hardly savage," I say with a sigh. Oliver rolls his eyes.

"You nearly had it. Like you said they are big but they are also strong. Horse power," he says smiling as the pieces click into place in my head.

"The towers?" I whisper. He nods.

"When I found out I was going to be looking after the work horses I wasn't thrilled, I'll be honest," he says. I nod remembering him asking what he was going to do with a bunch of horses when he was assigned them on the bus

214

here. I smile. He looks more cheerful now I'm no longer mad. "The horses I look after work the land around here; they can cart tons at a time. I even have a tower in my field for god sake; it's like it was meant to be. Now can you imagine a group of say twelve at one time working in unison? A tower has no chance against my lot."

"Can it really work?" I ask, he nods before turning to me smiling.

"Yeah, I've done test runs. I have one horse, Magnus, he's a monster. He has uprooted a tree on his own. So it will work just fine," he says. I stare at him in shock. I feel my face light up as excitement rushes through me.

"And Billy? He knows about the idea?" I ask feeling jealous and trying to hide it. I must do a good job because he smiles widely.

"Yeah, he knows. In fact, he encourages it. He has shown me all the right equipment to use and which of my horses we should use. We have the people and they are all up for it," he says. I run my hands through my hair feeling a little overwhelmed.

"How many people?"

"There are eleven so far. We're keeping it small until we find out people's reactions to the tower coming down, then we might reach out to others."

"Is this actually happening?" I ask, Oliver smiles. I feel myself smiling with him for the first time in what feels like forever.

"Yeah it is. I wish I had told you earlier to see you smile like that," he says. I feel my smile slowly slip from my face at the change and intensity of his gaze. I feel like I haven't seen him for an age. Now, as I look at him I notice the difference in him. It's distracting.

He's still pale but his cheeks have a constant red tinge to them from the constant exposure to the wind and rain. He has a few more freckles than before and his already wild red hair is longer and shaggier. I smile as I move it out of his eyes. He blinks and swallows loudly.

"You need a haircut," I say. He hums in agreement as I tuck it behind his ear. He turns his head pressing his lips to my wrist and his eyes meet mine.

"Would you do it?" he asks, my hand freezing in his hair.

"I've never cut someone's hair in my life. Are you sure?" I ask with a chuckle. He nods his soft lips caressing my wrist.

"Practice makes perfect," he says.

"I don't know. I don't want to make a mess of it," I say. He smiles as he looks at me.

"You won't, I trust you not to make me too hideous. Plus I don't think it can get much worse than it is just now," he says, tugging on it a bit.

"I like it." He looks at me doubtfully making me chuckle. "Ok, well maybe a little shorter wouldn't hurt, but I still think you should just go to the barber," I say and he arches an eyebrow.

"Nope. They cost money. Come on it'll be fun."

"You won't be saying that when I have made you bald," I say. He kisses the palm of my hand sending shivers up my arm, taking me completely by surprise.

"Hair grows," he says before he bounces off the bed and out of the room.

"Hey you still need to tell me what's happening."

"I have," he calls from the bathroom. I hear water running from the bathroom and frown at the doorway.

"I thought you would have done something already," I say and he's silent. He comes back into the room with a pair of scissors a towel and his hair dripping wet.

"We've had a lot to sort out, it has been nothing but talking so far but we're starting to move. We'll get there. A revolution takes a while to get off of the ground," he says with a smile. He holds out the scissors for me, throwing the towel over the back of the little chair by the dresser. I stare at him as he reaches for the hem of his t-shirt, pulling it over his head. I don't look away as he does. To be honest

216

I really don't want to. I recall him from our trip to the lake all pale and muscled but now... wow! These two months have been kind to him, I think, gawking at his torso as he throws his t-shirt onto the bed. I hear him chuckle a little as my eyes travel lazily up his body to his face then finally his eyes. He gives me a cocky knowing smile. I'm too impressed to be embarrassed, so I just give him a little smile and shrug. He sits down smiling and brushes his hair; I step up behind him watching him in the mirror. He meets my eyes in the mirror and smiles.

"Are you sure you want me to do this?" I ask again.

"Hack away," he says wrapping the towel around his shoulders. I take the comb form him giving him a nervous smile. I comb his hair again pulling it about trying to work out where to start. I recall my mum cutting my hair when I was much younger and she began at the top so I start there. I gather up a little section of hair; our eyes meet in the mirror again.

"Here goes," I say. As I cut he sucks in a loud breath between his teeth and winces.

"Oh god, you're a butcher!" he gasps. I shove his head making him laugh.

"Shut up," I say smiling as I pick up more of his hair.

I work for nearly an hour. He sits quietly while I move around him. He lets me move his head about as I finish off trimming any stray strands that I have missed.

"How is it looking?" he asks startling me as I snip the last few strands of his fringe. His eyes meet mine as I comb it down. I lean back a little to make sure it looks even.

"Ok, I think," I say straightening up as he smiles. I take the towel from his shoulders. I carry it to the open window shaking the hair out. I turn around; Oliver is looking at himself in the mirror ruffling his hair into its normal messy style.

"Not bad. Shorter than I usually have it but it's good." I smile as the wind howls past the window, rattling it.

"Thanks," I say, smiling, as I turn to close the window. I jump when I close the latch as something in the darkness moves in my peripheral vision.

"What is it?" Oliver asks as I squint out of the window.

"I thought I saw someone," I say frowning into the dark. I see Oliver come up behind me looking out as well.

"I don't see anything."

"Must have been a neighbour," I say, as Oliver closes the curtains with a frown.

"No one would be out this late Chloe," he says. I look up at the clock.

"Eleven o'clock, why didn't you say? You have work in the morning," I say. He shrugs.

"You were busy," he says running his hand through his drastically shorter hair drawing more attention to his exposed chest.

"Is it really ok?" I ask my voice a little higher than normal as I desperately fight the urge to ogle at him again.

"Yeah I like it. It's going to stay out of my eyes now," he says. I nod smiling at a little at him guessing my intentions. Oliver does have the most spectacular eyes having them on display is never a bad thing.

"Good. You should get to bed," I say.

"I should," he agrees smiling down at me. Maybe his eyes being on show wasn't such a good idea, I think as he asks, "Are you coming too?" His cheeks redden slightly, my breath catches a little but I mask it well with a fake yawn.

"Sure. I just have to brush my teeth," I say.

"Ok," he says. I make my way through the dark hallway into our little bathroom. I'm quick in the bathroom, as I leave, Oliver passes me with a smile. "Need to do mine too," he says with a smile. I smile back; I jump into the bed lying down heavily. I close my eyes sighing as I sink into the mattress. I feel like a weight has been lifted from me now we're talking again. I feel a tingling all over my body, I smile when I realise it's because of Oliver.

Since he took his shirt off I have been a mess. I smile up at the ceiling closing my eyes and listening to the running water in the bathroom and the creaks and moans of the house as the wind howls outside.

"Chloe."

"What?" I say my voice thick with sleepiness. I feel my whole body go cold, my spine tingling unpleasantly.

"Chloe," the voice says again, my eyes snap open.

"Mum?" I gasp, as an intense almost painful heat rushes through me, nothing like the pleasant heat I was feeling moments ago.

"Chloe," she calls, this time closer. I feel her. I smile feeling myself sit up. "Chloe," the voice is getting further away. I panic.

"Mum!" I scream as I leap out of bed sprinting towards the window.

I have to find her.

I hear a distant crash as I'm pulling the curtains open. I reach for the window latch as I look out of the window. I see myself smiling back at me. I push the window open I smile at myself as I stretch a hand out to myself. I put my foot on the windowsill ready to jump out. Then like an electric shock an arm wrenches me away from the window from the voice and the intense heat. I gasp like I have been submerged in water. I feel myself shaking, I grip Oliver's arm.

"Chloe what are you doing?" Comes a yell from inside the little house. Lillian feels the connection between her and her daughter lessen. She reaches her hand out, Chloe smiles at her as she begins to make her way out the window.

"That's it baby come to mummy," Lillian says, then like a hot iron to the stomach Lillian is thrown back into the darkness as a big arm drags her daughter back into the house. Lillian jumps up and rushes behind the bushes, as she tries to catch her breath. She frowns as she listens to the panicked voice of her daughter's husband.

"Chloe, can you hear me?" Oliver asks loudly, as he turns me to face him, gripping my shoulders tightly, I frown at him.

"Yes Oliver, I can hear you," I huff. He looks at me confusion clear on his face.

"I was yelling your name. You never said a thing. You were climbing out of the window, what the hell was that all about?" he asks, looking towards the open window. His hands tighten on my shoulders as my legs wobble. I stare at him unsure, myself, what the hell just happened.

"It was my mum," I say like it was the obvious answer. His head spins back to me so quick I swear I hear his neck click. I feel my lips begin to tremble. I blink rapidly fighting back the tears that burn my eyes. He rushes to the window to look out and after a few moments I stumble to the bed before I fall down. "She was here," I breathe. Oliver looks down at me his eyes wide and frightened.

Lillian looks back at the house, at the man in the window. She stares at the man with a look of pure loathing as his eyes scan outside flicking over her shadowed figure a few times. A flicker of recognition crosses Lillian's mind. He turns to look back into the house; she can feel the anger spilling from him. She straightens up her face falling when she realises who she is looking at; Oliver Hunter. Little Oliver Hunter, her daughters best friend and all grown up.

She backs up, as she senses his anger and his love for her daughter spilling towards her. The feeling is strong and almost overpowering. This may be harder than she originally thought, she muses as she backs away. She watches from the shadows as he closes the window and with great effort she turns away from the house deciding that she is going to have to rethink her plan.

Oliver yanks the curtains closed before turning to look at me as I tremble on the bed. As he looks at me I feel tears spill from my eyes.

"Chloe it's not possible. She can't be here," he says in a hushed voice like he doesn't believe a word of what he's saying. I shake my head.

"I felt her pull, I-I think I..." I feel my eyes widen at the reality of what had just happened. I had not seen myself outside or in the window. My eyes dart to the window then back to Oliver who is looking at me, scared. "She was here. She was just outside, I saw her," I gasp as I feel myself shudder at the thought of her outside my house. So close after all these years; calling to me. Oliver cups his hands behind his neck as he walks towards me. He kneels down in front of me looking unsure what to do with himself.

"She can't be here," he croaks.

"I saw her, I thought it was me but now..." I say and I sob. "Ollie I felt her. She was here. She was close. She just said my name and I nearly ran out of here. If it weren't for you..." His face scrunches in pain. He pulls my face to his. His lips meet mine desperately.

"Stop," he pleads against my mouth. I sigh against his lips. "I will look after you, I promise. She's not taking you anywhere. You're mine," he says mirroring my words from the lake as his eyes bore into mine my heart squeezes as I nod.

"Promise," I whisper.

"I promise Chloe," he says imploring me to believe him. I nod once bringing my lips back to his, needing him, needing his comfort. Our lips move together mingled with the salt from my tears. Oliver traces my lower lip with his tongue; I gasp wrapping my arms around his neck I pull him closer. He rests his hands on my hips before slowly lowering me back and moving us up the bed. "Chloe we need to talk about this," he mumbles against my lips. I shake my head.

"Not now," I say as one of his hands moves up my sides and our kiss becomes hungrier. When he traces my ribs with his hand I nip his lower lip making him groan.

221

"I'm not the only ticklish one then?" he says. I squirm beneath him; he chuckles before kissing me again. I feel the pleasant tingle begin to creep over my body again after the shock of seeing my mum. I start to move my hand down is bare back when he stops and pulls back. I stare up at him; I'm pleased to see he looks just as undone as I feel. He gives me a little smile before pulling away, taking all the pleasant tingles and heat with him. My hands drop from around him.

"Why are you stopping?" I ask breathlessly. He looks at me from the corner of his eye and he laughs.

"I don't want to," he says. I frown.

"Well why, did I do something wrong?" I ask. He turns and stares down at me.

"No. It's just…"

"I thought we could you know…" I begin. He lowers his head his gaze making the words die in my mouth.

"Trust me Chloe I want to, you have no idea," he says. I frown as he pulls the covers up over us. I reach up kissing him again, he responds but I can tell he's fighting to restrain himself. I pull back frowning at him.

"Then why are you stopping?" I ask. He groans and leans back.

"You're upset. You will regret it in the morning and worse hate me for taking advantage. It can wait. We can wait," he says sounding like it's killing him a little to say it. Despite it being very frustrating, I know he's right.

"Fine," I say huffily.

"You are not making this any easier," he chuckles. I smile up at him.

"Sorry. Thank you," I say. I roll on to my side as he lies down and smiles.

"Anytime," he says. I lean over, kissing him again. He groans after a while and I smile into his lips. "You're killing me here."

"Sorry. Good night Oliver," I say lying back down. He tucks my hair behind my ear.

"Night Chloe."

"Chloe where are you? I'm going to find you."

She will never find me. This place is the best hiding place in the world. No one has ever found me in here before. My heart beats in my chest; I feel it flutter at my wrist as I curl my arms around my knees. I hear her light footsteps getting closer. I hold my breath as they stop outside my hiding place. She's so close that I can hear her breathing. It's dark in here and I know I'm completely hidden. I'm being as quite as a church mouse. I can only hear my tiny breaths and my excited heart beating in my ears. They're the only things that could give me away, not even she could hear those things. It's gone silent. I can't hear her; my hiding spot has no peepholes. She must have moved away but I have to stay hidden. There is a bang from above me. I scream then the light blinds me.

"Ha, I found you!"

"No mummy, that was my bestest hiding place," I say grumpily as I climb out of my daddy's trunk. I cross my arms across my chest frowning angrily at her. Mummy copies me. I make myself crosser. She laughs. "Stop it mummy, it's not funny. How did you find me, did you peek?"

"Chloe Wood, I did not peek," Mummy says looking cross.

"How then?"

"Mummies always find their babies. It's just what we do," she says pulling me into her arms and nuzzling into my neck.

"Stop it mummy," I giggle.

"Chloe," she says. I feel the icy shuddering down my spine. My dream ends as my eyes snap open. I sit up but I don't feel the need to move. I look around seeing Oliver in the darkened room staring at me. His eyes wide and full of worry, I look down to where he has a grip of my wrist anchoring me to the bed. I look back up at him.

"Tell me you heard that," I say desperately, he nods. I sag back down onto the bed.

He lies down next to me wrapping an arm around me. He pulls me against his chest holding me tightly. I don't fight him because the closer he's the further away and the less the pull on me.

"Try to go to sleep. I've got you," he says his lips against my neck. I nod, closing my eyes.

"Thank you," I say quietly as sleep starts to pull me down almost instantly. I hear her again before I finally descend but it's nothing but a distant whisper.

Chapter 22

When Oliver's alarm goes off in the morning we slowly get out of bed, after untangling ourselves from each other. We're both so tired and sluggish that after he has eaten he's running late for the meeting. He's by the door jamming on his boots; I pack him a hurried lunch while making him a coffee to go.

"Don't forget to mention me this morning," I say as I stuff his sandwiches into his bag.

"I won't."

"And don't forget I will come anyway," I say as I rush over to him, coffee and bag in hand. He gives me an exasperated look.

"I know."

"Ok," I hand him his things. He smiles as he slings his bag over his shoulder.

"Thank you. You're a life saver," he says.

"I owed you," I say, with a little smile.

"We will talk about your mum tonight, okay?" he says, looking concerned.

"Sure," I say rubbing my neck. He nods pulling me towards him, with his free arm, kissing me soundly.

"Have a good day," he breathes against my lips. I nod up at him.

"Yeah, um you too," I say. He smiles, giving me a quick peck before bolting out the door. I hear someone wolf whistle as I watch him run down the road. I look over the street where Rose is smiling at me from her open front door clutching her milk bottles. I pick mine up throwing her a rude hand sign. I hear her laughing loudly before I close the door. I rest my back against the cool door looking around the small house unsure what to do with myself for the rest of the day. As the cold air and chilled milk begin to seep into my skin I decide a few more hours in bed will do me no harm. Passing the kitchen I put the milk away. I rush into the bedroom clambering under the covers, it only takes moments before I'm asleep.

I'm awoken a few hours later by a loud rapping on the door. I sit bolt upright in bed panicked, until I realise its daytime and she can't be here. I throw the covers off myself, rushing to the door. I freeze as my hands hover over the locks.

"Who is it?" I ask remembering Oliver's warning not to open the door to strangers. I hear a bored sigh.

"I have a delivery for Chloe Hunter. I'm from the postal office," says the man on the other side of the door. I reach for the handle then realise I'm in my pyjamas. I look around for a jumper. I pull it on and it falls over my head to midway to my knees.

Oliver's, damn it.

I shrug before pulling the door open. The Postman looks at me. Boredom and frustration clear on his face.

"Mrs. Hunter?" he asks. I nod.

"Yes," I say waspishly as he stares at me with an arched eyebrow. He holds out the parcel for me. I snatch it from him not liking how he's looking at me.

"Sign here," he says with a smirk. I snatch his pen and scratch my name into the paper. "Nice socks Mrs. Hunter," he says taking the pen back from me turning, chuckling to himself. I look down at my feet at my one white, one black sock. I slam the door.

"It was wash day," I mutter to myself as I pad into the kitchen with the parcel. I turn it around, smiling when I hear a rumble from within. I notice Michael's handwriting; I sit down, tearing it open as I do. My face breaks into a wide smile as my eyes land on a small tin. I pull it out, opening it quickly. The smell hits me instantly making my mouth water. The tin is full of little rock buns that Millie makes for me when she can. I take one before putting it in the middle of the table. I move the tissue out of the way gasping when I find a small wooden frame containing a picture of a beautiful little dark haired baby. It must be Alice my little niece. She's adorable; she looks just like Millie except she has Michaels blue eyes. I don't know how long I stare at the picture before I drag my eyes away. Hidden under the tissue I find a letter taped to the bottom of the box. I open the envelope, quickly, desperate to read something from home. I rip the envelope open carefully pulling the letter out. I smile at the sight of Michaels writing.

Dear Chloe,

You're welcome; I had to wrestle those rock cakes from the sharp teeth of Adam and Simon. I nearly lost three fingers! I'm not even kidding those two are a force to be reckoned with. Millie says she hopes you enjoy them. I just hope you appreciate them, that's all I'm saying.

Anyway how are you? We haven't heard from either of you since Alice was born, hope that means all is well. I don't have to beat Oliver up, or help you bury a body do I?

Everything here is great, Alice is a little bawler; she's keeping the whole neighbourhood up. I think we might have to move. You should see the looks we're getting. I'm just having to laugh it off like, she's a baby what do you want me to do? People are so irritating.

So Millie wants to know what you and Oliver are doing for Christmas this year. Does he even get time off? You can't just turn off a horse like you can a computer. I suppose I'm lucky, I probably shouldn't bitch. How is he getting on anyway, Oliver I mean? Has he been bitten or kicked yet, I bet that hurts!

How are you holding up? You bored? What're you getting up to? I miss you little sis. Take care of each other. Adam and Simon say, "Hello Auntie Chlo."

Love you,
The Woods.

I put the letter down rummaging in the drawer for the pad of paper. I flick though looking for a clean sheet, grab a pen and begin writing.

Dear all of the Woods,

Thank you. I'm very grateful for the cakes, I'm eating them right now. They are delicious. I may even save one for Ollie.

Michael, if Adam and Simon are anything like you and Joseph then I feel bad for you. You two were a nightmare!

Oliver and I are fine. No you don't have to beat him up and there are no bodies, yet. To be honest I doubt you could beat him up anyway. He's huge now! We have a lot going on here and we're really busy but we'll fill you in when we see you in person. Oliver is enjoying his job; it's coming in handy. He's feeling a lot better and like I said he's even bigger if you can believe that? They have also taught him how to drive a tractor! Nowhere is safe!

I love the picture. Alice is beautiful; she looks just like Millie, thank god! Did Joseph make the frame? It's really nice; it looks like something he would make. I can't wait to meet her. Just tell your neighbours to back off.

I don't know about Christmas, we haven't really spoken about it but I will bring it up. I guess he won't get time off unless he can get cover and no you cannot switch off a horse... as far as I know. Maybe you guys will just have to rough it up here for Christmas? In fact that might just work out perfectly.

I'm ok, I'm bored but I'm finding more things that are interesting me now so they should keep me busy. I hope. I will tell you soon what I'm up to, I promise.

Hello to Adam and Simon, I miss you guys.

I miss you all. Love you.

Chloe and Oliver.

I fold the letter and begin the hunt for an envelope before I realise I can just re-use the one my letter was given in. I scribble Michael's address on it before rushing to get dressed.

The wind and rain are in full force as I step outside. I nearly head back inside but I really want to get the letter off. So pulling my hood up and ducking my head I walk down the little path towards the gate. As I pass the side of our house I notice along the fence line a worn track and some footprints directly opposite our bedroom window. I stare at it for a moment before realising that this must have been where my mum was stood. By the look of the churned up ground she must have been pacing for quite a while. I bend down to examine the soggy ground looking a little closer. I see an imprint of some small flat-soled shoes and frown.

"What the hell are you doing?" Rose's voice comes from behind me making me jump.

"Nothing," I say standing up quickly and wiping my hands on my jeans as she eyes me suspiciously.

"What were you looking at?" she asks looking at the ground over my shoulder. I walk away and she follows after me chuckling.

"Never mind, what do you want?" I ask. She smiles at me.

"Well aren't you just a little ray of sunshine? You still pissed then?" she asks. I stare at her confused.

"What are you talking about?" I ask. Then it dawns on me what she meant. "No I'm not still pissed," I say and she raises her eyebrows like she doesn't believe a word. "Ok, well maybe I am, but don't dare tell me you wouldn't be if you were in my shoes."

"Fair enough, I would be mad but if it's not that, then what is tripping your face?" she asks. I frown at the floor moving further through the village and towards shops.

"Just had a rough night," I say. When she giggles I immediately regret my choice of words.

"Not the good kind of rough, I presume?" she says still giggling. I shove her making her laugh loudly.

"Shut up Rose," I say pinching the bridge of my nose, trying desperately to ignore the stares. A few people who are milling around, look at us with frowns. Rose doesn't seem to notice as she throws her arm over my shoulder smiling widely. I look at her from the corner of my eye.

"Tell Rosie all about it," I shake my head.

"I really don't want to talk about it, not yet," I say.

"Fine, boring," she says with a dramatic sigh. She drops her arm and nudges me. "Are you and the redheaded Adonis ok though?" she asks. I laugh loudly.

"Red headed Adonis?" I giggle. She shrugs looking down at the floor.

"Damien's words not mine. I saw you smooching this morning," she says. I nod a little and she smiles. "Good because if you two can't work things out there is no hope for the rest of us."

"Are you and Damien ok? I heard you shouting after I left," I ask, feeling a little guilty for their argument. She waves me down.

"Oh, we're fine," she says absentmindedly playing with her ring. I'm about to ask if she's ok when she smiles at me. "I saw you slap him."

Oh we're back to Oliver.

"I swear I heard it too," she chuckles. I cover my face in my hands while she laughs and tells me how much she thinks he deserved it. The walk to the postal office takes no time at all with Rose as company. We stop off at the grocery store to pick up the flour that she came out for.

"It's so expensive. I wish we got the wheat fields. I'm sick to death of eggs," she says as she pays the storeowner who gives her a little smile. We walk out into the street. I'm relieved to see that the rain has stopped. I let my hood down as I look around the village square. It's a lovely little area with white painted stone buildings most with thatched roofs or red slate tiles. The chimneys are all smoking and the square itself has a small, but no less beautiful, fountain of a man on his horse. I walk over to it, see coins littering the bottom of the pool and frown.

"Wishes," Rose says.

"What?"

"Damien told me people make a wish on a coin and throw it into the fountain. Load of old rubbish if you ask me." I frown at her before looking at the bottom of the pool again; there must be hundreds of coins in there.

"That's a lot of wishes," I say, I can't help but feel sad. I wonder how many of these wishes wished for freedom, for a way out. I fish around in my coat pocket I pull out a coin, clutch it in my hand and close my eyes. I wish for freedom. I open my eyes as I drop the coin into the fountain. I watch as it falls on top of the pile. I hear a plunk. I look over at Rose who smiles sheepishly.

"A little bit of extra hope can't hurt, right?" she says. I smile at her knowing what she wished for, as I'm sure she knows exactly what I did.

"Right," I say with a smile.

"Let's get back before it starts to rain again," she says linking her arm with mine.

I'm surprised by how close I feel to Rose, she's funny and sweet but I hardly know her. I suppose when you go through something like we have it's hard not to form some sort of bond. I feel bad that I have not made more of an effort with Rose, Mary as well, we talk but we could probably do a bit more together.

We walk through the town arranging to meet the next day. We agree that we should try to get a hold of Mary so she can tell us what she has found out. I was pleased to find out that Rose hadn't been to any of the meetings either but she's going to ask Damien if he can ask for her.

"I don't want to be the only one out of the loop," she says. I nod my head knowing how she feels. "I don't know how well that will go down though. Damien isn't quite as in with them as Oliver is."

"Why not?" I ask frowning at her.

"Oliver is the ideas man; they all look to him apparently. Before he came along all they ever did was talk about what they could do. Planning it but never doing anything. But now with Oliver's ideas and him pushing them to get things done, things are actually happening. Slowly but they are still happening," she says. I stare at the ground as I walk, overwhelmed with what she's saying.

"I can't believe it," I say quietly.

"Believe it Chloe. Oliver might just be the person to get us out of the hell. I wonder why he's doing something now. I mean he wasn't exactly quiet about it all at home, why now?" she says. I frown a little.

"I might have something to do with that."

"What do you mean?"

"I think, among other things, he's doing this for me. We spoke about running away," I say quietly. Rose's eyes widen. "I told him how much I hated this life and that I wanted out. We only talked about it for a minute or so but he looked pretty shocked that I was saying it. He said he wanted to do something since my mother died. Then after with what happened to his brother..." Rose gives me a sad smile.

"That was horrible."

"It was the worst, it changed Oliver. It made him so angry. Even after talking to him about it, that day, I never thought he would go this far." I look up at Rose who is staring at me with wide envious eyes.

"Wow. I knew he loved you but this is some other level shit for him to get mixed up in something this crazy."

"What? He doesn't..." I pause knowing that he does love me as I love him, as friends. "We're friends," I say lamely. Rose smirks.

"Friends don't kiss each other like you two did this morning or look at each other the way you two do. You love him admit it."

"I do but..."

"And he loves you. You have to admit Chloe you guys have changed, any moron with half a brain can see it," she says with a little smile. I look ahead staring at nothing while she continues to smile at me.

232

"Damien's helping too. If what you say is true, he must love you too," I counter. She looks away her smile slipping slightly.

"He says he does. I know he does. He'll never love me quite the way David loves Mary or Oliver loves you but I'm ok with that. He's great and he's trying. I know it's hard for him," she says but I can hear sadness in her voice.

"He doesn't look like he's suffering," I say. She gives me a little smile.

"It's fine, really. I know, we know how it is and we're working on it. It's hard sometimes like when he talks about how good looking Oliver is or whatever but we're trying," she says. I give her a little smile. "I feel bad for Damien more because he says these things then immediately has to back pedal. Then he feels bad for making me upset. Then I feel bad for getting upset over something that he can't help." She stops as her breathing begins to get more laboured. Despite her turning away from me I see tears in her eyes. She rubs her arm looking frustrated, like she has wanted to get this off her chest for a while.

"He likes girls, but obviously likes guys too, and is stuck with me right? Could you imagine having to spend every day with someone you're not only forced to marry buy you don't find appealing, in the slightest."

"Rose…"

"I mean, he says I'm beautiful. He kisses me, we sleep together but I don't know how he can stand it. I don't know if I would be able to handle it. He never talks about his other relationships, even the girls saying they're not important, but they are. I want to know, I wish he would tell me. I just wonder what will happen if this plan works," she says, her voice becoming more hysterical. Her lower lip starts quivering.

"What do you mean?" I ask, confused.

"If this plan works, Chloe, if we're free and able to do what we want, he'll leave me. I hate that I do but I love him. I'm going to lose him," she says as the tears that rimmed her eyes spill over and roll down her red cheeks.

"Rose I'm sure he wouldn't…"

"How do you know? You and Mary are *so* lucky having someone who wants you, who at the first sign of freedom won't leave you and go back to their old life," she says. I stare at her as she angrily wipes her eyes with her sleeve.

"I don't know Rose. I don't think Damien is like that," I say feeling completely useless. She sniffs but her tears continue to fall. "Come on, let's get you home," I say, as people start to stare. I wrap my arm around her waist as we walk towards her house. She cries, quietly, as we walk back. I keep my arm around her trying to comfort her. I really have no idea what to say to her. I don't know what is going to happen if this plan works or even if it will work. As far as I know Damien could leave her, I don't know what he thinks. Then again Oliver could leave me too for all I know. The thought isn't a pleasant one but also not that unlikely. He's under no real obligation to stay with me. I look back at Rose who is wiping her eyes as she reaches her house. Suddenly I can sympathize with her. I would be crushed if Oliver left me. She opens the door slowly peering in before letting me in. I head into the kitchen where Damien is stood in a white apron looking very domesticated. He turns smiling when he notices me.

"Hey you two, how…?" His smile vanishes as his eyes flicker over my shoulder. He sees Rose is crying. "Rose what's wrong?" he asks, dropping the dough he was kneading. He rushes over from the counter, past me and wraps his arms around her. She breaks down in his arms. He looks at me, over her quivering shoulder, for an explanation. I motion to the front door; he nods and pulls away from her.

"Hey, it's ok you're home now. I'm just going to see Chloe out, ok?" he says looking down at her and wiping her wet cheeks. She nods up at him, her eyes red and puffy. He kisses her nose before sitting her down on the couch. "I'll be right back ok?" he says, handing her a tissue. She nods at him. He unties the apron throwing it onto the kitchen table before he follows me outside. He closes the door, looking at me expectantly.

"She's upset," I say. He nods and crosses his arms.

"I can see that. What's going on?" he asks his tone full of worry.

"She's scared. I think," I say trying to make sense of the whole thing.

"Scared? Of what?" he asks with a frown.

"Everything, including the plan. She's worried about what happens after," I whisper. Damien's eyes widen and his cheeks flush red. "She's terrified that you're going to leave her at the first chance." He looks embarrassed for a moment then his dark eyes become angry. It's so shocking to see Damien angry that I take a step back from him but he doesn't seem to notice.

"Damn woman!" he growls as he clutches his hair, some of the dough that was on his fingers gets stuck in his hair. His eyes turn to me. I just stare back at him unsure what to do or say. Other people's problems are not my strong point.

"I don't know how many times I have to tell her… I'm sorry that you have been dragged into this. She drives me mad sometimes," he says with a little mad chuckle. "I will tell you as you might actually bloody listen that in the end I will not leave her. I swear it." He holds my eyes trying desperately to get his point across. "I do love her she just needs to get it into that abnormally thick skull of hers. I know she doesn't believe me when I say my feelings have changed. I'm still me but I adore her. She has made this whole shitty experience bearable. I will never forget that," he says. I nod, smiling at him, as I see the front door creek open. Rose stands in the doorway her face red and a little puffy but a lot happier than before. Damien just has time to turn before she launches herself at him.

"Ooof!" he groans as he wraps his arms around her.

"I heard everything," she says. He cocks his head to the side narrowing his eyes.

"Eavesdropping were you?" he says. She smiles before nodding.

"Yes," she says. I see him smile.

"Of course you were," he says. I hear the humour in his voice and smile at them.

"I'm going to go," I say quickly as they lean towards each other. They turn to face me in unison, staring at me like they forgot I was there.

"Thank you, Chloe," Rose says. Damien smiles at me.

"You just needed to talk. Or listen," I say. They both smile and nod. They look at each other staring into each other's eyes and Rose bites her lip. "I'm going now," I say feeling a little uncomfortable.

"Sure, oh see you tomorrow right?" Rose says as Damien pulls her into the house.

"Sure, tomorrow," I say with a smile as he grabs her around the middle making her squeal. Their door shuts loudly as Damien kicks it closed. I hear Rose giggle as I walk down their garden path. I make my way across the street pulling out my keys when the front door opens. I jump but smile when Oliver smiles down at me.

"Hey," he says, stepping aside to let me past.

"Hey, I didn't think you would be home," I say pulling off my wet coat and hanging it up.

"The rain kind of put a dampener on things so I finished up early. You're not pleased to see me?" he says with a pout. I roll my eyes.

"Sure, it's a nice surprise," I say.

"Everything ok over there?" he asks, looking out of the window to Damien and Rose's house.

"Yeah they just have a few things to sort out," I say. Oliver nods before walking into the kitchen. That's one of the things I love about Oliver he's never interested in gossip.

"I saw the picture Michael sent," he says looking into the living room where I had left the picture on the side table. I walk over picking it up and look down at my niece.

"Yeah, she's adorable isn't she?"

"For a baby. Nah she's cute, looks like her mum," he says, as he walks over to me, looking down at the picture. I slap his arm as I put the picture back down, and he sits at the table. I nod in agreement as I toe my boots off. "Oh, talking about her mum, I had a cake. They were great."

"Hey, they were for me. How many did you have?" I protest as I kick my boots into the corner. I make my way over to the tin and open it.

"One," he says. I arch my eyebrow at him. "Ok two but what is it they say? What's mine is yours right?"

"Oh, you're playing the 'husband' card now are you?" I ask putting the lid back on the tin. "Fine so the stash of chocolate your mum sent you that you think I don't know about is also mine then?" I say smiling. His eyes widen as I dart around him and run into the bedroom.

"You stay out of my stash!" he yells from behind me as I crash through the bedroom door, over the bed and into the closet. I yank open his chest before he runs through the door. I grab a bar of chocolate and stand up smiling. "Ok Chloe put the bar down and move away from the closet," he says moving slowly into the room holding his hands up. I lift the bar up, his eyes following it. They widen as I rip open the wrapper.

"Oops," I say, my mouth instantly watering as the smell hits me. He takes a step forward and I pull the wrapper down.

"You wouldn't?" he says, his eyes narrowing. I take a big bite my eyes almost closing in pleasure at the taste. He stops his advance, staring at me in horror as I chew.

"Yummy," I say as I swallow the bite.

"Evil," he growls before he rushes at me, grabbing me around the waist. I squeal as he lifts me over his shoulder. I laugh as he throws me down on the bed. I bounce a few times before he tries to pull the rest of the bar from my grip but it just gets mashed between our fingers.

"You mashed it," I moan, barely containing my laughter.

"You mashed it!" he groans, as he looks at the ruined bar squashed in my hand. I lick my fingers and I notice Oliver watching me intently.

"Still tastes good," I say smiling up at him, he shakes his head like he's trying to clear it. He blinks a few times before pulling himself up and wiping his hand on his jeans.

"I'm um, going to um…" He turns to leave but I grab his wrist holding him in place. He turns, staring down at me.

"I need to ask you something," I say remembering Rose's and my conversation from earlier.

"What?" he asks with a frown.

"Why are you doing all of this?" I ask.

"All of what?" he asks looking confused.

"The whole thing. The plan?" I say trying to clarify. He frowns.

"You know why Chloe. I want to be able to live my life as I see fit," he says.

"Is that the only reason?" I ask. He stares at me looking completely confused now.

"We've discussed this, what is going on?" he asks, his frown deepening. I drop his wrist as I sit up feeling embarrassed.

"Nothing," I say before I stand up.

"What is up with you? One minute you're all playful then the next you look sad," he asks, sounding concerned. I pause on my way to the bedroom door feeling a blush creeping up my neck.

"I'm just worried that's all."

"About me?" Oliver asks his voice close. I nod and turn around nearly bumping into him. "Don't be."

"I can't help it," I groan.

"I know."

"I'm stuck here all day and you're working and doing god knows what," I say shrugging making my arms flap at my sides.

"We're being really careful. Anyway you'll see what we're up to at the next meeting," he says.

"You can only be so careful Oliver, I mean if any of you get so much as a cut the Fanged will have you tracked down... sorry what did you say?" I say, my brain finally catching up with the conversation.

Chapter 23

"I got you in," he says smiling, as I stare up at him in shock.

"Shut up," I say making him laugh.

"I will not. Look if you really don't want…"

"No! I want to, I really want to. You really got me in?" I ask as he backs off trying, and failing, to hide his smile. He nods and I do the girliest squeal, I think I've ever done in my whole life, before throwing my arms around his neck.

"Glad you're pleased," he says as his arms wrap around my waist.

"Thank you Ollie. I love you."

"Love you too," he says. We both stiffen before he chuckles a little nervously and I drop my arms from around him. "I promised I would, didn't I?" I nod at him, my eyes still a little wide and shocked.

"So, um what did they say? When you asked," I ask and he grimaces.

"They kind of made some comments about who wears the trousers in this house and I said that we're a team."

"Damn right we are," I say punching his arm, making him chuckle.

"We're going to have to get you into some training. Everyone else is way ahead of you," he says. I frown at him.

"What do you mean training?" I ask, hesitantly, crossing my arms across my chest remembering the training I received on my arrival here.

"Not that kind of training, I mean to strengthen you. You're quite fit but a little weak. You need to work on your muscles. That's easily sorted though."

"Weak?" I say with raised eyebrows. He raises his hands.

"I don't mean anything by it, I just mean ARGH!" he calls out as his knees buckle after I stab a finger at his ribs. I do it again and he falls to the floor a big, giggling mess.

"Who's weak now?" I say triumphantly. He glares up at me still chuckling a little.

"You fight dirty," he breathes. I smile down at him with my hands on my hips.

"I was brought up by men. I know how to look after myself," I say holding out a hand to help him up. He takes it, I grip his hand before twisting his arm behind his back making him groan.

"Damn," he says through his teeth, I smile into his neck. I hear him let out a shaky breath.

"Give in?" I ask. He shakes his head as he smiles at me.

"Never," he says, standing up dragging me with him. I twist away as he tries to grab me. He smiles as he circles me. "So your brothers taught you a few moves did they?" I nod watching him. My heart pounds beneath my chest and I can feel my cheeks flush with excitement. "Is there anything else you're keeping secret from me?" he asks arching his eyebrow at me, making my skin tingle. I swallow hard as my stomach does a little flip at the looks he gives me.

Focus.

"So much," I say giving him a look that I hope is suggestive. He smiles widely.

"Interesting," he says, as he stops pacing around me. I watch as he eyes darken the way that makes my blood rush through my veins. All the playfulness goes out of the window as he grabs me around the waist and crashes into me. His hands thread into my hair as his lips meet mine fiercely making us both groan. I pull away smiling. He stares down at me, breathing heavily.

"I thought we were training?" I say my hands threading in his hair.

"Shut up," he growls and our lips meet hungrily. I back him towards the bed. He falls backward pulling me with him. Our lips don't separate as we move up the bed. I hover over him propped on one elbow. My arm soon tires so I throw my leg over his hips and climb on him making him groan into my mouth.

"Chloe," he sighs into my lips sending shivers down my spine. I stare down at him. He stares back up at me his eyes wide and his breathing heavy. I lift my hand putting my fingers on his cheek. I trace along his cheekbone and down his jaw. My fingers trail over his face, even down his nose. All the while he lies there still, letting me. My fingers ghost over his face exploring where I have looked a million times but never had a reason to touch before now. His jaw is strong and has a light, prickly hair coating it. I smile as it tickles my fingers as they move back towards his cheekbones. His cheekbones are covered in more freckles than it looks like from a distance, from a distance it just looks like a light dusting. I move upwards to his forehead where even at eighteen he has faint but permanent frown lines. I move up to his cropped hair, messy as ever but considerably tidier after his trim. I have always been envious of Oliver's hair colour it's a lovely dark red which matches his tidy eyebrows perfectly. Then there are his eyes the dazzling blue green framed by light almost blonde lashes. For now I ignore them moving down to his mouth that's open slightly and looking very inviting. I trace my thumb over his lower lip and he kisses it. My eyes shoot up to his and the normal blue green is almost swallowed completely by the black of his pupil.

"What are you thinking up there?" he asks his voice a little hoarse. His hands that are on my hips grip me harder as I bite my lip. He doesn't seem embarrassed by my staring so I give him a little shrug.

"I wasn't thinking. I was just admiring the view," I say honestly. A little crease appears between his eyebrows but he chuckles and smiles up at me.

"Like what you see?" he asks his hands running down my thighs until they rest at my knees.

"Yes," I say simply. A flicker of shock crosses his face at my honest answer before he smiles again.

"What were you looking at?" he asks sucking on his lip like he wants to chew on it.

"Everything, your jaw, cheekbones, nose, eyebrows, your lips. You have nice lips," I say meeting his eyes and they crinkle a little as he smiles.

"Do I?" he asks running a finger along them. I nod as he lifts his hand to my face and running his thumb over my lip. I feel myself blush. "So do you. I love your hair and eyes, your nose is cute and it's adorable when you blush," he says making my face heat up further.

"I hate it. You hardly ever blush," I moan. He smiles as he plays with my ponytail.

"You make me blush," he says making me frown.

"Do I?"

"Yeah sometimes. Some things you say, even if they are completely innocent make me blush," he says.

"That is just your filthy mind though," I laugh.

"Maybe, but it still does," he says with a little smile. His fingers are still playing in my hair, I watch him as he does. We're silent for a little while just enjoying being together until Oliver takes a deep breath. "I'm glad you're here," he says quietly his eyes flicking to meet mine again. "I know it's not what you wanted. I know we both didn't plan our lives to go like this to end up here and married but I'm glad it was you," he says looking at his ringed finger then back at me. I sit up a little.

"You chose me remember," I say. He leans up on his elbows keeping his eyes on my face.

"I know. I think I did it for this reason, as well as stopping you doing something stupid. I just didn't know it at the time," he says taking one of my hands as I bite my lip giving him a guilty look. "I knew I needed you in my life I just didn't think I needed you this much. I wouldn't have been able to handle the thought of you with someone else, even Damien. I think even if he out bid Jackson I would have still done it. It just feels right," he says his fingers playing with the ring on my finger. I feel my heart constrict at his words. I smile as my eyes prickle slightly making me look down. It takes all the courage I have to let the words I'm trying to say actually out of my mouth.

"It does," I say honestly. "I never, in a million years, saw this coming. Honestly, I never thought I could be happy with anyone like this. It kind of shocked me," I say playing with a loose thread in his t-shirt. I see him smile in my peripheral vision.

"That makes the two of us. Not an entirely unpleasant outcome though eh?" he says as his finger trails down my neck. I look up at him; he gives me a little smile. I narrow my eyes at him. I lean forward bringing my face and whole body closer to his. He stills under me then, much to my pleasure, he blushes.

"Not unpleasant at all," I say slowly. He practically growls before he kisses me again. I love it when he does that. He grabs me around the waist lifting me to roll us over so he's lying above me kissing me feverishly. He lies between my legs our hips pressed together. I groan as he moves against me causing my whole body to shiver and arch up to him. He pulls back looking down at me his eyes dark and full of lust. I stare up at him, embarrassed by my reaction but a small smile spreads over his face. He lowers his face to my neck trailing kisses down to my collarbone. The sound passes my lips again making him smile against my skin.

"Stop it!" I grumble half-heartedly slapping his shoulder. He looks up at me through his lashes.

"You want me to stop?" he asks with a knowing smirk. I shake my head quickly. "What do you want Chloe?" He moves so he's hovering over me. Our bodies pressed together, his lips a hairs breadth away from mine. "What do you want?" he asks me again as I stare up at him feeling shaky and completely overwhelmed. I stare at him, unblinking. He waits patiently as my mind races trying to catch up with what my body is screaming out for. It always comes back to how good this feels having him against me, how great his lips felt against my skin. I swallow back my fear and I take a deep shaky breath.

"I want…I…" there is a loud frantic knock at the door. Both of our heads snap towards the noise before it sounds again.

Oh come on!

"Damn it!" Oliver hisses as I stare into the hall and giggle.

"We should get it, it sounds urgent." I say begrudgingly making him sigh into my shoulder. He kisses me again and groans as he rolls off me. He swings himself out of bed as I pull myself up padding towards the door after him, feeling lighter than usual. I follow a step or two behind Oliver and the door rattles again. I see Oliver tense.

"I'm coming!" he yells as he reaches for the handle. He unlocks all the locks before pulling the door open angrily. David is stood on the doorstep smiling widely. Having known Oliver for so long he doesn't seem concerned by Oliver's angry scowl. "This better be bloody good David," Oliver says tensely. David just smiles more.

"You're not going to believe what Mary has found!" he says. I see Mary step out from behind him clutching a little book wearing a little smile. Oliver's eyes dart to her then the book all the anger vanishes from his face. He pulls them both into the house marching them into the bedroom without saying a word. They exchange a look of confusion but don't question him as he shuts the door and draws the curtains. I know he doesn't want us to be seen talking together like this and the only window in the bedroom leads to the garden.

"What've you found?" he asks turning to Mary who's looking around the small collection of pictures on my bedside table. She looks at David who nods at her encouragingly. She points to the bed.

"Is it ok if I sit?" she asks. I nod and trying not to blush at the messed up sheets but I catch Oliver grinning and my face reddens anyway.

"Would anyone like a drink?" I ask feeling very hot all of a sudden. David and Mary nod. I leave the room, shooting Oliver a glare, which makes him smile. I quickly make some tea. I re-enter the bedroom where Mary is pointing to a page in her book and Oliver leans in for a closer look. I hand them the cups. Oliver takes his without looking then he looks up at Mary his eyes wide.

"Does that mean what I think that means?" Oliver asks in a hushed voice. Mary looks at him with a little smile.

"I really think so. I found this book hidden inside another, it has to be significant," she says as David smiles at her. Oliver puts his cup down. I notice his hand is trembling as I try to get a look at the book.

"Mary if this is real... if this is true..." Oliver gets up gripping his hair. He begins pacing the room and I frown at him. All of our eyes follow him; he looks like he could explode.

"It means we can fight back," she says my eyes widen as I turn to stare at her.

"It means we actually have a chance," David says. Oliver stops pacing and looks at me. The smile that graces his face is the most glorious I have ever seen.

"What is it? What's happened, what are you going on about?" I ask feeling excited for some unknown reason. He walks over to me taking my head in his hands and kissing me. I stare at him wide eyed as he pulls away. I feel my face heat again as I see David and Mary exchange a smile. Oliver takes my hand and pulls me towards the bed. As he sits me down he hands me the book.

"Look," he says, his voice shaky with emotion, I look up at him. He nods at me. "Just look," he says. I look down at the book. It's old, with yellowed pages. I can smell the mustiness of it. The writing on the pages is like nothing I have ever seen before. I scan the pages and look at the many drawings on the page. There is one of a man drinking from the neck of a lady in a long flowing gown. Then on the next page the same lady with her fangs sharp and her face contorted in pain as a bulking man wielding a sword cuts her head from her body. At the bulking mans feet, a pile of heads all contorted and fanged. I look up from the book my eyes wide. They find Oliver's instantly. They are wide and full of hope.

"They can be killed?" I whisper fearing if I speak it aloud it will sound ridiculous. Oliver takes the book from my hands pulling me up into his arms to hug me tightly.

"Only one way to find out," he says his breath against my neck.

"No way Oliver. I'm not letting you do that, its suicide," I protest as Oliver scrubs the plates from dinner.

Mary and David left shortly after Oliver told them his idea and I hit the roof. They made a quick excuse that they were going to try and translate the words in the book. I didn't hear much of what they said as I was too busy staring daggers at Oliver. He managed to calm me down but now as he turns to me drying his hands, his face is soft, trying look reassuring.

"Chloe, come on, it's a good plan," Oliver says, trying and failing, to win me over.

"Yeah a good plan if you want to be killed, or worse, turned. I'm sorry Oliver but there is too much that could go wrong with this. It could get loose. It could bite you or anyone else. Could you imagine?" I say poking holes in his "lets capture one and test the sword theory out" plan. He frowns at me folding his arms as he leans on the counter.

"It won't get to that, we'll plan it carefully. Make sure we have everything worked out. We'll do it in daylight and then if cutting its head off doesn't work we'll just leave it out in the sun. We know that works," he says. I scoff really not buying into it.

"There are too many risks."

"Chloe we need to take these risks if we want to stand any sort of chance of fighting at all. We need to find at least one weakness of theirs that we can use against them. They aren't going to come out in the sun willingly so we need something else. If this is it then we have to take it," he says. I look at him frowning.

"You think you can do it?" I ask. He looks at me, confused.

"Yes."

"You will be able to cut someone's head off? As they plead, scream and beg you to stop. You would be able to do that?" I ask. His face pales a little.

"They're not people," he says in a small voice.

"They were once," I say and his eyes widen a little.

"I know but now they are just... it's not the same. Their heart doesn't beat Chloe, there's no life in them. I know they will fight maybe even beg but that doesn't stop them when they eat our elderly or infertile does it?" He pauses, his eyes burning into mine. "Or when they chase them down like prey or drink from them, keeping them alive for god knows how long," he says, his face angry now and I stare at him.

I hate it when he's right.

He must see my resolve crumble and he comes over and sits beside me and takes my hand.

"I know it's going to be horrible but this is war Chloe, it's not going to be pretty. I promise that I will try and make it fast so they don't suffer. I don't want to be like them. I don't want to see people suffer unnecessarily. That's why we're doing this to stop suffering for the living."

"Fine, I want to help though," I say. His smile falls from his face. "If you're going to do it then so am I," I say finally. He sighs as his head falls onto our linked hands.

He's silent for a moment then he sighs dramatically and looks up at me.

"Fine! Maybe you do wear the trousers in this house," he mumbles as he gets up and heads back to the sink looking upset. I smile as I pick up the dishtowel and start drying.

"Just remember that," I say. He shoots me a dangerous look making me chuckle.

"Oh, one last flaw in your plan," I say looking up at him. He turns to me frowning.

"I haven't told everyone yet Chloe but what is it?"

"Where are you going to get a sword? There aren't many of them lying about," I say. He stares at the wall for a moment.

"I will need to speak to Billy about that one. But there are other ways until we work that out," he says his eyes traveling out of the kitchen window into the rainy garden. My gaze follows his. My eyes widen when they land on the pile of firewood in the little hut and sticking out of one of the logs; an axe.

Oh god.

Later that night as we lay in bed Oliver is quiet and when he starts to fidget, I roll over. My eyes meet his and he gives me a little smile.

"Sorry."

"What is it?" I ask. He shrugs a little.

"I'm just worrying about you."

"Why?"

"This is going to be tough. I'm still going to have to go to work every day. I just worry about you being alone."

"I'll be ok. Like you say I should probably do some training or something to get strong and I have Rose or Mary for company," I say. He gives me a skeptical look.

"You don't talk to them that much," he says.

"I'll have you know that I plan on meeting them tomorrow after the meeting. Also, I never spent time with them before because I thought I was doing some useful research," I say. He looks away embarrassed.

"Yeah, I'm sorry about that."

"It's ok. I get why you didn't say anything. You thought you were doing me a favour. Just don't do it again," I say.

"I won't," he says smiling before he yawns. I pull the covers up, feeling a little chilly. "Are you cold?"

"Yeah a bit," I say as my teeth start to chatter. I feel coldness sweep over me as a sharp tingling shoots down my spine followed by a familiar burning, making me gasp.

"Chloe, you ok? Is it her?" Oliver asks. I clench my teeth together gasping when he pulls me towards his chest. He holds me tightly as I try to catch my breath.

"I don't know," I say in a shaky voice. As I tremble in his arms he caresses my face making me focus on him. I feel the heat slowly seeping out of me, leaving me the heat of Oliver's body, I sigh into his chest as I relax.

"Why is she here?" he asks, his voice tight, as he looks over my shoulder towards the window.

"I don't know," I say as his arm tightens around me.

"What're we going to do when it gets dark earlier in the day? Do you think she'll come around when I'm still at work?" he asks, sounding frightened by the idea. I shrug, unable to voice how awful that thought is.

"I don't know. It'll be too risky. She could be seen. Maybe I can come with you, to work. When I'm with you I don't feel the pull," I say. His breath catches a little against my neck.

"Really?" he asks, sounding surprised. I nod.

"I know it's happening but it's like, when you're here, you shield me from it. You keep me from going to her," I say. He hums thoughtfully as I turn in his arms to face him.

"Weird," he mutters as I bury my head in his shoulder. After a while I feel myself relax. I look around the dark room.

"I think she's gone." I say. Oliver loosens his hold on me slightly. When nothing happens I let out a relieved breath as I flop onto my back, feeling exhausted.

"Try and get some sleep Chloe, you look beat," he says. I nod in agreement as I close my eyes.

"Do we still have a meeting tomorrow?" I ask. I feel him turn onto his side. I peek through my lashes at him. He's looking down at me with his eyebrow arched.

"There is one, yes. Early in the morning."

"Ok what time?" I ask. He frowns a little.

"Will you be up for it? I mean after tonight." I narrow my eyes at him.

"I'm going," I say simply. He sighs loudly.

"Fine, it's at half five in the morning, before I start work. It should be interesting, they're a weird bunch," he says. I chew on my lip.

"They're going to hate me, aren't they?" I ask, he frowns shaking his head.

"Not if they know what is good for them they won't. You will be fine. Just don't let them intimidate you," he says smoothing his thumb over my cheek.

"I'll try," I say. He leans down pressing his lips lightly on mine, sparking the memory of earlier. I lean into him pressing my lip to his harder. He smiles against my lips before he pulls back.

"Try and get some sleep," he says, his eyes roaming over my face. I nod feeling a little disgruntled. I turn around as he wraps his arm around me, drawing me into his body. "Goodnight Chloe," he whispers against my hair.

Lillian is leaning against the tree outside her daughter's house, feeling completely exhausted when she hears a low chuckle. She spins around in a crouch her teeth snarling and eyes wide.

"Calm my love," Henry says with a smile as he approaches her slowly. Lillian sighs as she straightens up, frowning.

251

"What are you doing here?" she snaps as Henry continues to move towards her slowly.

"I came to see how you were doing in your bid to get back your daughter. I see it has not gone well," he says with a smug smile. Lillian clenches her teeth as she looks at his lips. Her eyes flicker up to his dark eyes before she looks away turning back to face the little house.

"She's in love. She doesn't know it yet but when he is around her she is unreachable," Lillian says angrily.

"Ah, yes I did notice their connection at the graduation. Such a shame," Henry says as he stops directly behind her. Lillian turns around with a frown.

"Why didn't you tell me? It would have been a useful piece of information," Lillian says between her teeth.

"Firstly, you left without alerting me," Henry says in a level tone while raising his eyebrows. "Secondly, I am as surprised as you are. I thought her resentment would have won out. I hoped she would be as stubborn as you my dear but apparently she is more like her father. You never felt how she felt as the boy bought her. She was so angry and sad. As was I because I think if that little boy had won her, I would have got the two of them, her and her partner."

"You wanted them both?" Lillian asks sounding surprised. Henry gives a noncommittal shrug. "You don't seem very sympathetic to my pain," Lillian scoffs. Henry places his hand on her cheek tenderly.

"When my mate is concerned I am always sympathetic. I think we were mislead when it came to our young lovers. I will see to it that this deception does not go unpunished," he says his tone gentle and deadly.

"What do you mean?" Lillian asks with a frown.

"You will see my sweet, you will see," he says, before kissing her lightly on the cheek.

Chapter 24

"So this is where you work?" I ask as Oliver and I walk hand in hand towards a large farm with a big red barn in the middle of it.

"This is where I work," he confirms as he opens a set of double gates allowing me to walk in before closing them behind us. I wait for him as he locks the gate. He holds out his hand for me as he approaches, I smile before taking it without hesitation.

"It is huge," I say looking around the open space. He nods as he looks around.

"It is, it's really peaceful here. It reminds me of the lake," he says with a smile. I look up at him grinning. "The farm is split into six different yards. We have everything from sports horses, ponies then my lot, the workhorses. Those who work for the Fanged, the high earners mainly own the sports horses. They are pets or racehorses; it's where all the money is. My lot are useful though," he says with a hint of affection. I grin up at him. "What?" he asks noticing my smile; I shake my head looking towards the big red barn we're walking towards.

"Nothing."

"No, what is it?" he asks giving my hand a squeeze.

"I just never saw you as an animal lover," I say. His eyebrows shoot up as he chuckles.

"I challenge you not to fall in love with this lot," he says. As we reach the big barn I hear a series of loud echoing bangs from inside. He smiles at me noticing my hesitation.

"What's that?" I ask my voice sounding nervous. He kicks the floor bolt open with a practiced move.

"They're hungry," he says. He shoves the doors open and the banging gets louder. The banging is combined with some whinnying and rumbling. I see some of the horses' heads over their doors looking at Oliver as he walks into the barn. There are around six horses either side of the long barn. I see the nearest doors rattling as the horses kick them with their front feet.

"Do they do this every morning?" I ask as the banging rings in my ears. He begins to throw big bowls into each of the stables.

"Every morning," Oliver confirms. He throws one bowl over nearly hitting the horse on the head.

"Look out," I say he turns to me rolling his eyes.

"Don't worry about him he's tougher than he looks," he says moving further down the yard throwing the last few bowls into the stables silencing the horses. The yard is now filled with the munching noises of the horses. Oliver looks over the stable door of the last horse. "Come and watch this," he says as I slowly make my way towards him not wanting to startle any of them. He holds out his hand noticing my hesitancy. He pulls me towards the stable door. The horse, a big black and white, is eating. It's taking big mouthfuls of its breakfast. I stare at him wondering what he wants me to see.

"What am I looking at?" I ask, sounding confused.

"Watch her, it's amazing how she eats. Watch her lips they are like fingers sifting through the food picking out the bits she likes best. They can feel even the tiniest bit of grain. One of them, Roman, leaves all the green bits in his bowl they are dried peas. He hates them." I frown looking down at the horse watching her for a while. It is pretty funny watching her snuffle through the food picking out the little nuts and munching on them. Oliver straightens up and I look away from her.

"Come on we should get a move on or we'll be late," he says. I almost jump as a big dirty nose presses to the side of my face as the horse snuffles around my hair and neck.

Victoria Nock

"What do I do?" I squeak, making Oliver chuckle.

"Pet her, she's nice," he says. I slowly move away from the big pink nose, which is covered in bits of food. I realise it must be all over my face but I will deal with that in a moment.

"Hello... um horse," I say as I raise my hand to its big black and white face.

"Her name's Emily," Oliver whispers in my ear. I frown keeping my eyes on the horse.

"That's a person's name," I say. The horse stares back at me, I look into its big brown eyes. I notice long, surprisingly pretty eyelashes and I smile at her. "It suits you," I say to the horse feeling a little foolish. The horse blinks at me and makes a little rumbling noise. I snatch back my hand and jump back into Oliver who chuckles.

"She likes you," Oliver says chuckling.

"I thought she was growling," I say feeling my heart race. Oliver laughs.

"They don't growl," he says with a smile. I smile feeling a little foolish.

Oh that's embarrassing.

"Can I pet her?"

"Sure. Emily is a good judge of character," he smiles as I carefully run my hand down her nose.

"Is she now?" I scoff. Oliver just nods.

"She bit that creep Norman. You remember him, the one who took you to that place?" he hisses.

"Vividly."

"Well he came in here one day all pompous and swaggering and she practically picked him up and threw him across the yard. It was hilarious," he says proudly patting her on the neck. I stare at him wide eyed.

"Good girl," I say. I pet her slightly less hesitantly.

"Come on let's go we have to make it to the next farm. They won't be happy if we're late," he says.

I follow after him, walking out, as he closes the barn doors again. We head across a big open field attached to

255

the farm. I look up at the tower; I feel a tingle of fear running through me.

"Are you sure that the towers are unoccupied?" I ask.

"Yeah, well we're pretty sure. I mean we haven't been caught walking across here yet so I'm assuming that Marcus is right."

"You trust him that much?" I ask doubt clear on my voice. He looks down at me, I see a flicker of worry but he just smiles.

"We need to trust some people. I see the hate he has towards them. That's hard to fake, especially with the amount enthusiasm that he shows," he says.

"I trust you," I say looking back to the tower. Oliver pulls me to a stop turning me towards him.

"Do you mean that?" he asks. I frown up at him.

"Of course I do. I have no reason not to," I say. He cups my face with one of his hands. I hear my breath catch. It becomes hard to look directly at him as my face heats up in his hand. He leans down pressing a light kiss on my lips before pulling away a little.

"I won't let anything happen to you."

"I know," I breathe. He takes my hand and straightens up.

"You've got a little something..." He wipes my cheek with his sleeve. I feel myself blush remembering the horse feed smudge on my face.

"I forgot about that."

"That's better," he says, lowering his hand, taking mine again. I give him a grateful smile as we walk toward the tree line along the field. He helps me over a crumbling stone wall then pushes through the thick trees and shrubs while I follow after him. I duck under a branch he's holding back for me. I'm glad when we finally get to a clearing. In the middle of it is a cute little stone house. In my eagerness to get out of the thick trees I trip on a tree root. I fall heavily on my hands with a groan. Oliver rushes towards me helping me up.

"Are you ok? Are you bleeding?" he asks, I shake my head feeling embarrassed. I quickly check over my hands and knees.

"No I'm fine," I say as I dust myself off. Oliver holds my arm pulling me to a stop.

"You sure you're ok?" he asks looking concerned.

"I'm ok," I say. He smiles giving my arm a squeeze.

"Just remember when we get in there I have your back so don't worry. I want you here, so do Damien, Mary and David so just relax."

"I'm fine. Come on or we'll be late," I say. I shove myself through the last of the bushes waiting for Oliver on the other side.

The clearing is small. The little house that sits at the edge is old and looks like it's crumbling but still completely adorable. I look up at Oliver as he steps up beside me. "Whose house is this?" I ask as I hear the rumbling of many voices coming from inside the small building.

"It's Marcus and Harriet's house."

"It's amazing," I say looking around the little clearing. It reminds me of the little cottage in my snow globe.

"Try telling them that," he says as he takes my hand. He leads me towards the front door which flies open as we approach.

"Ah, here he is!" says a tall thin man in the doorway. He has mousey blonde hair and a crooked smile. He looks down at me from the doorway. "And he has brought the little lady," he adds grinning at me. I scowl at him before I push past him into the house. I pull up short when I'm met by a room full of ten or so people who all look up at me.

"Hey Chloe," Damien says cheerfully waving. David and Mary smile at me from around a little table, which is covered in open books and paper.

"So this you are what all the fuss was about the other day?" says a short dark-haired woman from a small

257

wooden chair. I open my mouth to say something when I feel a hand on my back.

"Everyone this is Chloe. Chloe this is everyone," Oliver says. I wave awkwardly into the room. "You know those three," he points to Damien, David and Mary. I smile at them. "You know Billy and this is his wife Gillian." He points to a tall slim woman with short almost buzzed salt and pepper hair, her bright grey eyes sparkle as she smiles at me.

"Call me Gill," she says. I nod as Billy winks at me.

"Those three over there are Trevor," the blonde, "John and Cameron." I nod at them before looking at Oliver.

"Are those the three that tried to kill you?" I ask, he laughs and nods. The three look at each other smiling. The taller, dark haired one Cameron, smiles at me.

"Just a little misunderstanding," he says. I roll my eyes.

"Good thing your man is light on his feet or we'd have had to hide the body." the shorter dark haired one, John says. Oliver shakes his head.

"Anyway, last but not least we have Harriet," the small dark haired woman, "and Marcus," angry looking with buzzed hair, "who have let us use their home for these meetings."

"It made sense," Marcus says shooting me a wary glance.

"Nice to meet you all," I say. Some of them nod and others still look at me warily.

"How do we know we can trust her?" Harriet says from her chair. I stare at her knowing we're not going to get on. Billy groans loudly.

"Oh for god sake!" he nearly yells as he rubs his temples. Gillian pats his knee as he takes a deep breath.

"We've discussed this. If Oliver trusts her then I trust her," Cameron says his hazel eyes darting around the room.

"Doesn't fill me with relief," Harriet says.

"Well it should you insufferable woman," Billy groans.

"William!" Gillian scalds as Harriet gasps. Marcus puffs out his chest about to shout at Billy, no doubt, but he cuts him off.

"I'm sorry Gill but that boy over there," he points at Oliver, "has done more for us sorry lot in the two months he has been here than all of us combined. Give him some credit. If he says the girl is trustworthy then take him at his word. Plus if I'm not mistaken she has something to do with all of this?" Billy asks looking at Oliver. Everyone looks at me I feel myself turning red.

"She does, it was kind of her idea in the first place," Oliver says making me frown.

"It wasn't really," I mutter. The people who still seemed to doubt us look between the two of us smiling. Well all except Harriet and Marcus.

"Fine. You have one chance kid or you and your wife are out. Understand?" Marcus asks. I look at Oliver who nods.

"I wouldn't do this without her anyway," he says. I smile when I hear a little "Aww" from the table where Damien, David and Mary are sat. I see David rolling his eyes at Mary.

"Now can we get on with it, we're running out of time and I have a job to get to," Billy says. Everyone moves to the corner of the room around David and Mary's table.

"What have you found sweetheart?" Gillian asks Mary who looks up at her then around the others.

"I think I may have found a way to kill them. The Fanged I mean," she says. The room falls silent while people look at each other. Their eyes are wide, mouths gaping as they look at each other in disbelief.

"How?"

"Are you sure?"

"How do we do it?" Billy asks. Mary frowns a little.

"I'm not one hundred percent but I'm pretty sure. We would need to test it though just to make sure." She pauses looking a little worried. "We have to sever the neck. In the book I found it looks like the only way to kill them. It's possibly one of their weaknesses," she says. I stare at her still in awe of what she has found. The room is silent for a moment, while the others absorb this new

"How do you know?" Gillian asks.

"Well, like I said, I don't know for sure but it says, here," she points to the pages of the book in front of her, "something about the point of change. Something like because it's where they're changed they're most venerable there." She looks around us all and as she takes in a few confused faces she goes on. "Ok, for example, imagine a window. Tough to break with your hands but with a weapon or if you hit it in the right spot it will shatter."

"They will shatter?" Harriet scoffs. Mary shakes her head looking frustrated. I see a wave of annoyance wash over her.

"No I just meant… never mind. I just mean everything has a weakness and this may be theirs," she says. I look at Oliver who is chewing his lips nervously. Billy lets out a low whistle as he sits back.

"Well damn girl," he says. Mary closes the book looking at David who takes her hand smiling at her proudly. The room is silent for a moment before a little alarm goes off and John looks down at his watch.

"Next meeting we'll discuss what we're going to do with this information," John says looking up at everyone, they move to get up.

"Everyone start coming up with ideas on how we test this theory and have them ready for next time," Billy says we all nod.

"I'm already working on something," Oliver says giving me a sideways look.

"I'll bet you are," Gillian says smiling at him.

"We'll get into the nitty gritty next time, let's get out of here," Billy says. Oliver nods before heading to the door holding it open for people to pass. I hang back watching as people leave the house looking excited and congratulating

Mary. I join Oliver at the door; he takes my hand as we walk towards the trees. We stay quiet as we make our way through the thick bushes. I'm careful where I step this time not wanting to fall again. I'm desperate to say something about the meeting but Oliver remains silent. When we finally reach the stone wall Oliver jumps over before turning and helping me over. As I jump down he instantly scoops me into his arms and hugs me. He buries his face in my hair and sighs.

"Hey. You ok?" I ask after a silent moment. He nods and I feel him smile against my neck.

"I'm great. Will you stay with me today?" he asks straightening up looking down at me.

"At work?" I ask with a little smile feeling a pang of excitement.

"Yeah, it's only me and the horses so why not?"

"Sure sounds like fun," I say. He smiles a contagious smile setting me down on the ground. He pulls me along towards the barn with a big grin on his face.

Chapter 25

It's fun for me at Oliver's work. I watch him go about his duties while trying my best to stay out of his way. He leads horse after horse out to the fields, the yard becoming quieter with every horse that's removed. I can't help but think how small some of the horses look next to Oliver's tall, wide frame but as they pass me I look up at their high heads in wonder. Oliver returns with a smile after letting out a pale chestnut horse.

"What is it?" I ask as he stops at the last horse, Emily. He grins at me holding out her rope to me.

"You think I'm going to do all of the work?" he asks, making my eyes widen.

"No way Oliver. I wouldn't know how. I couldn't..." Oliver rolls his eyes stroking the horse's nose as I back away.

"I think she's chicken," he says to the horse making me slow to a stop. I scowl before I march towards him holding out my hand for the rope.

"Show me," I say, sounding more confident than I feel. He smiles triumphantly, I swear I see the horse roll its big eyes.

After showing me where the rope clips onto and giving me gloves and a hat that's slightly too big for me he opens the stable door. My hand automatically tightens on the rope expecting the horse to run out as soon as it senses freedom but she just stands there patiently. I relax slightly letting out a breath I hadn't realised I was holding onto.

"You're fine. Just remember you're the boss. It's just like walking a big dog," Oliver says. I nod making the hat slip downwards slightly. "Come on, I don't have all day. I have twelve stalls to clean out," he says as I push the hat back up. I narrow my eyes at him, making him smile widely. I step out of the stable slowly and Emily stays put looking a little hesitant to come out of her box, like she's not quite sure what is going on.

"Come on Emily," I say moving forward pulling the rope slightly. She blinks before taking a small step forward. When she seems sure of what is going on she moves forward a little quicker. I move out of her way as she swings her large body around and straightens up. I walk beside her down the length of the barn; Oliver joins me nodding encouragingly. I smile looking back at the horse that's walking calmly along minding her own business.

"Good girl Emily," I say feeling proud of myself. Oliver chuckles but I ignore him to focus on the job at hand. As we get to the field Oliver opens the gate for me and I walk Emily in. As I'm turning her around I hear a pounding noise from the other end of the field. I look up and see the other eleven horses thundering towards us. I panic but Emily remains still and waits patiently despite her ears turning to the noise of the approaching hooves.

"Ok Chloe, unclip her and back away slowly," Oliver says calmly as I fumble with the clip eventually getting it loose. I move away faster than I should've and trip on a clump of grass. I fall backwards landing hard. I watch with wide eyes as Emily spins around running towards the galloping heard sending clods of dirt flying over my head as I sit on the muddy ground.

That could have gone worse, I think as Oliver, who leapt over the fence helps me up to my feet. I give him a small smile of thanks.

"That wasn't so hard," I joke trying to wipe the mud from my jeans.

"You ok?" he asks, smiling.

"I'm fine," I say, he reaches for the hat straps and I look up at him.

"You look pretty sexy in all this," he says tapping the hat. I roll my eyes as he takes the hat and rope from me. I duck out of the field through the fence and watch as the horses gallop around playing for a while until they disappear over the crest of the hill.

"They're pretty amazing," I say as I watch the last tail vanish over the hill. When I don't get a reply I frown. I look round and notice Oliver isn't there. I see him in the dark barn wheeling a barrow towards a stable. I make my way back to the barn and walk to the stable Oliver is in before leaning on the door.

"I didn't hear you go," I say as he forks up the bedding. He turns giving me a quick smile.

"You looked like you were enjoying yourself," he says turning back to his work, smiling.

"Are they always that energetic?" I ask. He laughs loudly making my smile widen.

"No. They're only showing off," he says. I frown.

"Sure," I scoff, he looks at me smiling.

"Honestly. They did that on my first day. I haven't seen them do it again until now. They may not be your typical show horses but they are show offs," he says.

"They're beautiful," I say. He smiles as he begins leveling off the bed.

"They are," he agrees. I look in the wheelbarrow.

"Smell a bit though," I say. He laughs again.

"You get used to it," he says. I wrinkle my nose.

"I doubt it."

By lunchtime I'm starving, my stomach growls loudly as Oliver pulls out his lunch. As we hadn't foreseen my staying Oliver tries to share half his lunch with me. He hands me half of his sandwich I shake my head.

"No, you have it you have been working all day. I have just been sat here doing nothing," I protest as he tries to give me the sandwich.

"I won't feel right eating when you aren't. Please Chloe just take it," he says his eyes pleading with me.

"No," I cross my arms as my stomach growls treacherously.

"Fine," he says as he puts the sandwich down, crossing his arms in front of himself staring at me.

"What're you doing?" I say as he crosses his legs.

"If you aren't eating then neither am I."

"Oliver…"

"Chloe," he says mimicking my tone. I glare at him he returns it with a little smirk. I unfold my arms and pick up the sandwich making his lips quirk in a triumphant little smile. "See that wasn't ugh…" I jam the sandwich in to his open mouth. He stares at me in disbelief.

"Just eat," I order. He angrily bites the bread glaring at me as he does. After he finishes lunch and after persuading me to eat his apple we head down to a smaller barn where there is an old run down tractor sitting.

"Want a ride?" he asks as he climbs in. I see a little blush creep below his freckles. I smile up at him.

"Not right now," I say staring at the machine apprehensively; I walk around the old pile of metal as he jumps out. "You drive this hunk of junk?" I ask as my eyes dart over it. He gasps looking at me with a horrified look.

"Daisy is not a hunk of junk, she's great," he says patting the rusty wheel arch.

"Daisy?" I chuckle making him blush more.

"Yes Daisy. Now come on I have stock to do," he says brushing over the subject of his naming a tractor. I follow him into a little room.

"Is this your office?" I ask looking around the cluttered room. He nods as he squats down by some filing cabinets.

"Yeah, of sorts," he says.

"Does your office have a name?" I tease. He looks up at me from the filing cabinet with narrowed eyes.

"Shut up and make yourself useful," he says pulling out a folder full of invoices and pulling me back into the barn. He lifts me easily onto a big bale of straw kissing my forehead. "Read out how much of everything I'm supposed to have. I will count what I actually have and then I will call some people and yell down the phone if need be," he says, showing me where to read from and making me laugh.

"Got it boss," I say saluting him as he heads to the back of the barn.

"Enough of your sass, or I'll have to come over there and show you what for," he calls from behind a stack of hay. I'm grateful for the cover as my whole body glows red. I smile as I bite my lip and look down at the folder again.

"Ok it says seven pallets of haylege," I call; he's silent for a moment.

"Ok excellent. Next?"

It takes a while to get through the list. When we're finished he comes back round looking a little dusty.

"All done, we can go home now," he says, looking pleased.

"You're finished?" I ask, sounding as surprised as I feel.

"I'm finished. The horses are being left out for the weekend so I will be working half days. So you will have me all to yourself," he says taking the folder from me, tossing it to the side, while smiling down at me. I smile widely as he leans down to kiss me. We both start when someone clears their throat loudly. Oliver steps back quickly as I pick up the folder and jump from the bale.

"Billy?" Oliver says, sounding confused.

"I'm sorry kid," Billy says. I look up and Oliver is frowning. His back stiffens when Norman rounds the corner; I look away as Norman looks at me obviously surprised by my presence.

"What are you doing here?" Oliver asks sharply. Norman drags his eyes from me to look at Oliver.

"I could ask your wife the same question. Do you not have a dress to mend or something missy?" he asks looking back at me. Oliver steps between him and me.

"What do you want?" Oliver asks, sounding threatening. Norman snickers despite Oliver's dangerous tone.

"I want to borrow a horse."

"No," Oliver says flatly. Norman tuts loudly as he walks further into the yard.

"Now, now let's not be unreasonable. It's for a wedding in town. My son's wedding in fact."

"No," Oliver says again crossing his arms in front of his chest but Norman ignores him and carries on.

"My son lives in the south you see. He and his fiancé are coming here for the wedding, more scenic apparently. The bride has requested one of these nags; she is my future daughter-in-law so I am to make sure it gets done," Norman says walking around locking eyes with me again. I look away from him feeling uncomfortable under the intensity of his stare.

"I said no, and if you look at Chloe like that again I will break your nose," Oliver says, his tone dripping anger. Norman looks away from me when Billy clears his throat. We all look at him.

"Can I speak to Oliver alone for a minute, Norman?" he asks, his tone light. Norman looks between the two of them.

"Fine, but I haven't got all day," he complains as he stomps off. As he passes me I can tell he's making an extra effort to avoid looking at me. Billy pulls Oliver towards me and I stare between them.

"Look kid, I know you hate the guy, we all do but a weddin' can pay pretty well. His son is willingly goin' into this marriage and, from what I hear, he and his wife-to-be are well off. If it goes well there's always a chance you may get more business," Billy says reasonably. I can tell by the look on Oliver's face that he's not convinced.

"Billy I don't care. I have no interest in helping that rat. We're getting out of this hell hole I don't need or want to play nice," he says.

"Oliver, it might be worth…" Oliver looks at me and cuts me off with a glare. I look at Billy, for help, he throws me a quick wink before talking directly to Oliver.

"Kid, just think 'bout this for a moment. What happens if this doesn't work? What happens if this plan of ours goes to shit? Then what?" Billy says. Oliver looks at me, his eyes softer, as I stare up at him. I have never even entertained the idea of this plan not working. Of course I have my doubts and my worries but the thought of it not working was beyond horrible. "You always need to have a plan B. Remember it's the two of you now," Billy says looking at me and putting his hand on my shoulder. "Also you can charge whatever you want. Just think 'bout that," Billy adds with a devious smile. Oliver's mouth twitches before he sighs loudly.

"Fine. Fine!" he says louder. He turns to where Norman is stood in the doorway.

"I knew old Bill would talk some sense into you. It's a month on Sunday. You have a black one I assume?" Oliver nods stiffly as Norman face stretches in a horrible grin. "Good just make sure the old nag is spotless," Norman says. Oliver's jaw clenches but he nods stiffly. Norman leaves looking smug as Billy claps Oliver on the shoulder.

"Good man," he says as Oliver huffs angrily.

"I hate him," he says though clenched teeth.

"He's hard to like," Billy agrees. "Look Oliver I'm glad I'm hear actually, I have things I'd like to go over with you, if that's ok?" he asks. I suddenly feel like I'm not wanted there, I wrap my arms around the folder.

"I'll just um…" I say looking down at the folder as I head towards the office.

"I was meanin' the both of you actually," Billy says sounding apologetic. I stop and turn feeling a little surprised. "You're a team right?" he adds with a wink. I smile meeting Oliver's eyes.

"Yeah we are," Oliver agrees and I nod.

"What's up?" I ask, standing at Oliver's side.

"The others stopped me before I could leave this mornin'. They want to push our plan forward. This new theory has gotten them excited," Billy says. Oliver frowns.

"It's not ready, I haven't even told you my plan yet! We're not ready. No one is prepared," Oliver says. I can't help but nod along in agreement. We are nowhere near ready to go through with the plan. They haven't come up with any finalised ideas on how they are going to make it work.

"I know lad, but with this new information that Mary came 'cross and the fact you said you were working on a plan they're chompin' at the bit."

"We can't. They'll have to wait," Oliver says. I don't miss when his eyes dart to me then away quickly. I know he's reluctant to let me help.

"I said that, but they ain't havin' it. If they don't get somethin' they're gonna fire in there with some half-cocked idea and get us all killed. You have a plan right? Can you make it work?" Billy asks rubbing his neck. I look between them as they stare at each other, I can tell they are having a silent conversation, Oliver's eyes are pleading and Billy's sorrowful.

"When?" I ask, breaking them out of it and they look at me.

"Two weeks," Billy says. I feel my eyebrows shoot up.

"Two weeks? But that's…"

"Hardly any time, I know but we do need to move forwards," Billy says giving me a small smile before turning to Oliver. "Will you be ready? Will your horses be ready?" Oliver frowns.

"How did you know I was going to suggest doing it during the pull?" Oliver asks. Billy just shrugs.

"Because you're smart like that, that's why. Kill two birds with one stone, literally. So will they be ready?" Billy asks again.

"They'll be ready. I will have to work every day with them." He shoots me an apologetic look. I know our

269

weekend together is gone. I can't help but feel a little upset. I take his hand, giving it a squeeze. He turns back to Billy who is looking between us. "What about the group? Will they be ready?" Oliver asks, sounding doubtful.

"They're gonna have to be. Hey kid, it will work, don't worry," Billy says clapping Oliver on the shoulder. Oliver's eyes meet mine and he nods. He turns back to Billy with a sigh.

"It's not me I worry about," he says. I grip his hand tighter as the words nearly knock the air from my lungs. "Ok, let's do it," he says still sounding reluctant. They exchange a meaningful look. I look away knowing it's about me and I feel a little embarrassed.

"Chloe," Billy says softly, I look up and he smiles. "We'll work hard to make sure this goes off without a hitch." I nod unable to speak due to the burning tingle in the back of my throat. Billy nods and pats Oliver's arm again. "Meeting tomorrow?" he asks. Oliver nods. Billy gives us one last smile before he heads out of the barn leaving us in an awkward silence. I look up at Oliver who is staring out of the barn; he's as pale as a sheet. I wait patiently for him to break the silence but after a few tense minutes I realise he isn't going to. I put the folder down on the bale and slowly make my way over to him. I see him tense as I near. I slowly place my hand on his arm. He blinks a few times before he turns his head towards me. His face is unreadable, his eyes look strangely blank and it worries me.

"Oliver?" I say in a whisper as I take his hand. He grips me tightly and I pull him towards me; he comes willingly. I wrap my arms around his middle placing my head against his chest where his heart is beating rapidly. He lets out a deep breath as his arms circle me. "We will be ok."

"If anything happens to you," he croaks.

"Shh, we'll be fine," I say firmly. His lips press into my hair. "It will work. It has to."

"I hope so, Chloe."

Chapter 26

"Will you all pay attention?" Oliver yells over the loud chatter of the small crowd gathered around him. The barn falls silent as everyone turns to us as Oliver glares at all of them murderously. "If you don't pay attention then this is not going to work. I do not want any of my horses getting injures because you didn't pay attention for five bloody minutes," he says trying to reel in his anger.

"What about us getting injured?" Marcus scoffs. I grind my teeth as Oliver takes a deep steadying breath. Marcus and Harriet have been the bane of Oliver's life, and mine, over the last fortnight. Always being complacent or trying to rile Oliver at any chance they could get. As it transpired it was Marcus and Harriet who had gotten everyone fired up about moving the plan forward putting Oliver under all the pressure of having to ready his horses, while everyone relied on him to devise a plan that would work. Oliver had risen to the challenge brilliantly. With me at his side we worked out a plan and I was there to calm him down when he got too stressed.

"I will not say it again," Oliver says through his teeth. I place my hand on his arm. He glances down at me I give my head a little shake. He takes another deep breath letting it out through his nose. "If you can't see the importance of the horses you're not helping," he says calmly.

"I still don't see why we can't just use your tractor," Harriet says. I close my eyes as the room at large sighs in frustration.

"We are! But only for carrying the equipment back," Oliver says in a flat tone. "The horses are being used because the tower is in their field. Their tracks and scent will be all over the field so there shouldn't be too much suspicion. They can tear it down then be let loose. I'm leaving them out the day before to avoid any unnecessary suspicion. Let's face it if this goes south I will be the first one they're going to come after and if they come after me they come after Chloe. I will not allow let any of you endanger her life by not listening," Oliver says. I look around the group trying not to blush. Everyone nods while Marcus and Harriet exchange a look.

"Problem?" I ask staring between them. They look at me in surprise, Harriet with her eyebrows raised.

"I don't like it; I don't trust it and I sure as hell don't like your tone," she says making me scoff. Harriet and I have not got on since day one. She seems to hate everything I do, she'll argue until she's blue in the face that I'm wrong. I have no idea why she dislikes me so much but when I asked Oliver all he said was that they don't trust anyone. Apparently when they lived in Centrum they were sold out by a person they considered a friend. That's how Marcus lost his job and ended up getting sent here. They hate it here and apparently have trouble trusting anyone now. The fact they are even here is a small miracle but Billy thinks that their hunger for payback is stronger than their distrust of others.

"Enough! For god sake," Billy sighs looking tired.

"This is the best plan we have," Damien says as Rose, who was now happily accepted into the group, nods beside him.

"You guys wanted this hurried along and gave nothing but half cocked ideas so just shut the hell up and listen," Cameron says rubbing his temples. Harriet and Marcus exchange another disgruntled look but stay silent.

"Go on Oliver," David says sounding just as strained as we all feel.

"As I was saying some of you will be allocated a horse to catch and tack up. It's simple," he says bringing Emily out of her stable and tying her in the yard. "You put the bridle on first." He does this slowly to show us exactly what to do then backs up to let us see how it sits. I make myself remember the buckles to fasten and nod along with the others. "Next the harness, it goes over their heads like this. Then you will attach the ropes to these loops. Everyone got that?" he asks. We all nod again.

"Will the ropes be strong enough?" Rose asks. Oliver nods smiling. It's fair to say that he has a better tolerance for his friends asking questions.

"Yeah they will and then we can burn them after. Those of you who are getting a horse will be in charge of making the horse move. A simple loud click will do the job, they're well trained," Oliver says. Those of us who have been assigned a horse, nod. It will be Mary, Rose, Damien, David, Billy, Gill, Harriet and I who will be dealing with the horses while the other guys disable the cameras and drive the tractor.

"If this goes accordin' to plan it shouldn't take long for the tower to come down. They're in a sorry state, honestly I think one good kick from one of the horses would bring it down, so it shouldn't take much effort," Billy says. Oliver scoffs and I can't help sympathising with him. This has been nothing but effort to arrange especially on his behalf.

"What about the Fanged? How do we know they won't escape?" Trevor asks.

"They'll be too darn scared. Even if they do try it we'll all be there. Before they get too far they will burn. Our scent will draw them out but they will be reluctant to come out at first because of the sun but their hunger will win out," Marcus says with a sinister grin. I frown at him as his smile grows.

"You sure about that Marcus?" John asks, looking slightly uncomfortable at the look on Marcus's face.

"Positive. I have seen it before. They don't last long in direct sunlight; turn to ash like logs on a fire," he says.

273

"Better hope it's a sunny morning then," Damien says. Everyone looks at him making him flush a little. "Well it has been overcast for the last two weeks. If we need direct sunlight then…"

"They will still burn you stupid boy," Harriet snaps. His face turns red now.

"It'll just be slower," Marcus adds still smiling. The barn falls silent until Mary speaks her voice low and shaking slightly.

"Who… who is going to do it?" she asks looking round at us all. She's the only one who has had the courage to even bring up the thing that has been bothering me and, I'm sure, everybody else for the last fortnight. She looks around the room and when no one speaks her eyes fall to the floor. My eyes dart up to Oliver as he takes a deep breath and he opens his mouth to speak. I look away cringing.

"I'll do it," Billy says gruffly. I look at Oliver whose eyes are wide then back to Billy. Everyone is staring at him in disbelief and he looks around us all.

"I can't have you kids do somethin' like that on a hunch."

"We'll have to do it if it comes to a fight," Damien says a few of us nodding in agreement.

"Sure kid, if it comes to that. If it doesn't work I don't want you kids livin' with that hangin' over your heads," Billy says with a little smile.

"What about you?" I ask knowing how horrible it's going to be but Billy just chuckles.

"Well if it doesn't work I won't have to live with it much longer," he says. I see Gillian cringe at his words. I look at Billy frowning. Surely he cannot be getting farmed any time soon, he looks too young. As if reading my thoughts he smiles at me and winks. I look up at Oliver; he gives me a little shrug.

"Fine," Marcus says as I open my mouth to ask Billy what he means.

"We should all get plenty of sleep tonight. Tomorrow is going to be a long stressful day," Gillian says.

"We won't have much time so everyone go over and over what you're supposed to be doin'. We don't need any slackers," Billy says. We all nod.

"Now get out," Oliver says as he looks up at the clock on the barn wall. Everyone notices the time and that Oliver is in a bad mood. They all learned pretty quickly that he isn't very pleasant when he's in a bad mood.

In his defence he has been under an obscene amount of pressure. With that and the worrying about everything from the plan, to his horses, the others and I, he has been driven nearly mad. He has practically been begging me over the last twelve days to reconsider helping at all. *"No. I don't want to be left at home worrying about you,"* I would say over and over again. I yelled it at him after the one-hundredth time of asking me; he sulked and didn't talk to me for a whole day. I felt bad for making him worry but I was not backing down. I have even started filling my days with exercise. I started running, doing push-ups and sit-ups. One evening when Oliver walked in on me doing sit-ups he just sighed and walked away with a sad expression.

"Chloe you had best get going as well," he says snapping me out of my daze; I look up at him frowning slightly. I was hoping to stay behind and help him get organized for tomorrow but I can tell by the look on his face that he was not in the mood for company, even mine.

"Oh, ok," I say disappointment clear in my voice. I step away from Emily ducking under her head.

"Sorry," he says. I shrug giving him a little smile.

"It's ok, I should be training or something anyway," I say trying to sound like I don't mind. His jaw tightens and I see that he isn't happy.

"Right. I will see you at home then?" he asks.

I nod before I stalk off. I hear him sighing but I don't turn around. I pick up my pace and start jogging along the road. Not far down the track I spot Mary out on the road picking some late brambles, her cover for being out so early. I slow down when I reach her.

"Oh, hi Chloe, I thought you would be helping Oliver," she says lowering her voice.

"He doesn't want my help, he's in a mood," I say. She nods giving me a knowing smile.

"Yeah he did look especially tense this morning," she says sarcastically.

"Understatement," I say quietly.

"He's just worried. About you in particular," she says nudging me.

"I know he is. He just doesn't talk to me. I'm doing everything to show him I'm fine, I will be fine but he's being unreasonable."

"I don't think so," she says as we start to walk back to the village, my eyes widen.

"You don't?"

"No I don't. He's scared you're going to get hurt. What we're doing is stupidly dangerous so it's not that unlikely."

"I know, but I bet David isn't bitching about it though," I say, jumping a little when she laughs loudly.

"Are you kidding me? He's been a nightmare. He just doesn't show his protectiveness quite as much as Oliver does. Oliver has never been very good at hiding his emotions," she says stopping and picking berries from another bush.

"I guess so," I mutter as I help her pick.

"I mean look what he was like in school, for instance. He was always so passionate about how much he hated the Fanged and how shitty he thought our situation was. He's passionate and he cares about everyone. He feels responsible for us because it's his plan, which is really sweet," she says smiling. I stare at her frowning.

How the hell does she know all this? I think. Then I realize that she has been with David for a long time, and

276

whenever Oliver wasn't with me he would've been with the two of them.

Or Rachel Hunt, my teeth grind loudly as I think of the two of them together and I wonder if Mary knew about the two of them. I'm about to ask when she goes on.

"He especially cares about his family and the people he loves," she says shooting me a meaningful look. I look down at the ground when we fall silent.

"So do you think I should stay at home?" I ask, all thoughts of Rachel shoved to the back of my head.

"Absolutely not!" she scoffs. I look back at her totally confused. "Look I get why he's worried, he's scared to lose you or have you hurt and that's admirable. If the tables were turned he would insist on coming with you. I don't see why it's any different. Don't do something that will make him happy just because he says so. That's not you Chloe. He will not thank you when you're angry with him for making you do it. He will just have to get over it," she says firmly. I smile at her.

"Is that what you said to David?" I ask. She laughs as she picks up her basket.

"Yep and I withheld sex until he saw the error of his ways. It didn't take long for him to come around," she giggles. "Try it, it'll work, I guarantee it," she says with a wink. I shake my head smiling at the floor.

"Well I um… we aren't… we haven't…" I mutter. Her eyes widen and I feel my face flush.

"No way!" she says, muffled behind her hand, her eyes wide and staring.

"It's not a big deal," I mutter feeling mortified.

"Well no it isn't but no wonder he's so wound up! Why haven't you? I thought, well the day David and I came around, I thought you were…"

"No," I interrupt, before chewing on my cheek. I remember that day vividly, it was the first day I was ready to move our relationship further. After I had taken in every detail of his face after he kissed me making me melt into the bed. I feel a warmth rush through me as I remember the feel of his body against mine. Then him asking me what I wanted; in that moment I only wanted him. "No we um…"

"Oh god, we interrupted didn't we?" Mary asks sounding apologetic.

"Maybe," I say honestly.

"I'm *so* sorry. No wonder he looked so pissed," she says with a big smile as I chew my lip.

"It's fine. Ever since then everything has been about the plan and we have not had time to do anything, let alone that," I say. She pats my shoulder.

"It'll happen," she says. I shrug; I was starting to doubt if it ever would. "Come on, we had better get home."

We walk quietly back towards our houses. She pauses when she reaches her gate.

"It'll be fine tomorrow. We'll all be fine," she says. I nod giving her a little smile.

"See you tomorrow then," I say as she heads towards her house. I wait at her gate waving as she closes the front door.

I turn my back on our house running in the opposite direction feeling frustrated and like I really don't want to go home just yet. I decide on running through the village. I try and turn off my mind as my feet hit the ground rhythmically. Once I have lapped the village once it starts to rain. I scowl up at the sky as fat, icy droplets fall on my face. I decide to head home not needing to get sick before the big day. Oliver would love that. I slow down as I reach the edge of the street. I see Rose and Mary huddled under my little porch hiding from the rain. When Rose sees me she nudges Mary before walking down my path.

"Where have you been? We have been here for ages," Rose says swinging open my gate.

"I was…" She lifts up her hand cutting me off. I feel my eyes widen a bit. Rose has never been the subtlest of people. I raise my eyebrows at her.

"Never mind. I need to talk to the both of you about tomorrow," she says.

"Shall we just go for a walk?" Mary asks pulling us along.

"But it's raining," I moan. She just ignores me as she pulls me down the road. I reluctantly allow Mary to pull me along as we walk behind Rose back into the village. Despite Rose's eagerness to talk to us she remains silent was we walk along.

"So, what do you want to talk about?" I ask. She slows before she pulls us into the empty little play park and looks around. I look at Mary who shrugs. "There is no one here. It's raining," I sigh.

"Rose what is it?" Mary asks kindly. Rose lets out a long shaky breath.

"I can't help out tomorrow," she says. Both Mary and I frown. She turns around looking back at us she looks so desperately sad.

"What's wrong?" Mary asks, sounding worried. Rose looks between us before her hands rest on her stomach. My eyes fall to her hands. I hear Mary gasp as my hands shoot up to my mouth.

"I'm pregnant," she says, confirming what we both guessed.

"Oh my god," I say through my hands. Mary puts a hand on her shoulder.

"How far along?"

"Six weeks. I just found out this morning. I haven't told Damien," she says. I drop my hands from my face taking a deep breath.

"You have to tell him," I say.

"I will but not tonight. I don't want him to be distracted tomorrow I will tell him after," she promises quickly, as I open my mouth to argue with her. I nod but Mary frowns.

"How are you going to explain that you're not helping?"

279

"I'll fall over and pretend to twist my knee or something. He doesn't want me doing it anyway so he'll be easy to persuade. Just don't tell him, don't let it slip. I don't want him getting hurt because he's not focusing on what he is supposed to be doing," Rose says, sounding desperate.

"We won't say a thing. Just be careful," Mary says. Rose nods letting out a big breath.

"Thank you. It feels so good to tell someone. I have been going mad for the last few hours," she says linking her arms with both Mary's and mine dragging us along back to our houses.

Mary's and my eyes meet, I can tell she's shocked as I feel. I look ahead quickly when Rose stumbles slightly. I see Miss Love marching towards us her nose held high. Her beady eyes narrow at us beneath her umbrella.

"Oh god not his old hag, my day just keeps getting better and better," Rose sighs. Mary and I giggle as Miss Love stops in front of us eyeing our linked arms suspiciously.

"Ladies," she says with a tone that drips sarcasm. I see her eyeballing each of us; her eyes lingering on me for the longest obviously taking in the running gear I'm in. She shakes her head disapprovingly. We all remain silent. I can imagine her feeling nothing but hostility pouring from the three of us as we stare up at her. This fact doesn't seem to bother her. I'm sure that she's little liked in this village by any of the women she has 'instructed'. "I am glad to have caught you three."

"Oh really?" I say disbelievingly. Shocking the others and myself as well, Mary gasps and Rose snorts. Miss Love turns to me her dark eyes narrowed. She breathes in sharply through her pointed nose staring at me like something slimy she wants to get far away from.

"I was just on my way to the postal office to drop off these letters for your husband's but as you are all here I shall not waste my valuable time," she says. She thrusts a letter at each of us with a tight-lipped smile. I look down at mine seeing it's addressed to Oliver.

"What's this?" I ask, Miss Love smiles.

"It is for your husband. Good day ladies," she says, pushing past us, heading down the road.

"What the hell is this all about?" Rose asks, looking at her letter.

"I don't know but I don't like the look of this," Mary says, looking down at the letter in her hand. I nod in agreement as I stuff the letter in my back pocket. We walk home slowly chatting about nothing in particular. As we reach Rose's house she smiles at us as she walks through her gate.

"Good luck tomorrow. Let me know how it goes. I'm really sorry I won't be there."

"It's not like you planned it," Mary says with a little smile.

"We should've been more careful. I can't believe this is happening. I'm so pissed I can't help," she groans as she hugs us both.

"See you tomorrow," I say.

"I'll make a cake," she says, as she lets me go. I stare at her in confusion.

"Cake?" Mary laughs.

"I have to do something so I will make some cake. Everyone likes cake," she calls over her shoulder, as she walks into her house. Mary and I walk; staring at her closed door and Mary starts laughing quietly.

"I don't have the heart to tell her I hate cake," she says. I snort with laughter. We hug before I hop over the fence still chuckling.

Chapter 27

Mary's pregnant! I keep thinking as I approach the door making my smile falter. The very thought makes me feel uneasy. As I enter my house my eyes land on the crib room's door. It's the first time I have looked at the door willingly since we've moved in. I normally actively avoid looking at it. It usually blends in with the wall but now it sticks out like a sore thumb. I walk towards it my hand reaching for the handle before pulling it down slowly. I push open the door staring into the blank room. I try imagining it with some colour on the walls and in the crib a little red headed baby. The shock of my thoughts makes me blink a few times in shock. I grab the door swinging it shut and backing away. I jump and spin around when the front door opens. Oliver walks in looking tired. He spots me and smiles before his face falls.

"What's wrong? You look like you've seen a ghost," he says obviously reading the shocked and probably horrified look on my face. I shake my head sighing.

"It's Rose," I begin then I stop rethinking if I should tell him or not. I mean, Damien won't be getting told until the next day; it's hardly fair if we all know before him.

"Is she ok?" Oliver asks looking alarmed.

"Depends."

"On what?" he asks looking worried.

I have to tell him.

"If you think her being pregnant is a good thing or not?" I say. Oliver's eyes widen.

"Shit," he breathes as his hands scrape through his hair. I nod in agreement. "Does Damien know?" he asks. I shake my head. "Shit. She can't help tomorrow, not if she's..." he says looking unable to say it out loud. Like if he says she's pregnant it will make it real.

"That's why she told us."

"Us?"

"Me and Mary. She's not helping and she isn't going to tell Damien until after either. She doesn't want him to be distracted."

"Damn. Is she ok though?" Oliver asks, his hands in his hair.

"Honestly I don't think it has sunk in yet, she seemed ok."

"Really?" Oliver asks looking puzzled.

"I think she's in shock. It probably won't sink in until she tells Damien. Is the plan still going to work?" I ask. He sighs loudly dropping his arms to his side.

"It will. I'll just have to rethink the layout but it'll still work," he says taking my hand and pulling me towards him. "I'm sorry about earlier, I shouldn't have sent you off like that."

"It's ok," I say but he shakes his head.

"It's not. I shouldn't be mad at you for doing something I suggested. It's good you're doing all your exercise. Just seeing you do it, how determined you are, makes me scared."

"About what?" I say hugging his middle.

"Losing you. There are so many ways you can get hurt or worse. I don't want that," he explains.

"I know but I know it's going to work. You're not the only one that worries you know?" I say. His chest rumbles against my ear as he chuckles.

"I know," he says as he holds me tighter. We stand clinging to each other for a while when Oliver chuckles. "Chloe?" he murmurs.

"Yeah?"

"You kind of reek," he says. He holds me tighter as I try to wriggle away from him feeling embarrassed.

"Let me go!" I yell as I laugh.

"Never!" he says loudly. I try with all my power to wriggle out of his arms and as a last resort I poke his ribs. His arms instantly loosen allowing me to spring free. "Evil!" he gasps trying to catch his breath. I smile.

"I'm going for a shower," I say backing up.

"Probably best," he says pinching his nose; I scowl at him as I close the bathroom door and switch on the shower. As I undress the letter from Miss Love falls out of my back pocket. I pick it up and place it on top of my towel. I smile as I enter the shower.

Payback will be sweet.

After a nice long shower I climb out and wipe the fog from the mirror. I dry my hair with the towel, brush it and tie it up in a loose bun leaving a few strands hanging around my face. I tuck the letter between my towels smiling at myself in the mirror. I open the door and lean against the doorframe.

"Oh Oliver?" I call as the steam billows out of the door behind me.

Ooh nice touch.

I hear him walk towards me. I feel my heart flutter and try not to smile.

"What is it?" he asks his eyes on the floor as he comes around the corner. I watch as his eyes widen and travel slowly up my legs, over my body then to my face. His mouth hangs open as I smile at him.

"I have something for you in this towel," I say pulling at it slightly; his mouth closes. He looks up at my face again and I motion him forward. He almost trips over his feet as he moves forward. I bite my lip trying not to laugh.

"What do you have?" he asks his voice a little hoarse and excited. I pull the towel his eyes falling to my hands as they hold it together.

"You want to see?" I ask with a smile.

"Yes," he answers quickly and without embarrassment. I drop the towel to the floor. He frowns as his eyes lift up to mine looking thoroughly cheated by the other towel that's wrapped around me. I smile as I hold out the letter for him.

"There you go," I say he looks at the letter then back at me like I'm joking; it's the perfect reaction. "Is dinner nearly ready? I'm starving," I say kissing his cheek putting the letter in his hand. He opens his mouth to say something but I press a finger to his lips. "Never tell a girl she "reeks" Hunter. We don't like it." I wink before walking past him and into the bedroom.

"You evil little…" I close the door laughing loudly.

I rejoin him in the kitchen after getting dressed. I smile as he starts serving up some baked potatoes. He sees me coming in and shoots me a narrowed eyed look, making me smile wider.

"What was the letter about?" I ask seeing it sitting on the counter top. He turns around crossing his arms.

"They want you back at the training centre," he says. My eyebrows shoot up.

"Really? That's a surprise. I got the feeling I wasn't liked much there. Why were you sent the letter and not me?" I ask.

"I'm the "husband", that's how it works apparently," he says as I frown.

"Well that's just stupid. When do I have to go?" I ask. He frowns deeply.

"You aren't going. Although after your little striptease I might just have to rethink," he says. I narrow my eyes at him and we stare each other out.

"You wouldn't," I say. I see him trying not to smile. I get up walking towards him pouting a little. "I think you like it when I misbehave." He smiles briefly before he tries to make his face a blank mask again.

"Misbehaving wives are supposed to be punished right?" he asks pulling at my t-shirt lightly. I blush.

"That's what they say," I say trying to sound like I'm unaffected by his words. "What do you have in mind? A week of no going outside or..." He silences me with a hungry kiss. He pulls back leaving me breathless.

"I'll think of something," he says as he hands me my dinner with a smile. We eat in our normal comfortable silence, as Oliver re-organises the horses for the pull tomorrow. He sits back looking satisfied with his new plan before getting up to help me with the dishes. After we head into the living room where he picks up a book and begins reading. I flick over the few television shows before deciding on a documentary. I just stare at the screen not really paying attention to it. My mind is otherwise occupied with worrying about the next day. I can't help but think about how dangerous it's going to be. Yes, we have planned for every possible scenario, but anything could go wrong. If we're found out Oliver and I will be the first people who're questioned. The thought of someone hurting Oliver is painful. I shudder at the prospect of one of us getting bitten or killed. I know we would all rather die than have to live like this but I can't help the fear I feel.

"Chloe you're staring," Oliver says startling me. I blink when I realise he's looking at me. I hadn't realised I had turned away from the television.

"I'm sorry," I say sitting up and stretching.

"Are you tired?" he asks. I nod as I fight back a yawn.

"A little bit yeah," I say. He puts his book down as he gets up. He holds out his hand and pulls me up from the sofa.

"Come on," he says walking towards the bedroom. I pull my hand free of his to head into the bathroom, to brush my teeth. As I come out, Oliver walks towards me from the bedroom in nothing but a towel. I stare at him with wide eyes. He swoops down kissing me before backing into the bathroom, smiling. I stare as he closes the door, as the shower turns on I shake myself. I smile as I walk into the bedroom, I throw myself into bed settling into my pillows. I sigh as my whole body tingles after his short but no less amazing kiss. He really is a great kisser. I close my eyes as I hear the shower switch off. I pull the covers up around my neck as I hear the bathroom door open then close. I feel my heart beat faster as I hear him coming into the room. He chuckles quietly as he closes the door. I listen as he pads around the room. I hear the whisper of his towel falling to the floor. I have to use every ounce of self-control not to open my eyes.

Eventually the bed dips as he lies down and the room falls into darkness after the soft click of his light going out. I realise my breathing is loud so I try and control it but the smell of him is over powering my senses. He smells clean, soapy, the smell is intoxicating. He's breathing lightly beside me and he's unmoving. I open my eyes slightly and he chuckles again.

"I knew you weren't sleeping," he says. I close my eyes again but not before I notice he's shirtless.

Damn him.

"I was so," I counter lamely.

"Liar, you breathe differently when you're sleeping," he whispers in my ear making my skin prickle pleasantly where his breath warms me.

"How am I breathing different?" I ask with a frown.

"When you're asleep it's slower and less often but now, it's like you have been running," he says as his fingers move over my lips. My eyes find his in the dark. Even with the limited light in the room I can see his pupils are big and black.

"You're breathing fast too," I say in a quiet voice. He nods.

"That's because I can't stop thinking about you in that damn towel," he says gripping my vest top. I stare at him and he smiles. "You looked..." he pauses and leans over me making sure I'm looking at him, "...beautiful." I gasp at his words as he captures my lips in a searing kiss. My eyes close of their own accord as he presses me into the mattress. I wrap my arms around his neck pulling him closer making him groan into my mouth. I wrap a leg around his hips. Before he knows it I have rolled us over and he stares up at me his eyes wide. I lean forward to kiss him as he runs his hands up my thighs and sides. I moan into his mouth as his fingers tickle my ribs.

"This ok?" he asks between kisses. I nod quickly. He slowly runs his hands down my sides again. I sit back watching him as his hands roam over my body. I place a hand on his bare chest making his breath hitch as I run my fingers down and across his firm stomach. His hands have frozen on my waist. I look down at him and I'm shocked to find he looks a little frightened.

"Are you ok?" I ask. He nods as he sits up suddenly wrapping his arms around me. I put my arms around his shoulders while I run my hand through his hair. "Ollie what's wrong?" I ask feeling concerned.

"I just wish things were different. I wish this could have happened for real," he says quietly. I lean back as he looks up at me.

"This is real," I say with a confused frown.

"I know. I just mean..."

"Do you think I'm doing this because I have to?" I ask he looks down nodding. I climb off of him sitting down on my side of the bed while his eyes follow me looking hurt.

"I don't blame you for it. You're trying. I can see that but I feel like I'm taking advantage of the situation," he says as I pull my legs towards my body feeling slightly embarrassed.

"You're not," I say looking at him. He gives me a little smile.

"Try and see it from my point of view. You're my best friend and like I said I'd thought about us being together before, while you remained oblivious," he says with a little smile. "Now because of this whole situation you're my wife and you're expected to have my children. I don't want that for you. I feel that if we, you know, had sex that I'll be ruining your life. Now with the whole thing with Rose it's made me think." I stare at him feeling angry for some reason. Yes, everything he said is true, except for one thing. I don't feel any pressure from him to reciprocate any sort of feelings. They're all real. I enjoy kissing him, I have enjoyed getting to know this side of Oliver and I definitely don't want to stop.

"I wish you wouldn't think, just for once," I say softly. His eyebrow arches at me. "Oliver, you're not taking advantage of me. I'm mad that you think I would let you take advantage of me and that I would do any of this just for your benefit. You know me better than that." He smiles a little. I return it. "The fact that you chose me at graduation was probably the best thing to happen to me that day and ever since." He opens his mouth to say something but I shake my head.

"Please let me finish. I'm grateful for everything you have done for me and that you continue to do for me. You've saved my life; I would have been utterly miserable elsewhere. I think that if I was to choose someone it was always supposed to be you," I say honestly his eyes are wide in surprise. I feel the sting of tears in the corner of my eyes. I push on before I do something stupid like actually cry.

"Please believe me when I say everything I'm doing is my decision. This situation has nothing to do with how I feel about you. You gave me the option to find someone else and I chose you. Get it into your thick skull that I want you and you're stuck with me whether you want me or not," I say. He nods and smiles.

"Come here," he says pulling me towards him sounding a little gruff. I smile as slide into his open arms. "Thank you," he says into my hair. I nod; he pulls back a little chewing on his lip. "Can we just wait a little longer?" he asks. I smile nodding.

"Sure there is no rush," I say, he kisses my hand.

"You're the best."

"I know, I know," I say smiling as I climb under the covers.

"And oh so modest," he chuckles as he lies down lifting his arm so I can slide in next to him.

"That's me," I say closing my eyes. I rest my head on his chest and he kisses my head. He chuckles again wrapping his arms around me. I begin to drift off quickly just before I'm pulled under I hear him whisper, "Sweet dreams."

Chapter 28

Despite waking up several times in the night from dreams of varying degrees of horrible bloody situations that could arise during the plan, I feel surprisingly rested as the alarm finally goes off at four o'clock in the morning. I listen to the shrill alarm for a moment while the gravity of the coming day washes over me. Oliver reaches over me turning off the alarm before looks he down at me. I see in his eyes that he has not slept as well as I have. I feel immensely guilty about that. I reach up putting my hand on his face, his tired eyes flutter closed. He lifts a hand holding my hand to his face.

"Chloe," he starts but I shake my head knowing where he's going with this. His eyes open and he sighs.

"No. I'm not letting you do this without me. Please don't ask me again," I say. He leans down giving me the lightest, sweetest kiss before nodding.

"Come on we have a lot to do," he says. He rolls off the bed moving slowly towards the cupboard in the dark. We have agreed to have the lights off, as four o'clock is too early even for Oliver to get up. We have to do anything to avoid any suspicion. He hands me my pile of nondescript clothes, another counter measure just so we don't stick out like sore thumbs. We change in silence, him with his back turned. When I'm dressed I touch his shoulder lightly. He turns around as he pulls on his black wooly cap to cover his fiery red hair. I smile as he tries to tuck it under the hat. I reach up to help him with the last few strands.

"Thanks," he says a small smile flickering as he looks down at me. The alarm goes off again we both look over at it before I turn it off. I pick up his dressing gown wrapping it around myself as we walk into the dark living room. I hold out his backpack for him as he pulls on his work coat. He pulls up the hood before taking the backpack from me.

"I will see you later," I say as he pulls me into a tight hug. He's going ahead to make sure all the equipment is ready. To avoid any suspicion I'm going to follow after him with his lunch, which he's going to forget.

"See you later," he says. I lean up to kiss him, he sighs as he turns away opening the door. It's a cool but clear morning. I smile up at him as he looks out. His shoulders seem to relax a little at the sight of the clear morning sky. I can't help but feel some fragment of relief rush though me. Damien was right it's been horrible over the last few weeks. This clear day might just make the whole thing easier.

I spot David and Damien heading off to their farms. I wave at Rose, like I do every morning. She looks pale and her wave is half hearted.

"Have a good day," Oliver says, kissing my cheek.

"You too," I say. He gives me a weak smile. He rushes off in the opposite direction of David and Damien and I turn and slam the door closed. I look at the clock, pulling off the dressing gown. I pull on my boots before I make a quick lunch for Oliver. I wait anxiously for another ten minutes before I grab the bag and run out the door. I jog through the street and once I hit the cover of the trees I pick up my pace. I slow to a jog as I near the stables still clutching Oliver's lunch bag in my hand. My stomach is assaulted with butterflies as the red barn comes into view. I slow to a walk as I enter the barn, which is eerily quiet.

"Oliver?" I call. His head sticks out of a stable at the end. I walk down tossing his lunch onto a bale of straw. "What can I do?"

"We're done," he says closing the door to the stable behind himself.

"We?" I ask stroking the horse on the nose.

292

"Mornin girl," Billy says from an empty stable making me jump slightly. I turn around when he comes out hauling a big metal container behind him noisily causing the horse, Hugo, to scuttle to the back of his stable and snort. Oliver rushes over to Billy, helping him by picking up the other end and walking with him down to the end of the barn, leaving it outside.

"I didn't know you were here Billy," I say as he smiles.

"I couldn't leave the kid to do all this by himself. I'm here for some feeds," he says with a wink and I smile.

"I see. Is there anything left for me to do?' I ask. I look at Oliver who looks sickly pale and who has apparently become a mute.

"Nah, I think we're 'bout done now. It's nearly time, Cameron and Trevor should be on their way up there now," Billy says. As I look up at the clock I hear a rumble form behind me. I turn and see Oliver's tractor coming towards us. John is bumping along inside the cab; he waves his hand in a greeting. The tractor is carrying a fork on its arm and as he approaches John lowers them slowly before picking up the heavy metal crate. He switches off the tractor before jumping down. I see others coming towards the barn as Billy goes out to shake John's hand. Oliver steps up beside me, when I move off to go join the others, Oliver grabs my arm. I turn around as he looks over my head.

"Come on Oliver, we don't have much time."

"Please Chloe," he pleads as is eyes meet mine. When I see the unshed tears in them my heart nearly breaks. "I'm begging you, please stay behind," he says quietly. The look he gives me nearly makes me agree but I shake my head before pulling my arm back.

"I can't, I'm sorry. Please don't make me." I turn, rushing over to the others just as Damien is explaining about Rose falling and hurting her knee the night before.

"She's really sorry she can't be here," Damien says looking slightly relieved that she isn't here.

293

"Convenient," Harriet says in a carrying whisper. I'm not the only one to throw her a dirty look but no one says anything, it's tense enough without her causing more of an atmosphere.

"Let's get this over with," Oliver says moving past us all, heading towards the field. We all follow after him; Gillian's eyes meet mine as she gives me a quick one-armed squeeze.

"Don't worry sweetheart," she says. I give her a little smile. We reach the field gate and Oliver holds it open for us. He leaves it open, walking ahead of us, his long legs used to the rough terrain.

"Follow me and be quick," he says as he hands each of us a rope from the bucket he left the night before. I turn around when I hear the tractor coming up behind us. As we near the tower I see Cameron and Trevor waiting for us. They give us the thumbs up meaning they have disabled the cameras. We weren't sure if they actually worked but we needed to make sure we weren't caught. They've also attached the ropes to each of the tree legs of the tower; they're laid out waiting for us to hitch them to the horses. John rushes past us on the tractor dropping the crate so we can reach it. He jumps out of the cab making his way over to the tower. We spot the horses and Oliver whistles loudly making them all look up. Magnus, the biggest, moves forward slowly. Then like setting off a chain reaction the others follow picking up speed as they do. They come running at us and I nervously back up.

"Stand your ground, they'll stop," Oliver says to us who moved. Sure enough the horses all slow as they near us allowing us to approach and secure them with the ropes. Oliver and Billy begin tacking up their horses while Cameron, John, Trevor and Marcus run around handing out tack and help us tack up quickly. I have Emily and she's as patient as ever as I put on her tack. Oliver's first to have Magnus hitched up to the tower. He watches as I tie the ropes to Emily's harness, with shaking fingers. Our eyes meet and he frowns a little before directing everyone to move forward so the ropes are pulled tight. There is a creak from the tower, as the ropes are pulled taut. John stands under the tower looking up at it warily. After a few seconds he relaxes a little giving us a little nod. All the horses look excited at the prospect of work, which throws into sharp contrast how nervous, and sickly we all look. I look back towards the tower where John has his ear against the tower as he looks at his watch. He's listening out for the Fanged heading back up the tower for their watch. I watch him with baited breath, awaiting his cue. I tear my eyes from him briefly looking around our small group. Everyone looks worried but determined. I can't help but think how ridiculous we must all look, standing in an open field holding onto ten horses doing nothing. I hope more than anything that this works because if it doesn't then we're all doomed. My eyes flick to Oliver who's looking at me with a stony face but I can see the fear and pain that lies beneath it. He opens his mouth to say something when I hear a loud but distinctive bird call form John. I spin, staring at him. He's nodding as he holds up three fingers, which means he can hear at least three Fanged inside.

Oliver clicks loudly as John gives us the thumbs up, they're in the tube. The horses move forward a step, there's an instant groan from the tower. I look back; John is running out from under the leaning tower, his arms above his head as wood splinters rain down on him. There's a crack of breaking wood then suddenly the furthest away leg snaps in half causing the others to shiver and splinter. Then with one mighty tug form the other horses they too snap like matchsticks. The tower groans as it falls. I hear a faint scream as the tower bends and snaps the metal pipe leading into the ground. The horses continue moving forward as the tower falls. With a shuddering bang, I feel in my legs, it crashes into the ground. The blacked out windows explode sending glass everywhere. There's a moment of shocked silence before the screams of the Fanged inside fill my ears.

"Uncouple the horses," Oliver calls. I move feeling like I'm going in slow motion, the screaming having unnerved me. I look at Oliver as my fingers fumble with the tack; he has already untacked one of his two and is working on the second. The horses move off as they are released. I try to unbuckle Emily as some of the other horses run off. A big hand covers mine. I look up as Oliver quickly removes Emily's tack handing it to Marcus who rushes off with it throwing it in the metal chest. Oliver slaps Emily's back end and she runs off with the others. I stare at him feeling confused and strangely disconnected from everything. He takes my hand pulling me towards the tractor.

"Wait here," he pleads. I nod, unable to resist or do anything else as Mary comes over towards me. She looks at me. We exchange a shocked and slightly dazed look.

"It worked," is all she says as I nod mutely. We watch as the guys all huddle around the pipe. I freeze when a scream of agony comes from inside the tower. I look around my eyes darting around the tower. I gasp as a charred body climbs out of the wreckage and comes running towards Mary and I. The pain and anger in the Fangs' eyes startles me out of my daze. I move in front of Mary instinctively, she holds onto my shirt tugging me back a little. The Fangs skin is smoking and he's breathing heavily as he shakily moves towards us. I hear someone shouting, I don't know who it is and I don't care. I turn around to run pushing Mary in front of me. We reach the tractor together. I shove Mary up into the tractors cab. I spot a tire iron on the floor; I grab it before slamming the tractor door shut in Mary's face.

"Chloe!" she screams as she bangs on the door. I jump down from the tractor, as the Fang barrels towards me. His skin is charred and falling off in some places. He's screaming in agony but suddenly he leaps from a good ten feet away. I jump out of the way as he hits the tractor window. I hear Mary scream as he tries to break into the cab but as he hits the window his arms begin to crumble and break. He stops his attack, looking at his ruined arms in horror. He screams in anger. I gag as the smell of his burning flesh hits my nose; it's a sweet perfumed smell. He turns his head at my gagging, his scream dying down as he spins at me. I don't have a chance to think before he's on me. I fall hard to the ground my head slamming to the wet mud, as his weight crashes down on me. He tries grabbing me, screaming all the while but I stick the tire iron against his throat as his useless arms flail at its sides. His body presses down on me hard, I fight against him, pushing the iron away from me as his jaws snap angrily above me. I manage to get my legs under him to kick him off. His eyes go wide and his body blackens as he's pushed backwards. He hits the ground with a puff of black ash and with a couple dry, heaving breaths he gasps and stills. The sickening smell of perfumed burnt flesh fills my nose as I scrabble up, ready for another attack but his body just crumbles at my feet. As I stare at the charred remains I gag again, as sound and feeling returns to me. I heave as I grip my knees; David rushes towards me looking sick with panic.

"Are you ok?" he asks quickly gripping my arms; I nod. His eyes travel over me before he rushes over to the tractor where Mary is still trying to get out. I hear Mary yelling as she's let out, she's furious with me but I block her out as I look around. I see Oliver looking at me his face drained as he holds another armless, burning Fang against the splintered wood. The Fang wrestles with Oliver and Cameron as they pin him to a tower leg. Despite the struggling Fang Oliver's eyes don't leave mine.

"You won't get away with this," the Fang hisses angrily. With a swift, practiced move Billy swings his axe. My eyes close tightly with the sickening thud of metal on wood. I open my eyes to Oliver and Cameron letting the body fall to the ground. The head rolls a few times before coming to rest at Damien's foot and bursting into a pile of black ash. He steps back a little before he looks up at the others, as the body crumbles at their feet. Mary sobs into David's chest as he looks on at the group. The smell of the Fang's burnt bodies is overwhelming and I move away to take a breath of fresh air. I hear an angry hiss from behind me and I gasp, tightening my grip on the tire iron. A third Fanged rounds the corner before leaping into the group sending them all off in different directions.

"Murderers!" she screams from the middle of the circle. She looks at all of us as she burns under the sun. She jumps at Billy who is still holding the axe. She collides with him heavily. Billy grunts loudly as I rush forward. Billy wrestles with it hard. Oliver rushes to grab the axe at Billy's feet. He swings it hard against the Fang's side. The impact knocks her off Billy who's dragged away by David and Damien. The Fang, crazed with pain, screams as she launches herself at Harriet, who's stood staring at the whole scene in shock. Harriet screams as the Fang flies at her. Trevor jumps in front of it taking the hit full on. The impact crumbles the right side of the Fang, her arm and leg charring and crumbling. Trevor lands heavily with a grunt but he uses the momentum to roll over, pinning the burning Fang below him. I seem to be moving in slow motion as I watch Trevor struggling with the Fang. Everywhere he grips seems to crumble and after a near miss with her sharp fangs he panics.

"Hunter!" he yells as her teeth snap at him narrowly avoiding his wrist. Oliver rushes over with the axe raising it above his head. I gasp as he swings the axe downward. The Fang goes silent and stills. He drops the axe at his feet backing away as the Fang crumbles completely. Trevor drags himself off the ground stumbling away from the smoking ashes, coughing and spluttering loudly as he grips his right shoulder.

"We need to move," Damien says suddenly as he makes his way towards Trevor who is doubled over. He helps him straighten up and looks round at us all, frowning at us as we all just stand staring. "Now, move it!" he says tensely. Everyone moves off slowly, looking as dazed as I feel. I gather some ropes pulling them towards the tractor while others begin throwing the last pieces of tack in the crate. John has already started up the tractor he picks up the crate as Cameron slams it shut. David and Mary are already half way across the field he has his arm wrapped around her supportively. Gillian is fussing over Billy who grumbles, "I'm ok", which doesn't deter her. Harriet who looks like she's completely in shock is thanking Trevor. There are tears falling down her face as Marcus stands by her looking concerned.

"It's ok. We're a team," Trevor says with a shrug that makes him wince, before he turns away his arm wrapped around his chest like he's in pain. Harriet stares after him. Marcus takes her hand leading her out of the field. I look back to Oliver who is still standing by the charred remains and the dropped axe. I'm about to go over to him when Billy walks over, picking up the axe and whispering something in his ear. Oliver nods stiffly as his eyes flick over to me. He pats Billy's shoulder before walking towards me.

"Let's head out!" Billy calls. Damien waves to me before he takes off at a run towards his farm. John and Cameron help Trevor climb into the tractor and then the three of them ride it out of the field. Eventually it's just Oliver I left. He puts his hand on my arm.

"Go home Chloe, it's done, you need to go home. This never happened," he says giving me a shaky smile. I blink at him. "Go. I will see you tonight," he says shoving me forward. Before I turn he gives me a swift kiss, let's me go and follows after Billy towards his farm. My feet move on their own, clearly they are still alert enough to realise we still have a job to do. Before I know it I'm on the road jogging home. I run blind as I try to absorb what we all just did. We killed three Fanged. Oliver killed one with his own hands, did I? I certainly helped it die, we all did…The fact that we can actually kill them that we can actually fight back is greatly overshadowed by the imagery of that Fang trying so hard to take a chunk out of me. It even does wonders to make me forget Oliver's face after he cut the head off the Fang. I would do anything to never see that look on his face again. I'm not foolish enough to pretend that I won't see it again, after today I fear I will be seeing a lot of it. As I take a deep breath through my nose I get a waft of the sweet-smelling, burnt flesh from my clothes. I stop suddenly on the road coughing and spluttering trying to rid my head of the smell. Shakily, and after I have caught my breath again, I move off at a slower pace. When I see my house approaching I slow down to a walk trying to calm my still shaking body.

Unsurprisingly, Rose is waiting for one of us to get back. I'm a little shocked to see her in her garden pruning her shrubs. As soon as she sees me she drops her clippers on the floor and she rushes towards me.

"Hey Chloe. How was the run?" she says in a calm tone not matching her panicked wide-eyed look. I shakily smile and look around the street seeing some of our neighbours hovering around tending to their garden in this rare sunny morning. It must have been where she got her idea.

"It went fine," I say trying to smile. Her shoulders relax as she smiles.

"Great, really great," she says walking out of her garden and towards me. "I'm off to give Damien a hand today," she says loudly. "Is everyone ok?" she whispers as she passes me. I nod.

"Trevor got hurt but he's ok, saved Harriet. Everyone is ok," I say quickly trying to calm he worried look. She sighs with relief.

"Ok, good. You might want to wash your clothes," she says smiling as she pinches her nose. I see the warning in her eyes. I sniff my clothes nearly gagging again. I rush towards my house throwing the door open before slamming it shut behind me. I tear off my clothes trying not to breathe the acrid smell any more than I already am. I take everything off in the living room before stuffing it in the machine. I pour too much powder in the machine before slamming it shut. I put it on the hottest setting uncaring if something shrinks. I stand watching the machine as it goes around until I start to shiver. I wrap my arms around myself and realise I'm naked, I quickly look around. Seeing Oliver's bathrobe on the floor I pick it up and wrap it around me breathing in the now fading, comforting smell. I rush into the bathroom switching on the shower turning it up as hot as I can bear and step under. My skin turns red under the hot spray. I grab the soap and scrub my skin until it's raw. I shampoo my hair three times and even brush my teeth to get any residual smell or taste of the brunt flesh out of my body.

I leave the bathroom feeling raw but smelling clean. I slump down on the sofa and lie down. I close my eyes as I feel tears burning the back of my throat. It worked. We can fight. We can take back our lives. I keep repeating in my head. I can't help the small smile that crosses my face. I laugh at the ridiculous notion. My eyes spring open when the telephone rings. I jump out of my seat and run into the kitchen.

"Hello?" I breathe as I answer.

"Hey kiddo," Dad says from the other end. I smile as I grip the phone tighter.

"Hey Dad."

"You ok there you sound a little out of breath."

"Oh, I have just got in from a run," I say frowning as the lie rolls off my tongue.

"When did you start running?" he asks with humour in his voice.

"I have to keep myself occupied somehow," I say trying to sound natural. I can picture him rolling his eyes.

"Well, I have some good news," he says.

301

I sit down at the table, desperately in the need for something to distract my mind for a minute. "We're coming up there for Christmas. Your brothers and I have got time off over Christmas. So we're coming to stay with you guys since Oliver won't get time off," he says. I smile at this news.

This is definitely what I need to distract me.

"Really? Dad that's great, hang on how did you know he was going to be working?" I ask frowning.

"I asked him," he says like it was the most obvious answer. I suppose it was.

"He never told me that," I say as dad chuckles.

"That's because it's supposed to be a surprise but I couldn't stand not telling you. Don't tell Oliver I said anything," he says sounding very guilty.

"I won't. Dad it's so great to hear from you. I miss you so much," I say. He sighs sadly.

"I miss you too; it's so quiet around here without you guys. I can't wait to see you, both of you. Are you keeping well?"

"Yeah Dad everything is fine. We're fine. One of my friends is pregnant," I add. Dad groans.

"So soon?" he asks sounding a little upset by the news.

"Yeah she found out yesterday."

"You have no idea how much I wish you didn't have to go through all of this kiddo. I wanted something better for you two," he says making me smile.

"We're ok Dad. We've kind of accepted it; we're happy. Well as happy as we can be. I'm just glad I have Oliver."

"Me to kiddo. It nearly broke my heart when I saw that other kid looking at you. Oliver is a great man. I know he will respect you."

"He is, he has been. He's doing everything he can to make me happy. I can't help it but I think…" I pause, as the realisation of what I was about to say, hits me.

"What?" Dad asks. I frown and bite my lip.

"I'm in love with him Dad," I say quietly.

302

"Well it's about time. I've been waiting to hear you say that for the last five years or so," he says shocking me. I can't help but laugh.

"Really?" I say through giggles.

"Yep. It's been a long time coming. Me and your mum used to talk about you guys getting married one day," he says pausing. I chew my lip waiting for him to go quiet and closing off, like he normally does after mentioning mum. So when he goes on I'm happily surprised. "Tell me kiddo does he know it yet?" Dad asks. I shake my head before I realise he can't see me.

"No, he doesn't know yet," I say chewing on my thumbnail.

"Yeah I do," comes Oliver's voice form behind me. I spring out of the seat spinning around quickly to stare at him. He's in the doorway wearing a shocked but happy expression. I hear dad laugh.

"Oh my god, is that him?" Dad asks chuckling. I nod my head.

"That's him," I confirm in a small voice. He laughs again.

"Go. I will call you later. Hello Oliver!" he calls loudly. Oliver's eyes flick to the phone and he waves.

"He says hi," I murmur as dad chuckles happily.

"Love you Kiddo," he says quickly before he hangs up. I put the phone down as Oliver closes the front door. I turn back to him as he pulls off his coat.

"So," he says hanging it up.

"So," I repeat feeling my heart pumping fast.

"You love me?" he asks. I open my mouth and nothing comes out.

Oh man.

Chapter 29

"You weren't supposed to hear that," I breathe out. He laughs before looking at the floor.

"What's so funny?" I ask as he lifts his head shaking it at me.

"Nothing, but tell me Chloe if I wasn't supposed to hear it why did you say it?" he asks looking at me intently. I gape at him completely lost for words. I'm no romantic but when I envisioned telling Oliver that I was in love with him this was not what I had in mind. I had imagined it being in a slightly better setting, maybe at our lake. Not in our kitchen room, with me standing in his dressing gown, my hair unbrushed and him in his work clothes, covered in mud and having hay in his hair. I blink at him unable to think of anything to say.

"You weren't supposed to be home," I blurt out.

"But I am and I heard you say it. Did you just say it to make your Dad happy?" he asks sounding slightly upset. I shake my head quickly. Sure it had made my dad inexplicably happy but that was not the reason. Oliver slowly makes his way towards me like I'm a scared animal that he's trying not to spook. Suddenly I do feel very exposed even a little scared.

"I didn't expect... I didn't want to say it like that," I say backing up against the counter as he advances.

"How did you want to say it?"

"I don't know," I say gripping the counter top.

"Did you mean it?" he asks his eyes wary.

"Yes. Yes I meant it," I say quickly. He smiles widely as I blush.

"Chloe are you sure?" he asks stopping in front of me his voice sounding hopeful.

"I mean it," I say. I take the last step towards him. I stand on my tiptoes to kiss him. He pulls away tucking my hair behind my ear.

"Say it again?" he asks in a low voice making me smile.

"I'm in love with you Oliver," I say as his eyes burn into mine. He smiles as he presses his lips to mine. I can't help but smile as well. It's the clumsiest kiss we have ever shared and we pull apart laughing.

"I love you too," he says after taking a shaky breath. "I have for a while now."

"I'm sorry it took me so long to catch up," I say smiling. He laughs as he picks me up around the waist holding me tight against him.

"Oblivious as ever," he says. I smile down at him as I pull a few strands of hay out of his hair. He looks up at me his eyes bright and happy. I smile at him before I kiss his nose. I wrap my legs around his waist his Adams apple bobs as he swallows.

"Take me to bed," I say making his eyes widen.

"What?" he breathes. I lean down and kiss him. I kiss him until we're both breathless. I move my lips to his ear.

"Take me to bed," I whisper. I feel him shiver and I smile against his ear. This seems to snap him out of his daze he grips me harder he walks us both through the house kicking open the bedroom door. He places me down on the bed kissing me soundly before backing away. He must notice my eyes widen and he smiles.

"I have to have a quick shower, I can still smell it," he says. I realise he must still be covered in the smell of the Fanged.

"Ok go," I say with a little smile. He bites his lip as his eyes roam over me.

"I will be right back. Stay right there," he says holding up his finger. He practically runs out of the room. I watch as he slides down the hall and into the bathroom. I spring off the bed rushing to my drawers, hunting for my nicest set of underwear. When I can't find it I realise it's sitting in the wash basket. I really should be more organised, I think as I look at myself in the mirror. In my own defence, I never expected this to happen at this precise moment. I look over myself deciding to just stay in the dressing gown; it's easier to remove after all. I pull a brush through my snarled hair then with one last look at myself in the mirror I sit down on the bed and wait trying to calm my nervous heart.

The realisation of what is about to happen nearly sends me jumping out of the bedroom window again but as I focus on the sound of the shower running I reason to myself that I really do want this. It has been a trying day. When I think of all the times today that I could have lost Oliver it only makes me want to show him how much I love him and that I'm happy he's safe. I block out the sudden image of him swinging the axe and focus on the fact we're still together. We're alive, we all are. If he didn't do what he did someone, even himself could have died or been bitten. I nearly leap out of my skin when I hear the bedroom door clicking shut. I spin round and feel my racing heart stop for a few beats at the sight of him in a fluffy white towel. I look over him; his skin is still wet and slightly red from the shower. His stomach is rising and falling rapidly. My eyes dart up to his when he runs his hand through his hair nervously.

"Are you ok?" he asks sounding as nervous as he looks. I can't help but smile, he's always so unsure of himself when it comes to me. He frowns slightly as I make my way on shaky legs towards him. "You know we don't have to. Like I said last night we can wait," he says in a reassuring tone. I frown up at him but it fails when I see the fear and uncertainty in his eyes. I take his hands in mine. He looks down at them as I pull him towards the bed. His eyes dart to mine as I give him a reassuring smile. His shoulders relax a little.

"I trust you. It was always supposed to be you," I say my eyes not leaving his despite the nerves I'm feeling. He smiles as he takes a deep shuddering breath.

"I thought I was going to lose you today. When that Fang came at you, you were so brave. You saved Mary, I shouldn't underestimate you," he says his hand coming up to my face tucking my hair behind my ear.

"Shh. I don't want to think about it," I say as the vision of the scorched Fang flashes in my mind.

"I only say it because I want you to know that if anything had happened to you and I never got to tell you…"

"Tell me what?"

"How much you mean to me," he says his eyes burning into mine. I grip his hand.

"I already know," I say feeling my eyes stinging.

"You do?" he asks in a doubtful tone. I narrow my eyes playfully making him chuckle.

"Yes I do. Only someone who cares this much for someone would do all the stupid things you're doing. Like starting a war with the Fanged," I say. He laughs loudly making me smile.

"You got me," he says his eyes sparkling.

"Good, now are you going to help me got out of this dressing gown or shall I…" I start to untie it but his hands stop me.

"No," he says quickly. I look up expecting him to tell me he thinks we should wait but the look on his face tells me he's done waiting. "I want to do that, eventually," he teases. He picks me up bridal style before throwing me onto the bed. I giggle as he climbs on after me he hovers over me as I smile up at him. "I love you Mrs. Hunter," he says in a low soft voice. I smile widely; it's the first time being called my new name has made me happy.

"I love you too Mr. Hunter," I say bringing my hand up to his face. He smiles before lowering his head to kiss me slowly and tenderly.

A while later as I lay in the now dark room with Oliver's arms wrapped around me I smile to myself. I can't help but bask in the afterglow of making love to Oliver. It was nothing like I was expecting. From all of the stories I heard at school and from what we were taught, even the things Mary and Rose told me I expected it to be horrible. But I was wrong. I never knew I would feel this happy. Nothing I was told came close to the reality of being so close to someone that the feeling over powered you, the feeling of being so close but even that was not close enough. I had expected it to be awkward, fumbling even a little embarrassing but I couldn't have been more wrong. It had been the most terrifying experience of my life so far but Oliver made me feel relaxed. He was gentle and sweet. The way he looked at me made me feel brave and beautiful. I will never admit it to him but I'm secretly glad of his previous experience because it seemed effortless and natural. Him knowing what he was doing, while making me feel so relaxed, made the whole experience, for the lack of a better description, mind-blowing. Oliver's hand ghosts down my back and I look up at him. He smiles down at me moving my hair out of my face.

"Are you ok?" he asks concern clear in his voice.

"Is it always that nice?" I ask. He chuckles and shakes his head.

"Not that I know of," he says his finger still playing in my hair. I move up his body resting my head on my hand.

"Thank you," I say as I run my fingers over his stomach. He laughs taking my hand and lacing his fingers with mine.

"Chloe you don't have to thank me. I should be thanking you," he says pulling me closer to his side with a smile.

"Shut up. I just meant thank you for being patient for waiting for me, for putting up with me all this time. I promise I won't make you wait again," I say. He smiles.

"I would have waited forever for you," he says leaning up to kiss me. I smile at him before lying down and stifling a yawn. "Get some sleep," he says pulling the covers up over us as I snuggle into him. After a few minutes of silence I hear Oliver snore lightly. I smile before I drift off.

A violent shiver awakes me from my deep sleep. It takes a minute for me to realise that it wasn't me, but Oliver. I sit up looking down at him. His face is scrunched up and he's shivering. I touch his head carefully. He's cold; I notice there is a sheen of sweat over his body. I panic and start to shake him.

"Oliver," I hiss shaking him harder, his eyes spring open and dart around the room before they land on me, wide and staring. "You were having a nightmare."

"Chloe?" he groans. I place my hand on his face as his chest rises and falls rapidly. "I killed someone," he croaks. I sit up on my knees holding his face lightly not letting him look away.

"You saved Trevor's life," I say fiercely. He frowns at me.

"That's what Billy said. I still did it. I didn't even think," he sighs. I do the only thing I can do to comfort him knowing nothing I say will make him feel better; I lean down and kiss him. His eyes close.

"I have no idea what you're going through," I say against his lips. "I don't know what to say except you saved someone and that we now have a way of winning this," I say. His eyes open slowly and meet mine.

"This is what we wanted right?" I ask.

"It is." He nods slowly as I run a hand through his hair.

"It was never going to be pretty but we have a way to take back our and our families lives, I think we can do it."

"You do?" he asks sounding doubtful. I lean forward to kiss him again.

"Yes, I do. Don't let this get to you, you're stronger than this," I say. He takes a deep breath before nodding.

"I'm sorry for waking you," he says sounding a little embarrassed.

"It's ok," I say as I straddle his hips, his eyes widen slightly but his hands come to rest on my waist. "You feel better?" I ask as I lean down to press my lips to his. He hums against my lips.

"Much," he sighs as I smile against his lips.

"Good.

"This is a good vintage," Henry says licking his lips as he lowers his glass. He turns smiling over at Lillian who is staring into the fire her glass untouched. He sighs as he places his glass down heavily snapping Lillian out of her daze. "Your mood is really starting to grate on me my love," he says in a tense tone. Lillian shrinks down in her chair slightly under his angry gaze.

"I'm sorry; I'm just upset that my daughter has forgotten me," Lillian says sadly. Henry lets out a long breath through his nose.

"Can you blame the girl; you abandoned her and her siblings. Broke her father's heart then left your young children to pick up the pieces. She has every right to hate you, my love," Henry says as Lillian stares at him in disbelief. She was shocked to be spoken to so frankly and it irritated her.

"She is my daughter," she says tensely barely keeping her own temper in check.

"And you her mother but when you break a bond like that it is hard to remake. She has moved on and I would advise you do the same."

"I can't."

"You will not be able to get her now she is in love. Her mate protects her too fiercely," Henry says as Lillian's eyes narrow. The subject of Oliver Hunter was a sore spot. "He is not her mother," Lillian says through gritted teeth.

"Nor are you in her eyes, Chloe's mother died the day you abandoned her," Henry says matter of factly. Lillian ignores him.

"I thought you were going to take care of the one who mislead us about their relationship. If I would have known I

could have done something sooner!" Lillian says standing up frustrated.

"Calm my sweet I will be speaking to Eric soon," Henry says dismissively waving his hand at her.

"When?" Lillian asks spinning around glaring at him. Henry stares at her with a raised eyebrow, a dangerous look on his face. "I am sorry my love," Lillian says rushing over and falling to her knees before him. "I am sorry, I am just so angry," she growls. Henry's hand comes up cupping her cheek. She looks into his black eyes.

"I will make him pay; no one makes a fool of me and gets away with it," he says squeezing her face a little too tight. Lillian smiles despite the discomfort knowing it's a warning to her as well. She crawls into his lap peppering kisses along his jaw. The drawing room door bursts open. Lillian jumps up hissing in the direction of the intruder. The man stoops low waiting to be acknowledged. "Samuel, how can I help you?" Henry drawls as Lillian stares between the two of them.

"Sir, miss, I'm sorry to interrupt master but news had just reached us of an incident," Samuel says looking nervous as Henry stiffens.

"An incident?" he repeats. Samuel nods looking incredibly nervous.

"Sir, a tower has come down."

"When?" Henry asks standing up slowly making Lillian back away cautiously.

"Two days ago Sir."

"And we are just hearing about this now, why?" Henry asks frowning.

"Sir they lost three. They were not prepared for this; they didn't know what the procedure was. It has never happened before and..." Samuel snaps his mouth shut as Henry raises his hand to silence him.

"Where?" is all he says. Samuel's eyes flicker to Lillian before he addresses Henry again.

"The Greenbelt Sir, the west farms," Samuel says. He stands quietly as Henry paces the room before stopping in front of Lillian.

"It seems we will be visiting your daughter sooner than expected," he says. Lillian nods fighting hard not to smile.

Chapter 30

The next week for Oliver and I goes by with startling speed. The morning after the tower collapse we awoke to the rapid knocking on our front door. We jumped out of bed pulling on clothes. Oliver ran to the door wearing only his sweatpants while I tied the dressing gown around myself as I followed him out. Damien was standing at the door wearing a grin that was instantly infectious.

"Rose is pregnant!" he almost shouted as I rounded the corner. Oliver shook his hand and invited him in. I gave him a quick hug and he smiled at me in a daze. "She told me last night. It's why she didn't come yesterday. I'm going to be a dad. I'm going to be a dad!" he said. His face fell a little bit, like the realisation of the whole thing had just hit him. He stared at Oliver looking like he was going to pass out.

"You ok man?" Oliver said gripping his shoulder. Damien stared at us with wide eyes.

"Damn, this isn't good is it?" he said his voice low and frightened. Oliver and I looked at each other unsure what to say. He looked franticly between the two of us before covering his face with his hands. "Oh god what've I done? What am I thinking?" he said desperately as he dropped on the sofa with his head still in his hands. I looked hopelessly at Oliver as I sat down next to him.

"Go make a tea," I whispered to him as I placed my hand on Damien's tense shoulders. Oliver, who looked very awkward nodded and rushed into the kitchen.

"Chloe what've we done? We can't have a baby," he groaned. I patted his knee as I tried to think of something to say.

313

"Don't worry about it everything will be fine. We'll work something out," I said. He looked at me with wide pleading eyes. "We are a team remember?" I added trying to smile. He gave me a shaky smile as Oliver came in clutching a tea. Damien took it with a grateful smile before looking into the steaming cup.

"Chloe's right we'll work something out," Oliver said. Damien nodded and took my hand and gave it a squeeze.

"Thank you, both of you," he said smiling at us both.

After that morning, when the news of the fallen tower got around the village, it was all anyone talked about. Oliver's field had been cordoned off the day after he called the authorities like planned. He was to call in furious about the fact that the tower could have killed one of his horses. From that day Oliver had become a bit of an unwilling celebrity. Whenever someone saw him he was asked about what he saw or what happened. He managed to get rid of the nosey neighbours but he couldn't deny the local police officer when he asked some questions. The whole evening had been tense for me as I sat around our small kitchen table listening to Oliver expertly lie about what he had seen.

"So like I have said in my previous statement detective the tower was already down when I arrived at work. I went out to bring in my horses, like I do every morning when I've left them out. I didn't notice that the tower was missing at first; you know you just kind of ignore them when you see them every day. They just kind of blend in, but when I got closer I noticed something was off so I ran towards my field and that's when I found it," he paused for dramatic effect. "The tower was down. I ran towards it thinking I was going to find one of my horses underneath it," Oliver explained calmly as the officer, a large, round man, took notes on his little notebook. He stopped to look up at Oliver his brow creased.

"So you ran towards a tower that you knew would have Fanged in it?" the detective asked looking confused.

"Yes, of course I did," Oliver said sitting back crossing his arms.

"You're aware, aren't you that was a foolish thing to do? You could have been killed," the detective said leaning back in his chair, eyeing Oliver warily. My heart had stopped in my chest as I looked between Oliver and the detective. Oliver leaned forward looking completely unfazed.

"I wasn't worried because it was a particularly sunny morning; I was just concerned for my animals," he said in a level tone as my palms started to sweat. The detective looked at him for a moment frowning, after an agonizing silence he nodded. I let out a big breath I didn't know I was holding. Oliver took my hand and gripped it.

"Are you ok Mrs. Hunter?" the detective asked as his eyes flickered between Oliver and me.

"I'm ok," I said my voice small and scared sounding.

"I'm sorry officer my wife has been worrying ever since it happened, she yelled at me for being reckless," Oliver explained. I nodded as I gripped Oliver's hand. The detective looked at me giving me a pitying little smile.

"I'm sure it was all very upsetting but your husband did the best thing calling us," he explained in a patronising tone. I nodded like a mindless idiot despite wanting to slap him for talking to me like a child. "So Mr. Hunter once you had checked the damage you called us, is that correct?"

"That's right. Then your partner questioned me. After that I got my horses in the barn, due to the glass all over my damn field. Then I was sent home," he said calmly as the detective nodded, continuing to take notes.

"Sure. So the damage was cleared away and you dug out the field is that correct?" The detective looked down at his notes then back up at Oliver.

"No, it was some of the other farmers. I don't know how to do it," Oliver explained. It was true that the same day the tower was dismantled and dragged from the field by neighbouring farmers. John and Billy had come to Oliver's rescue digging the topsoil out of the cordoned off area of the field to remove any of the glass and unknown to others, the ashy remains of the three Fanged. They were sure they had got most of it but there could always be some in the field.

"I want to know who I complain to, when one of my horses gets injured, due to that damn tower exploding glass all over my field?" Oliver asked. The detective stared at him like he was talking a different language.

"I don't know Mr. Hunter, perhaps it's a question for the Mayor," he said frowning. Oliver huffed angrily. He played his part well.

"So no one then?" he said sounding angry. The detective gave him an apologetic smile.

"I think I'm done here Mr. Hunter. If there are any other questions…"

"I will be here or at work," Oliver said standing up. The detective stood up nodding at me.

"Mrs. Hunter, sorry to have bothered you."

"It's ok," I squeaked as he gave me a little smile. Oliver opened the door holding it open as the detective left with a quick nod to Oliver who returned it stiffly. I noticed a small crowd gathered outside of our house before Oliver slammed the door shut. "What're they all doing out there?" I asked as Oliver locked the door.

"They were probably hoping for an arrest," he said locking the last lock before turning to me and holding his arms open. I walked into them and he held me tight.

"You were amazing," I said into his chest as he sighed into my neck. That night he woke in a cold sweat again, I calmed him down, and held him as he tried to get back to sleep.

The rest of the week has been hard work, for us both. We started working on a makeshift fence to protect the horses from the possible dangerous area of the field. I had been helping him hammer posts into the ground as the rain poured on us. I think he just wanted me there to keep him company but I was glad to help. It made it easier on me as I was not worrying about him all day long. Since the day of the tower coming down and our first night together we have been inseparable. As we walk back home hand in hand from our fifth and final day of fence building we laugh at how exhausted we are.

"I can't wait to get you back home and into bed," Oliver says as he pulls me into his side. I shove him slightly but not enough for him to leave my side.

"I thought you were tired?" I smile. He raises his eyebrows giving me a heart-melting smile.

"I'm never too tired to…"

"Get your mind out of the gutter," I say blushing slightly, making him smile.

"I can't help it. Watching you get hot and sweaty all day has been killing me."

"I've been checking out your butt all day," I admit making his eyes widen.

"Oh really?" he says smiling widely as I grin at him. "I love you," he sighs. Since my unknowing confession of love for him he makes sure to tell me every day, at least once, that he loves me. It never fails to make me smile.

"I love you too," I say as he kisses my head. He holds me close as we walk towards the edge of the village. When we near our house I hear a rumble of many voices. I look up at him and he's frowning.

"What the hell is that?" he says under his breath. He takes my hand before he pulls me along behind him. We jog along pulling up short when we see a crowd of people at the bottom of our street. I spot David and Mary in the middle of the crowd. I pull Oliver along with me as I make my way through the crowd towards them. David nudges Mary as he spots us; she turns around giving us a tight-lipped smile.

"What is going on?" I ask. They both shrug.

"I don't know. We were all just called out and told to wait here for further instructions," David says as I look into the crowd.

"Can you see anything?' I ask Oliver he shakes his head.

"Nothing, oh wait people are moving off," he says. I frown when I hear Roses' voice through the throngs of people.

"Excuse me, pardon me," she says as she shoves past the last few people. Damien follows her looking embarrassed.

"Sorry," he says as a furious looking neighbour glares at her.

"It's about the tower," she says ignoring the mad man. "We are all to attend a town meeting. Well everyone who doesn't have to look after the children. Apparently we're to go now," she says as I fight back a sudden nauseous feeling that washes over me. I look up at Oliver whose jaw has gone tight.

"Well we had better go then hadn't we?" he says, his voice strained. I notice the crowd has thinned considerably as we follow the now mainly male group towards the centre of the village. Only silent whispers can be heard over the crunch of gravel under the feet of the villagers. I'm hyper aware of the looks that the six of us are getting. I notice also that there is a small but noticeable gap between us and the other villagers, like if they get to close they will catch something.

"These people have no idea what we are trying to do for them! If they knew what we were risking for them, they wouldn't be treating us like this," Damien says in a hushed voice so even we can barely hear him.

"Don't be so sure," Oliver says. He pulls me in closer as we walk.

"They're scared, we all are but if we don't have their support when we need it we're not going to survive this," Rose says sounding a little frightened. I look at her.

"If that happens, we'll deal with it then," I say trying to sound confident. As we walk further into the Village I spot the town hall and see people spilling in from the other surrounding farms. I see Billy walking ahead of us. He gives us a quick wink.

"Apparently someone's been naughty," he calls over the crowd. I feel my eyes widen.

"He doesn't seem worried," Oliver says with nervous smile as he shakes his head at Billy who is grinning.

"He's going to get us all killed," David chuckles nervously. Billy strides into the town hall followed by Gillian who looks like she's going to kill him. I shake my head at him and grip Oliver's hand as we near the wide double doors.

Lillian paces up and down the room with her hand over her mouth trying not to breathe too deeply. The overwhelming smell of fresh blood is almost too much for her. Henry looks at her with humour and she scowls at him.

"How can you stand the stink?" she snaps he shrugs giving her a small smile.

"I am more in control of my senses than you are my young mate," he says caressing her face. "Why so restless my love?" he asks, she huffs as she continues pacing.

"I'm anxious to see her. I want to be able to talk to her," Lillian says. Henry shakes his head at her and she slows to a stop.

"Always thinking of yourself my dear, three of our kind have been murdered yet you think of only yourself," Henry says calmly. Lillian knows him well enough to know that he is truly angry under his cool exterior.

"I am saddened by the deaths. I want to find out what happened to them as much as you do…"

"But you care more about getting to your daughter," Henry says. She knows this is not a question but a statement of fact. "Tell me Lillian why do you want her so much? You never cared this much about your sons. Why Chloe?" Henry asks with a little frown.

319

"She's my daughter."

"And your sons are too much like your human mate, to have them with you would only remind you every day of what you left? A man who loved you with his whole heart but was not enough for you," Henry says coldly.

"Stop it," Lillian says as Henry approaches her.

"I speak the truth don't I?" Henry says with a smile. Lillian does not meet his eyes but she nods. Henry lowers his head to her ear and kisses it. *"When your daughter disowns you again, and it will happen, I want to hear nothing more of this, do you understand me?"* he says his voice tense.

"Yes, but it will not come to that," she says defiantly. Henry just chuckles as he straightens up.

"We will see my love. We will see."

We're all squeezed into the small village hall our backs pressed against the walls to allow people to squeeze in. Even with the crowd pressing on us they have still managed to make a small circle around us. Some of the latecomers actively avoid looking our way as they squeeze past us as they walk in the doors we're stood beside. I look up as the room falls silent as Norman walks onto the stage wearing a suit and a very smug look.

"All right everyone, settle down," Norman calls from the front of the hall before he steps aside. I never knew he had such a high-ranking job.

"Mr. Mayor," he says bowing slightly as the Mayor of the Greenbelt steps forward, frowning.

"Yes, thank you Mr. Clark," he says tightly. Norman backs off with another little bow.

"Slime ball," Oliver says under his breath. I can't help nodding and smiling. He really couldn't be more accurate when describing Norman.

"Ladies and gentlemen this meeting has been called this evening due to the fall of the tower in the western farms. I'm aware that a full investigation has been carried out and that no arrests have been made," the Mayor says looking around the room as people murmur under their breath. I don't miss the many glances that are directed our way. They catch me looking back at them and turn away looking embarrassed. "However due to the seriousness of the incident an official from the Centrum has paid us a visit," he says. The murmurs grow louder before they die when we hear the groaning of rusty shutters. I look around in horror as the door behind us is blocked by a solid metal shutter, much like all of the other exits in the place. I look up at Oliver just in time to see the flicker of fear cross his face. I feel my heart turn to ice before the room is plummeted into darkness. There is a low rumble of terrified villagers when a door creaks open eerily. The room falls into another deafening silence. It's so quite that I'm able to make out the soft click of some heels on wood before they stop suddenly. I squint up to the front of the room. I can just about make out two shadowy figures standing where they Mayor was moments ago. I feel a shiver travel down my spine and Oliver's hand tightening on mine.

"Shit," he whispers. I look up at him frowning.

"What? Who is it?" I breathe. The next voice I hear is most unwelcome.

"Good evening," says the smooth but deadly voice of Henry Caldwell.

Chapter 31

The sound of Henry's voice makes my whole body run cold. Oliver stiffens next to me and even the breaths of the villagers have ceased. I hear a low amused chuckle.

"I do love a dramatic entrance," Henry says laughing to himself. "Come now, don't be frightened my loyal flock. There is nothing to be frightened of. I have merely come to visit you in this the saddest of times. I am sure once the investigation has been finalised all of this will be just a horrible accident and we can all go back to our normal lives. I am sure you all have nothing to fear," he says sounding very unconvinced by his own words. It's too dark to see his face properly but I'm sure that he's not amused. I feel for the poor souls in the front who will be feeling the full impact of his anger. "I am lead to believe this has been a horrible accident is that correct Mr. Mayor?" he asks in a level voice. I see a shadow step forward as Henry turns to him.

"Yes sir. That's the conclusion our detectives have come to."

"And why would you think anything else Mr. Mayor. I am sure you believe in all of your people. Your law enforcers wouldn't neglect their duties or ignore any vital evidence even if the deaths were nothing but "Leeches" am I correct," Henry says his voice so low I can almost hear the growl in it.

"No s-sir. I don't believe they would. They serve you sir. The issue has been given the fullest attention."

"Issue? I would say the loss of three souls was more than a mere "issue" Mr. Mayor," Henry says slowly his tone dark and curious.

"I-I-I only meant..."

"Silence!" Henry shouts. The shadowed figure of the Mayor backs away quickly. "I am sick of your kinds' sniveling ways." I stare transfixed at Henry as he tries to school his features back to their normal calm and uninterested way. He seems to be having some difficulty reining in his anger so he turns away from the crowd. His partner walks over to him. The click clack of her heels on the floorboards echoes around the room as she puts a comforting hand on his shoulder. Oliver steps in front of me as the woman comes into my view but he's split second too late. I gasp as my eyes widen and my legs wobble. I grip Oliver's jacket hard and groan at the pain that shoots through my chest.

"No," I say quietly but the sound carries in the silent hall. Several people turn around to look at me including Henry and my mother. As I stare into her dead dark eyes, it feels like the room has emptied and it's just the four of us. My mum's eyes seem to burn into me as she smiles and waves, wiggling her fingers at me.

"Hello Chloe," she says her smile wide and her tone completely casual. With a shuddering breath I look up at Oliver who looks tense. He grips me tightly to his side as I look back towards her with wide eyes. It's then that the room comes back into focus and I notice that every person in the room is looking at me. Henry glares out into the room having had enough time to compose himself.

"Before I leave you all to your lives, know this. I will find out what happened here. If any of you precious lambs are involved I will skin alive every member of your family and feed them to my dogs piece by tiny piece," he pauses and looks round us all. "Then after you have watched everyone you love eaten alive I will set you amongst us, like a fox amongst the hounds and you best hope they are hungry because if they are not you will die slowly in the most painful way you can imagine," Henry says slowly, his words sending a violent shiver through the whole room. Through Henry's whole speech I have been unable to look at him as my mother, who I have not seen for eleven years, has my full attention. Despite that his words still have a profound effect on me; I feel the threat of his words. I believe them to be, not only true, but also something I feel he would enjoy doing immensely.

"Mrs. Hunter," Henry says loudly. The directness of him calling my name makes me turn to him. "You will wait behind, I think it is time we get this reunion over and done with, don't you?" he says with a tone of finality before he sweeps out of the room with my mother scampering after him like a dog at its master's heel. As soon as the doors have closed behind them the shutters roll upwards. The villagers begin moving quickly and clumsily towards the exits tripping over themselves to get out of the room. I notice David and Damien have not moved. They're looking between Oliver and me, like they're waiting for instructions.

"Just go," Oliver says. They look at each other tensely.

"Oliver..." David begins to argue but Oliver shakes his head.

"It's ok, we'll be fine," he says looking back at Rose and Mary who are hovering in the doorway looking nervous.

"Go guys," I say. They frown looking very unhappy about it but after a few tense moments Damien nods.

"Be careful and don't do anything stupid," he says looking directly at Oliver who flashes him a quick smile. Damien pulls David out of the room before he can do or say anything else. We watch them leave until the door closes. I clutch Oliver's arm tightly as we turn towards the door in the corner of the room. I'm squeezing so hard I'm surprised that he doesn't complain.

"Chloe," he says sounding very far away. I look up at him my eyes wide and rimmed with tears. "Don't worry ok; the whole village knows where we are. If anything happens well..." he frowns when he struggles to finish his sentence. I cringe at the thought of what may happen.

"Remember I won't leave you. No matter what," he says wiping a tear that has escaped my eye.

"We're a team," I say shakily. He lets out a choked laugh before he kisses me.

"Always," he says kissing my forehead. I look around when I hear the door in the corner of the room open. My eyes widen slightly when the Mayor walks towards us his face tight and his eyes tired.

"They're ready for you," he says and I nod. "In the room at the end of the hall," he adds giving us a sorrowful look. We walk towards him hand in hand. As we pass him he quickly grabs my arm, I stare at him in shock. "Thank you," he says looking at us both. He drops my arm quickly and walks off out of the building.

"What…" I start but the smile on Oliver's face shocks me so much the words die in my lips.

"He knows," Oliver mouths barely whispering. I feel my eyes widen as they shoot to Oliver's. He knows, how does he know? And if he knows who else knows? "I don't know," Oliver says answering my silent questions.

The fact that the Mayor of the Greenbelt knows about my and Oliver's involvement in the tower coming down, or even the fact that he knew people were involved has put an unconscious spring in Oliver's step. He almost seems buoyant as we walk towards the door at the end of the hall. I can understand why, if he thinks others know and they are not doing anything about it means they are with us. I think if it weren't for the reason we were back here he would be wearing a huge smile but as where we were headed was no laughing matter his face is unreadable. I frown at him. He pulls me to a stop and puts his hands on my face.

"It'll be fine," he says almost convincingly. He pushes the door open walking slowly into the darkened room before me.

"Come in and close the door tightly," Henry drawls from the shadows. Oliver closes the door tightly and we stand with our backs against it as we try and focus our eyes.

"I don't believe I asked you to stay behind Mr. Hunter," Henry says sounding mildly irritated.

"No you didn't," Oliver says gripping my hand harder.

"And yet here you are," Henry says now sounding annoyed.

"Here I am," Oliver says sounding unfazed. I squeeze his arm as Henry's irritated growl echoes around the room.

"You forget who you are talking to," Henry says, his tone thick with threat.

"I don't actually. You're Henry Caldwell, the leader of our country. You have been trying for the last few months to recruit Chloe who has turned you down at every turn." Henry passes us in the shadow, pacing up and down the small room. Oliver moves in front of me slightly and continues. "When she declined your offer you sent in her mother to lure her away from me and the life she's choosing to live," Oliver says. I stare out into the room trying to look like I agree with everything Oliver is saying. I do but I'm too scared to be that brave. I hear Henry chuckle making me jump when he moves in front of us stopping before turning and facing us.

"You have got me Mr. Hunter. However you are wrong about one thing," he says. I see his white teeth flashing in the dark.

"Oh really?" Oliver says almost laughing. I see Henry's eyes flicker to me.

"I have absolutely no interest in Chloe," he says shocking me. "I am sorry my dear everything I have done is for another. I could not care less if you were to die today and I never see your face again. I am saddened however that you will be wasted to grow old and fat and have some sniveling infants running around you. That is wasteful." He looks away from me. I frown at him unable to comprehend what he had said. "You however Mr. Hunter,

I did want. I liked your attitude. You are strong minded and brave, if not a little hot headed. You are nothing like your runt brother!" Henry hisses. Oliver growls before he lunges at Henry gripping him around the neck and squeezing hard. The action shocks Henry so much I see a flash of panic in his eyes as he stumbles backwards.

"Stop!" I yell, when Henry finally gets over the shock and in a flash pins Oliver to the wall, his forearm crushing Oliver's windpipe.

"You have a fire in you that I admire Mr. Hunter. I would so love to sample it," Henry says as I try to pull his arm off of Oliver.

"Please stop!" I scream as Henrys mouth lowers to Oliver's throat. My mother is at Henry's side in a flash. I stare at Oliver who is turning red as his airways are squeezed harder.

"Henry my love, you must be careful. Remember where we are," my mum says calmly. This seems to snap Henry out of his rage and with a little shake of his head he drops Oliver who, despite coughing loudly and taking ragged breaths lands, on his feet. I rush to his side helping him stand steady.

"Get on with it Lillian. I want to leave this place," Henry says sounding out of breath as he slinks off to the back of the room. I catch him rubbing at his neck before he vanishes from my sight completely. The shock of seeing Oliver nearly bitten has completely erased the reason as to why we were here in the first place out of my mind. I frown into the darkness ignoring my mother's attempt to get into my line of sight and look at her.

"What do you want?" I ask Henry, he chuckles darkly.

"Like I say I am not interested in you. I am here on behalf of someone else," he says. I focus my eyes on the spot where his voice is coming from as my mother's shadow moves closer to me.

"Stay back," Oliver croaks as she nears. I see her freeze and hear a low growl coming from her.

"Hello Chloe," she says slowly. My eyes close as the memory of her voice stings my eyes. Oliver straightens up stepping in front of me again. I look up at him knowing that if I look directly at her I will lose my already shaky grip on my nerves.

"She won't even look at you. Can you see my dear how much she loathes you?" Henry says from his dark corner. I scoff loudly. I'm surprised to hear him chuckle. "I am correct I see Mrs. Hunter."

"Nailed it," I say tensely. I hear Oliver snort and I try not to laugh. The ridiculousness of the situation is not lost on me. I have wanted nothing more to see my mother again to tell her exactly what I thought of her. How I hate her for what she did to my family and me. I want to tell her that I wish she had really died, that I'm embarrassed to be associated with her. However as she stands mere meters away my body and mouth seem to have stopped working.

"Oh my dear Lillian can you not feel the hatred pouring off of your dear daughter? It is thick and strong it's as potent as any poison," Henry says. I see my mother back away from me a little. Like it's, in fact, a real solid thing that's deterring her.

"Are we done here?" I ask still ignoring the dark stares of my mother and holding Oliver tight.

"You are free to go," Henry says dismissively. My mother hisses.

"No, I'm not done. Chloe I want you to look at me, you are my daughter. I am your mother," she says moving into my eye line. I frown as my eyes land on her unwillingly. Oliver pulls me tighter to his side. I hold his hand as I feel a shiver down my spine.

"Stay right there," Oliver says his voice warning as she steps towards us. She stops but doesn't look at him.

"You look like my mother," I say frowning. She smiles slightly, happy that I finally acknowledged her existence. I stare at her as the shiver runs through me again.

"I am your mother," she says happily.

"No. My mother died," I say with a frown.

"I am still here baby. You look so different." I glare at her, as she looks me over.

"Well, eleven years will do that to a human," I say shortly.

"I would have recognised you anywhere. When I saw you at graduation in my dress it was like looking into a mirror," she says. I shrug at her.

"Well unfortunately I look like you so... Michael and Joseph remind me of that on a regular basis." I say. She looks a little startled at the mention of them. "You remember them then, your sons?" she nods and looks away. Her eyes flicker to Oliver.

"You, I did not recognise Oliver," she says with a little smile, ignoring my question. I pull him backwards stepping in front of him. He grips my arms tightly but doesn't move me.

"Don't talk to him!" I snap. Her eyes dart back to me wide and startled as I glare at her.

"I only want to talk," she says backing away from me slightly.

"Then talk to me. That's what you dragged me back here for is it not? Oliver is nothing to do with you," I say through gritted teeth. I feel the pull again but this time I just laugh. My laugh dies when Henry slides out of the shadows next to my mother. He lowers his mouth to her ear as she stares at me looking confused.

"It will not work my love. Can you not sense it?" he asks in a carrying whisper. I frown at him. They both look over my shoulder at Oliver. Henry smiles while my mother starts breathing heavily. "Look how she protects him from you. Look how he is ready to spring to her defence despite my choking the air from him. It is too late my dear, her heart belongs to him. They have become one." My mother's eyes flicker between us. Oliver steps next to me, I take his hand before looking at my mother.

329

"No, it can't be," she says. Henry smiles as he straightens up.

"It seems you are too late my love," he says looking a little bit pleased. She growls angrily and in a flash she rushes towards us. My eyes widen as Oliver pushes me aside. I hear him grunt as he and my mother fall to the floor in a heap. I scrabble to get up as my mother and Oliver wrestle on the ground. My mother has him pinned but he's struggling hard as she screams at him.

"You stole my daughter from me! You had no right to her!" she yells into his face.

"Neither do you!" Oliver growls back. He bucks his hips throwing her off balance. I run at them hard throwing my full body weight into my mother. She calls out as she's thrown off Oliver. I'm on top of her, pinning her arms on the ground with my legs. I do the only thing I can think of, I grip her neck hard making her eyes bulge.

"STOP!" echo's the collective cry from Oliver and Henry. I grip her harder. She stares up at me with wide fearful eyes. I don't see my mother anymore but a monster, a monster that must be put down. I feel her neck begin to give beneath my hands when a warm arm grabs me around the waist and I'm dragged off of her. I gasp when the room comes back into focus. I scream as Oliver drags me back from her.

"No let me go!" I yell. I watch as a wide-eyed, panicked looking Henry helps my mother to her feet.

"I think we are done here," he says tensely. Oliver tugs me hard spinning me out of the sight of my mother.

"We're going," Oliver says walking me to the door. I wriggle hard out of his arms turning to face Henry, locking eyes with him.

"Tell your mate that if she comes near me or my family again I will kill her," I say as Oliver pulls my arm.

"Chloe!" he says angrily.

"Is that a threat?" Henry scoffs. I smile at him shaking my head.

"No, it's a promise," I say then before he can reply I throw the door open and walk out.

Lillian stares in shock as her daughter storms out of the room. The shaft of light that pours in the room stings her sensitive eyes but she cannot tear her eyes away. The sound of her daughter's threat rings in her head as the pain from her hold on her neck makes her feel disorientated.

A loud bang pulls her from her shock. She turns slowly to find Henry pressed against the now closed door. He looks at her with a mixture of fear and pure rage. It makes Lillian nervous to her core.

"That was an interesting development." he tries to joke but his tone is far from humorous. Lillian's hand moves to her neck as Henry's eyes follow it there.

"How did they know?" she croaks when Henry's eyes meet hers. His black soulless eyes darken further. She realises his breathing has accelerated.

"I don't know, we can't be sure they do," he says. His fist bangs on the door punching a hole through it allowing a beam of light to come through. He steps away from it hissing. "We have to eliminate the threat. They have to be involved in the death of the three in the tower," he says. Lillian's eyes widen.

"I doubt my daughter would have killed…"

"Wake up Lillian!" Henry rages making Lillian shrink back. "This foolishness is over. You are not to try and contact her, I forbid it. As of now, she and her mate are the enemy. Look how she nearly ended your life without so much as a second thought. You are her mother, despite how much she denies it. If she can do that to you imagine what she would do to those she had no connection with. They must be stopped," Henry says as Lillian stares at him.

"How?"

"We cut out the disease and we will start from the bottom, at the roots."

"You mean…"

"I think it is time I paid Eric a visit.

331

I rush forward trying to get as much space as possible between my mother and me. I only slow when I can no longer catch my breath. I stop in the street putting my hands on my trembling knees. I tried to kill my mother, I wouldn't have stopped. I would have kept going until...

"You stopped me," I say still gasping slightly for air. I hear Oliver breathing heavily behind me. "I didn't want to even look at her but when she spoke to you I couldn't... she has no right to expect anything from me. Does she?" I ask standing up and turning to Oliver who is clutching his side. He shakes his head and I nod. "I don't know what she was expecting from me. Did she expect me to run at her and hug her, tell her that I missed her? That I forgive her?" I say angrily, I wipe away the tears that have escaped my eyes. "She abandoned me, my brothers and my dad. I could never forgive that," I say. He nods at me. I groan loudly gripping my hair. "I hate her! I hate that she has made me cry, again! She doesn't deserve my tears. It's not even my mum; the thing in there is just wearing her like some sick costume. My real mum would never have attacked us; the thing may look like her but inside it's a monster. I want them gone; we have to end this Oliver," I say getting hysterical. I realise that I'm shouting. The houses around us can probably hear what I'm saying but I'm too angry to care. Oliver takes my head in his hands he leans down giving me a quick kiss. I take a deep steadying breath.

"We will Chloe, I promise. This is the first time in my life where I can say that I'm glad Elliot is not here, that they declined him. If they had him to use against me I don't know if I would be able to do what you did," he says sounding sad.

"Why did you stop me? That was not my mother," I say angrily pointing back towards the town hall.

"I don't know, seeing you there with your hands around her neck scared me. All I could think of was how I would feel after I did it if it was Elliot looking up at me.

Seeing the pain on your face was hard to witness," he says. I give him an apologetic smile.

"I'm sorry. I didn't think it just kind of happened. I thought she was going to kill you," I say honestly remembering the feeling of complete anger and fear that propelled me towards her.

"You don't have anything to be sorry about, you saved me. Twice," he says. I frown remembering that Henry had nearly bitten him as well.

"I was so scared when he had you against that wall. I honestly though he was going to bite you," I say. He chuckles humorlessly.

"I did too. I had no idea what he was doing, that he wanted me," he cringes. I take his hand as he shivers. "You have to tell your dad about this," he says making my eyes widen and my head automatically shake. "Chloe he would want to know. We should've told him about this before but now..." He takes a breath as his hands tighten on my arms. "Things are different. They are going to get bad quickly, its best if he knows what is going on," he says reasonably. I know he really means that we're in more danger. We're surely going to be figured out just from the fact we both just exposed our greatest weapon and the only bit of knowledge we had about killing the Fanged.

"We're in trouble aren't we?" I ask in a low voice. He smiles a little.

"I think we are going to be if we don't end this soon," he says.

"I still don't think I can tell him though. What he doesn't know won't hurt him," I protest.

"And if you get hurt or killed do you think he'll feel better not knowing why?" Oliver asks. I look down frowning at the ground. I hate when he's right. "He's your dad Chloe you have to tell him. He may even be able to help," he says.

I chew my lip as I ponder the idea. I know he's going to be furious with me that I have kept my mother a secret.

He'll be even worse when he finds out how long it has been going on for.

"I don't know if I can," I moan and Oliver puts his arm over my shoulder.

"Come on let's get it done, what's the worst that could happen?"

"Why the hell am I only hearing about this now!?" Dad rages down the phone. I hold it away from my ear staring at Oliver who eyes the phone wearily, like my dad might come out of it. I had called him after a lot more persuasion from Oliver who now looks like he's regretting it.

In dads defence he had stayed silent until I got my story out. I told him everything from mum being at the graduation to her being outside my window then what happened tonight. There was a long silent pause, I thought the line was dead until he took a deep breath and yelled down the phone.

"I told you he would be mad," I hiss at Oliver who gives me an apologetic look. Dad laughs manically down the phone.

"Damn right I'm mad Chloe. For god sake you should've told me or you Oliver," he says angrily. Oliver looks guiltily at the phone. "What else are you two keeping from me?" he asks angrily.

"Nothing," I say quickly. Even I can hear the guilt and lie in my tone. I look at Oliver who is chewing his nail anxiously.

"Chloe..." Dad says warningly. I frown knowing I cannot tell him over the phone.

"I can't say," I say, I hear him take another big breath to shout at me. "I want to but I can't right now," I say desperately. Dad releases his breath loudly. He must hear the pleading in my voice and what I'm trying to say, they're always watching.

"What is it? What have you done?" Dad asks sounding worried.

"We'll explain at Christmas," I say, Oliver's eyes widen.

"That's supposed to be a surprise," he says. I groan and glare at him.

"Shut up," I hiss. I hear my dad grunt in agreement.

"I want the full story. Don't you dare miss anything out you hear me?" Dad warns.

"Yes Dad," I mumble.

"Your brothers are going to hit the roof when I tell them."

"Ugh Dad don't tell them, they have enough on their plates," I groan. Oliver rolls his eyes. He knows my brothers well enough to know how badly they are going to react to this news.

"We're a family Chloe; we don't keep things like this from each other," he says sounding extremely disappointed.

"I said I was sorry."

"I know you are but this is unforgivable. You can let Oliver know I will be telling his parents about this too." My eyes dart to Oliver whose eyes have become saucers.

"Please Christopher don't tell them," Oliver begs.

"Sorry Oliver, they have a right to know," Dad interrupts. Oliver leans back in his chair looking very worried. I can't help but feel bad for him. His parents are a force to be reckoned with when they are mad. Jimmy who is normally so quiet and mild mannered is terrifying when he's angry. Oliver's only saving grace is that he's miles away.

"Please Dad we're both really sorry," I beg.

"And so you should be. I'm going to call your brothers," he says with a sigh.

"Dad please…"

"Love you kiddo," he says before the line goes dead. I stare at the phone for a moment before hanging it back up.

"Well that was horrible. You still think it was a good idea?" I ask.

"Well at least he knows," he says as he gets up and wraps his arms around me, kissing my forehead. I nod and give him an apologetic look before burying my head in his chest.

"Yeah but your parents are going to know as well," I say. I feel him sigh.

"They would've found out eventually."

"How are we going to tell them about the tower?" I ask in the hushed voice we normally take on when we want to talk about something we shouldn't be discussing.

Just in case.

"We'll just have to tell them, maybe now they have found out about this they will realise we had something to do with it. It's been all over the news," Oliver says, playing with my hair.

"Well if that's the case then maybe they'll want to help?" I say hopefully. He pulls back to stare down at me.

"You think they will?"

"Yeah we're not the only ones to think like this. I know Michael will agree with us after he calms down. There has to be others outside of our families who care enough to do something. I mean the Mayor knew. He knew and he didn't say anything," I say. Oliver smiles and I see the hope in his eyes again.

"It could happen. Once they know they could find some people willing to help," he says. I smile when the realisation of what he said moves me.

"Everyone working together?"

"Like it should be," he says.

"Could this really work?"

"Only one way to find out."

"You'll have to tell the others. They'll listen to you," I say. He shakes his head.

"No it's your idea, you should tell them. It's a great idea," he says his hands gripping my waist.

"You're only saying that because you think you have to," I say. He laughs before kissing my forehead.

"When do I not say what is really on my mind? If I thought it was a bad idea I would tell you. Trust me," he says with a smile.

"I do," I say winding my arms around his neck.

"I'll tell them what happened today. I'll explain that we may have made a mistake in attacking them. I think they know we know that their neck is their point of weakness," he says. I shrug as I bite my lip.

"They were going to find out eventually right?"

"Yeah, but now they could do something to protect themselves," he says. I shake my head and he frowns down at me.

"I doubt it."

"We can't be sure though," he says.

"I know but if I have learned something from you Oliver is that people always leave their weaknesses unguarded," I say. He frowns at me before I tickle his sides making him gasp. I freeze when I realise that his gasp was not a gasp of surprise but of pain. He groans as I step back my eyes wide. "I'm sorry," I say as he tries to school his pained face and holds his ribs. I move his arms away from around his ribs and pull his jumper up slowly. My free hand covers my mouth at the sight of his bruised ribs. "Oliver I'm so sorry. Why didn't you say?" I say angrily. He shrugs.

"I didn't realise they were so bad, the adrenaline must have worn off," he says prodding his ribs gingerly. "Your mother hits hard."

"Are they broken?"

"I don't think so," he says. I see his hand begin to shake. He moves it away like he doesn't want me to see but I do and I frown up at him. "I'm ok," he says as I let go of his jumper. I stare at him in disbelief.

"Are you sure?"

"Yeah I'm ok." He looks over in the direction of our bedroom. "Maybe I should go and have a lie down though," he adds. I smile at him knowing he's only trying to act nonchalant so I don't worry. I roll my eyes at him as he gives me a sheepish smile. I help him get into the bedroom and he groans as he sits down. I pull off his shoes before I help him undress and lie down. The phone rings and our eyes meet.

"I'll be back in a minute," I say. He nods before closing his eyes.

"Ok," he says in a tight voice. I lean down and give him a quick kiss before running into the kitchen and snatching up the phone. I cringe as I answer realising too late that I should've left it to ring out.

"What the hell are you two playing at?" Joseph yells down the phone. I cringe as I sit down.

"Hi Joseph, Dad called you then?" I say trying to be funny, he doesn't find it very funny and the phone vibrates in my hand as he screams at me.

Chapter 32

Christmas time in the Evans house hold used to be met with enthusiasm and laughter but this year as Eric Evans finishes wrapping the last of his children's gifts he's in a sombre mood. Once they are hidden he stretches and moves towards the tree, in the corner of the room. He places a fallen decoration back on the tree and the back of his eyes prickle; he straightens up swallowing hard as he fights back the tears. He looks at the picture of his son on the mantelpiece and a sob escapes his mouth. He's reminded that this will be the first year without him after his untimely death at the beginning of the year. The whole house is missing his presence. His wife had been sobbing quietly all evening while his daughters sat at in front of the fire toasting marshmallows; it was Daniel's favourite part of Christmas. Eric extinguishes the last of the candles and makes his way through the dark hallway into his daughters' room.

They are huddled together in the same bed, the elder of the two with her arms wrapped around her younger sister. His heart breaks when he notices they have been crying their sweet faces red and their eyes puffy. The sight of them lying together makes him feel helpless. He kisses each of them before backing out of the room a tear falling from his nose. He leans against their door so he's facing Daniel's room. He reaches for the door his hand trembling, as he turns the handle the hairs on his neck stand up and his eyes catch a slight movement in the living room. He sees a light from within the room; he frowns as he looks around. He was sure he had blown all the candles out. His hand falls from the handle and he walks slowly towards the source of the light. He stops in his tracks when his nose picks up a familiar choking scent, the sickly smell of citrus and pine smoke. With every ounce of courage he can muster he rounds the corner. His eyes land on Henry Caldwell, sitting comfortably in his chair holding his family picture.

"Merry Christmas Eric, your house looks lovely," Henry says looking up from the picture with a smile.

"What're you doing here?" Eric asks in no mood for pleasantries. Henry's eyebrows raise and he laughs.

"I have a problem," Henry says standing up smoothly, throwing the picture on the chair behind him. Eric backs away instinctively.

"A p-problem?" he asks his courage wavering as the severity of the situation dawns on him.

"Yes. I have an issue regarding Miss Wood or should I say Mrs. Hunter," Henry says. Eric frowns.

"I did everything I could. She chose to not become one of your kind," he says rooting himself to his spot. Henry sighs and pinches between his eyes.

"Don't I know it? I have been reminded of it every day since," he says. He breathes deeply before smiling. "My mate happens to be her mother and she was very keen to have her daughter back."

"Was?"

"Yes, was. I have demanded she drop the subject."

"It's out of my hands now. I did everything I could you must know that," Eric says backing away further towards the hallway.

"Oh Eric I am sure you did. However you were not truthful to me about the girl's relationship. If we had known about her connection to the angry red head we would have assured he would be out of the picture."

"W-who are you talking about?"

"Don't play coy with me Eric it aggravates me," Henry says through his teeth.

"Please I had no idea they were anything other than friends. I don't see how this could have swayed her decision at the time."

"Like I have said before I do not care for the girl but your mistruth with the information seems to have caused some sort of problem," Henry says and Eric frowns.

"I assure you that was not my intention."

"You are full of lies. Anyone with eyes could have seen their connection; even the dumbest of your herd would have seen it."

"I never..."

"Liar, I detest liars!" Henry yells and Eric hears a startled gasp from his bedroom. The bedroom door flies open and his wife comes rushing out colliding with Henry who shoves her towards Eric in disgust.

"Who are you?" she says shakily. Henry smiles.

"You have come to the end of your usefulness Mr. Evans. You are to be made an example of," Henry says. Eric shoves his wife behind him and she rushes to the door of their daughters.

"Please, please don't, my family won't survive," Eric begs. Henry chuckles darkly as he moves towards Eric his eyes flash darkly and he runs his tongue over his teeth before leaning towards Eric and whispering in his ear.

"I will personally see to it that they won't," he says before he sinks his teeth into Eric's neck filling the house with screams.

The past few months have been hard. With Oliver's injuries, given to him by Henry and my mother, being worse than we had thought and him taking longer to fully recover it has been difficult. The morning after the incident with my mother I awoke to a horrible rasping noise from beside me. My eyes instantly flew open and I sat up looking down at Oliver whose lips were slightly blue and his skin was a sickly pale colour except from the black bruise on his neck. The sight of him lying there his eyes closed and his breath rattling made my heart stop. After a split second I was out of bed shaking him hard.

"Oliver?" I called but he was unresponsive. I did the only thing I could think of, I let out the loudest scream I could muster.

"HELP!"

It was moments before the front door was being pounded on. I rushed from Oliver's side and unlocked all the locks with trembling hands. Damien and David almost fell through the door their eyes wide and worried.

"What is it?" David asked hurriedly. I pointed to the bedroom and Damien ran in.

"Oliver. He won't wake up," I croaked. I could hear Damien calling Oliver's name. His voice rose and called out to David.

"David, get a doctor, now!" he said his voice firm and commanding. David left without another word, sprinting down the street as Rose and Mary rushed down the path.

"What's going on?" Rose asked running up to me.

"Oliver is..."

"Chloe," Damien called making me jump. I rushed back into the room followed by Rose and Mary.

"Oh my god," Mary said from behind me. I stood frozen as Oliver's eyes met mine.

"Oliver!" I squeaked. His lips that had gone from blue to bright red lifted in a smile. I ran at him crashing to my knees by his head.

"Careful," Damien said pushing me back a little. I frowned at him but he just he lowered his eyes to where there was a foamy reddish brown puddle inches from my knees.

"Is that..." I stared at it wide eyed and horrified.

"Blood, yes. I think he was choking on it," Damien explained calmly. My eyes widened almost leaving my head. "He coughed it up when I pulled him out of bed and put him in the recovery position," Damien explained. I just nodded dumbly whilst stroking Oliver's sweaty hair.

"Chloe," Oliver croaked making me jump a little. His eyes met mine again. I took his hand and squeezed it tightly.

"I'm so sorry Oliver. I never knew! You could have..." I gasped. Oliver gave my hand a soft squeeze.

"I'm fine. You aren't getting rid of me that easily," he added his voice raspy but his tone joking before giving me a toothy smile.

"Not really a time for jokes," I snapped as I glared at him and frowned.

342

"I'm fine," he said soothingly as I dropped my head. He kissed my hand as angry, terrified, relieved tears began to fall from my eyes. My shoulders shook with quiet sobs. I was relieved when the doctor finally came in behind David who ushered Mary and Rose out of the room. Damien moved out of the doctor's way and I jumped up to hug him before he left the room.

"Thank you," I said and I caught David's eye. "Both of you." They smiled at me and I closed the door behind them. I turned back into the room noticing Oliver looking at me as the doctor examined his blackened ribs. I bit my lip hard at the sight of the other huge black bruise. I walked over to him and knelt down. I took his hand while the doctor looked over him. Oliver didn't make a noise as the doctor probed and prodded him but the pressure of his grip on my hand told me how much pain he was in. The doctor was listening to Oliver's heart and lungs when he looked up at us both and spoke for the first time, since arriving.

"How did this happen?" he asked in a soft calming voice as he examined Oliver's neck. I looked down and waited for Oliver to answer.

"I fell," Oliver croaked. The doctor's eyebrows rose looking thoroughly unconvinced.

"You fell?" he asked and Oliver nodded. "Ok when did you fall? Was this before or after the meeting last night?" he asked giving Oliver a knowing look. Oliver stared at him his mouth open and the doctor smiled at him. "I've heard a bit about you lot. I need to know how this happened um..." The doctor froze looking at us a little embarrassed.

"Oliver and this is my... this is Chloe. And I told you I fell," Oliver said his voice pained. The doctor chuckled and shook his head.

"Ok Oliver, I get it you don't know me but just know you guys are not alone ok. For future reference I'm Ray," he said as he smiled. Oliver and I looked at each other quite shocked about the openness of the young doctor. "You are lucky to be alive Oliver," Ray said getting back to business. "These are some quite serious injuries. I'm surprised you haven't punctured a lung, you definitely have a few broken ribs but they will heal, eventually. You have some fluid in your lungs but I can see you coughed up some of that," he said, looking at the puddle of foamy blood on the floor. "And by the look of that bruise on your neck you're lucky it wasn't broken." My eyes widened in horror but Ray just went on. "You are going to have to lay off of work for a while until you're able to breathe without pain at the very least. I will bandage you up but that's the best I can do."

"That's fine but I can't miss work," Oliver said. I frowned at him as he looked at Ray.

"You can't work, not like this," Ray said firmly. Oliver opened his mouth to argue.

"I'll do it," I said quickly. The both turned and looked at me. "What? It makes sense you won't have to pay me."

"Ok, I will train you," he said. Ray nodded in agreement.

"Just make sure you don't let him do anything until he's ready." he said to me and I nodded.

"I promise."

So here I am, on the coldest of days, tending to Oliver's horses while he sorts out his paper work. He has been able to do the work for himself for around a month now but I found I enjoyed it and he has enjoyed my company so I stayed longer than needed. It's not so bad if you don't mind the cold but there are plenty of things to keep you busy and warm. It's been pretty rough all round since winter hit, the days are horribly cold and the nights are even worse. The only thing that has been keeping me going and working hard is that my family is visiting. Today is the first day I will have seen them since my graduation. Granted they have been calling me almost every day since I told them about my mother. They assure me they are just calling to check I'm ok and coping with doing all the work but I know they are looking for some more information. I have told them countless times that I will tell them everything and that there is nothing new to report. Since the town hall meeting I haven't heard, seen or felt my mother's presence near me and for that I'm glad.

Maybe she finally got the message?

"Are you done in there?" Oliver calls down the barn. I stick my head out of the stable with a big smile on my face.

"I'm done," I say quickly sweeping back the bed grinning at my work.

"You're very neat," Oliver says sticking his head over the door. "You know they are just going to come in there and mess up all your hard work, right?" he says with a smile. I roll my eyes.

"True. But it doesn't mean it can't look nice even if it's only for a few seconds," I say. He chuckles. It's nice to hear him laugh without sucking in a pained breath or gripping his ribs. He was miserable for a good few weeks because of that. I put all my tools away as Oliver comes back around the corner, carrying two bales of straw. I frown as he drops the bales at me feet.

"What? I'm fine, I feel great," he says. I roll my eyes.

"I give up," I sigh dramatically. He laughs loudly as he wraps his arms around my waist lowering his head to my neck.

"I thought we were a team," he says as his hot breath tickles my neck followed his chilled lips. My whole body shivers as I feel him smile against my neck.

"We are," I say as his lips trail down my neck. "Doesn't mean you're any less of a nightmare," I say desperately trying not to get side tracked. I wriggle free of him and turn around, he stares at me with a pout and I smile.

"Behave; I want to get back home, now go lock up," I say. He salutes me with a big smile.

"Yes ma'am, I like it when you're bossy," he says with a wink and I shove him.

"Go!" I say giggling. He laughs as he walks down the yard.

"What time is your family coming?" he calls over his shoulder.

"Noon."

"Are you ready to tell them about everything?" he asks. I frown at him.

"So much for us being a team," I scoff. He smiles as he locks up the tack rooms.

"We are, but your brothers are probably going to re-break my ribs," he says. I shake my head.

"They won't. Dad and my brothers might overreact a little more than the others did when I told them we were going to tell our families everything," I say. Oliver nods in agreement.

"Yeah I was surprised how well the others took that news. I'll be right back," he says before rushing off. I chew my lip as I imagine how badly Dad, Joseph and Michael are going to react when I tell them everything. Oliver is right though, I was shocked to the core when we told the others we wanted to tell our families about what we had all been up to. I was expecting a lot of yelling and arguing but I was surprised by the looks of acceptance and trust that filled the room, well almost...

"This is unbelievable. You can't just spring this on us the day they're supposed to be arriving. We're supposed to discuss who we're telling and if we all agree, then it's passed. You can't just expect us to be ok with this," Marcus cried out as soon as I had told them.

"I'm sorry but that's bull shit!" I snapped. He blinked at me and straightened up. "I don't recall all of us being asked when you told your friends or when everyone else involved people." I looked around the room to see a few people wearing an amused look and others wearing a surprised one. "I don't see how we're not allowed to tell anyone. I don't see how that's fair," I snapped and Marcus scoffed.

"Well you have hardly been discreet in the past, have you girl?" he shot back. I frowned at him knowing he was right but not wanting to admit it.

"That was a mistake," Oliver said defensively. Marcus rolled his eyes.

"Oh yeah great. You two possibly giving away our best and only piece of useful information is a pretty big mistake," he scoffed.

"What did you expect them to do Marcus? They were in danger," Mary said looking at him with a mixture of exasperation and anger. Marcus groaned loudly.

"That's what they say happened. How do we know it was the truth?"

"Oh, shut up Marcus!" Harriet said from her chair. The whole room fell silent and we all looked at her. She was massaging her temples and eventually looked up at him. "You saw the state Oliver got into. You saw the damage those Leeches caused. The boy was nearly killed," she said in a measured tone. Marcus stared at her like he had been slapped.

"Listen to your wife Marcus," John said smiling. Marcus's mouth closed and he sulked in the corner for the rest of the meeting.

"Are we done here?" he calls, as I finish locking up the tack rooms. He comes around the corner with my jacket.

"Yeah we're done. Are you sure we're going to be able to fit everyone in the house?" I ask, pulling on my jacket as Oliver closes the barn doors. He looks at me rolling his eyes.

"Yes Chloe," he groans. I shake my head smiling. It has been something that had required a bit of thought. What with my dad and brothers being so big and then Millie and the kids. We were able to borrow blankets and pillows from Rose and Mary. They even donated the little mattresses from their baby cribs for the twins. The little room had been made up for Michael and his family while dad and Joseph would have to fight over the sofa and the cushions on the floor. I had offered Dad our bed but he was not hearing anything on the matter. "It's going to be a squeeze, but we'll manage," Oliver says taking my hand after we climb the entrance gate. Oliver looks back over his shoulder then up at the sky. "Do you think it's going to snow?"

"I don't know," I say. He nods his head like that was all he needed to hear. After a busy end of year Oliver had turned the horses out for the winter. The harvest and plowing is over as the ground was too hard to do any sort of work with them so he turned them out. It had freed up a lot of time for him, which was good considering he needed to recover. It was also great as he was getting more offers for special occasions after the success of Norman's son's wedding. Despite his injuries Oliver made it to the wedding, with my help. Except for the bride, the horse was the talk of the event. Much to Norman's annoyance and Oliver's delight. Oliver was paid handsomely for the work and hire. Every penny of the money he has raised has gone straight into the pocket of Terry, one of our new recruits who just so happens to be the village blacksmith.

He's a heavyset man with thick strong looking arms. His hands are scarred and burned and as big as dinner plates. His whole scruffiness and size is intimidating, he was a great choice. On the day Billy took us to meet him he certainly noticed that I was, at first, a little scared of him.

"What's up kid?" he asked me as I eyed him warily.
"Nothing," I said trying to make my voice a strong as I could.

He drew his eyes off me and turned back to Billy who'd been doing all the talking.

"So you're telling me that the Fanged can be killed and you're wanting me to make you weapons to do just that?" he asked. Billy shrugged.

"That 'bout sums it up," he said using a nail to pick out the dirt from his nails. Terry shook his head as he looked at Billy.

"This sounds like some fairy tale bull shit to me," he scoffed. Billy looked up from his hands and laughed.

"It sure does," he said simply. Terry stared at him for a moment.

"You aren't joking are you?" he asked with a frown. Billy shook his head. Billy has a remarkable way of not actually talking to someone but being able to convince them to do something or win them around. I was not surprised when Terry laughed loudly and shook Billy's hand. "Fine but I want in," he said. Billy's eyebrows rose slightly then fell back to their normal position.

"Are you sure?" Billy asked eyeing Terry carefully. Terry nodded his light eyes darkening under his bushy eyebrows.

"You say they can be killed. I want the pleasure of doing that. They took my girl from me just because she couldn't have kids. I want them all dead," he said his tone level but full of anger. I stared at him in shock. I had never met someone who had their child taken from them like that and I felt a surge of sympathy towards the big man. He looked over at me and frowned. "You look like her kid," he said nodding at me.

"I'm sorry," I said not really knowing why I said it. He nodded before looking at Oliver then back to Billy.

"So is it just you and these kids?"

"We're not kids," I said loudly. I was tired of being called that, enough was enough. Everyone looked at me Terry with surprise, Billy and Oliver with a little bit of humour in their eyes. "Well, we're not."

"You look like kids to me, girl," Terry shrugged. I ground my teeth as I stepped forward.

"Well this bunch of 'kids' has done more in the last few months to free your 'old' assess than you have done in your whole lifetime. So if you have a problem working with us then fine forget we asked. We'll find someone else or another way," I said crossing my arms. Terry stared at me then burst into a loud echoing laugh.

"Is she for real?" he hollered pointing his thumb at me. Billy smiled at me as I stared at Terry feeling mortified that he was laughing at me.

"She's the real deal," Billy said giving me a wink. Terry looked back at me and crossed his arms mirroring me. I saw the faintest hint of a smile before he spoke.

"Well girl…"

"It's Chloe," I snapped. He held up his hands in surrender and smiled at me.

"Well Chloe, you have yourself a blacksmith," he said holding out his hand for me to shake. I took his hand and I smiled. "When do you need them for?" he asked. I stared between Billy and Oliver who were both smiling at me.

"Um, well as soon as possible," I said as Terry let go of my hand. He clapped his big hands together as he stood up from his bench.

"I'll get right on it," he said with a wink. I smiled at him.

"Thank you."

I smile as Oliver and I near the edge of the village. A large flake of snow floats in front of my eyes and I stop in my tracks as Oliver drops my hand and gives me an apologetic smile.

"I will be home in a bit," he says backing up. I just smile and nod before he turns and runs back towards the yard. I decide to have a little jog as the cold seeps in through my coat. I'm glad to get home and smile when I open the door and a rush of warm air greets me. I close the door and begin pulling off my many layers. I head into the kitchen to finish off the cleaning from breakfast. Before our guests arrive.

Chapter 33

I'm off in my own little world when I hear a loud rumbling laugh. I rush out of the kitchen as the front door opens and smile widely as Joseph and Michael wrestle to get through the door first.

"Chloe!" they both call as they pop through the doorway pulling me into a chilly but no less amazing hug. I hug them both individually; Joseph picks me up like I'm a small child and gives me a bone-crushing squeeze.

"You look like a real mountain man," I say as he drops me. He smiles as he ruffles his beard.

"Keeps my face warm." He shrugs. I chuckle as I turn to Michael and smile. He pulls me into a hug and spins me around.

"Put me down!" I squeal as I laugh.

"Jeez you got heavy, you putting on some pounds Chloe?" he asks chuckling. I hit his arm.

"Jerk," I growl.

"Bitch," he says with a big smile making me laugh. "Missed you sis."

"I missed you guys too. Where are Millie and the kids?" I ask looking around for them.

"They have gone to Millie's parents. Dad said it was for the best," he says looking out the door. I sag a little.

"I wanted to meet Alice," I pout. He smiles nudging me with his arm.

"Next time," he promises. I turn around as Oliver brings in their bags. He smiles at me before I turn to Dad who is standing in the doorway smiling.

"Hi Dad," I say smiling back at him.

352

"Hey kiddo," he says. I run at him slamming into him and squeeze tightly. "Oh look out, you're going to bust my back," he says. He pulls away holding me out at arm's length his eyes darting all over me. "You look different. You look well, how are you?" he says slowly and I smile.

"I'm good," I say. I pull him in the house closing the door behind him. He looks around the house. I stand with him as he does.

"Nice little place you have got here," he says.

"It's ok," Oliver says with a shrug.

"Nicer than the hut I was given," Joseph says as he peers around the kitchen.

"That's not hard though you basically live in a shed," I say. He nods in agreement.

"A fair point."

"So are we getting a tour?" Michael asks. I look at Oliver who is chewing his lip. He meets my eye and nods slightly.

"Actually we were hoping that you would want to go for a walk. We can catch up then. We have got some things to tell you," I say as Oliver moves to stand beside me. In perfect synchronisation Dad, Joseph and Michael's eyes move downwards to my stomach and then to Oliver where they shoot him a death glare. My mind is slightly slow but when it catches up I groan.

"God no, not *that*!" I snap. Their faces relax and Oliver lets out a quiet, relieved breath.

"Well if it's not about that what is it about? Your mother?" Dad asks. I stare at him.

"Partly," I say quietly and he narrows his eyes at me. "Please can we just go out and I will explain," I beg. Dad reaches for the door and opens it.

"Lead the way," he says.

We are all silent as we walk towards the outskirts of the village. The only sound I can hear is the crunch of the fresh snow beneath our feet and the irritated huffs from Michael.

353

"Can we just get this over with I'm freezing," he finally says. Joseph shoves him.

"Sitting in an office all day has made you soft Michael," he says as Michael scowls at him.

"Yeah well not all of us are covered in a disgusting layer of hair," he snipes. Joseph grumbles in laughter.

"You're just jealous because I can grow a beard and you have the face of a little girl," Joseph says and Michael narrows his eyes. I look up at Oliver who is trying not to smile. I look away in fear I might laugh. I had forgotten how much the two of them squabble. I suddenly realise it's going to be a long week with the two of them in our tiny house.

"Will you two knock it off?" Dad says with a sigh. I can't help the smile that crosses my face. I see Oliver smile as he catches my eye. He rolls his dramatically. "Are we nearly there kiddo?" Dad asks. I turn and nod my head.

"Yeah we're just going to see the horses," I say. The three of them frown at me but don't say anything. We finally get to the gate and I look into the field. I see the horses all crowded around two large bales of hay. I chew my lip as my eyes move to the large cracked wooden legs of the fallen tower. I turn around; Dad, Joseph and Michael are eyeing Oliver and me strangely.

"Are you telling me you really dragged us out here to look at some dumb horses?" Michael asks frowning into the field.

"That's what you are going to say, yes," I say. He frowns at me clearly confused by our strange behaviour.

"Chloe what is going on?" Dad asks carefully. I know he's anxious to know why I dragged them out here.

"Just have a look into the field," Oliver says as we step aside to let them at the gate.

"I'm really not interested in horses," Michael complains. Oliver sighs.

"Just look," he says. Michael frowns but joins Dad and Joseph at the gate and looks into the field.

354

"What am I looking at?" Joseph asks after a moment. I roll my eyes at the back of his head.

"Just look around," I say imploringly. He shakes his head. I imagine him rolling his eyes right back at me.

"I don't see…" Joseph's voice trails off, he has gone still and rigid.

"What is it?" Dad asks following the line of Joseph's eyes towards the three splintered legs. Joseph slowly turns around his wide eyes land on me.

"How did that happen?" he asks. His eyes dart to Oliver and then back over his shoulder towards the horses. I see the pieces fitting together, as his eyes momentarily go blank and he breathes deeply. "You didn't?" he says staring at us in disbelief. When we don't reply his face turns furious. "Tell me you aren't that stupid!" he rages. I step back, a little frightened while Oliver holds his ground.

"What is it?" Michael asks as he moves away from the gate while I watch Joseph's fists clench.

"What have you done?" Joseph says through gritted teeth. Oliver holds up his hands in a calming way.

"Hang on Joseph it wasn't …" Oliver doesn't get to finish is sentence before Joseph lunges at him. I'm so shocked about what is happening that I just stare as Joseph grabs Oliver's arm. Oliver ducks quickly to avoid Joseph's flying fist, he spins around ending up behind Joseph holding his arm behind his back.

"Hey!" Michael calls looking startled as Oliver and Joseph struggle. Dad and Michael pull them apart.

"Enough! What the hell is going on?" Dad asks stepping between them, looking a little stunned.

"Let us explain," Oliver says, his eyes on Joseph, wary of another attack. I rush up to his side taking the arm that Joseph grabbed and look up at him. He looks a little shaken. He was obviously not expecting an attack from my brother.

"Are you ok?" I ask. He nods and swallows hard.

"I'm fine," he says. I look around to my family as they stare at us with a mixture of confusion and anger. It's probably weird for them to see us like this I hadn't realised that until now. I take Oliver's hand and he squeezes my hand.

"Someone better start talking," Michael says with a strained voice. I take a deep steadying breath.

"They destroyed the tower," Joseph says angrily. I hear a shocked gasp coming from Dad and Michael and I frown down at the ground. When I look up I notice three sets of furious eyes are on Oliver. I step in front of him and they all land on me.

"Stop it. It wasn't his idea," I say defensively, lying slightly. It *was* his idea but I was not going to let him bear the brunt of the anger. "We came up with the idea. We helped to carry it out and it worked. I'm not sorry," I say, as Dads face begins to look pained.

"I heard rumours about this at work. It's been all over the news but they never said where... that was here? You did this?" Michael says, sounding shocked. "Chloe if they find out..."

"They will, they probably already know," Joseph says angrily. I shrug.

"Maybe they have but I don't care. We don't care," I say. Michael frowns looking completely shocked.

"They'll kill you," he says. I smile a little making his eyes widen.

"They are going to kill us eventually anyway. What if I cannot live up to their rules? What if I can't have children, or Oliver? What then? They will kill us anyway. I'm fed up of just living and waiting to be farmed. I want to do something," I say looking at Michael. He frowns looking down at the ground. I know he's remembering the many talks we had when we were younger about being free to do what we want to do. "The tower was just the start, we're fighting back. We're going to take back our lives," I say with as much conviction as I can muster. I can feel my resolve crumble under the devastated stare of my dad but Oliver takes my hand; I feel myself become stronger.

"We know how to kill them," he says. They draw a collective breath and Dad shakes his head.

"They can't be. Someone would have found out by now," he says his tone sad. I shake my head and he frowns.

"Well we have. We know for sure," I say. Michael groans, looking slightly ill.

"Oh Chloe, you didn't?"

"No, I didn't but I did fight one, he came at me in the sun. He tried to bite me but I fought him off before he burst into ash," I say trying to ignore the horror and anger in Dads and both my brothers' faces.

"I did it, I killed it. We know for sure they can be killed," Oliver says giving my hand a squeeze. I know the whole thing is still affecting him. He still wakes me every now and then whilst having nightmares. When he wakes he's groggy and scared he doesn't say a word he just burrows into my chest and holds me tight until he clams down enough to fall back to sleep. He has never mentioned any of it to me, which makes me think he doesn't know it's happening. The thought of him suffering makes me indescribably sad but I don't want to bring it up in fear of him being embarrassed or even reminding him, just in case he's unaware he's still having the dreams.

"How?" Joseph croaks after a few moments. He looks like he might pass out.

"Their necks, they are delicate. You need to…"

"You cut off someone's head?" Dad asks in a shocked whisper looking at Oliver with sad eyes. I feel Oliver stiffen and his hand tightens around mine.

"It was a Fang. Oliver saved someone's life," I say defensively.

"A life that wouldn't have needed saving if you hadn't been so stupid!" Joseph says angrily. I can't help but think he's making a good point but I can't afford to think that way, I believe in what we have done and what we're going to do.

"You don't get it," I say lamely. He scoffs.

"Is that so? Explain to me then little sister, what am I not getting?" he asks stepping forward Michael steps between us glaring at him.

"Calm down," he says tensely and Joseph backs up.

"You never had your life sold off," I say, my voice low as I look at Joseph. His eyes narrow at me. "You were one of the lucky ones. You can choose how you want to live your life. You can fall in love without it being forced on you. You don't have to live with the guilt of bringing children into this life."

"You think I don't suffer?" he interrupts loudly. "God Chloe, you don't know anything do you? I suffer just fine. I have to watch the people I love go through hell. I can't allow myself to like someone in fear they will want children. I won't do that," he says barely containing his anger. I blink at him shocked at his confession.

"Joseph I..."

"You think I'm lucky? You don't know shit sis. I have to watch the people I work with suffer as well. I see abused women walking around with pregnant bellies knowing full well it was their scumbag husband that did it to them. I see the suffering I see the pain. I hear the stories of the poor souls who get taken or lose a child. I may not be a part of it but I know. The worst part of it for me is watching you and Michael going through this knowing I can do nothing to help," he says his body shaking slightly with anger. I stare at him in shock.

"You can," I say desperately. The words leave my mouth before I have even realised.

"I won't help you kill yourself sis, because that's what is going to happen," he says his voice sad now.

"It might not," Michael says quietly. My eyes dart to him.

"It will," Joseph snaps, looking angrily at Michael for not backing him up. Michael ignores his angry stare and turns to me.

"They've gotten this far. You've seen this story on the news; they have no idea who did it. I had no idea that was you guys," Michael says with a little proud smile and I can't help but return it.

"This is hardly a smiling matter!" Dad snaps. Our smiles fall off our faces. "Joseph is right, what you have done is immeasurably stupid and reckless. You could have been killed, you still may be. They may not know now but they could still find out," he says giving us both a stern look. "When did this happen?" he asks his eyes darting back into the field.

"Around three months ago," Oliver says and Dads jaw clenches.

"About the time you got injured?" he asks quickly, connecting the dots. Oliver nods.

"He didn't get hurt that night. That was something different," I speak up. Dad silences me with a look.

"Was that the night you phoned me and told me about your mother?"

"Yes. He got hurt a week or so after the tower came down," I say. Dad nods looking like he's trying to put all of the pieces together.

"How did you get hurt? I want the truth son," Dad says looking at Oliver. Oliver looks at him with wide shocked eyes looking unsure how to put it.

"It was mum," I say saving him. They all look at me. Oliver with relief and the others in horror. "She tried to attack us and Oliver protected me," I say. Dad visibly pales. Michael growls and swears under his breath.

"Chloe fought her off. She saved my life," Oliver says quickly. Their shocked faces turn to me again.

"You did?" Joseph asks looking impressed despite his obvious anger. I nod and he runs his hands over his shaggy face.

"I had her on the ground. I wasn't going to stop," I mutter. They all exchange a worried look.

"I'm glad you did," Dad says, finally. My eyes widen.

"Really?" I ask in a quiet voice. His jaw hardens as his eyes take on a glassy quality and he gives me a tight smile.

"She's mine," he says his tone final. I stare at him as he stares unseeing into the field. The thought of him killing my mum or the monster inside her terrifies me for some reason. I know in the back of my head it's not really her. My real mother died; a cold dead thing replaced her, but he loved her or he had.

I remember what Oliver said about if it were Ethan he wouldn't be able to do it and it makes me wonder if Dad would be able to kill her when it came to it. I look up at Oliver and I'm unsurprised to see he's staring at me. I don't think I would be able to kill Oliver if he was turned. The grim look on his face tells me he's thinking the same thing as I am. I pull my eyes away from him and that worrying thought to glance at Michael and Joseph who are also wearing the same worried looks.

"What did she want?" Michael asks. I frown, as I'm not sure what she actually wanted.

"She wanted Chloe," Oliver says. I stare at him.

"What did she want with you though? Did she want to turn you?" Joseph asks and I shrug.

"I don't know," I say honestly, the whole thing was strange to me. Yes, she had said she wanted to see me and she was furious when she couldn't influence me anymore but I was not certain if she did want me to change or not. I hadn't really thought about it.

"I think she did. That head Fang tried damn hard to change her mind at graduation," Oliver says frowning. I stare at him and he gives me a little smile. He has obviously been thinking about this a lot more than I have. I wish he'd told me.

"It didn't work though," Joseph says, stating the obvious, but I shake my head.

"Mum tried again later. She tried to draw me out of the house in the middle of the night but it didn't work either," I say. Dad turns back around to face me.

"Why did it not work?" he asks looking confused. I chew my lip before I answer.

"Well it worked for a while. Oliver was out of the room then when he came back in he stopped me from going to her. Then when we saw her the night Oliver got injured she couldn't reach me anymore. I could feel her try but it didn't work," I say trying not to blush.

"I don't understand, what changed?" Michael asks. I look at Oliver who is smiling despite the touchy subject matter.

"Henry said that we were joined, that Chloe's heart didn't belong to her mother anymore," Oliver says. I feel myself blushing. Even Oliver shuffles and looks down at his feet.

"So what Chloe's heart belongs to who? You?" Michael asks with a chuckle. Oliver blushes and shrugs.

"That's just what he said," he mumbles. I chew my lip as I try not to smile.

"It does," I say in a small voice. The smile that crosses Oliver's face is glorious. We smile at each other until I hear a groan. I see Joseph frown and let out a loud long breath while dad stares at us, his face unreadable.

"Gross," Michael says and I shake my head at him. "I always knew you two would fu…"

"That's quite enough! That's my baby girl you're talking about," Dad says to Michael he shrugs and smiles evilly as Oliver and I burn crimson.

"We all knew it was going to happen."

"Can we stop talking about this?" I beg.

"So let me clear this up, you two being in 'love' or whatever this is," Joseph says waving his hands at us, "saved your life?" he finishes, looking at me.

"I guess so if you want to look at it like that," I say with a shrug.

"Well then Oliver I'm sorry I tried to knock your head off," Joseph says. I stare between them trying to work out if Joseph is pretending to forgive Oliver.

"It's fine," Oliver says. Joseph nods accepting his forgiveness and I let out a relieved breath.

"So tell us about your great plan. I'm assuming since you brought us out here to look at the scenery in a blizzard, it's something you are not wanting over heard?" Michael asks.

"You could say that," I say and he nods.

"I'm also assuming that since you have dragged us out her you want us to be involved?" Michael asks. I nod at him. "Well spill, I'm freezing. I'm losing the feeling in my toes" he says.

"You want to join us?" I ask unable to keep the surprise out of my voice.

"It could get really bad," Oliver says carefully. I know right away he's thinking about Michael's family.

"I don't doubt it won't. You two aren't the only ones to think like this you know. Millie and I have talked about what we would do if this were to even happen and how we would deal with it if it went tits up. We're ready," he says. I stare at him in shock, he shrugs and smiles at me. "What?"

"Why didn't you say anything?" I say quietly feeling bad that he didn't tell me considering all the times we talked about it when we were younger.

"I don't know... you had your heart set on working for them, I thought your opinions had changed," he says sounding apologetic. I frown knowing where he was coming from, after all, that's what Oliver thought as well. I had been working hard to get an occupation and I did always talk Oliver down from his rants about the Fanged. I see how it might have looked.

"I wish you would have told us about this sooner," Dad says looking between Oliver and me then to Michael who he looks more shocked at.

"I'm sorry Dad it really wasn't something I could have spoken openly about," I say apologetically and he frowns.

"It would be wrong of me to let you go through this alone. So I suppose you better count me in," he says. I smile and hug him. We all look at Joseph who is staring at us like we have all gone insane. Who knows, maybe we have.

"You are all doing this? Seriously?" he asks with a frown. We all nod and he shakes his head in disbelief before he lets out a big sigh. "Fine, it's not like I have much of an option. I'm in."

"You have an option," Oliver says but Joseph shakes his head.

"We're family. We stick together. I'm in," he says with a tone of finality.

"Thank you," I say smiling. He waves me down.

"I still think it's insane but whatever."

"Now we've all agreed will you tell us what the plan is?" Michael asks.

"Tomorrow. When you meet the others," I say making his eyes widen.

"Oh, come on!" he says loudly. I spin around quickly when I hear a crunch of snow from down the track.

"What was that?" I say quietly. As soon as the words are out of my mouth Norman rounds the corner red faced and puffing heavily, he's followed close behind by the two detectives that were investigating the fallen tower. They stop in their tracks as we all look at them. Norman looks over my family suspiciously.

"What do you want?" Oliver asks in a clipped tone as we all stare at each other.

"We were told there were strangers at this field," Norman says warily eyeing my dad and brothers.

"We're Chloe's family," Dad says stepping forward holding his hand out to Norman who stares at him looking very irritated. Dad let's his hand drop when it's clear Norman isn't going to shake his hand and looks at me with a frown. "Friend of yours?" he asks trying not to laugh.

"Definitely not," I say staring angrily at Norman who has kept his eyes averted from me. His eyes dart to Oliver who's at my side and he looks to the police officers, that both look frustrated. They look at each other and the older one, the man who interviewed Oliver at our home, sighs loudly and walks off angrily muttering about a waste of time and energy.

"We told you it was nothing," the younger grey-haired officer says to Norman. "We're sorry to bother you," he says to us, as Norman stares at us looking cheated that he didn't catch us doing anything untoward. He huffs and storms off after the older detective. The grey-haired officer waits behind with a big smile on his face, while the other two walk off.

"Thanks Malcolm," Oliver says with a smile. The officer, Malcolm, another of our new recruits winks at us.

"See you tomorrow morning. Nice to meet you," he says shaking Dad's hand. Dad nods at him looking a little perplexed.

"You too," he replies calmly. I smile.

"You got good kids there," Malcolm says cocking his head to Oliver and me.

"Thanks," Dad says with a bemused smile.

"Well I best get off, Norman will be furious," Malcolm chuckles to himself. I smile widely before he turns and jogs off. We're all silent for a moment when Dad speaks up.

"That really just happened didn't it? Was he really a police officer?" Dad asks looking shocked. I nod and he shakes his head looking completely startled. "This is all for real. There really are people helping you?" he asks. I nod and smile at him.

"Yeah, Dad there really is a lot of people in on this. Malcolm, even the Mayor knows," I say as I look to Joseph who is looking a bit more relaxed, he's even smiling.

"Damn it Chloe, what have you done?" he says in awe. I look at Oliver who is also smiling. Only now, now that I have my whole family at my side does this all feel real.

Now I know we can do this.

Chapter 34

That evening as I'm getting ready for bed I can hear the low rumbling noise of Oliver, my dad and brothers coming from the living room. They seem to be having some sort of silent but heated debate. I smile remembering all the arguments they used to have back home, about the school football team or something stupid like that. I realise that despite the obvious frustrated tones the noise is comforting. As I walk out to join them I realise that their tone is not one of frustration but of worry and sadness.

"I don't think we should say anything," Michael says. The serious tone of his voice makes me feel cold despite the cozy warmth of the house.

"I'm sorry Michael we need to tell her, she hates being kept in the dark. I'm not about to keep something from her again," Oliver says and I smile. I hear the sound of a whip followed by a loud chuckle. I round the corner and four pairs of worried eyes meet me.

Oh god.

"What is it?" I ask looking at them all individually. Michael and Joseph drop their eyes and Dad frowns.

"We have some bad news from home," he says sadly. My blood chills knowing bad news from home means only one thing.

"Who?" I ask my voice tight.

"Mr. Evans, your head teacher," Dad says. My eyes widen and they land on Oliver who looks sad and angry.

"Why?" I croak feeling my throat tighten and burn as I fight back the tears that fill my eyes.

"No one knows," Dad says. I sit down at the table putting my head in my hands.

Poor Mr. Evans.

Sure he was in my bad books in the end for allowing me to become a breeder but he was a nice man. He cared greatly for all of his students, which was evident during graduation; he looked ill with worry on the day.

"There is more," Oliver says sitting down next to me, taking my hand. I look up at him. His face has become stony and anger radiates off of him.

"Oh god, what?" I ask as he takes a shaky breath.

"His…" his voice shakes and he clears his throat loudly. "His wife and kids have gone missing." My eyes instantly fill with tears and spill over. I look at Dad in horror and he nods in confirmation.

"When?" I squeak. I see Dads throat bob like he's swallowing his tears.

"A few days ago. His body was found drained and his home empty. They believe it to be an unprovoked attack but I don't think it was nor do most people."

"It was definitely a Fang?" Oliver asks. Dad nods and sighs loudly.

"That's weird," I say slowly. Everyone looks at me frowning.

"It's sad Chloe not weird," Michael says looking mad.

"I know it is, it's horrible." I wipe away my tears looking at Oliver. "Did Marcus not say that the Fanged can't come inside our homes without previous invitation from us?" I ask. Oliver nods slowly.

"He did and it must be true otherwise your mother would have come in here. It must've been someone he knew," Oliver sighs. He stills then looks over at me his face is pale and full of realisation. It's only seconds before I'm on the same page as him.

"You don't think?"

"It has to be who else would do it?"

"Will you two stop talking in code? Who the hell are you talking about?" Joseph says looking between us.

"Henry Caldwell," I croak. Joseph's eyes widen.

"It couldn't be he..."

"He's the only Fang Mr. Evans would have ever invited into his home," Oliver says as Joseph sits back heavily in his chair.

"They have his family," I say angrily.

"They?" Dad asks. I frown at him knowing that I have missed one vital piece of information out of this whole mess. I suddenly wish for the house to fall on me and save me the pain of having to tell my dad this. I look to Oliver who seems to have read my mind and is staring at me with a look of pure shock and embarrassment.

"Dad," I start in a slow, calming voice. "I didn't mean to not tell you it just slipped my mind. I'm so sorry."

"What is it?" he asks looking a little frightened.

"Mum she, well she's with Henry. They're together," I say. He looks at me blankly, blinking a few times. I stare at him nervously very aware that the room has fallen deathly quiet. Dad closes his eyes and before I realise what is happening, he's laughing loudly. I stare at Joseph and Michael who are staring at him with matching frowns.

"I should've guessed really," he says eventually. "Your mother was very taken by him during our graduation. Much like a lot of the girls and some guys to be honest. I'm hardly surprised she wormed her way into his bed," he says still chuckling darkly, I frown at him totally confused.

"Are you ok?" I ask carefully.

"I'm fine kiddo. I got over your mother a long time ago," he says taking my hand. "You kids, my grandkids that's what is important to me," he says. I smile at him.

Lucky escape there, I think with a dark chuckle.

"What you guys are doing is important too. We need to help as many people as we can. It might be too late for the Evans' but there are many other families that need our help," Dad says squeezing my hand. The vision of Mr. Evans's little girls at the graveside at their brother's funeral flashes in my mind and I frown.

"His kids, his little girls, do you think they are still alive?" I say my voice full of pain.

"I hope not. But if they are there is nothing we can do for them just now," Michael says. I look down at the table trying to get their faces out of my head.

"Michael's right, best we can do is hope that this plan works. That we can stop this happening in the future," Joseph says. I feel anger bubble up inside of me.

"The plan will work. It has to," I say through my teeth. I get up from my seat, storming out of the room, leaving the four of them speechless in my wake. I slam the bedroom door closed behind me. I stand uselessly in the middle of the dark room not sure why I got so angry. Sure I have plenty to get angry about but it just seemed to take me over, much like when I was choking the life out of my mother. I shake my head at the unwelcome thought. I slump down on the floor and start doing some sit-ups. Knowing the anger isn't going anywhere fast and that this is the best way to work it out.

My thoughts drift to Mr. Evans. Although I was immeasurably angry with him at the time for changing my life without warning me, I realise it was not his fault. He was a sweet, kind man and during our many meetings I found him to be very funny. I know now, despite the responsibility of his job, he had no real power.

I want to get back at all of those who have caused this pain and suffering. I want to avenge his death and I want the person who did it gone, forever. I also realise with an angry clench of my jaw that it's thanks to my mother that I'm in this mess. She must have known I wouldn't have wanted this life but for the first time ever I'm grateful for what she has done. If it weren't for   her interfering I would be working mindlessly under the Fang's watchful eye. But now, thanks to her I'm here with my family and friends preparing to fight back. It was her biggest mistake trying to get involved in my life again and maybe her most fatal.

The bedroom door opens and Oliver's eyes instantly fall to the floor meeting mine. He cautiously steps into the room eyeing me warily as I sit up and cross my legs. He looks at me like I might start hurtling things around the room or attack him. He closes the door and I stand up slowly.

"I'm ok," I say. He relaxes a little.

"Are you sure? You still look really pissed."

"I am," he nods and steps towards me slowly, I roll my eyes at him. "We are going to make this right," I say. He nods as he stops in front of me.

"We will," he says putting his hand on my face lightly; I place mine over his and close my eyes.

"I hate this," I say with a huge sigh. He leans down and kisses my forehead lightly.

"I know. We're going to get through it. Things will get better. I promise," he says. I open my eyes and smile at him.

"I hope so," I sigh again. He leans down and kisses me. I stand on my tiptoes wrapping my arms around his neck. He smiles into the kiss. I pull back frowning slightly.

"You know when you kiss me like that you make the 'no sex while family visit' rule really hard to follow," he says in a low voice. I smile as I play with his hair.

"I'm sorry," I say kissing him on the cheek. I let him go and climb into bed. He runs his hand through his hair and I chuckle. "You ok over there?"

"This is going to be a long week," he sighs before climbing in next to me.

"It'll fly by. Once we get everything sorted with the plan we won't have much spare time anyway," I say as I lie down. "It'll be interesting to find out what those three make of this whole plan. If they think it'll work or if they think we're in way over our heads." Oliver looks down at me as he chews on his lip.

"You don't think we can pull it off?" he asks worry clear on his voice.

"No I think we can, but what we're asking them to do is dangerous. Especially for Michael, he's going to be risking a lot. I don't want anyone to get hurt," I say moving his growing hair out of his eyes.

"I know but Chloe you've got to know that some people are bound to get hurt, or worse, through this whole thing. Not everyone will make it," he says sadly. I can't help the shiver that wracks my body.

"I know," I say in a small voice. I have accepted it but the fact that we might lose one of our own makes me sad. I have also accepted that I might be one of the people who might not make it. If that's the case then I'm going to make sure that I take out as many Fanged as I possibly can. I blink away the sickening image of Oliver laying broken on the ground his eyes wide and vacant. I have not and will not accept that outcome. Oliver takes my hand, pulling me from my dark thoughts. I look up at him his eyes shining in the light from the bedside table as he strokes my face.

"Hey, what're you thinking about?" he asks. I let out a long tired breath.

Lie.

"Tomorrow," I say flatly. He frowns at me looking unconvinced. I ignore the look as much as I can and go on. "I just hope they've remembered to bring a coat for Rose," I add lamely.

"I'm sure they have, we told them it was important. Rose will need to get them done while they are here," Oliver says.

It's a strange thing, when someone is told they cannot help fight for their freedom they become more and more determined to do just that. Rose told us in the most colourful language imaginable that she was not going anywhere after her bump started to show and we all started getting nervous about her being involved. She eventually agreed to avoid any physical work. Then after she had a two-day sulk, came back to us with the most brilliant idea. She walked into the cabin followed by Damien who was smiling ear to ear. She gave us all a quick wave before she switched off the living room lights.

"What're you doing girl?" Marcus said from his little table in the corner.

"Oh shut up," Rose said as she drew the curtains. I smiled at Oliver who looked at her like she was a maniac. The guys had quickly learned not to mess with Rose as pregnancy had made her short tempered and very, very dangerous to be around. "Since all of you have decided you don't want my help, and I refuse to be told what to do, I've come up with an idea. Just keep your mouth shut Marcus."

"I didn't say a thing!"

"You were thinking it so just shut it," she said. I stifled a laugh as I saw her rubbing her temples in the dark room. "Now, Damien if you could please turn it on," she said in a tight voice. I heard a rustling of fabric and a loud frustrated sigh from Rose.

"Rose I can't find, oh wait I got it," he said and with a little click Damien's jacket lit up making us all squint in the room. We all stared at him in awe as he smiled out at us from his bubble of light.

"What's it for?" John asked from Damien's side. Rose rolled her eyes as she sat down on the arm of Gillian's chair.

"It's for when you're all in the tunnels. Since I can't be there I will be making each of you one of these. If I can't have your backs in there I will make sure you're as safe as I can," she said folding her arms and chewing her lip. I smiled at her as she looked up at me.

"That's a great idea," I said with a huge grin. She chuckled and smiled at me.

"I know," she said and winked at me. "Basically the lights can be dimmed." Damien's jacket dimmed and then went bright again. "It has lights in the front and back so depending on the order you all go in depends on the lights you have on. It should be enough to dazzle the Fanged enough for you to get away or if need be…" She ran her thumb under her neck.

"You really out did yerself Rose," Billy said as he looked over the coat.

"Thanks, they're not expensive to make. I just need a couple of lights and these are low energy but really bright so they should last a while. You will just have to make sure they work before you go down," she said fidgeting with the sleeve of Damien's jacket.

"Amazing," Oliver said with a little smile.

"I will just need an old coat you don't want and I can get to work," she said and everyone agreed willingly. We all applauded her and she burst into tears, she was a little over-emotional.

Although Rose had been working on our coats for the last two months she was beginning to struggle with all the new recruits that we'd been getting. There was a point a month or so ago where she couldn't work due to contracting the flu. She was really unwell for a long time and whenever Damien wasn't working he was looking after her when she let him. She pulled through, luckily, and she was getting better and stronger. It had weakened her and what with being four months pregnant she was really struggling. She's feeling much better now and she has been constantly working on the coats. She had done Oliver's and mine in the first batch; they were both hidden, along with the short swords from Terry, behind our bath panel. We, along with Billy, had been given our tools form Terry first. He handed me them in a long package one day at the yard while he was shoeing Oliver's horses. He said absolutely nothing about them but gave me a wink before he continued with his work. After he left Oliver and I hid in a tack room and opened up the package. We stared down at the two short swords in the wrapping. They were sharp, shiny and new with a tightly wound leather handle and a strap for your wrist.

"I can't believe he did it," Oliver gasped. I nodded at him in agreement unable to speak. We quickly wrapped them back up and I took then home that evening in a sack full of compost. I threw them through the open bathroom window and went inside and hid them away with the coats. We're slowly getting organised. The thought that nearly everyone had been given what they needed to protect themselves and that my dad and brothers were going to be given the same treatment made me nervous beyond belief.

"Do you think that your dad and brothers are going to be able to gather up enough people to help?" Oliver asks his voice low and rumbling in my ear.

"I don't know. I'm sure they know enough people to change some minds," I say hopefully.

"I hope so."

"Oliver?"

"Yeah?"

"Your parents what are they going to say about all of this?" I ask. He chuckles and kisses my hand.

"They will probably just yell a lot. After they have got that off their chest they will be ok with it, they'll want to help."

"It's a start." I roll onto my side, resting my head on his chest.

"It is," he says holding me tight.

"We will be ok, half of the village knows and we're yet to get dragged out of here," I say trying to sound comforting. "You think someone will let it slip?"

"No I don't. I think everyone is pretty much in the same boat. If one person lets slip we're all dead. You heard Henry, no one is safe," he says his grip on me tightening still.

"I just want this to be over," I murmur against his chest. He squeezes me and kisses my hair.

"It will be soon."

374

The next morning I wake Dad, Joseph and Michael with a cup of tea and leave them to get dressed. Telling them they have fifteen minutes before we leave for the meeting. They grumble about the cold as soon as we step out of the house but as soon as we began walking they settled down. They look nervous and excited in equal measures.

"Where are we going again?" Joseph asks as he climbs over the crumbling stone wall.

"It's a small house in the middle of these woods," I say as he, Dad and Michael follow Oliver and I through the bare shrubs. The woods are still dark due to the early hour. It's cold and slippery making the three of them stumble and curse behind us.

"Just lift your feet the path is pretty clear," Oliver says over his shoulder.

"Easy for you to say," Michael grumbles. I hear him swear under his breath as he hits his head off a low branch. It's true, Oliver and I are used to walking through here in the dark but it's muddier than usual due to the snow. It's also painfully early and I know the three of them couldn't have gotten a good sleep in their uncomfortable, makeshift beds.

"We're nearly there," I say as I see the lights of the little house through the thinning tree line. Oliver pushes through the last bush holding the branches back for us. I keep walking up to the house; I knock once before pushing the door open. I'm met by Gillian in the hallway and I hear the others follow me in. She smiles at me before she looks over my shoulder to Dad, Joseph and Michael.

"Morning Chloe, is this your family?" She asks smiling.

"Yeah," I say looking back over my shoulder at them.

"Nice to meet you. I'm Gillian. We're just waiting on you," she says before she walks back into the little living room. It's much more crowded in here now, what with our other recruits. The five of us squeeze in the room, I wave at a few of them and roll my eyes as Ray winks at me.

"Mornin' you two," Billy says to Oliver and me as he makes his way over to us pushing through a few people who grumble tiredly at him. "You three must be the Woods?" he says holding his hand out to my dad.

"Christopher, Chloe's dad," Dad says as Billy shakes his hand vigorously and smiles.

"Hell of a kid you've got there," he says, winking at me.

"Dad this is Billy, he's sort of the boss here." Billy waves me down and laughs.

"Hardly, I'm just bossy. We don't have boss's here we all work together," Billy says, indicating around the room.

"Good to hear," Dad says. Billy nods and looks to Joseph and Michael.

"Billy these are my brothers. Joseph," I say as they shake hands and Billy stares up at him.

"Big bugger aint ya?" Billy says. Joseph's lips twitch in a smile and he shrugs.

"'Spose," he says gruffly. Billy chuckles and turns to Michael.

"So you must be Michael, am I right?"

"Yeah, that's me," Michael says shaking Billy's hand.

"You're the computer whizz? Chloe told us 'bout your skills," Billy says nudging me with his elbow. Michael looks at me questioningly and I smile.

"I'm ok," Michael says, turning back to Billy who smiles widely.

"I'm glad you could all join us. I take it these two have filled you in on the plan?" he asks and they nod.

"Something to do with decapitating a bunch of Fanged. Seems a little mad to me," Joseph says frowning. I know that he's still not fully convinced that it's going to work and that he still might need a little convincing.

"It is son, but it's all we got, so what the hell," Billy says with a shrug. Joseph stares at him, frowning but to my surprise he laughs.

"This is mental," he murmurs.

"Sure is son," Billy chuckles but I see Joseph's lips twitch. "Now we have the introductions out of the way can we get on with it? I want us all out of here by sunrise. First things first did y'all bring a jacket like Rose asked?" Oliver pulls off a backpack throwing it towards where Rose and Damien are sat. Damien catches it easily and hands it to Rose. She pulls out the jackets, inspects them and nods.

"I'll have these back to you before you leave," she says. Billy claps his hands together loudly.

"So, Malcolm you had some news... what's goin' on?" he asks and Malcolm nods.

"Norman knows something is going on. He has reported it at the station. I said I would have a look into it but he's like a dog with a bone. He's going to be talking to the Mayor today." Malcolm smiles.

"So he'll be ignored again," Cameron says smiling and many people laugh.

"Even so everyone be on alert, that little weasel would just love to catch one of us up to something," Oliver says over the chuckles. I hear the hatred in his voice.

"I also have some codes here for 'the computer whizz'," Malcolm says looking at Michael. "These codes have not been changed for years, my wife works at the Fang HQ in the city. She says nothing has changed in that place since she started there." He hands Michael a small list of numbers. I look at them as they pass me. They just look like numbers to me but Michael whistles and looks up at Malcolm.

"These are their access codes," he says, sounding impressed. Malcolm shrugs.

"I don't know what the hell they are, I was just asked to get them so here they are."

"These codes can get me into any system in their buildings. I can do something with this," Michael says in awe as he looks at the paper.

"Really?" Cameron asks.

"Oh yeah," Michael says. I stare at him and he smiles, there's a strange, dangerous glint in his eyes and it scares me a little bit.

"You have the technology?" Marcus asks causing Michael to laugh.

"I live in the south, I have *the* technology. If I'm able to do enough digging I may even be able to access other regions systems," he says and Marcus smiles.

"Bring them down from the inside out?"

"Maybe?" Michael says. Joseph slaps his shoulder smiling widely.

"Ok, now I feel better about all of this," he says.

"Sounds better than just decapitatin' some Fangs eh son?" Billy says, winking at Joseph who smiles.

"You're all still insane but I'm coming round," he says. He meets my eyes and I smile at him.

"Mountain man," John says making Joseph frown, we all look at John but he's looking at Joseph.

"What did you call me?" Joseph asks frowning deeply; I look between them and John smiles.

"You work up north, right?" John asks. Joseph folds his arms and nods. "Thought as much, only a northerner would sport a beard like that," John laughs as Joseph continues to frown at him.

"What do you know about it?" Joseph asks sounding defensive. John doesn't seem worried by Joseph's reaction in fact he just laughs.

"My family all live up there, they are all aware of what is happening down here and they are all in," John says.

"Who're your family?" Joseph asks sounding curious now.

"The Simmons family," John says making Joseph's eyes widen slightly.

"You're John Simmons?" Joseph asks sounding a little awestruck. John smiles as. Joseph lets out a low whistle.

"Who the hell are the Simmons's?" Michael asks. Joseph scoffs and runs a hand over his shaggy beard.

378

"Only one of the richest timber families in the north, they also happen to be my employers," Joseph says looking at John in admiration.

"They know why you're here. They want to see you when you get back," John says. Joseph nods looking a little intimidated by the smaller man.

"Sure thing," Joseph says. I smile when I see Joseph's mind change.

"Ok, so we want you to try and recruit as many people as y'all can. Christopher," Billy says looking at my dad, "Chloe tells me that you're quite well known and respected."

"I don't know about that but I will do what I can," Dad says sounding embarrassed.

"In your line of work you must meet a fair amount of families who have gone through some traumatic times. We need those people. We need them to fight for their lives. I imagine those people will want to fight, they will be angry," Billy says.

"Perhaps. I will do what I can, I can think of a few people who will be willing. Leave it with me," Dad says scratching his chin. Billy smiles gratefully.

"Once you have gotten people you must arm yourself. I will be making you three something to use but others will have to improvise," Terry says from the far wall.

"You don't have to waste your time making me anything, I'm set," Joseph says and Billy nods.

"Use anything that will remove a head anything that will sever their neck," David says.

"They're really weak there. I felt her throat give way under my hands," I say and they all look at me.

"We can't rely on that," Oliver says quickly. I look up at him with a frown.

"You're right we can't risk strangling anything, it's too close to the mouth and you will not be able to remove the head. We only do that if we're desperate or it's a last chance," Gillian says, the room nods in agreement.

379

"Yeah," I say as I stare down at my feet until a rough hand lifts my head up.

"You were brave Chloe," Billy says kindly. "Saving Oliver and Mary that day but you just remember, be smart," he taps my head lightly. I nod and he smiles.

"Are we all clear on what we have to do?" Trevor asks standing up as John looks at his watch. We all nod and look outside; the sun is rising.

"Looks like our time is up today," Billy says. There is a loud sound of movement, as we all start moving. "Oh and, Merry Christmas," Billy calls as we stream out of the house.

Chapter 35

The next morning, Oliver and I walk out of the bedroom, after being woken up by the smell of cooking chicken we pad sleepily into the living room.

"Merry Christmas, dad calls over his shoulder as we enter.

"Merry Christmas," Oliver yawns, as I walk into the kitchen and hug Dad.

"Merry Christmas Dad. Where're Michael and Joseph?" I ask, noticing their absence.

"They've gone for a walk, they have a lot to think about after yesterday," he says. I nod and look up at him.

"What about you?"

"Nah, I'm pretty much sold," he says. I smile and give him another squeeze.

"Do you need a hand in here?" Oliver asks, looking into the kitchen. Dad shakes his head.

"I'm good just now everything is done for now so why don't you guys just sit and relax. Play some games or something?" I look at Oliver expectantly and he gives me a sorry smile.

"I should go and check on the horses but I won't be long." I move off to get ready to help him but he stops me. "Stay with your dad I promise I won't be long."

"You sure?" I ask, he smiles and kisses my forehead.

"Positive, no point us both getting cold and wet. You deserve a break," he says. I smile as he rushes off to get changed and I turn to Dad who is smiling.

"It's nice seeing you two happy despite everything," he says. I feel myself blush but I smile.

"Thanks dad."

"I brought my old chess board. Fancy a game?" he asks. I nod and smile.

"Prepare to get beaten old man." I say as I sit down. He laughs as he rifles through his bag and pulls out his set.

"Challenge accepted kiddo."

We're half way through our first game when Joseph and Michael walk in shaking off the fresh layer of snow on their jackets.

"It's freezing out there!" Michael says, unwrapping his scarf. Joseph rolls his eyes at him as he pulls off his one jacket and smiles at me as Michael starts pulling off his many layers.

"Soft southerners," Joseph mumbles as he passes Michael who punches his arm. They scuffle as they make their way over to the table only stopping to look down at the board. I stare up at them as they look at the board. They both look exhausted, like they have hardly slept and I can't help but feel bad.

"Oh Dad, she's got you in two moves," Joseph says. He smiles slightly as Dad's eyes widen.

"You're kidding?" Dad groans.

"Nope. When's dinner going to be ready? I'm starving," Michael asks, sitting down next to me. "Merry Christmas sis," he says, throwing an arm over my shoulder.

"Yeah Merry Christmas," Joseph says stuffing half a carrot in his mouth.

"Merry Christmas," I say with a smile.

"It'll be ready when it's ready," Dad says grumpily. I chuckle as he stares at the board his eyes darting around the remaining pieces and smiles. He moves his bishop and sits back smiling. Michael sucks in a breath through his teeth and Joseph smiles.

"Stop it you two," I say as Dad looks frantically at the board not realising his mistake. "Go make yourself useful and sort the vegetables out," I say shoving them away from the table. They both get up snickering like children as

Dad stares at the board. His eyes widen and he slumps back in his chair when he realises what he has done. I slide my queen in front of his king and smile at him. "Check mate," I say grinning. He sighs angrily; he never has been the best at losing games.

"Stupid game," he mutters making me laugh.

"Well I learned from the best," I say. He reluctantly smiles at my compliment. The four of us have a mini tournament whilst we take turns cooking dinner and wait for Oliver to get home. I beat Joseph and Michael quickly much to their displeasure. I watch intently as Dad and Joseph battle it out. I turn when I hear the door open and Oliver comes in with is head held high taking in a deep breath through his nose.

"Smells great in here," he says as he hangs up his coat. I get up and walk over to meet him.

"Hi," I say smiling up at him.

"Hi," he says with a smile as I hug him. He smells like snow and he just as cold but it's quite pleasant in comparison to the heat in the house. He wraps his icy arms around me and kisses my hair. I hear a disgusted noise from the kitchen breaking our little moment and I scowl in its general direction. Michael is stood in the kitchen with his arms crossed and a frown on his face.

"That is so gross," he says grimacing. I roll my eyes at him. "Just you keep your hands to yourself Hunter," he says pointing at Oliver with the potato masher. Oliver takes a step back from me holding up his hands.

"Shut up Michael!" I snap. I hear Joseph laugh. "You too."

"I didn't say a thing," he complains.

"But you were thinking about it," I say and he shrugs knowing I'm right.

"It's just weird seeing you two so..." he pauses as he takes dad's queen.

"In looove!" Michael sings from the kitchen. I pick up a little wooden bowl and aim it at Michael's head.

"Chloe," Dad says warningly not moving his eyes from the board.

"Wow, wow, wow," Oliver says wrapping his arm around my middle pulling the bowl from my grip.

"Hey," I moan as Joseph laughs loudly. "I hope you lose," I shoot at him. He looks at me hurt as dad takes his queen with a triumphant yell.

"Come on we'll go get the gifts," Oliver says pulling me out of the room as dad and Joseph start to argue.

"They don't deserve gifts," I call over my shoulder. I hear loud laughing and scowl. Oliver pulls me into the bedroom and walks over to his chest where we pull out the little wrapped gifts that we managed to get for them.

"You ok?" he asks looking up at me and I nod. We hear a loud groan and Joseph swearing. "I think he lost."

"Good," I say smiling, Oliver laughs.

"Oliver you're up next," Michael calls from the dining room and Oliver smiles. I take a few of the little packages from him and he smiles.

"Just coming," he calls. I turn to leave but he pulls me back. He smiles before he lowers his lips to mine. I crush myself against him. He chuckles deeply before backing me against the closet door. I drop the gifts on the floor as his cold hands slide around my back and I weave my hands in his hair. He pulls back reluctantly. I let out a little moan and he sighs deeply. "Longest week ever," he says before unwrapping himself from me. I giggle as I bend down picking up what I dropped.

We walk back out into the living room and I pile the little packages under the tiny tree along with the few gifts that were already there. Oliver and Dad are getting set up for their game. I take a seat next to Oliver who smiles at me making me look away and fight a blush.

"Ugh you two kissed didn't you?" Michael says. I stare at him mortified.

"Michael, leave them alone. We didn't harass you when you and Millie stuck your tongues down each other's throats," Dad says calmly as he places his pieces on the board. The room falls silent as Michael stares at him in disbelief.

"Dad!" he squeaks, as his face turns scarlet. I burst into a loud fit of laughter Oliver and Joseph join in while Michael takes himself and his red face over to the stove to check the food.

"If you can't handle it then don't dish it out son," Dad says as Michael scowls at him. "So Oliver are you ready to be beaten?"

"I highly doubt that'll happen," Oliver says clicking his fingers.

"Go easy on me now I'm an old man."

"Don't listen to him," Michael says as he mashes some potatoes. Oliver smiles at him.

"I don't intend on. Chloe told me all about your tricks." Dad's eyebrows rise in humour and Oliver smiles. Dad turns to look at me with mock horror.

"Turn coat!" he hisses making me laugh. Joseph and I watch the game from the kitchen as we start serving up lunch. Joseph pulls out the chicken that was a gift from Damien and Rose as Michael laughs loudly.

"Dad's just lost his queen," Michael says as I watch Joseph carving the chicken. It's absolutely huge and smells amazing. My mouth waters as he slices it evenly. I turn and look over at the table; Oliver is smiling as he moves a piece.

"Check," he says calmly. Dad shakes his head in disbelief.

"What the hell just happened?" he asks shaking his head.

"Oh, he's good," Michael says slapping Oliver on the back. Oliver's eyes lift meeting mine and he winks at me. I smile and turn away feeling myself blush. I bite my lip as I start heaping vegetables on to the plates.

Longest week ever indeed, I think as I move out the way as Joseph starts serving the chicken.

"There's plenty of this left for the next few days," he says. I nod as I pull out our mismatched glasses.

"Checkmate," Oliver says triumphantly. I hear Dad groan.

"Good game son," he says, I smile widely. I love that Dad calls Oliver son it makes me ridiculously happy.

"Thanks," he says. I hear his chair scrape and I turn as he comes into the kitchen looking very pleased with himself.

"Well done," I say smiling.

"I had a good teacher. Do you want me to set the table?" he asks leaning around me to the cutlery drawer. I feel my face flame and my heart race.

"Yes please," I breathe. He chuckles as he gathers up the cutlery.

"Are you ok? You're looking a little flustered," he asks innocently. I throw him a death glare.

The git, he knows exactly what he's doing.

"Shut up," I hiss at him, he smiles widely, scoops up a hand full of napkins and kisses my hot cheek before he heads back to set the table.

"This looks amazing," Michael says as we all sit down. The smell of lunch is delicious and I dig in greedily. We eat in silence, which unnerves me slightly. Normally meal times with my brothers are loud. Full of arguing and a lot of laughter but as they sit eating in silence I begin to worry.

"Ok guys what is going on? Are you ok?" I ask, putting my cutlery down.

"Yeah," Michael says as Joseph nods. "Fine why?"

"Well firstly, you're quiet," I say. I see Dad's lips quirk in a smile as they look at each other like I'm offending them. "Secondly Dad said you were walking to think about things." They both look at Dad who has become very interested with a carrot on his plate. Oliver rolls his eyes. I stare between them and they exchange a quick look.

"We've had a lot to think about," Michael begins delicately. I nod at him bracing myself for him to say they are out. "Me in particular, I have my family to think about. They are everything to me and if anything were to happen to them, because of me, I would not be able to forgive myself." I feel myself sag in my chair. He's right I can't ask him to do something this stupid.

His family comes first.

"That said, I want the best for my family. I think this is the best way to give them it," he says. I sit up in my chair staring at him.

"Michael, are you sure?" I ask. He nods.

"I am. I have spoken to Millie. She's going to stay at her mothers. The further away she's from me the better. She won't be seen near the house, I will tell the neighbours that we have spilt for the time being."

"Do you think people will buy it?" I ask. Michael shrugs and stabs at his chicken.

"If the shit hits the fan it's not the people I'm worried about," he says. I stare at him. "If anything happens to me she'll have to look after the kids," Michael says. I feel my body chill.

"Nothing will happen, this is going to work," Oliver says sounding a little half-hearted.

"I appreciate your optimism, Oliver, but you don't know that, if something does happen I want my family to be safe. I'm going to have to do some serious hacking to get into the controls of these places. If I'm discovered that's it for me," he says. I frown at him, not liking the thought of him getting hurt.

"You think you will be able to?" Joseph asks. Michael takes a bite of chicken and nods.

"I'll be able to. I was part of the team who designed these systems but I'm going to need some help. I can't keep my eyes on everything at once," Michael says thoughtfully.

"You know some people?" Dad asks, Michael nods.

"I do and they will be there to help me cover my tacks and keep an eye on you all. That's going to be the hardest part to keep on top of."

"But not impossible?" I ask.

"No, not impossible. It should be fine. The south controls most of the country's major amenities like power, gas and water. It's all done remotely so if I can take over that I will be able to do a lot. I will be able to keep the lights on when it's their time so they stay out of the villages. Even better I should be able to disable the sun shields, I hope," he says. I stare at him in awe.

"Force them underground," Oliver says. I turn to him and he's smiling.

"That's what we were thinking," Michael says looking at Joseph.

"We're going to have to find a way to keep in touch," I say looking hopefully at him. He looks down at his plate, frowning. Then smiles as he looks up.

"That guy." He points his fork between Oliver and me. "What's his name, Malcolm? He's a cop right?" I nod. I see a smile of understanding cross Oliver's face.

"Yeah he is," he says grinning. I frown between them.

"He will have access to radios and walkie-talkies he should be able to hook you up," Michael says nodding happily.

"We have them already in the woods for the guys' miles out. They're more reliable than phones up there," Joseph says. Michael smiles before taking a big drink of his beer.

"It's the best idea we've got," Michael says. Dad and Oliver nod in agreement. "I should be able to fix together some radios for as many people as I can whilst I'm here."

"I'll ask Rose if you can borrow her tools," I say. Michael nods his head.

"Excellent."

"One more thing," I say looking at Oliver who meets my eyes.

"What?" Joseph says looking between us suspiciously.

"Oliver and I were talking. We were thinking we should come up with a plan B."

"What, why?" Michael asks.

"Well, if this doesn't work, if we get found out we'll need to run," I say and Dad frowns at me.

"You can't," Dad says.

"We've packed a bag. We have a tent and we're going to run if this goes south. We won't be coming back here," I say as they stare at me like I have grown a second head.

"We're hoping if we call that our home we can't be touched inside it," Oliver says as they stare at us wide eyed and, to my shock, with disappointment. "We will travel through the day to get further away," I say lamely as I feel the strength of our plan crumble away before me. We were so certain it would go down well but the way we're being looked at makes me feel like a five-year-old. Joseph sighs and puts his fork down.

"Sounds to me like you two are certain this plan is going to fail," he says folding his arms.

"No we just need a plan B," I say quickly.

"Plan B is going down fighting," Michael says. I stare at him shocked. The thought of Michael or anyone around this table dying like that is repellant to me. I chew my lip hard as it starts to tremble.

"It won't come to that," I say lamely. Oliver is looking down at the table looking as embarrassed as I feel and Michael shakes his head.

"So there is no need for plan B is there?" he says sounding angry. I see Dad placing a hand on his arm.

"What about all you have here?" Dad says quietly going for the reasoning as opposed to the angry route to get through to us. "What about the people here? The ones who are going to be fighting with you, your friends? Your friend, the pregnant girl... she won't be able to run. Will you just leave her behind?" I stare at him and shame washes over me. "Say the plan fails but we're not found out? What then? Would being together here be so awful?" I look at Oliver and drop my eyes to the table.

"Yes."

"No," he says, I cringe and my eyes shoot up. I don't miss the pang of pain that crosses his face.

Oh no.

I look at Dad trying to look angry but the guilt on his face makes my anger fade.

This is not his fault.

"Oliver, you know I didn't mean it like that. Oliver I…"

"Excuse me a minute," Oliver says in a low voice, as he stands up. I watch wide-eyed as he walks out of the front door.

"Chloe I'm so sorry," Dad says taking my hand. My eyes haven't left the door. I get up tugging my hand free. I rush to the door and pull on my boots. I yank the door open and run through it.

"Good going Dad," Michael says, as the door slams. I rush to the end of the path and look down the street; Oliver is walking slowly down the street huddled in the icy, snowy breeze. I rush after him the cold chilling me through my wool jumper instantly.

"Oliver," I call, he stops. I slip slightly on some hidden ice and slow myself. I finally catch up with him. I see the frozen rapid breaths puffing out of him. "Oliver, I'm so sorry I didn't mean that the way it came out."

"You mean how it came out like a life with me would be repellant?" he says sounding hurt. I pull him round to face me.

"I didn't mean that. I meant that coming back to this life would be my last choice. I want a life with you just not this life. You said yourself you hate what is expected of us here," I say and his eyes meet mine.

"I do."

"So do I, I don't want this to be what we have left. We deserve better than this."

"But what if we're stuck then what?"

390

"Well…"

"Your brothers are right running is a stupid idea. We were idiots to think it would work, we couldn't leave everyone here to suffer because of something we started," he says sounding frustrated.

"I know we can't. I know that now. We just got carried away," I say, feeling irritated at myself.

"Would you rather run, be caught and feasted on than stay here with me and our children?" I stare at him, my teeth chattering against the icy wind and fear. He has never mentioned our possible children before and hearing it from his lips makes it all the more real and terrifying. I don't ever want to be the subject of a feast, considering Henry's last words at the town meeting. *I will skin alive every member of your family and feed them to my dogs piece by tiny piece.* I could never handle that part alone, never mind what would follow so I shake my head. "No, I didn't think so. So let me ask you again, what if we're stuck here?" he asks again.

"Then I guess we make the best of it. We try to live the best we can," I say feeling like my whole world is about to crumble around my feet. Oliver takes me in his arms as I fight the urge to cry and I squeeze him tightly.

"We will only have each other if this goes bad we have to work together," he says. He pulls away keeping old of my arms. "But remember, I promised you I would make this better and I'll make sure that it happens," he says with a little smile. "You're not the only one that this life doesn't appeal too. I promise, I will not leave your side when we're free."

"We're a team," I say. He smiles for real.

"We are, plus I love you, so I'm in this for the long run," he says.

"I'm sorry I made you upset," I say looking up at him. He gives me a little smile.

"Don't worry about it. We've never really discussed it, probably should've, before it got to this. It's ok."

"I love you," I reach up to kiss him but he stops me. I frown as he chews on his lip his eyes burning into mine.

"Chloe, I was going to do this after the raid but I don't want to wait until then. I might not get a chance," he says quickly.

"What is it?" I ask, feeling my heart begin to race. He digs around in his back pocket and smiles at me. He holds out a silver ring with a small teardrop diamond on it. I stare at the ring in shock and miss it when he gets down on one knee. My eyes meet his. He looks up at me his eyes wide and frightened. I gasp covering my mouth with my icy hand and take a little step backwards.

Oh sweet lord!

"Chloe when this is all over and we're safe would you do me the honour of marrying me?" I stare at him wide eyed. "For real," he adds with a smile. My eyes flicker between him and the ring, it really is pretty. I feel like all of the oxygen has left my body. He's asking me to really marry him; he's on one knee and everything, oh my god. Yes. My mouth doesn't seem to be working and I notice him starting to look a little worried.

"Say yes for god sake!" I hear Rose yell form down the street. I turn around and see a little crowd has gathered. Damien, Rose, David and Mary as well as my dad and brothers are all staring at me expectantly.

"Chloe," Oliver says quietly I turn slowly to face him. He's staring up at me steadily and I smile. I nod slowly and his eyes widen. His smile is breath taking; well it would be if I had any breath left in me.

"Yes," I gasp. He gets up taking my hand he pulls off the standard issue ring and pockets it before slipping the silver ring on my finger.

"It's perfect," he says sounding relieved, as I smile down at it. He puts his finger under my chin. I look up at him smiling.

"What did she say?" I hear Michael call. Oliver smiles widely at me.

"Say it again," he says in a low excited voice.

"Yes," I say louder as I grin. His eyes crinkle, as his smile gets impossibly wider.

"She said yes!" Oliver calls. I hear a loud cheer and a soft sobbing that could only be Rose. "Can I kiss you?" he asks looking over my shoulder to the crowd. I nod. He captures my lips quickly. I can't help the smile that crosses my face. I wrap my arms around him and he pulls me closer. The sound of the others becomes distant; the only thing I can hear is my heartbeat in my ears and our mingled breaths. I pull away giving him a little smile.

"How long?"

"A while, I had to ask your dad first," he says still smiling. The fact he asked permission makes me smile even more.

"You're adorable," I say before I kiss him again.

"I know," he says with a huge grin. I giggle before I'm scooped up into a big hairy hug.

"Congrats sis," Joseph says putting me down. I smile as I'm passed from person to person hugged, kissed and congratulated. Dad who, along with Rose and Damien, looks on the verge of tears eventually scoops me up.

"He's a good man," Dad says gruffly. I nod and laugh as Rose gives Oliver a tear filled kiss on the cheek.

"He is," I say, watching as he wipes the tears off his cheek with the back of his hand, he meets my eyes he smiles widely.

"Everyone back to ours for a glass of Champagne," he says. I roll my eyes as he takes my hand. "About time we drank that bottle don't you think?" he adds with a little smile at me.

"It's as good a time as any," I say. He chuckles as we all rush back into the warm house.

The nine of us all crowd in our living room while Oliver pulls the cork out of the bottle. It pops loudly and the others cheer, he fills up the mismatched glasses and mugs after giving Rose a glass of milk. She gives him a grateful smile and looks on enviously as everyone picks up a drink.

"To Chloe and Oliver," Dad says happily. I can't help the smile as they all raise their glasses to us. Oliver leans down to kiss my head and my smile widens before I take a sip of the Champagne. The bubbles tickle my nose and it wrinkles as the drink slides down my throat.

"It's an acquired taste," David says as he scrunches his face. I chuckle as Joseph downs his and sighs loudly.

"I like it," he says. His eyes widen before he lets out a huge burp. "Scuse me," he gasps as we all laugh except for Dad who rolls his eyes. After everyone finishes their drinks they congratulate us again before heading home back to their families.

I'm curled up in the chair feeling full after eating the rest of my dinner and happy after receiving my gifts. My head seems fuzzy and I attribute that to the glass of Champagne. I stare down at my new ring and smile.

"You like it?" Oliver asks from behind me I look round at him as he kneels down resting his arms on the back of my chair.

"I love it, its very pretty," I say as he smiles. I chew my lip feeling guilty as I inspect the shining piece of jewellery. "Was it expensive?"

"No, it was my grandmothers. She left it for me or Ethan to give," he explains. I feel a pang of sadness knowing that it must have been hard for Oliver to give this to me considering it should've been Ethan's first.

"I love it even more now. Thank you," I say. He moves some hair out of my eyes.

"No thank you," he says his eyes roaming over my face. I smile under his intense gaze.

"Ugh, you guys are gonna be all gross and lovey dovey tonight?" Michael asks from the table where he's playing a quiet game of chess with Joseph. I turn to him and cross my arms.

"Yes we are you got a problem with that?"

"Well screw that. I'm off to the pub," Michael says getting up from the table.

"Hey what about the game?" Joseph says and Michael looks down at him.

"You really wanna be here while these two are bumping uglies?"

"Michael!" I squeal. Dad looks at me with wide eyes and a red face. That was probably the last thing he wanted to hear.

"Since you put it that way," Joseph says getting up and walking towards the door after Michael. I stare at them in disbelief and complete embarrassment. As Dad gets up I look up at him. He clears his throat looking extremely awkward.

"I'll um..." he pauses before he turns on his heel and catches his coat as Michael throws it at him. He's first out the door followed by Joseph. Michael looks back into the room smiling. I imagine that Oliver's face is just as horrified as mine and Michael laughs.

"You're welcome by the way. Don't do something I wouldn't do," he says and with another big laugh he's out the door. It's either seconds or minutes that pass before I turn back around to look at Oliver. I'm not surprised to see his shocked expression. He lowers his gaze, meets my eyes and blinks.

"He's a complete..."

"I know," I say still feeling stunned. He stands up and walks around my chair offering me his hands. I take them wordlessly. I feel the rapid flutter of his pulse under my fingertips.

"Say it again," he says running his hands up my arms.

"Yes," I say smiling. He smiles before scooping me up into his arms and carrying me into the bedroom. He closes the door loudly with his foot and I giggle. "Someone's excited," I say looking up at him. He grins at me.

"You have no idea."

Loud crashes echo through the house as my dad and brothers stumble back into the house clearly drunk. I chuckle quietly as I look up at Oliver, who is still sound asleep, and I smile.

"I'm taking the couch," Dad says in a loud whisper. I hear him groaning loudly as he lowers himself into it. There is some loud whispered conversation then the house falls silent. I lay my head back on Oliver's chest and his arm tightens around me. I'm almost asleep when a loud rumbling snore echoes through the whole house I jump and my eyes shoot open. I look up and Oliver's eyes have opened he's looking down at me.

"Was that you?" he asks chuckling but looking shocked.

"It was not me!" I scowl at him as it sounds again. We both look at the door. We hear an angry groan then a loud thud.

"Shut the hell up Joseph," Michael moans. Joseph swears at him before they fall silent again. I lie back down and Oliver kisses my head.

"Sleep," he orders. I smile into his chest all too willing to do as I'm told.

Chapter 36

The week has been crazy. It's been great seeing my family and more than that, we have all managed to get so much done. Not only have Rose and Terry managed to get the coats and weapons done for the three of them, Michael had made some real progress in keeping us all connected. He was given a box of old dusty walkie-talkies on Boxing Day that Malcolm said were just sitting in the basement of the police station. He has spent the last three days with Rose mending as many as he possibly could with her assistance. The two of them have been sat together in our kitchen for days with a number of little tools laid out in front of them.

"I'll need your help to make sure these are in working order and when I'm gone, fix up some more," Michael had said to her on their first day together. He was so impressed with what she did with the coats that he was sure she would be the perfect apprentice. They worked well together and I watched as they fixed up a few radios, just so I knew what was expected of her and if I were ever needed I would know how they worked but after the first few hours on their first day I left them to it while I went on a run. I was surprised, when I came home, to hear Rose laughing loudly as Michael chuckled at her, and she really seemed to get on well with Michael. I was just glad to see her smiling. It seemed like a long time since I had actually seen her happy. When Damien came to get her on the last day of their working together he stared at Rose in shock as she smiled up at him as she packed away her things.

"How did you do that?" he asked desperately, pulling Michael to the side. Michael frowned, looking confused.

"How did I do what?"

"Make her laugh," Damien said sadly. I felt sorry for him as I tried not to listen. I knew he was struggling with everything. It looked like he had lost weight due to the stress. He was working hard and was constantly worried about Rose; he seemed way out of his depth. Michael looked at him sympathetically.

"Just treat her like you normally would, she's pregnant not sick. She doesn't want or need to be babied. Just look at her," he said. They both turned and I found myself doing the same. She was lifting up a big box of spare parts. "She can handle it," Michael said patting Damien's back. Damien frowned and nodded but he looked like he was itching to help her out.

"Ok thanks," he said after a moment. "It was great meeting you. Take care of yourself."

"You too man," Michael said as he shook Damien's hand.

"See you later Chloe," Damien said waving at me as he went over to Rose smiling. "Need a hand?"

"No, I've got it," she said tightly. I rolled my eyes but Damien just nodded and walked to the door.

"Ok, after you," he said as he opened the door for her. She frowned as she stared at him for a moment. He waited patiently then she smiled widely. She turned to us and wiggled her fingers giving us a little wave.

"Thank you for everything," she said smiling. Michael shrugged.

"It's fine. Just you take care," he said smiling at her.

"I will, thank you again," she said before she left the house. I moved beside Michael as the door closed and he looked down at me.

"Nice couple."

"They are. They have been through a lot," I said and he chuckled.

"We all have sis, we all have."

The week has gone too quickly. I'm sulking, quite spectacularly, as I watch my dad and brothers pack away the last of their things. I'm in a horrible mood and I'm dreading having to say goodbye to them all over again. Oliver has already gone to work so he's already said his goodbyes. It was a sombre affair with lots of meaningful looks and unspoken promises of keeping safe. I'm very reluctant to think that, as the raid goes on, one of the people I love the most in the world is not going to see the other side.

"Chloe," Dad says kneeling down in front of me. I try to avoid looking at him as my throat and eyes burn painfully. "Chloe, honey, we have to go and catch our busses."

"Right," I say getting up so quickly I nearly knock Dad over. I stomp to the door and hold it open. They all stare at me looking worried and a little bit sad.

"Chloe why are you acting weird?"

"I'm not acting weird."

Lies.

"I'm fine."

More lies.

"You don't look it, you've had a face like a slapped arse all morning," Michael says sounding frustrated.

"Maybe that's because I don't want you to go," I snap angrily. "Did you think about that? This could be the last time I see your stupid faces," I say, my voice cracking as my anger is replaced with fear. I feel myself start to tremble. I take a shaky breath but I sob loudly. I cover my mouth and close my eyes.

"Aww kiddo," Dad says, sadly. He pulls me into a tight hug. I bury myself in his coat gripping it tightly. "We will see each other again, really soon."

"You can't know that," I sniff as I wipe my eyes on my jumper.

"I do. I believe this is going to work. We'll see each other again. This is not goodbye but," he pauses and looks at Joseph and Michael, "see you later."

"See you later?" I ask in a shaky voice.

"Yeah, you'll see my ugly mug again soon," Joseph says. I stare up at him.

"And my dashingly handsome one," Michael says. I laugh despite my sadness.

"Ok. I'll see you later then," I say straightening up and wiping my wet face feeling slightly better.

"You too baby," Dad says before giving me a quick hug. I squeeze him tightly before I let him go.

"Take care sis," Michael says holding me tightly before handing me off to Joseph who picks me up like a little kid.

"Look after yourself and Oliver won't you?" he says. I nod as he puts me down.

"We'll be fine, just all of you be careful," I beg. They all nod.

"I'll contact you as soon as I have everything set up," Michael says picking up his bag. "Then well…"

"We can get moving," I say. Michael nods and smiles.

"Come on boys we have to go," Dad says. They nod sadly then with one last quick hug they all leave. I grip the door hard, willing myself not to cry again.

"Oh and Chloe," Dad calls from the street I stare at him and he smiles. "We love you and we're so proud," he says. I look at Joseph and Michael who nod.

"I love you too. All of you," I say my voice staying strong despite my shaking grip on the door keeping me together. They all smile and wave.

Remember that, I think grimly as they turn away.

I watch with blurred eyes as my family walk away from me. I watch as they disappear round a corner as I shiver hard in the frigid air. I don't know how long I'm standing there staring out into the street but I jump when I hear the squeak of the front gate and see Mary walking towards me looking worried.

400

"Chloe are you ok?" she asks in a low voice. Worry and embarrassment are clear on her face. I give her a little smile. I nod before looking back down the street.

"Hello," I say in a tense voice. I see her wince slightly.

"Hi. Are you ok Chloe? You have been standing here for quite a while now," she says as she stops next to me but I don't look at her. I have enough to deal with at the moment I can't be bothered dealing with her guilt or whatever this is.

"I'm fine," I say not even convincing myself. I see her frown. I sense she's going to question me further so I turn to her smiling. "What can I do for you? I haven't spoken to you properly since the tower," I state. She looks down at her feet blushing furiously. She looks so embarrassed that it almost makes up for the fact she has basically ignored me for the last few months ever since I locked her in the tractor. It bugged me for a little while, not that she didn't thank me; I didn't do it for the thanks. Just the fact she acted like I was invisible that pissed me off. Then we got so busy I hardly had any time to think on it.

"I was just checking you were ok. I saw your family leaving," she says talking to the floor and shifting from foot to foot.

"That all?" I ask sounding bored. Her eyes dart up to me and I nearly crack when I see her sad expression.

"That's all."

"Ok, well, thanks for your concern," I say. I turn and start to close the door but she sticks her foot in the door her face going from sad to angry.

"Why? Why did you do it?"

"Why did I do what?" I ask, frowning at her. She groans angrily.

"Lock me in that damn tractor. Why did you do it?" she looks so angry that I think carefully before I answer.

"I don't really know," I say honestly.

"It was stupid."

"I know."

"You could have died."

"Look, I know. I really didn't think there was the space for the two of us, and if he got in when we were both squashed in there, one or both of us could have been bitten."

"You didn't know that. He started to fall apart when he tried to get in."

"I didn't know that would happen either. Otherwise I would have just got in." I say defensively.

"You could've been killed. I couldn't have forgiven myself for you risking your life for me; imagine you were hurt or killed. Could you imagine what Oliver would have been like? It makes me so angry just thinking about it," she says her eyes flashing angrily like they are proving a point.

"Is that why you haven't spoken to me before now?" I ask with a sigh. I see her mouth quirk up a little.

"David says I'm the worst for holding grudges." I snort out a laugh. She squints her eyes at me.

"He might be right."

"Look I don't need my friends dying to protect me. I couldn't live with that. Thank you for doing it but don't ever do it again," she says sounding cross. I smile at her despite the ridiculousness of her request.

"Fine. I promise never to save your life again," I say with my hand over my heart. She smiles and laughs.

"Thank you. I'm sorry I acted like a complete bitch. Can you forgive me?" she asks in a pleading tone.

"Hmm, I don't know about that," I say tapping my chin but she smiles. "Fine, I suppose I can let it slide. Just this one time though."

"Thanks," she says happily as she steps up and hugs me. "You're freezing," she says.

"I'm ok," I lie. She narrows her eyes at me.

"You're ok though, like now?" she asks. I bite my lip as it starts to tremble. She gives me a little knowing smile. I lower my head as my eyes start to sting. "It's hard I know.

I hate not knowing what is going to happen. It's driving me insane."

"I know. We're really risking everything for this," I say in a low voice.

"It'll be worth it," she says sounding so convincing that I can't help but smile.

"You want to come in for some tea?" I ask. She smiles widely.

"I thought you'd never ask," she says dramatically. I open the door for her she walks in smiling and rubbing her chilled hands. Just as I'm about to close the door I hear a bang from outside. I see my garden gate swinging hard back into its lock as flame-faced Rose storms down the garden path through the mushy slush. I smile at her but she glares at me wiping my smile off my face.

"Don't you smile at me missy," she says, pushing me out of her way and marching into the house. I close the door following her hurriedly into the living room where she casts Mary a death stare, as well, as she sits in my chair and folds her arms angrily.

"What is up with you," I ask with a nervous chuckle. She arches her eyebrow at me and her nostrils flare.

"You two are having a girly day and I resent not being invited," she states matter of factly. I stare at her in shock.

"We weren't..."

"Bull shit!"

"I was just making tea," I say casting Mary a nervous glance as Rose sighs angrily.

"I'm not supposed to drink tea I'm pregnant. In case you haven't noticed."

"I would never have guessed," I mutter. She narrows her eyes at me. "Damn Rose, it was a joke. What can I get you to drink?"

She really is quite terrifying.

"Water," she says. I cross my arms arching my eyebrow at her. "Please," she adds sweetly. Mary laughs loudly as I shake my head.

"You've gone insane with hormones," Mary says as I walk into the kitchen. Rose sighs loudly.

"You're telling me."

Chapter 37

"*Sir, there is someone here to see you,*" Samuel says. Henry looks up from his book before placing it on his lap.

"*I don't have any meetings,*" he says frowning at his loyal servant.

"*Yes sir, but he has travelled quite a way to speak to you personally.*"

"*Who is it Samuel? I have no time for your cryptic guessing games.*"

"*He is a human Sir, from here in the Greenbelt,*" Henry sits up in his chair his curiosity piqued; no one was supposed to know where he was.

"*Send him in,*" he says, standing up and placing the book on the table. Samuel bows and backs out of the room. Henry listens intently for his visitor; he hears the approach of a raspy-breathed human. His nose curls in disgust at the noise and the smell that blows through the open door. There is a hesitant knock on the door and he sighs.

"*Come in,*" he says in a level voice. He watches as the human steps into his shadowed room. He watches as the human's eyes adjust to the dark; his pupils blowing wide as they try at adjust to the dull light. As his eyes dart around the big room a flicker of recognition crosses Henry as he observes the seedy man in front of him.

"*I'm sorry to interrupt you Master,*" he says, his breath rapid as his heart thuds wetly against his ribs.

"*To what do I owe the unexpected visit?*" Henry says making the man jump and his eyes finally find him in the dark. He bows low and Henry rolls his eyes.

"*Master, I come with news of misdoings. I fear my fellow villagers are up to something,*" he says. Henry's eyebrows shoot up.

"*Up to something? Be more specific, human,*" he says. The man bows his head lower.

"*There have been meetings. Secret meetings, I should know as I'm in a position of some power and I know nothing of these meetings. The villagers are in cahoots and I have a bad feeling about it.*"

"*What have you heard?*" Henry asks feeling his temper rising. He knew something was not right with this place. Now he is hearing it from this human's own mouth he knew it to be true.

"*I know no facts Master but I know when something is not right and I have that feeling now,*" the man says, still talking to the floor.

Henry walks forwards.

"*Stand up,*" he says slowly. The man straightens himself but keeps his eyes firmly on the ground. "*Tell me how long have you had these 'feelings' exactly?*"

"*For a while Master. I just don't know who is doing it,*" he says. Henry smiles coldly, knowing full well who is to blame.

"*It is just a case of proving it,*" Henry muses out loud and the man nods.

"*Yes, Master.*"

"*Tell me, what is your name?*" Henry asks. The mans eyes dart upwards in surprise and he smiles.

"*Norman Clark.*"

"*Well, Norman, my dear fellow. I think you and I should have a little chat don't you?*" Henry says. Norman smiles up at him happily.

"*It would be my pleasure Master.*"

Why is it that whenever you're awaiting something the time seems to go slower?

The waiting is slowly driving me insane. It has been a month since Christmas and we're ready. All of us have been kitted out and we've been tested and drilled in every aspect of the plan. Now, we just have to be patient. Michael has made his presence known to us all by taking control of our street lamps. Each of them burns a little bit brighter at night and at exactly ten in the evening they blink on and off twice. His little way of telling us he's still in control and more importantly that he's still with us. It has become a ritual for me to wait at our bedroom window every night for his signal unable to rest until I see it. When the lights flicker I smile to myself and close the curtains feeling more at ease. I've heard from Joseph, as well, when he called me to inform me of his 'promotion'. I knew instantly that it had everything to do with our take-over and him being accepted into the North's resistance circle. Despite my knowing, I played my part well.

"Wow Joseph, that's great, but are you sure it was for you and not someone else?" I joked making him laugh. I could hear the falseness in his laugh but we were just playing a game now.

"Oh sis, it's definitely for me. I'm exactly where I want to be," he said. I smiled knowing he was putting my mind at ease after his reluctance to originally join our cause.

The only person I haven't heard from was Dad and I'm starting to get really worried. "Maybe he's been found out," I groan as I pace the kitchen floor while Oliver looks up at me worry clear on his face.

"Or maybe he's busy," Oliver offers in a calming voice. "Like you said last week he has his work too. No news is good news and remember if something was wrong my mum and Dad would tell us." I stop pacing and look at him before sitting down heavily in the chair next to him.

"You're right," I say. He moves off his chair kneeling in front of me he takes my hand and kisses it as he looks into my eyes.

"Everything is fine, don't..." Our heads snap up as the sound of radio static fills the room.

"Testing, hello can anyone hear me? Over." I spring out of my seat nearly knocking Oliver on his ass but he rights himself before joining me at the radio.

"Answer it," he says quickly. I pick up the receiver, pressing the side button.

"Hello, I can hear you. Is that you Michael?" I hold my breath as I wait for a reply. The seconds tick by. I stare at the radio my hand shaking slightly. I begin to fear something has gone wrong and I look up at Oliver who looks as tense as I feel. The radio crackles again and our eyes dart back to it.

"You are supposed to say 'over' when you're finished speaking. Over." he says. I let out a loud laugh that turns into a sob. Oliver takes the radio from me as I cover my mouth trying to muffle my sobs.

"Michael it's us, it's Oliver. You did it man! Over," he says excitedly. I stare at him through my tear-filled eyes he crushes his lips to mine and rests his forehead against mine with his eyes closed. I try and steady my breathing as another crackle sounds.

"Of course I did brother," Michael says proudly. Oliver chuckles. "Did you like my little trick with the lights? Over."

"I knew it was you. Over," I say happily into the radio as Oliver holds the button down.

"Damn it's good to hear your voice sis. How are you? How is everyone doing? Over," Michael asks. I can hear the smile in his voice.

"We are fine, I'm fine. Michael we're ready. Over."

"Good, we are too. I have been able to do everything you guys wanted of me, with a little help. I did a little recruiting of my own. Over." I smile at how pleased he sounds with himself and Oliver chuckles.

"Great job, son," Billy's voice booms, making me jump slightly. I frown at the radio.

"Everyone can hear us," Oliver explains. I had forgotten momentarily about all our radios being connected in the secure frequency.

"Are we sure this line is secure?" someone asks, I don't recognise the voice or the accent and it hits me that we're connected all around the country so it could be anyone. Its then that I realise that we're a lot bigger than our little group here in the Greenbelt.

"Of course it is. I've made sure of it. Over," Michael says exaggerating the last word. I smile.

"So when do we move?" I hear the familiar voice of Damien ask. "Over," he adds hurriedly. If his question hadn't sucked all the oxygen out of my body I may have laughed.

"Tomorrow," Michael says. I let out a shaky breath as I look up at Oliver. His face has paled considerably and his eyes have darkened making him look scary. "We need to move quickly before we're found out. We can't do what we're doing for too long before they find us and I don't want that to happen. Over." The line is silent for a long time, obviously, all of us stunned into silence. The radio crackles again and Michael's voice comes out clear and business-like. "Rose? Are you there? Over." I wait patiently for Rose to answer imagining her all round-bellied and vulnerable as she picks up the radio and whispers, "Yes."

"Hey," Michael says in a calming voice making my heart hurt. "Did you manage to get all those ear pieces done? Over."

"I did, everyone has one here. We're ready. Over," she says her voice shaky but determined.

"Good girl," Michael says sounding proud. "I think we do this now so we'll have the element of surprise."

"I think they're going to be pretty surprised," Billy says. I can't help but chuckle. There is a flurry of voices. I try to focus on what they are saying.

"So we're doing this?"

"Tomorrow?"

"About bloody time."

"Bring it on."

The line finally goes quiet after a few minutes and I stare at the radio in Oliver's hand waiting to hear one of the voices I want to hear most. The radio crackles and I gasp.

"Chloe are you still there?" Michael asks. Oliver pushes the button.

"I'm here," I say quickly.

"And Oliver?"

"I'm here Michael," Oliver says. We both stare at the radio like it's the most precious thing in the world.

"See you soon?" Michael says. I gasp quietly and my eyes fill instantly. Oliver wraps his arm around me as he swallows and lets out a shaky breath.

"See you soon," I say trying not to sound too sad. I hear Michael chuckle before the radio goes silent. I feel my eyes spill over and Oliver pulls me into his arms. I don't know how long I'm crying but I jump when the phone rings. Oliver lets me go to answer it. I see him wipe his eyes before he picks up the phone.

"Hello?" his voice is hoarse as he rests his head on the wall. "I know mum, I love you too. We'll be careful I promise." He's silent for a while. I get up and go to him when I see his shoulders tremble slightly. I wrap my arms around his middle and he grips my arm. "Hey Dad," he says his voice shaky. I feel his breathing accelerate and a tear drop onto my arm. "Look after each other, I love you too Dad." He unwinds my arms from around him as he pushes off the wall. He turns, holding the phone out to me. I take it from him and raise it shakily to my ear.

"Hello?" I say quietly as Oliver wipes his tears away and sniffs.

"Hey Kiddo." The breath rushes out of me and I grip the wall. Tears instantly spill from my eyes at the welcome sound of Dad's voice.

"Dad, you're ok?" I squeak as I wipe my eyes roughly.

"I am kiddo. We have been busy at the office," he says apologetically.

"Everyone ok there?" I ask when I hear a quiet sob, in the background. I look up at Oliver who looks wrung out.

"We are, it's been a hard day but we're ok," he says letting out a long breath.

"Ok," I say. I chew my lip unsure what else to say.

"Chloe we just want you to know that we're all so proud of both of you. We have raised some pretty extraordinary kids," he says. I try and smile but the sadness I'm feeling is just too overwhelming.

"Thanks Dad."

"We're with you one hundred percent, no matter what happens. Ok?" he says. I hear him gripping the phone tightly.

"We know Dad."

"We better go kiddo," he says sadly.

"Wait Dad," I blurt out. "I just... I'm scared." I admit for the first time. I notice Oliver look up and stare at me.

"I know, I am too but it will be fine. Be strong and stick together. I love you so much," he says. My heart breaks when I hear his voice catch.

"I love you more," he chuckles and sighs.

"That's not possible Kiddo." There is a little pause before he sighs again. "See you soon," he says and before I can answer the line goes dead.

"Dad?" I say into the phone. I wait for a few moments but the line just beeps at me.

"Chloe. He's gone. Come on, put the phone down," Oliver says in a soft voice. His hand comes up to mine as it grips the phone tightly.

"I'll see him again won't I?" I say in a tiny voice, pain flashes across his face and he looks down at his feet.

"Chloe, I can't..."

"Just say yes," I beg. He pulls me into his arms but doesn't say another word. I know he's being doing me a favour by not lying to me but I can't help but feel hurt and a little angry.

"I just want them to be safe," I say, against his chest.

"I know. Come on, we should go to bed, we need to rest," he murmurs into my hair. He pulls me towards the

411

bedroom and sits me on the bed. "I'll be right back," he says as he backs towards the bedroom door. I watch him leave, feeling numb. I hear a loud banging and a crash before he re-enters the bedroom. He's holding two backpacks and the long thin package from Terry. I meet his eyes. He gives me a little smile before closing the door behind him. "I'm just making sure everything is ready," he says, I nod. I toe off my shoes before climbing onto the bed. He puts my bag down in front of me. I pull it towards myself and pull out my dark green jacket that Rose has modified for me. I push the little buttons in each of the sleeves, right for front left for back, and the jacket lights up in my hands.

"Still works," I say more to myself but Oliver nods as he rummages through his bag. I fish in my right pocket and pull out the little ear bud that Rose also worked on. I flip the little switch on it and the light glows a bright green, it works. I tuck it back in my pocket and pick up the bag, emptying the rest of the contents onto the bed. There is a bottle of water, a small pile of crackers and some dried fruit for the trip into Greenbelt City. I get up off the bed and walk into the bathroom. I feel Oliver's eyes on me as I round the corner. He has done a number on the bath panel so I step over the splintered wood. I grab the small first aid kit out of the cupboard and bring it back into the room. His eyes land on it and his face falls. I sit back down and stuff it into my bag along with my jacket. I fasten the bag up and turn to the long, wrapped package that sits between us. Our eyes meet over it. I can't read what he's thinking and I feel my own face mirroring his expressionless mask.

"You ok?" he asks. I see him frown at his own question.

"Not really, I'm nervous and…"

"Scared?" he asks. I frown at him.

"You aren't?"

"Chloe, I'm terrified," he says. I feel my eyes widen at his confession.

"Really?" I ask, feeling a little blind-sided. I have always thought of Oliver as a rock, unbreakable and solid but as I look at him I can see his fear as clear as day and that scares me.

"I'm scared to death. It's like I'm in a nightmare that I can't wake up from. I can't control what is going to happen and I don't like it."

"I feel the same," I say, taking his hand. He looks up at me. "We will get through this together. We're a team." He pushes the package to the side. As it thuds loudly to the floor he pulls me into his arms, holding me tightly.

"I love you, Chloe." He kisses my head as I wrap my arms around his middle, holding him tight.

"I love you too. You know that, right?" I ask desperately, as my heart breaks for the tenth time today. When I realise I haven't told him enough. If this all goes wrong I will hate myself for never telling him as much as I should have.

"I know, Chloe," he says into my hair. We stay wrapped in each other for a long time before he releases me to look down at me. "As long as we stick together tomorrow everything will be ok," he says. I know he's trying to comfort me but I can hear the doubt in his voice loud and clear.

"Sure," I say. I forgo trying to smile and kiss him. We lay back and I look down at him. We seem to stare at each other for hours just taking in every last detail of each other's face before I lay my head on his chest and wrap myself around him.

I don't think either of us sleeps through the night. We both just lay on our bed wrapped up in each other not talking or moving. Just holding on. The shrill sound of Oliver's alarm jolts us both and he reaches over and switches it off. He rolls onto his side and looks down at me, his eyes tired and full of sadness.

"Did you sleep at all?" he asks. I shake my head.

"No, you?" He shakes his head.

413

"Come on, we need to get up, it's nearly time," he says. He rolls off the bed as I sit up. I throw off the covers and my teeth instantly begin to chatter in my head. I would like to think it was the cold but I know it's the almost numbing fear coursing through my body. I dress in a daze occasionally locking eyes with Oliver then looking away quickly. I don't know why but every time I meet his eyes I feel a part of me crumble away. It's like I'm losing grip on everything and I can do absolutely nothing about it. I push the feelings back and try to focus on our task. We have to be focused, we have to be strong and we have to succeed.

As I pull on my jacket I turn around and our eyes meet again. I freeze under the intensity of his gaze. He looks nothing like my Oliver. He's dressed all in black and he looks tired but also determined. His jacket is zipped up, his heavy boots fastened and his short sword hangs at his side. His grip on the sword is tight I can see it tremble slightly.

He's ready.

"I'm not going to ask you to stay behind," he says, slowly, as he steps towards me.

There would be no chance of that.

"All I ask is that you stick with me." This is not really a request but a command, one I will do everything in my power not to break. I nod at him, unable to speak. He nods quickly back at me.

We have gone over this a thousand times; I know the drill back to front. Get in; stick together. Take the control room; stick together. Move to the towns and always stick together. I'm sure Oliver knows that may not always be possible but I know we'll both make sure it happens while it can.

"Come on, we have to eat," he says, snapping me out of my thoughts. He takes my hand and pulls me into the kitchen. He sits me down before he makes a quick hot breakfast of porridge and tea, which wakes me more and makes me feel a little more alive.

Henry crashes into his living quarters after a tense drive back to Centrum. He just made it before the sun started its deadly ascent through the sky.

"You're back," Lillian says from her place on their bed as Henry walks into the room. Henry gives her a little smile but she tenses when she sees the tightness of his mouth. "What's wrong?"

"We have a problem," he says tensely. Lillian sits up as he sits down on the bed.

"Henry, you are worrying me. What is it?"

"They are planning an attack of some sort," he says, in a hushed angry voice. Lillian gasps loudly.

"Who are? The humans?" she asks in a whisper. He turns to her. His eyes flash angrily.

"Your humans. Their village, for all we know the entire country," he says. Lillian's eyes widen.

"What do we do?" she asks crawling out of the bed. Henry's eyes follow her actions staring at her as she paces.

"You realise I am talking about your child," he says slowly. She slows for a minute before remembering the hurt and pain of her daughter's rejection.

"Yes. Like I said, what do we do?" she says and Henry smiles as he stands up drawing her into him.

"We strike them where they are weakest; their hearts," he says kissing her lightly.

I eat my breakfast slowly as a strange feeling of immense fear and dread courses through me with a strange undercurrent of excitement and hope. Even way down buried deep under my shattered nerves is a small fragment of humour. I can't help but think how ridiculous we both must look sitting in our kitchen hours before dawn in our jackets and boots. Our legs jiggling with nervous excitement with two, twenty inch swords sitting on the table between us. With a dry scoff I push my empty bowl away from me. Oliver looks up at me.

"We should go," I say. He nods and stands up as I pick up my sword sliding it into the holder on my belt and pop the ear bud in my ear. "I'm ready," I say, looking up at him. He nods and picks up the radio he presses the side button and looks into my eyes.

"Hunters ready," he says clearly. There is a pause before the radio crackles in our ears.

"Wood ready," Michael says through our little ear buds. I see the streetlights glow brighter in the still darkness outside.

"Hunters and Wood ready," Rita says. Oliver frowns at the sound of his mother's voice.

"Greens ready," David and Mary.

"Youngs ready," Damien and Rose.

"Craigs ready," Billy and Gill. The names keep coming thick and fast. I catch a few more I recognise and smile when I hear Joseph. As the list of names continue to stream in the sense of dread lessens.

"That is a lot of names," I say as they keep sounding off. I cannot help the hopeful tone in my voice. Oliver nods as the radio crackles for a moment.

"That is everyone accounted for," Michael says, sounding relieved. I swallow hard.

"Stage one everyone. Be safe, be smart," Billy says in our ears. I nod and make for the door; my hand is on the handle when Oliver's covers it. I spin around looking up at him before his lips crash into mine as he kisses me fiercely.

"Just in case," he says, against my lips. I nod, knowing it could be our last kiss.

"I love you," I say. He smiles and opens the door.

"I love you," he says. I smile as he pulls out his sword. He gives me one last smile before his face clouds over and the dangerous Oliver takes over. I copy him and I nod at him before I walk ahead of him out into the brightly lit street. The streetlights are emitting a low humming from being turned up so bright but without them we would be in the pitch black. The lights are never on at this time in the morning as it should be *their* time and the lights aggravate them. I know they will be out; they will just be away from the brightly lit areas.

Damien, David and Mary are waiting for us in looking all around the street. They all look for lack of a better word, badass. David turns, nodding at us both as we approach.

"Come on, we need to get to the tower," he says. We move off without another word. We walk quickly, but quietly, down the path. At the end of the street it's like there is a dark curtain blocking out the rest of the way as the streetlights run out. We need to head down that way towards Oliver's field and the fallen tower but it's as dark as night. I don't miss it when the three guys surround Mary and me as we enter the darker part of the village. As we near the end of the street, I see some curtains opening and house lights coming on. Lighting our way a bit more as the lights thin out more. More and more houses light up as we move down the street, I stare at them in disbelief.

"Do they know?" Damien asks. I shrug but as the houses at the edge of the village light up I can't help but think they know. I see a small smile creep on Oliver's face as an older man opens his front door and nods his head at us. My heart swells seeing the whole line of houses light ahead of us, my spirits are instantly lifted.

"I think they know," David says. I can hear the hint of happiness in his voice. My spirits deflate slightly as we reach the last of the houses and I start to hear noises all around us in the dark.

"There is someone coming down the path," Damien says from the front. I squint over his shoulder into the darkness.

"I can't see…"

"Shh!" David hisses, interrupting Mary and she falls silent. I can see it now a lone figure and it's walking quickly towards us.

"Well, well, what do we have here?"

Chapter 38

"What are you humans doing out at this time?" croons the voice. I can't help but think I recognise it. "Shouldn't you all be tucked up in your little houses?" he says and the familiarity of his voice hits me before he steps close enough for me to see his face. It's Jack, the Fang with the crazy mate. None of us answer him as he steps forward again before coming to a stop. I see his dark eyes flicker down to our hands and he straightens up. "What do you have there, little humans?" he asks, trying to sound playful but the panic is clear in his voice. I can't help but smile at the slightly wide-eyed look he's giving us all.

Where is his mate? I think as my eyes dart all around us. I hear a rustle in the bushes and a snap of a twig and Jack's eyes widen as Damien lifts his sword.

"Now!" Oliver yells and Jack gasps.

"Sara no!" he screams. The lights of our combined jackets make him stumble back and shield his eyes. They illuminate the female who has launched herself out of the bushes. She's in midflight when our lights turn on she screams and covers her eyes.

Big mistake.

We leap out of her way as she lands heavily on the ground. I hear a scuffle and see David wrestling with a still blinded Jack. He seems unable to concentrate on the person on his back as he claws his way towards his mate who is now ready to spring again despite being unable to see. However that's her downfall, as she hisses at us there's a whistle and a flash of silver as a sword falls. In one clean swipe her head falls to the floor beside her crumpled body.

"No!" Jack rages, throwing off David only to be pinned by Oliver and Damien. Mary stands over Sara's crumbling body, breathing heavily, as Jack scrabbles towards her, screaming angrily.

"Finish it, he'll attract more," she says as Jack roars and screams on the floor.

"You won't get away with this!" Jack yells, as David steps up to him and Oliver and Damien throw him to the ground. David swings his axe then with the sound of metal hitting stone Jack falls silent. David coughs and stumbles back.

I had forgotten about the smell.

"Let's move," Oliver says as he gets up, he claps David on the back and they exchange a look, before David nods and moves off, I follow after him staying close as Oliver brings up the rear. We finally make it to Oliver's field and the site of the fallen tower. We make our way towards the hole our jacket lights helping us navigate the rough terrain. We're slow and cautious as we move towards the hole. As we reach it I hear a distant crash and I spin around quickly. In the distance just in front of the horizon and the rising sun I see a bright orange flash followed by another loud echoing bang.

"That's not supposed to happen is it?" I ask quietly. I see Oliver shake his head. He unclips the radio from his belt and presses the button.

"We saw an explosion. Everyone ok?" he asks. We all patiently wait for a reply.

"We're fine," someone says in my ear startling me. I had forgotten about the ear bud. "John's tractor caught fire. We're fine." I let out a little relieved breath and Oliver clips the radio back onto his belt as we move closer to the hole.

"I can't see a thing in there," I say as I look down into the dark hole.

"I have a little torch," Mary says, pulling it out of her pocket. She clicks it on and a surprisingly bright shaft of

419

light shoots out. David takes it from her, moves to the edge and shines it down.

"There's a ladder. We can go down that, I think it goes right to the bottom."

"I'll go first," Damien says. I'm about to argue when he stops me. "I'm quicker."

"Are you sure?"

"Someone has to, let's go," he says as he takes the torch from David who pats him on the back. "Here goes," he says, as he lowers himself into the hole, legs first. I shuffle to the edge as he gets deeper into the hole, his jacket lights casting an eerie glow in the narrow tunnel.

"How much deeper?"

"Not far," he whispers back. I hear a thump as he jumps from the last few rungs and he lands in a crouch. David is already half way down and I wait behind Mary. I hear David and Damien whispering as Oliver helps me lower into the hole.

"Wait for me," he pleads. I nod as I begin to climb down. It's slow going as the ladder's rungs are slippery. I shiver slightly in the artificial chill blowing up the tube.

"It's horrible down here," Damien says as he shines the torch down the long dark corridor. I sigh as Oliver climbs down.

"Michael, we're in," Oliver says into the radio and there is small hum in my ear before he responds.

"Billy and the farmers are in too. I'm just waiting on three teams your end. I will let you know when everyone is clear. Head down the corridor and you will reach two doors one is storage and the other is where you want to be. You want the door on the left. Let me know when you're ready. Over," Michael says in my ear and we all nod.

"Ok," Oliver says and he clips the radio back on his belt. I pull out my sword, gripping it hard.

"It's tight in here. Just watch where you're swinging," Oliver says as we begin walking slowly down the corridor. Mary and I are in the middle again. David and Damien at the front and Oliver taking up the rear and constantly looking over his shoulder. There's a loud echoing bang ahead of us followed by raised voices.

"Lights off!" Oliver hisses. We're plummeted into darkness as the jackets switch off. We continue to move slowly forward not breaking pace.

"They have blown up the west tower and the control centre is overrun," one angry voice says. I smile internally, thinking of John, Cameron and Trevor's team barreling through the Fanged in that control room. I hear a crackle of a radio and an angry growl.

"Give me that. Is anyone there? All of the towers are down, the vermin have followed through!" a second voice rages louder than the other but there is no response on the radio. I smile realising Michael must have something to do with it. We all stop and listen and the footsteps stop as we do.

"Shh," the first voice says, "Can you hear that?" he says and my eyes widen when I realise how loudly we're all breathing. There is a low throaty rumble.

Damn.

"Can you smell that?" the second voice says hungrily. I feel Oliver shuffle behind me. I hear the footsteps begin moving quicker than before and I see two dark shadowy figures round the corner.

"Lights," Oliver hisses. The corridor fills with our combined lights making the Fanged hiss and shield their eyes.

"You stupid meat sacks, we know you're there!" the first voice hisses. They move forward, noses in the air and eyes scrunched shut. We move forward slowly making them stop in their tracks listening to us. Their faces are scrunched up in confusion as we advance on them. We're nearly on them when they begin to move back. Damien scrapes his axe against the wall with a grin on his face. The sound is eerie and it clearly scares the Fanged as they turn to run. David and Damien rush them. The Fanged, blinded

421

and panicked, stumble over each other. David wraps his arms around a Fang, tackling him to the floor, while Mary runs after them and slices through the air with her sword. Oliver helps Damien with his struggling Fang. It kicks him hard in the gut sending him flying against the wall next to David. I turn as Damien is thrown back against the wall and pinned by the neck. His eyes widen as the Fang opens his mouth his fangs shining in the light.

"Duck!" I shout. Damien shoves the torch hard into the Fang's eye socket. The Fang screams and lets him go, he squeezes out of the way of the Fang and his snapping mouth. He slides to the floor, as the Fang tries to right itself. The Fang groans loudly, gripping his head, and spins around to face me. His eyes are squeezed shut but he's completely focused on me and judging by the angry snarls he's completely pissed. I swing my sword but he hears my movement and my sword cuts through his raised arm. His mouth opens to scream but the thick blade of Damien's axe that's wedged in his neck cuts off his scream. His eyes open and the black pupils stare at me in shock. The axe is removed and swung back into his neck removing his head. It falls to the floor but I don't look at it. My eyes meet Damien's over the crumbling body of the Fang and he lowers his axe. The room is deathly silent as Damien and I stare at each other.

"Thank you," he croaks, his voice sounding pained. I see a red mark on his neck where the Fang had him held. I nod at him as I kick the fragrant ashes off of my boot.

"Anytime."

"Everyone ok?" Oliver asks breaking the tense silence. He has a cut above his eye but otherwise he looks ok. I meet his eyes and I see the panic there that he's struggling to contain.

"We're fine," I say, my voice betraying me, making me sound far from ok. I move forward avoiding the disbelieving look he's giving me, I peer around the corner and see that it's clear. "Come on," I say. I start to move off but I'm roughly tugged back. I almost call out but I remember where I am and clamp my mouth shut. I scowl up at Oliver instead.

"Stop. Stay in formation, don't just go charging off," he hisses. I frown at him.

"I wasn't." he gives me an angry look. He's right, I was being reckless.

"Just stay in formation," he says through his teeth as he struggles to rein in his temper.

This is no time for a domestic.

The others exchange a look clearly thinking the same thing. I look down at the floor feeling embarrassed and a little bit angry for being spoken to like a child. David and Damien move ahead again. We stop outside the little door on the right.

"This should just be the storage closet but I don't want any surprises," David says with his hand on the handle. Before he turns the handle there is a shuffle and a small gasp from inside making us all freeze.

"What was that?" Mary breathes. I hear it again a small shuffle and a sob.

"Open it," Oliver hisses. I see his hand tighten on his sword. David swings the door open and we all still when we spot the source of the noise. A small figure is cowering in the corner of the cupboard gripping the shelving unit tightly. She looks up at us and her eyes squint in the lights.

"Please don't hurt me," she begs her voice quivering.

"Stand up and come out," Oliver says in a tense voice. I can feel the heat leave my body as I watch this small, skinny child stand up and make her way out of the cupboard. I have to fight down the bile that rises in my throat at the horror of this young thing being turned. I stare at her as she moves towards us on shaky legs her eyes almost closed in the brightness of our combined light.

Wait.

"Stop," I say quietly but no one hears me. The little girl slides along the wall her eyes wide and terrified. "Wait.

What is your name?" I ask, my voice louder. The others stare at me like I'm mad. I step forward and Oliver grabs me again.

"Damn it, Chloe, stop!" he growls. I shake him off turning back to the girl.

"She won't hurt us," I say as calmly as I can, considering the delicacy of the situation.

"She's a…"

"She human," I say firmly. The others gasp as I look at the girl and try to smile. Her hair is unwashed and dirty. I can smell the mustiness of her unwashed skin but most of all I can see the bright brown of her eyes looking up at me. "You're the Evans's daughter aren't you?" I ask. Her eyes widen even more and fill with tears. I remember her now. Dressed in a pretty white dress her hair in a tidy bun as she stood at the edge of her brother's grave. "Elisabeth, am I right?" I ask, as her lip trembles.

"Lizzie, how do you know who I am?" she asks, in a small mousy voice.

"I went to your school. I knew your dad," I say. She looks around us all. I see a flicker of recognition cross her face.

"What's happening?" she asks, looking around us again this time to our weapons and our glowing jackets.

"We're um…" Damien says croakily rubbing his neck. Her eyes widen again.

"It's true," she says breathlessly. I frown at her.

"What's true?" I ask, quickly, making her jump.

"That you're taking over. You really are fighting back?"

"How do you know that?" Oliver says, stepping forward, making Lizzie cower.

"I-I heard rumours," she says, looking at Oliver with wide eyes.

"Where?"

"The Fang who took me. When he brought me here last night someone spoke to him. Someone from here. Told him that the villagers were up to something."

"Did he say what? Did this person say what we were up to?" I ask. She shakes her head.

"He just said he was suspicious. That things were going missing and that he thought the tower falling was not an accident. The Fang already knew that," Lizzie says scrunching her eyes shut as she tries to remember what she heard.

"How do you know all of this?" Damien asks sounding awed. Lizzie looks up at him her face filled with pain.

"I heard it last night, I was brought here for a feast but they just had me locked away until I was needed. They locked me in the cupboard after the man told the Fang about it. I was supposed to be feasted on last night but they were told to leave me alone until they sorted out what was happening..." she trails off as she starts shivering. Damien sighs and unzips his jacket. He pulls it off shoving it in David's arms. He pulls off his jumper and holds it out to Lizzie. She looks up at him frowning slightly. He clears his throat.

"Take it, you're freezing," he says with a smile. She reaches for it and pulls it over her tiny frame. It hangs loosely around her shoulders. She smiles up at him. "Go down this tunnel right to the end and you will come to a set of ladders. At the top walk out of the field and head straight into the village and look for house number twelve, that's my house. My wife Rose will be there. Tell her I sent you and that we're all ok. She'll be worrying. Tell her Damien sent you and that we're in," he says. Lizzie stares up at him her eyes wide and filled with tears. She launches herself at him wrapping her arms around his middle. He straightens up and pats her awkwardly on the back before she lets him go. She wipes her eyes on the long sleeves.

"I'll tell her," she says nodding. Damien smiles at her.

"Here take this, it's dark down there," Mary says, pulling the little torch out of Damien's back pocket and pressing it into her hand. "It's clear down there, don't worry."

"Th-thank you," she says, then with surprising speed she runs down the corridor her bare feet slapping off the concrete. We watch as the light fades and finally disappears.

"Do you think she'll be ok?" Mary asks.

"We shouldn't have let her go," David says. Mary turns on him frowning.

"She was a child, if it wasn't for Chloe we would have killed her!" she says, sounding outraged. David looks a little guilty but stands his ground.

"I know but we didn't, I just mean she knows who the inside person is, she knows everything. How do we know she isn't going to get out of here and tell all the wrong people?" he says. I frown and bite my lip.

"He does have a point."

"He does but would it really matter? According to her all the wrong people know already so what difference does that make?" Oliver says.

"Ok, so what do we do?"

"We keep going," he says as he pulls the radio off his belt. "Michael we're going in. Over," Oliver whispers into the radio before putting it back on his belt.

"Ok the other teams are in, shields going up in ten seconds, be careful. Over," Michael says in our ears. I let out a breath as I grip my sword hard.

"Let's do this," Oliver says and David and Damien grip the door handles tightly and I count down in my head. Three, two, one… On one I hear raised voices form behind the doors. Those voices become yells, as the doors are swung open. As we march in a wall of brilliant sunlight and the sweet burning smell of the Fangs hits us. My eyes quickly adjust to the scene in the room. There are six Fanged lying on the floor screaming and writhing, the room goes quiet for a moment when they catch our scent. Their heads snap up as one and they leap up, their instinct to feed stronger and more primal than their burning alive.

Marcus was right after all, figures.

Their crumbling bodies move with surprising speed towards us. In the scurry towards us two off their group get knocked over and trampled. Their blindness gives us a big advantage. David kicks a leg off of one male as he swipes for him. Mary finishes him off with a smooth swipe of her sword. A female rushes towards me all teeth and flailing arms. I duck under her outstretched arms and use all my strength to kick her to the floor. She lands heavily and spins around grabbing my ankle. I swing my sword at her. Her dark eyes shoot open as my sword connects and slides through her neck. Her surprised face crumbles as her head rolls off her shoulders. I kick her hand off me and make my way further into the room. I pass Damien and David, as they make sure the fallen Fanged are dead. I cross over to Oliver who is stood at the control panel scratching his chin as he talks into the radio.

"What do I have to do Michael?" he says looking confused by the whole set-up. His eyes are darting around the panel in front of him. I put my hand on his arm and I prize the radio out of his fingers.

"Help the others clear the rest of the room, I've got this," I say. He nods and kisses my cheek. "Michael its Chloe what do I do? Over."

"Hey sis. Ok there should be a monitor in front of you. There will be a menu bar and a system tab," he says and I look all over the screen and click it when I find it.

"Ok, got it."

"Good, ok. Click in the tab and there will be a security section, press unblock," he says and I do as he asks. The whole screen goes black and my heart stops.

"Damn it, what've I done?" I hiss as I hit the screen. "Michael it's dead, something happened." I look at the radio when nothing happens and I frown. I turn to look at the others and they stare at me in shock.

"Chloe look out!"

Chapter 39

The whole room seems to go into slow-motion as I see everyone rushing towards me, eyes wide and mouths open in shouts I don't hear. I feel a vice like grip on my ankle and call out. I feel my eyes widen, all the air leaves my lungs as I'm tugged to the ground. The little oxygen left in my lungs whooshes out of me as I slam into the floor hitting my head hard. I scrabble to grab the smooth marble floor, my hands clutching nothing but ash, as I'm dragged under the desk. Oliver slides across the floor and grabs my hands, pulling me back towards him. The hand on my leg grips me tighter and I scream.

"Hang on, Chloe!" Oliver yells as crashing and scrabbling sounds behind me. I meet Oliver's eyes as they widen and terror spills from them. "No!" he yells. I feel a tight sharp pressure on my foot and I wince. There is a series of thuds and screams then the grip on my leg is gone. Oliver tugs me hard towards him and scrabbles around to right me. I shake violently as he tears at my bootlaces; he yanks my boot painfully from my foot. The realisation of the pain hits me like a punch to the gut. I try and stop him from looking.

"Oliver stop, it bit me," I breathe as he pulls the sock from my foot. He shakes his head. I yank my pained foot from his grip. "Ollie, please…"

"NO!" he yells, glaring up at me angrily. He snatches my foot back and looks over it. I can't look as I feel the throbbing all the way up to my ankle.

"Oh Chloe," Mary says, sadly, as she crouches down by me, tears sparkling in her eyes.

"There is no blood," Oliver whispers but he could have shouted it. I heard it loud and clear in the silence.

"What? I saw it bite her," David breathes his voice disbelieving.

"There's no blood, it didn't make it through the boot," Oliver says his fingers running over my sore foot. "He missed!"

"But it hurts," I say frowning. He laughs manically looking beyond thrilled.

"There's no bite mark, you're not bitten," Oliver says smiling like I have never seen before. I look down at my foot barely able to believe it.

"But it hurts," I say dumbly. He laughs loudly again and smiles before leaning over me kissing me soundly. I feel a tear land on my cheek. I pull back and look up at him, his green eyes are filled with tears, as he smiles at me.

"You're ok," he sighs. I close my eyes as he rests his forehead on mine. It seems like time as frozen and when I hear my name being called it takes me a minute to realise where I am and I sit up.

"Chloe, are you there?" I hear Michael's voice a little more clearly. I pull my sock on trying to ignore the pain that shots through my leg.

"He's on the monitor," David says with a chuckle.

"She's here Michael, give her a second," Mary says, wiping her wet eyes.

I feel my foot throb as I wriggle it back into my sock. I don't miss Oliver's concerned look as I squeeze my rapidly swelling foot into my boot. He helps me to my feet sticking close to my side as I walk gingerly towards the monitor.

"Are you ok?" Oliver whispers in my ear. I nod quickly.

"I'm fine," I say. I walk over to the monitor and stare down at Michael as he smiles up at us.

"Well done guys, I'm in. We'll be able to keep control from in here for a while. Is everyone ok?"

429

"We're fine," I answer quickly not allowing Oliver time to tell Michael I'm injured, knowing they would gang up on me and prevent me from moving on to the next part. Michael nods looking pleased as Oliver scowls at me.

"We found something out before we got in here," Mary says reminding me about Lizzie and what she said, I had completely forgotten about her.

"What?"

"Someone has leaked that we were planning something to the Fang's here," I say. Michael's eyes widen.

"What? Who?"

"We don't know. We just know that a Fang was told and that it was someone here that spoke to him. They know we're up to something," Oliver says. Michael runs his hands down his tired face.

"Ok, so they know, they definitely know now. I suppose it doesn't make any difference. They might have known something was happening but they didn't know it was today. We still have the element of surprise," he says finally. I see him looking over his shoulder. "Tell Gary to pull over we have to get this out to the others. They have to know." I frown at him as he turns back around.

"Where are you?" I ask. He shakes his head.

"I can't tell you sis, just that we're moving. Ok, just stick to the plan. It's still early, the sun is barely up but you have to get moving to the next stop. I will try and think of something," Michael says.

"What if someone got news to the south?" Damien asks. Michael shakes his head.

"No messages were sent as far as we can see but the news will spread and they will try to regain control."

"Ok, so we better get moving to the cars," David says. Michael nods at us.

"Stay safe," he says. The screen flickers and his face vanishes, before I can say goodbye.

"So we keep going?" Damien asks, looking between Oliver and me.

"We keep going," I say. Oliver nods in agreement.

"Well let's go, the others will be waiting," David says shouldering his axe as he leads the way back out of the door. Now that the building is cleared, we know the area will be clear until at least sundown, giving Michael and his team plenty of time to gain complete control of the center. We make our way cautiously through the still dark tunnel but when I see the orange beam of daylight ahead of us I let out a little sigh of relief. We climb the ladders slowly with Oliver bringing up the rear. My foot throbs as I haul myself up the ladder but I push the pain to the back of my mind. As my head reaches ground level the heat of the sun washes over me making me feel better. David and Damien lift me clear of the hole taking an arm each and setting me down lightly. I give them a grateful smile and Mary hugs me.

"I thought we'd lost you back there," she says, squeezing me tightly. I meet Oliver's eyes over her shoulder and try to smile.

"Take more than that to get rid of me," I say to her but keeping my eyes locked on Oliver. I know he knows I'm trying to lighten the mood but I can tell that he's seriously struggling to contain himself. I know that given any chance he would have me locked away while he goes on. I will not let that happen. I pull away from Mary as she wipes her eyes.

"I'm glad you're ok," she smiles. I squeeze her shoulder. A few moments pass and she looks around us frowning. "Is it just me or is it really quiet?" She asks. I nod as I look around us. I see the smoke rising from the tower John's destroyed tractor. As I scan the rest of the horizon, I have a strange sense of pride at the lack of towers marring the beautiful landscape. The sight is almost freeing.

"It looks so weird, I like it," Damien says, his voice still a little hoarse. I smile and shake my head.

"Come on, we aren't done yet," Oliver says.

I shake myself out of my daydream and follow Oliver as he sets off. As we reach the edge of the field we start running and now the pain is hard for me to ignore. I feel something in my foot clicking and grinding and every time it hits the floor a sharp pain shoots up my leg. Despite my months of running training I'm quickly out of breath and begin lagging behind. I push myself harder but as I stand on a sharp stone a moan of pain escapes my lips. Oliver falls back; I shake my head at him.

"I'm fine!" I say, through my teeth. I don't need to look at him to know he's throwing me a disbelieving look.

"Please don't lie to me!" he says, in a low angry voice. I look round at him. There is no anger on his face just sadness. His face is pleading. It makes my heart ache and I look away.

"I think something might be broken," I mumble. I don't miss his silent groan.

"Chloe," he says. I look ahead, ignoring his pleading voice, I push myself on and he speeds up to keep up with me. "Please Chloe."

"No Oliver." I hiss. I see him look away. We run for a few more minutes then, eventually, I hear him sigh. I tense for the anger or the begging. I almost trip when he takes my hand and squeezes it.

"I will wrap it up when we're in the cars," he says in a calm voice. I look up at him; he gives me a little smile.

"Thank you," I say, returning his squeeze.

"Guys, you have to see this," Damien says, over his shoulder. I look ahead almost running into a slowing David. I slow to a halt and my eyebrows shoot up as I take in a large crowd of people looking right at us. There is a mixture of emotions across the faces of the people who stand before us, some angry, some scared and some looking mighty pleased with themselves.

"Well aren't y'all a sight for sore eyes," Billy says happily standing atop a big red pick-up. I see Gillian shaking her head at him from the ground. I look around

432

and as I see more and more familiar faces my spirits lift substantially. Cameron, John and Trevor grin at us as they wave from another car. I'm even thrilled to see Marcus as he helps Harriet into the back of a smaller pick-up. "What took you kids so long? I felt myself gettin' older," Billy says, his smile contagious. I roll my eyes at him.

"What happened?" Malcolm asks as Ray wraps up a cut on his arm, I bite my lip.

"Nothing, we just ran into some unexpected trouble," Oliver says. Billy nods as his dark eyes dart all over us.

"Everyone ok?" he asks. We nod.

"Everyone here ok?" David asks, looking at Malcolm who nods, but Billy's eyes fall to his feet.

"Tom's team lost three," Billy says sadly. I frown as I look around for Tom.

"Is he ok?" I ask quickly.

"He and one of his lads made it out. His youngest didn't make it. They are just getting treated now while we waited for you. They're with Rose," Marcus says, coming over and handing each of us a bottle of water. I thank him with a nod and he squeezes my shoulder, surprising us all.

"They're still coming with us?" Oliver asks, looking shocked.

"Oh yeah, he said if we leave without him he'll kill us all. I don't wanna risk that. He's handy with a cleaver," Billy says, trying to joke despite the sad moment.

"So is no one going to mention what's going on?" Damien asks looking around at the gathered village people. Billy chuckles and opens his arms wide.

"The people have risen, son," he says. I feel that niggling sense of hope again as I look around at the numbers.

"We want to help," a man, not much older than myself, says stepping forward holding a menacing looking scythe. Oliver's eyebrows rise looking impressed.

"They all do," Billy says, as the crowd nods in agreement.

I look at Oliver as he turns to look at me. His lips twitch in the first real smile he has given me all day.

"Ok, so what are we waiting for?" he says with a shrug. The crowd cheers, making me smile.

As we wait, for the people who are being patched, up the group is divided into teams who will secure the towers' control centers while we're all away. Others have been given jobs to make sure the work doesn't get missed, we'll need food and we can't fall behind on production.

Oliver gives his yard keys to two teenage boys and asks them to take care of his babies until he returns. Rick steps forward, offering to teach the boys, as he's unable to fight. Once they have all promised to return home as soon as they are done they head off towards the yard. We fill the others in on what we learned from Lizzie, that someone let the Fanged know that we were up to something. Despite a few angry words from a few, the revelation doesn't seem to come as a surprise to the majority. After a few tense moments and edgy stares, silence falls over the remaining crowd as Tom and his son approach us from the inner village. I can see his son, Craig, limping and hard-faced as he marches towards us beside his dad. Tom makes his way over to Billy and shakes his hand. I can't help but feel pity for them at losing someone. I don't know if I could be as strong as them if I was to lose anyone.

"Thanks for waiting for us Bill. I know we're on a tight schedule," he says. Billy nods at him.

"You know you and your boy don't have to come don't you?"

"No, we go," Craig says tightly. Billy looks at the boy and nods.

"We lost family and friends back there Bill. My girl is fighting elsewhere. I can't just sit back and wait for news. Shawn would want us to go on, so we're going," Tom says and Billy nods and claps Tom's shoulder while Craig stares into the distance, anger and sorrow clear on his face.

"Ok Tom, you're your own boss. I ain't gonna try and tell you what to do," Billy says. Tom nods.

"Appreciate it Bill," Tom says. I feel a sickening shudder as a sense of realisation hits me.

"Hang on," I say as people start to make their way to their cars. Billy looks over at me.

"Kid, we can't hang around much longer."

"I know but we need to find someone," I say and I look around at all the frowning faces. "Norman."

"Why in the hell would we do that?" John asks and I roll my eyes. I look to Malcolm whose eyes widen.

"Shit, it was him," he says like it was the most obvious thing in the world.

"Only person I know who would snitch," I say. Oliver steps up beside me.

"We need people to look for him," he says. A small group of men and women step forward including Malcolm's partner.

"We'll find him," she says. I smile.

"Make sure to ask the little girl at house twelve if he's who she saw last night..." Malcolm says then he trails off looking a little shocked. I turn to see what he's staring at. My mouth pops open when I spot our Mayor stepping forward from within the crowd. I stare at him in shock as he marches towards us wearing combat wear.

"Then lock him up," the Mayor says as he joins us by the trucks and looks at the search party. They move off looking a little startled. I watch with a satisfied smile as they spread out to look for him. "Is there room for on more in your convoy?" the Mayor asks, looking at us all. I stare at him still not really believing what I'm seeing.

"There's room, but Mayor..." Billy starts but the Mayor shakes his head.

"It's Frank," he says. Billy stares at him and shrugs.

"Sure Frank. You can ride with me in my truck. Let's go," Billy says as he hops into the driver's seat of his pick-up. Oliver jumps in the back and holds out his hand for me but I ignore it. I'm looking at Damien who is looking out towards his house. I put my hand on his arm.

"She didn't come," he says quietly as he looks at me.

"She's probably busy. Lizzie will be with her, she'll probably be feeding her up," I say, he smiles a little before his face falls again.

"She'll be ok won't she?" he asks. I look up at him and bite my lip.

"She will," I say, knowing how strong and stubborn Rose is. She wouldn't go down without a fight.

"If something happens to me…"

"Damien…"

"No please, if something does, please just keep an eye on her and the baby," he says. I nod before he pulls me into a hug.

"I promise," I say, into his jacket.

"Thank you," he says as he lets me go. He pulls me towards the pick-up and boosts me up. He leaps in after me sitting between Mary and Malcolm.

I sit between Oliver's legs and he wraps his arms around me as he rests his head on my shoulder.

"Everything ok?" he asks in a whisper. I look at Damien, his face a stony mask, as he talks to Malcolm.

"Yeah, everything is ok." I say. Oliver's arms tighten around me.

"I can't image what he's going through. As much as I hate that you're here risking your life, I don't think I could let you out of my sight," he says in a breathy voice. I nod and sigh as I close my eyes.

"Alright every one, let's move out!" Terry calls as he slams the doors of his van shut.

The vehicles around us roar to life and as we move off the crowd gathers around and, over the rumble of engines I hear talk of organisation and planning. I look up at Oliver and when I see him smile I feel my body relax slightly.

"We're, going to be ok," he whispers in my ear.

Henry paces up and down his drawing room angrily as his advisors stare at him nervously. They have come to him with nothing but bad news. He is seething as he goes over their words.

"So what you are telling me is that they are in control?" he says, through his clenched jaw.

"Sir, as far as we can see, from in here, they have hacked our systems," one cowering employee says in a low voice. Henry stops to stare at him.

"As far as you can see? Are we not supposed to be the superior species here?" he asks, dangerously, as his advisors look intently at the floor.

"As soon as the sun goes down we will get back up there and work this out sir."

"YOU WILL DO IT NOW!"

"But sir…"

"Do not question me!"

"I'm sorry Sir, but we, we just can't"

"You can't?" Henry spits as the advisors swallow loudly.

"No sir. They have disabled the sun shields." Henry freezes and stares at the men in front of him.

"How? Is that even possible?"

"We have been locked out."

Henry stares at his most trusted advisors and for the first time in his life he feels something he never thought he would feel again; fear. He slumps down on his chair where Lillian stares at him, worry radiating from her.

"What do we do?" she asks in a trembling voice. Henry meets her worried eyes. He takes a steadying breath and closes his eyes before he answers.

"We…"

"Hello people of our great country," comes a loud familiar voice from the television in the corner of the room. Henry's eyes snap open and land on the television as Lillian gasps next to him.

"Is that not your boy?" Henry asks in a low disbelieving breath. Lillian nods, staring wide-eyed at her tired looking son on the television.

"It is," she says through her hand as he smiles out at them.

"My name is Michael and I'm here with a special announcement so listen up…"

The journey by road to Greenbelt City takes about an hour but a while before we arrive we can see the city coming towards us. I have managed to eat and drink. I have even had Ray clean Oliver's cut and wrap my foot up good and tight. He assured me he thinks that it's just sprained but insists that I should take it easy. After I tell him firmly that's not happening he just nods and casts worried looks my way, which I try to avoid. There is a feeling deep in my stomach that something is not right, everything has gone too smoothly so far and it's unnerving me. On the outskirts of the city, the streets are silent. I know something is wrong.

"What time is it?" I ask, frowning, as I look around the tall multi-storey buildings.

"It's nine in the morning. The streets should be full of people," Malcolm says, his eyes darting all around us. I look up at the buildings. I see curtains twitching and even people staring down at us.

"They look scared," Mary says frowning.

"Wouldn't you if you saw us roll into the village? They probably don't know what we're doing here," David says, tucking away his axe. As we near the middle of the city we notice that the people seem to be a little bolder and start coming out of their homes to look at us. I see a few smiles and a few disbelieving faces. I don't quite know what to make of it but when a truck and a few cars come rolling towards us, Billy stops. I sit up crouching in the pick-up's bed to look over the roof. A car door slams as four men climb out of the first car. Billy kills the engine.

"Who's in charge here?" a man calls as I look over the roof. He stands in front of the pickup.

"What's going on?" Cameron hisses from the car behind us. Oliver waves him down.

438

"There ain't anyone in charge here," Billy says as he slides out of the truck. Terry, who'd pulled up beside Billy, climbs out of his van. The man and his followers look a little worried, as he stands next to Billy wielding a huge axe. The man eyes him suspiciously and Billy raises his hands.

"We're all friends here," Billy says with a smile.

"Can't help but be a little cautious," the man says his eyes flickering over to Terry. "We have a snitch amongst us," he says looking over Billy's head, meeting my eyes. I freeze as he looks at me with a frown.

"I know what you mean brother, but us lot are from the west farms. Don't you worry we're hunting the snitch down as we speak," Billy says. The man's eyes dart from me to Billy and scoffs.

"Is that right? You lot are from the west farms?" he says, looking unconvinced.

"That's right." Billy nods.

"You expect me to believe that you and those children are the reason for all of this?" he asks still sounding very doubtful. Oliver makes and angry noise behind me but Billy just chuckles.

"Well we just kick started it, but if that'd how you wanna word it, we'll take it. The name is Billy Craig," Billy says. I hear the smile in his voice. I frown as the man considers him for a moment, still looking unconvinced.

"Richard Smith. Smithy will do," he says. Billy nods at him. "Chloe Hunter," Smithy says suddenly, still looking at Billy. My breath catches, his head snaps back around to me, as I stand up.

"How do you know my name?" I ask, trying to sound less scared than I am. I feel Oliver move behind me. I straighten my back feeling braver knowing he's there with me.

"You're Chloe Hunter?" Smithy asks looking me over and I don't fail to notice he looks very disappointed. I nod.

"I am."

"I have a message for you." He looks over his shoulder to the others standing by his car, then back to me.

"A message? Who from?" I ask feeling my whole body go rigid.

"The man on the screens," he says, my eyes widen.

"Michael?" I gasp. A look of acceptance crosses his face; he was clearly testing to see if I was really who I said I was. "What did he say?" I ask quickly ignoring his changing expressions.

"He says that he knows where the leader is. He's in Centrum, they have him contained. For now," he says. I frown at him.

"Why didn't he tell me himself?" I ask. I realise that there has been no noise from my earpiece for a while now. I feel a little ill as I await his answer.

"He lost radio connection, he's working to get it back. He managed to get a television broadcast out before we lost him," Smithy explains.

"Lost him? What do you mean a television broadcast?" I breathe but Oliver's voice drowns mine out.

"What did he say?" he says stepping up behind me gripping my waist. Smithy looks at him for a moment then I see his eyes fall to Oliver's arm around my waist.

"He told all humans who can to head north but don't do so unless they can. We're to expect an influx of people in the coming days. He's going to be away for a while until he can insure that they remain in control. He also mentioned to everyone that they should be prepared to fight," he says, looking around us.

"What does this mean?" David says from behind me. The crowd, that I hadn't noticed, waits silently for an answer.

"I think it means that the Fanged are planning on fighting back," I say to David but the crowd hears and they murmur anxiously.

"What do we do?" Smithy asks. I look back at him as stares at me almost expectantly. I look over at Oliver who nods to me encouragingly, a small smile playing on his lips. I turn back to Smithy with a little smile on my lips.

"We do as he says. We fight."

To Be Continued...

Printed in Great Britain
by Amazon.co.uk, Ltd.,
Marston Gate.